Lonz Cook

*To Claire (Selvin),
It's a treasure having
your support"*

DIMINISHING VEIL

Lonz Cook

ELEVATION BOOK PUBLISHING

DULUTH, GA 30095

© Lonz Cook 2022

All Rights Reserved

No part of this book may be used or reproduced, stored in a retrieval system or transmitted in any form, or by any means, electronic, mechanical, photocopies, recorded or otherwise, without the permission of the publisher except in the case of brief quotations and embodied in critical articles and reviews.

Published by: Elevation Book Publishing Duluth, Georgia 30095 www.elevationbookpublishing.com

Cook, Lonz, 1960-

BISAC FIC027020
BISAC FAM029000
ISBN: 978-1-943904-17-4

Contents

Contents ii

Dedication iv

Part I   The Beginning 0

Chapter 1   I'm the Lucky One 1

Chapter 2   College - 8 Years Ago 5

Chapter 3   It's Him 26

Chapter 4   Her First Professional Job 41

Chapter 5   The Meeting 53

Chapter 6   Developing the Chance 80

Chapter 7   His Move 96

Chapter 8   Committed 123

PART II   Current Day 149

Chapter 9   The Coffee Shop 150

Chapter 10   The Coffee Grounds 162

Chapter 11	One Step at a Time	173
Chapter 12	The Divider	189
Chapter 13	What's Missing	200
Chapter 14	Sister's Surprise	219
Chapter 15	Visioning	229
Chapter 16	The Break	244
Chapter 17	Is it Really You?	261
Part III	A Year Later	274
Chapter 18	Realization	275
Chapter 19	His Move	294
Chapter 20	Let's Talk	313
Chapter 21	The Date	326
Chapter 22	When Hearts Pay Attention	346
Chapter 23	The Incident	373
Author's Biography		394

Dedication

To all who suffered at the hand of another.

To all who endure the scars.

To those who seek refuge of the heart.

This book dedication is to you.

The worst experience in life is falling below an ant's foot. Your lowest moment does not have to be the end. Accepting pain is the first step to rising. This story attempts to show your recovery, which is the path from the greatest disappointment to enjoying a full life. This book shares your struggle and tells others to have hope for a happier life after survival.

I am grateful for the friends and relatives who shared their stories of abuse. I appreciate their candid responses despite reliving the anguish during a period of their lives. You have given me the tool to aid others and maybe share a path of hope to love again.

We are in this fight together. We need each other's support, regardless of level. I know we can defeat unacceptable behavior. It is our determination to identify the process, react to it, and deny the horrible act people face when love matters the most.

In the end, I pray for the abused to accept the message I share. I believe there is an ability, within us, to love *again*.

Part I

The Beginning

Chapter 1

I'm the Lucky One

Renee walked by the head of the kitchen table, ran her fingers across the curvature of the chair, and brushed Marvin's shoulder. She swayed her hips to a soft piano melody playing in her mind, headed to the bottom of the stairs near the front door. Renee grinned when she heard Marvin's footsteps in her shadow. She glanced at Marvin and looked at the top of the stairs. *Ready, set, go!* Renee ran as fast as her legs could carry her to the second floor. Marvin followed with his best speed to beat Renee to the master bedroom at the end of the hall of their two-story, colonial, home.

Renee arrived at the foot of the king-size bed, looked at the full-length mirror, and felt Marvin's arms wrapped around her. His rigid muscles were a secure blanket, and his chest pressed against her back adding to her comfort. Marvin breathed in, raised his chest, and lowered it when he exhaled, encouraging her to respond to his rhythm. She closed her eyes, held his wrists below her breast and pressed her butt against him. The rise of his manhood signaled her to free herself and turn to him where her lips connected to his. Renee responded to his kiss and took the liberty of tilting her head and kissed him again. Her closed eyes, slight grinding indulgence, and the mindful act of grabbing his butt, all placed her in a trance. She flashed to the Mexican restaurant where her eyes connected to his from across the table. His glance over the laptop's soft light was a beacon of safe passage to his heart. The flash changed to a scene acknowledging his interest, the moment she saw their reflection on the elevator door, where he kissed her, ignoring the security cameras.

Renee stepped back and pushed him onto the bed. She giggled, jumping on top of him. Marvin placed his arms around her neck, and she mirrored his breathing. Her skin began to perspire, sweat beaded on her forehead, and accumulated to a gigantic drop on his arm. She closed her eyes, positioned herself over his manhood, and danced to an unheard rhythm. She laid down next to him, reached between his legs and pulled his rope of change with a lifesaving grip as if climbing a mountain.

Sunlight blared through the window, striping the room as if a music sheet for playing different melodies. She heard harmonizing strings fill the air and his arms were around her leading to a sway with the rhythm. They danced a hundred times over the years of marriage. She covered her mouth and pointed to the source next to the large speaker that suddenly appeared. Marvin reached for the speaker across the room without moving closer to the dresser. His arm became elastic and stretched to where his fingers rolled the volume control. His arm snapped back to the heat of the moment, and he repositioned himself for control.

He led her like a trained bear, performing their ritual after the habitual race. She responded with excitement, knowing their play would turn into passion. Marvin looked into her eyes, lifted his hand, and pointed his forefinger into the air. He moved it left to right, "I'll be right back," he said.

Marvin rose from their embrace and went into the master bathroom. Renee looked at the bathroom door only to see a flashing light behind it. She jumped under the covers to the bridge of her nose and kept her eyes peeled on the door. Marvin swung the door open, and the flash blinded her for a moment. Her vision returned in time to Marvin in the door donning an open fireman's jacket with matching pants, and the fireman's hat, referencing Engine 9. His sexy chest, abs, adoring smile and handsome features were on full display. She took notice to the hose in his hands, and watched Marvin pull the lever releasing a thrust of liquid. In blink speed she closed her eyes to the powerful thrust on her face. Renee's head pressed into the pillow, her eyes shut tightly closed and her mouth became a sli ver at keeping whatever pressing her head from going inside her body. She pulled the covers over her face only to protect her from the white foaming substance. The foam blanketed her body. Renee raised her hands, palms outward, shielding her face the best she can.

When the foam stopped, she wiped her cheek with the palm of her hand and rubbed her fingers on the foam. What she felt rolled like melted cheese. She opened her eyes to the content in her hand and reached to her face. Her fingers touched an exposed cheekbone and unprotected back molars. Renee sat in bed, opened her eyes and screamed. She touched her face, and bed cover, then looked around the room. She realized the room was exactly the same before she went to bed.

Renee placed her feet on the floor and walked to the

bathroom and peeked around the door before she entered. She shook her head, stood in front of the sink, and splashed cold water on her face. The water touched the rugged resurfaced edges of her face. She moved from the bathroom and stood in front of the mirror. She watched her hand move to touch the scars on her face. Renee mumbled, "They say you're the lucky one."

Chapter 2

College - 8 Years Ago

Renee Chadwick woke to the cell phone's alarm. Her eyes dilated to the coal of night and the comfort of her bed made it easy to ignore the time. She gazed at the ceiling fan taking form and with full focus, pushed the bedding back, and put her feet on the fuzzy rug she loves. Stretching her arms above her head, she rose to her feet. *Five, six, seven, eight,* she counted on her way to the apartment's bathroom. She grinned realizing the distance to the bathroom is the same as the freshman dormitory three years ago. Her excitement grew when she first moved in, living without a roommate and embraced the quiet environment it offered. A ten-minute drive and she's on campus utilizing various amenities. Renee flicked the light switch, turned on the water, splashed her face, and wiped her eyes. The routine she had done at least a hundred times. She looked at her curly hair, shook her head and grabbed a brush, comb, and a little oil, then tackled the tight ends.

After dressing in workout gear, she went to the front room,

turned on the television and listened to the weather forecast and walked into the kitchen. Renee mixed energy powder, fruit, and coconut water in a blender. She poured the drink in her travel cup and tightened the lid. "Rain and cool; the same beginning of every college year." Renee returned to the bedroom closet and retrieved a University of Maryland pride jacket, jeans, underwear, and a long sleeve shirt. She put the items in a gym bag and returned to the kitchen to retrieve her drink. Renee stopped at the couch with the gym bag and tumbler in hand, grabbed her backpack with camera and books, picked up her keys, and walked outside of her apartment. She secured the door, strode to her car, and drove to the school's gym. Renee started the school year as she'd done three prior years.

While Running on the tread mill, Renee listened to the rhythm of her feet hitting the moving rubber. She controlled her breathing and ignored everything around her. She allowed her thoughts to the coming school year; *Fifteen credits are all I need.* She increased her pace. *Four upper-level classes for my major and one damn elective.* Renee watched cars cruise by the gymnasium. *I could have taken in summer instead of going to an internship. I made the right decision.* She kept her pace while breathing easy. Twenty minutes later, she stopped running and moved to weight training. When she finished working out, she showered and dressed. Her routine continued with a visit to the cafeteria for breakfast.

***

Vincent Mathis entered the campus cafeteria, chose the second to the last table for two in the back, closest to the window wall; a perfect view to every angle except behind him. The cafeteria is his perfect setting to catch up on assignments. He incorporates the sound of his surroundings while studying or working on a project. Something he managed to learn in an Asian - African American household. Mom insisted he focus on his studies regardless of his dad's loud music of Miles Davis, Satchmo, Joe King Oliver, or Duke Ellington.

Fall semester and tree leaves are changing colors and fallen red or golden remnants of green scattered in the wind. Shortly after Vincent's first class of the day, he walked into the cafeteria in search of brunch. He skipped breakfast avoiding a late arrival to class. Without thinking, he didn't grab an oatmeal bar to take along and munch during the session. In the cafeteria, he glanced at the Japanese vendor and noticed the menu items his mom cooked. He shook his head in disagreement and moved to a Greek vendor. He stopped, stared at the listing, and moved along to a Mexican Cantina. He read the menu board and ordered a quick meal. "I'd like quesadilla breakfast special with beans and rice," he smiled.

"The beans and rice are extra," the clerk responded.

"I know, and it's okay." Vincent pulled the exact amount from his pocket before the cashier rang the order. "Here you go." Extending the money to the cashier.

"Thank you," the cashier smiled, entered the money and closed the register. She ripped the receipt from the dispenser and handed it to Vincent. "It'll be right out."

"Thanks." Vincent moved aside, waiting for his order. He looked around and his eyes gazed upon the beauty he thought never existed. Her curves were a figure that accented the hourglass, but slender to fitness. Her pulled back hairstyle did not hide one blemish of her skin and accented her natural features. He caught himself staring and quickly turned his head towards the cantina. He rolled his eyes in her direction but refrained from staring and fought his feet from moving closer. He took in another full glimpse, enough to admire her face, dark caramel sun kissed complexion, and exciting curves that would seemingly fit a sculptor's dream a second time. Vincent smiled, closed his eyes, and reflected on the picture memory of her face, a picture-perfect painting – beyond an artist's imagination. He recognized her as the beauty he periodically saw on campus. With open eyes, he moved aside with his order ticket in hand. *Should I?* He glanced at her when he stepped from the counter. He looked at the ticket and walked directly into her.

"Hey, watch it!" she said.

"Oh, ah ah ah." He stopped in his tracks and looked up. "Sorry." Vincent lifted his head, smiled, and stared at her without masking his action. He moved next to her, noticed the camera case strapped around her neck and shoulder, and listened to her order. He familiarized himself with the natural soft alto sax tone of her voice. *I should say something.* He slightly rocked side to side, closed his eyes, and smelled her scent. He stood beside her, peeping, and seeking courage to introduce himself.

"Forty-four!" the counter clerk yelled. "Forty-four!"

"Here!" Vincent looked at the clerk and approached the counter, grabbed the tray, and walked to his table. He sat next to the large wall window and periodically turned to glance at the Mexican Cantina counter. He shook his head. "Will I ever become brave?" he mumbled.

"What?" His friend Mel pulled out a chair and plopped his book and tablet on the table. He sat across from Vincent and stared at him in the eyes before asking, "Brave for what?"

"The girl over there." Vincent nodded.

"Which one?" Mel looked opposite where Vincent indicated and spoke loudly. "There are a lot of girls in here."

"The girl with the dark caramel complexion ...over there," Vincent spoke soft and used his head to point.

"I have no idea who you're talking about."

Vincent frowned, looking at Mel. "You know who I'm talking about."

"Oh, I know now. The one you keep talking about." Mel sighed, "She's okay, bro. She's okay."

Vincent shook his head. "You have no taste."

"Whatever." Mel grabbed his burger and bit into the soft sesame bun, changing the diametric of the sandwich.

Vincent took his plastic knife and fork, positioned them and coordinated his hand and eye movement, slicing the quesadilla into bite-size pieces and looked out of the window. "Damn, some people," he said. He forked a bite to his mouth and chewed while he watched events on the street.

"What?" Mel looked up. "What people?"

"The guy in the blue shirt, over there." Vincent pointed. "See him?"

"Yes, I do. What happened?"

"He ran into a girl and knocked her pack off her shoulder. He didn't try to pick it up. He waved and kept going."

"Some people aren't like you, man." Mel picked up his burger and changed the geometrics of a three-quarter moon.

"Manners aren't common."

"I know, I know." Vincent shook his head and bit into another piece of his quesadilla. He continued looking at the crowd and traffic.

"Will you ever change?" asked Mel.

"What for?"

"You have a routine you never modify." Mel raised his eyes from his burger and scanned the cafeteria. "Look at all these gorgeous ladies. Aren't you at least interested in talking to one?"

"I am in the one I like. When I get the chance, I will talk to her." Vincent looked around the café sitting area.

"You said that last semester." Mel picked up a fry and held it inches from his mouth. "I have a date, and she has a friend. You should come with us."

"Ah, no," Vincent said, shaking his head. "Can't do it." "Why? It's not like you have plans. I know what you are doing tonight, and tomorrow night, and the night after. It's the same routine."

"I'm here for an education."

"You sound like my dad."

"He's a smart man," Vincent nodded. "Plus, your dad wants a return on his money."

"Damn, dude—are you 19 or 40?"

***

Vincent opened the door to Crown Hall, a theater type classroom. He headed down the stairs passing row after row until he settled on the center aisle, center row, and sat at the end. He looked around examining the empty spaces. He arrived early in time to watch arriving students periodically glancing from his laptop when he heard a voice. The first day of class and he doesn't recognize anyone from last year, nor the summer session he attended. Mel walked over and sat one seat abreast from him leaving an empty seat between them. "Why didn't you wake me?" Mel asked.

Vincent looked at Mel. "You made it." He put the laptop down, pulled out a notebook from his backpack and placed both in front of him.

"For being a friend, you aren't friendly." Mel frowned. "How would I know you hadn't left? We aren't in the same room."

"You could have called when you didn't see me going to class."

"Are you that dependent?" Vincent scowled at Mel. "You're here on time."

"Let's make a pact. If I do not hear from you in time to get to this class, I'll call. You do the same."

"Damn." He glanced at Mel before shaking his head. "... okay, okay."

Mel turned towards the professor's podium at center stage. "I bet the professor won't show any films."

"Probably not." "Yea, no nap time."

Vincent turned his focus behind him. He watched his heartthrob enter the row. She slid three rows behind him and sat towards the center. He turned to the front and penned his name on the front of his notebook. "Don't look now, but I think she's…"

"…freaking awesome!!!" Mel turned and waved in Renee's direction.

"Damn, I thought before you said she was average."

"Dude, that was yesterday. Today I have new taste."

"I shouldn't have said anything." Vincent opened his laptop and booted it.

"Is she…"

"From the cafeteria yesterday."

"I remember." Mel looked back. "Dude, if you don't move now, you'll miss a second time."

"Okay." Vincent looked up. "I'll take a chance when it's time. It's not now."

Mel focused on the stage in time to watch the professor approach the podium, introduce the class, and instruct everyone to count across the theater. "All are here. 42 – a suitable number." He randomly locked eyes with students before he said, "Every six people will make up one group. I know you can figure this one out, right?"

"Yes," half of the students responded.

"Good," he nodded. "Get to know each other quickly, and I'll start your instruction in 15 minutes." The professor picked up a folder and walked to the other side of the room, where he watched students create groups. The professor looked left at the first group noticed a second as nearly organized. He watched the third and fourth groups and shook his head to their difficulty gathering the required numbers. He wrote his observation on the legal-sized tablet in front of him. When his eyes scanned Mel and Vincent, he nodded in approval. He looked at his watch and announced, "5 minutes."

Renee introduced herself to three classmates who had gathered one row ahead of Vincent. Mel spoke to her, "Hi, I'm Mel and this is Vincent."

Vincent closed his laptop turned to Renee and waved. The other three spoke announcing their names.

Renee looked at everyone and said, "We should share our contact information." She paused. "You know - email, cell numbers, and dorm room." She opened her notepad and ripped a sheet of paper out of it, and organized columns with her pen. "Here, I'll start with mine." Renee finished her entry and passed it along.

"Thanks." Vincent smiled, wrote his information, and passed it to Mel, who asked everyone their name and information, and recorded it. "I can write them faster than passing it around."

"Thanks." Renee shook her head. "I can take a picture of everyone just as fast." And she nodded towards her camera.

Vincent smiled watching Mel throw himself towards the other woman in the group. "And what's your name?"

"Hey, let me see that." Vincent said, "I should ask."

"No, let me get her info first."

"Okay but remember the date." Vincent winked.

"Man, are you... never mind."

Renee watched the professor rise from his seat. "Guys, look."

She pointed at the stage. "He's ready."

"Seems like you've completed the first task at being successful in this class." The professor glanced around the room. "I can imagine what you'll do if you aren't prepared to follow specific instructions." He walked behind the podium to the other side of the stage. He picked up a remote control and pressed buttons. The room lights dimmed while a presentation simultaneously flashed onto the big screen behind him. "Let me get to the syllabus."

After the class overview, the professor assigned topics for group papers. He numbered every group and established expectations for each. "Now that you have your paper objective, we can get to the lecture." He smiled, opened a notepad on the podium and scanned the class. "Let me start the course by welcoming you." He paused, "It's going to get interesting."

"I wonder how interesting," Vincent whispered to Mel.

"The group paper is 50% of your grade. Look at your syllabus. Notice the highlight, 'No plagiarizing from previous students.' This paper must be unique. Further in the syllabus, you'll see these areas of research are not typical." He turned a page closing the syllabus. "One representative will present your papers at the end of the course." The professor placed the paper into a folder on the podium and, in a final swoop, grabbed the folder before exiting the platform.

Renee could not fathom the intensity of the term paper. She frowned with a raised eyebrow before scanning the group. "What angle are you guys thinking?"

"I think the history of man and the evolution of human behavior," one member said.

"That sounds good, but not so great for a grade…" Renee paused, looking at the others before continuing. "I am sure it's been done already. The professor said to be unique in the subject."

"Well, I have a proposal." Mel reached into his book bag and retrieved a paper. "Here's what I've done so far."

"What?" Renee took the paper and read the cover and premise before she nodded. "It's old."

"Look, I did this by looking at the syllabus, and decided it would do." Mel smiled. "I try getting ahead."

Renee looked at a snip of content. "I don't think this works for a good grade. Plus, it's not exactly what I know the professor is looking for."

"How would you know?" Mel asked.

"Listen." Renee paused. "I'm only here because it's the last lower-level class I need to graduate. I cannot afford to get less than a 4.0. If you want an A, you will listen to me."

Vincent stared at Renee and glanced at the other four. "I think we should listen."

"Sounds good to me, since she put it like that," Mel agreed.

The others nodded in agreement, "We'll do what you need."

"Good," Renee said. "I'm glad you see it my way."

***

Five weeks into the fall semester, Renee dressed in a hooded heavy winter jacket, difficult for her backpack and camera to stay on her back, and she managed to hook an umbrella to her backpack, appearing like a wildebeest in winter. She walked to the campus cafeteria passing Vincent on the way. She caught his direct stare, glazed with moisture and a sparkle from the soft fallen snow. He lifted his glove covered hand, showing her the black palm in a greeting. Renee tightened her lips, elevated one corner and continued moving her feet toward the cafeteria.

Renee dropped her backpack and umbrella at the bay window table closest to the entrance of the cafeteria. She grabbed her purse and strapped the camera around her neck and shoulder before making her way to the counter to order. "I'd like the blueberry fusion pancake special, please." She looked down and then up, catching the eyes of the cashier. "Can you add cheese to the eggs?"

"Sure." The cashier entered the order into the register. "$5.50, please."

Renee pulled her card from her purse and swiped it on the point-of-sale machine. She smiled, knowing it's near the end of her college experience. "I'm going to miss this place." Renee mumbled.

"What was that?" the cashier asked.

"Oh, nothing." Renee placed the receipt and card in her wallet. She walked to the table and secured her wallet in her backpack before sitting closest to the window. She looked beyond the sidewalk in front of her, scanning for whatever is picture worthy. Renee had seen most things on campus and was not excited to see the same people or similar cars passing by the cafeteria.

Her eyes focused on a man with a confident walk, someone she had not seen on campus. His Navy-blue overcoat, dark like the sea, and light color khaki pants contrast gave her a picture of class. She squinted for a better view of him while he walked closer to the sidewalk in front of the glass window. She raised her camera, looked through the lens and focused on the guy, admiring his stylish dark hair. She zoomed in at his stone-chiseled features that jumped to recognition and re-adjusted her lens to see a tight-fit clothing display, enough to confirm 'sexy' to the imagination. She snapped pictures of him walking across the street. Her eyes followed him down the sidewalk until he was out of sight. Renee closed her eyes, fanned herself, and then enhanced the image she had watched disappear. She looked at the few snapshots of him on her camera and admired the impressionable youth that had recently arrived at adulthood.

Renee assumed he's a visitor because she had not seen him or heard about him from other girls on campus. She looked around the café in case another woman saw her drooling and felt relieved that no one had paid much attention to her.

"Sixty-three!" The clerk announced on the PA system. "Sixty-three!"

Renee looked at her receipt and rose from the table.

***

At the end of the semester Vincent accidently met Renee on his way to class. He looked at her, swallowed, and moisture increased on his forehead. He stood with one foot in cement and the other pointing to the open field while facing her. "Uhm... Hey, I...uhm." He looked down. "We're getting the group together to go hang out. You want to come?"

"What?" Renee responded. "I didn't hear you."

Vincent looked at Renee. "Ah," he swallowed, "we're getting together at Scarborough for pizza and beer. You should come."

"Who are 'we'?"

"The group. I thought it would be good for us to show you our gratitude and get to know each other."

"That's nice, but not necessary."

"I know." Vincent paused; his eyes focused on beyond her, where the sky and the horizon meet, pretending to stare into her eyes. "The group said to make sure you come."

"Okay." Renee looked at her phone. "When is it?"

"Friday, around 7. I'll get there early to make sure we get tables."

"Okay, Friday at 7...see you there." Renee smiled.

"You sure will," Vincent grinned before whispering, "You sure will," and watched her sway her hips and took long strides. "If I only...wow!"

***

Friday evening flashed to existence. Renee entered her apartment, dropped her bag and book, before opening the fridge. She grabbed a half full bottle of wine, pulled it out and looked at it, contemplating if she should finish it. The gurgle, rumble, and popping sound from her midsection ignited the human need for substance. She moved a box of left-over fried rice aside, pulled a plastic container from the shelf and popped the lid. She sniffed, perked her nose, and her stomach pressed for air, gag reflex, pushing empty air to her mouth. Renee dumped it into the trash pressed to look for more. She picked up a Styrofoam container and looked at the content she saved from the cafeteria. Renee shook her head and returned it to the refrigerator shelf. "I know that project group is meeting at Scarborough's for pizza and beer. I shouldn't go." Renee looked at the wine. I can save it for another day before graduation. "It won't hurt going," she told herself. She grabbed her sweater, picked up her purse, walked through the door and locked the apartment.

***

Vincent arrived at Scarborough's, an old wooden home turned pizzeria, walking distance from the campus' main entrance. It's a unique environment, open space inside and a covered porch at its entrance. The side yard has a covered area where brown wooden picnic tables included sketched names of past alumni. He walked in 90 minutes before arrival time. Vincent scoured around and decided on a perfect table for his group. He tipped the waitress to reserve the area. Vincent went to the table, picked up a menu and pre-ordered pizza, requesting she enter the order at a time he thought most would arrive.

Vincent sat in a chair near the area he cornered for the group. His eyes scanned counting on Renee attending alone. He looked around the table and nodded imagining where everyone would sit at the table. He charted his next move on seating arrangements.

Mel and Christine strolled past the receptionist podium in the restaurant. Vincent rose from the table and walked towards them. "Hey," he greeted Mel, and spoke to his girlfriend. "Hi...Christine."

"Good boy, you remembered," Mel smiled. "Christine, this is... "

"... your old roommate Vincent." She offered her hand to

Vincent, who stood, shook her hand, and took his seat. "Yes, I've heard a lot about you." Christine leans over to Mel and whispers, "I can see Asian."

Mel shook his head before sharing. "Oh yea, I ran into Renee on the way. She was headed in the opposite direction."

Vincent glanced at his cell phone. "I didn't get a message saying she's not coming."

"No worries, she'll be here." Mel winked. "I have faith she will."

"She's the girl you stalk." Christine interjected, with her arm around Mel. "Is she really all that good?"

"Stalk?" Vincent frowned. "How do you come... never mind." He looked at Mel.

"You follow that woman around campus like a lost parrot. Man, I thought you'd talked to her by now." Mel shook his head in disapproval.

"I plan to tonight." Vincent looked towards the front entrance.

"She's graduating, so if you don't talk to her now, you never will." Mel added, before his eyes connected with Christine.

"She's a senior?" asked Christine.

"She is and she marches next week," Vincent nodded.

"And you think you have a chance?" Christine raised her eyebrows.

"He's got one." Mel nodded in agreement.

"She has his interest," Mel said. "I even introduced him to a few of my friends' friends, but he never did anything with anyone."

"I wasn't interested," Vincent said. "Besides, a great catch is better than fishing in a pond of solid bites."

"What the hell?" Christine asked.

"He's trying to say that a good catch is all he needs," Mel explained.

"How would he know she's all that?" Christine tapped Mel on the shoulder and frowned at Vincent.

"He knows." Mel nodded, "I trust he does."

"Thanks guys, you can stop talking about me." Vincent glanced around the table. "I know what I'm doing, and don't be surprised if she talks to me all night."

Mel shook his head left to right and looked at Christine. "You want a beer?"

"Yea, sure."

"Come with me and we'll order one." Mel moved towards the bar and paused before leaving. "I got you covered, Vincent."

"Thanks, Bro."

Vincent glanced at his watch and noticed the time when four of the old group arrived at Scarborough's heading for their table. Mel saw the group and scooted closer to Christine; both sat across from Vincent, leaving several open spaces around the table. Vincent scooted to cover one third of the bench ensuring the end is open. He knew Renee would sit within his earshot if he saved her a seat. Vincent waived at the waitress he spoke to earlier, holding a thumb up in the air. "He walked to the bar to order."

"What would you like?" the barkeeper asked.

"Eight pitchers of beer." he showed his identification and gave the barkeep a credit card. After signing the slip, he left for the table. He returned to his end of the table, glanced at his watch and took notice to the group's interaction.

When the waiter delivered the beer, Mel placed the pitchers around the table and happened to look up at a perfect time, noticing Renee's approach to the table. He kicked Vincent and nodded towards her.

"Hi, Renee." Vincent rose from his seat, smiled, and pointed his arm towards the reserved section of the table. "Glad you made it."

"Yeah, me too." Renee grabbed a folding chair from another table and set it between Vincent and Mel opposite Christine. "I thought I'd come by for a brief time," she admitted.

"Yeah, I don't think Vincent would have gotten over it if you had not made it." Christine looked at Renee. "You're popular with these guys." She nodded towards Vincent and pulled Mel closer with her arm around his shoulder.

"I am?" Renee raised her eyebrow.

"Sure, because we scored an A on that paper." Mel raised his beer mug to his mouth and sipped.

Others acclaimed in response, raising their mugs of beer. "We appreciate you."

Vincent raised his beer mug. "Thank you, Renee!" he shouted.

"Thank you!" Mel responded.

"Can I pour you a beer, Renee?" Vincent asked.

"No, I have to drive." Renee paused. "But I'd like a Sprite." Renee looked for a waiter.

"No problem, I'll get it for you." Vincent jumped from his seat and headed to the bar.

Christine waited for Vincent to get beyond earshot and then looked at Renee. "That guy has the biggest crush on you."

"I...I'm surprised," Renee smirked. "I'm flattered." Renee looked around the table. "I wouldn't go out with any guy in the group."

"Then tell him now, so he can move on," Christine suggested.

"Are you ...?" Renee asked Christine.

"I'm with him." Christine kissed Mel on the cheek.

"Thank you, baby." Mel smiled, before adding. "You had to have noticed how he likes you."

"No, I never..." Renee shook her head, "never noticed."

"Don't you see him around campus all the time?" Mel sipped beer and placed the mug on the table.

Renee thought about Mel's comment, *see him around campus.*

"Yeah, I saw him a lot, come to think of it."

"Then you know it's no coincidence." Mel refilled his mug from the pitcher.

"I thought it was." Renee frowned. "I should leave. I don't want him thinking the wrong thing."

"I don't think you need to leave." He paused, "Let him off easy. I mean, let him know there's no future." Christine smiled at her suggestion.

"He's stronger than he looks," Mel nodded. "I'm sure he is," Renee responded.

Vincent returned with a sprite and placed it in front of Renee. "You're graduating soon. What are you planning next?"

"A job." Renee looked at Vincent before grabbing the soda in front of her.

"Not grad school?" asked Vincent.

"Not at the moment. I've had enough of college." Renee grabbed the drink in front of her and held it. "I'm ready for a big corporation to give me a chance."

"Didn't you intern at one?"

"I did." Renee sipped her drink. "They hadn't hired me nor my friend who interned there, but I hope they do."

"That's okay. I hear that happens to quite a few interns. They eventually get hired from a company they interned with." He looked at Renee. "At least I hope that's the case." Vincent added, lifting his mug to his lips before asking, "Is there someone you're connected to, in life?"

"What are you asking?"

"I mean..." Vincent stuttered, "...ah."

"Are you dating?" Christine got to the point.

"No, I'm not focused on dating right now. I will when the time comes, I guess."

"Not even when you've met the right one?" Mel asked.

"When the time comes." Renee smiled. "No more questions about my dating life." She said, looking at the pizza slices.

"Let's eat. I'm starving."

Chapter 3

It's Him

Renee wore a light-color flowered dress, brown laced heeled sandals, and sported a new hairstyle - loose braids in a bun and walked to the car with her parents. They drove to the campus stadium. She nodded back into the seat's headrest, and her flirtatious giggle started. She covered her mouth and closed her eyes for the ride. When dad pulled into the parking lot and parked in a space near the stadium's entrance, she grinned, her skin became moist, and her heart raced. Renee breathed as if she were running on the treadmill pushing herself for physical excellence.

"Mom, I did it!" Renee screamed.

"Yes, I knew this day would come," Mrs. Chadwick responded.

"Really?" Renee's voice arched.

"Of course. You never stopped short of doing anything in your life." Mom smiled.

When dad opened his car door, Renee jumped out of the car and put on the graduation gown without zipping the front. She looked at the stadium's entrance and lead the way with her family close behind. The dark graduation gown slightly exposed the flowered dress she wore. Carrying the square cap in her hand, she looked at the ground with a careful eye for each step on the sidewalk, to avoid a catastrophe from the sandal heels she wore. Renee turned towards the football field and chose a spot in the stadium bleachers.

Vincent approached Renee and her family holding a floral bouquet.

"Oh, my...." Renee covered her mouth, and her eyes slightly grew. She glanced at Candi who caught up to her reaction and waited for her remark.

"Who's the clown wearing a bowtie?" Candi asked.

Renee looked beside her with canted eyebrows. "We took a class together."

"He's not your type." Candi shook her head.

"Too boyish."

"Candi be nice," Mrs. Chadwick scowled.

"I'm sorry, Vincent, my sister can be a pain," Renee smiled.

"Ah, okay. Umm, congrats, Renee." Vincent handed her a floral arrangement of daisies, lilies, and four (red and white – school colors) roses all mixed with baby's breath leaves.

"Thank you." Renee pointed to her parents. "Mom, Dad, this is Vincent, a sophomore I had a class with, the past semester." She breathed. "That's my sister, Candi." Renee pointed.

"Hi," Mr. and Mrs. Chadwick greeted in unison.

"Nice flowers," Mom complimented.

Vincent slightly nodded. "It's nothing, and the least I can do, since she helped me in class." Vincent grinned.

Renee stepped ahead. "You shouldn't have but thank you."

"You're welcome." Vincent stepped aside for the family to pass and closely followed. "I don't want to interfere with your day." He smiled before looking down. "But I hope we can meet later."

"Vincent, I don't think that's a good idea. I am moving right after graduation. I won't have time to see you."

"I..." Vincent looked at Renee. "I can help you move."

"My dad and I packed everything. We don't have much else but a few boxes for the truck."

"Well, maybe..." Vincent looked at Renee, with hope.

"Thanks for the flowers. I have to go." Renee stepped quick without looking back, creating distance between her and the persistent horse fly buzzing in her ear, the unwanted pimple on the dark side of her bottom. Her smile returned when she heard the faint voice from the field bleachers. She did not look back at Vincent.

"I..." Vincent raised his hand towards Renee.

"Good luck!" He dropped his hand and focused on the opposite side of the field. *That didn't go well.* He thought during his walk to the stands.

***

Renee sat in her seat facing the makeshift stage in front of the goal post at the football field's end zone. The row of seats stretched sideline to sideline split at mid-walkway making two sections. Each chair positioned in a specific major for graduating students. Renee sat four rows behind the front row closest to the stage in engineering. She watched other anxious graduates take their seats in anticipation. Her eyes scanned the stadium and stopped at the guy she periodically saw on campus throughout the year. His freshly styled hair, square shoulders, and tanned complexion were no match for the graduation robe and square hat. His appearance snapped Renee blushed with her thought. *I would love to see him on a beach.* She fanned herself and turned left seeing the young woman seated next to her. "I... how embarrassing."

"Not at all, I think the same way," she responded.
"Have you seen him before?" asked Renee.

"No, it's my first time." She pointed. "That's the graduate school row. I think he's getting a masters."

"I bet it was a hell of a class." Renee looked at the row, counting seats and trying to pinpoint it his name on the program. "I bet it was." The classmate smiled and fanned, like Renee.

Nearly an hour into the program, the guest speaker finished his speech. "Like most worthy seafarers share on their exit... fair winds and following seas. I wish you well. Godspeed!" The graduating students stood during their applause and, like a well-oiled machine with a pushed start button, the Master of Ceremony announced the beginning of the march. Renee scanned who'd attended graduation practice and looked for familiar faces she had met over the years.

She remembered the first day of move-in into the dorm, and laughing with her first roommate, and later the part-time job she'd held at the local market during a semester. Renee giggled, remembering how she rushed, skipped brushing her teeth, and ran barely dressed to class, only to find that the professor arriving late. She nodded before whispering, "I made it!"

Renee listened for the graduate's name to start the procession to the stage. "Abernathy," the young woman called, and the first row of graduates rose in unison. Renee pulled the program to her face and counted names to positions. She listened to each name and watched for the mysterious handsome guy to respond. It was near the end of the graduate list when he walked across the stage. "Marvin Yarbrough." She watched him step with pride to receive his master's degree. He raised his hand towards the bleachers and smiled for the cameraman who snapped every graduate's picture.

Renee noticed his smile and stared as if he had the power of persuasion. She noted his tall, slender build, which showed despite the flow of his graduation gown. A gust of wind blew across the stage and his dress slacks became visible which impressed Renee. His wingtips shoes became noticeable with every step closer to Renee's attentive view. She smiled, loving a well-dressed man. Something she recognized while working as an intern. Renee focused on his left hand but could not see if he wore a ring. Her snapshot of his face produced the perfect picture memory making the wait worth every second.

The clean-shaven, chiseled chin man with a straight nose, has a pair of perfect lips. Her eyebrows raised and she stood clapping for him as if she were one in his visiting circle. She watched him until her eyes lost full view of him. Renee sat down and looked at the program to confirm his name once more before creasing the paper.

Renee's row stood when the announcer called the lead student's name. She moved through the chairs, following the steps like rehearsed. She listened for her name, heard chatter, and watched the person in front of her step up the stairs. Her eyes glanced left, then right, and a whisper of excitement sparked her heartbeat to kettle pound with anticipation. She heard "Renee Chadwick!" and the tightness in her face caused pain on each cheek from her smile. Renee carefully watched her step walking up the stairs and strode better than a pageant contestant to receive her bow-rolled paper. Her eyes glanced at Marvin even though she kept her head straight. Power overcame her and she looked at him, full view and turned her head to the front. She slightly bit her lip at the sight of him even though she saw his side silhouette because he was talking to the person next to him. Renee raised her bow-rolled paper when she heard her mother shout, "Renee Chadwick – yoo- hoo!!!" Renee waved and smiled at being the first non HBCU (Historical Black College or University) family graduate. She returned to her seat and waited for the rest of the ceremony.

After hundreds of black and red hats were thrown in the air, Renee picked hers up and held it above her head to block direct sunrays. She looked for Marvin to make his acquaintance. She scanned left, turned around, and searched again. Her eyes became empty, dropping her focus to the ground. Renee walked slower without smiling towards her family. "You didn't see me?" Candi asked.

"No, I..." Renee paused, looked beyond her in case Marvin walked by, and responded. "I didn't see you."

"Who are you looking for?" her sister asked.

"No one." Renee shook her head. "No one."

"Yeah, he must have been a really good-looking guy to get your attention."

"Let it go...okay?"

"Yep, he must have been hot." Candi followed Renee to their parents at the edge of the bleachers. "Congrats, baby, you did it!" Dad hugged Renee.

"Yes, sweetie, I'm so proud of you." Mom embraced her after Dad let go. "Now, what's the next step after your vacation?"

"Vacation?"

"Yes, your dad and I want you to enjoy yourself before you get serious looking for a job. At least a week at the beach, and then you're out into the world."

"That's nice, Mom, but I have a job interview next week. Its where I had the internship, once."

"Oh, my...Did you hear that, Dad?"

"I heard," he responded. "Where is it, again?"

"It's at a factory, with great opportunities. I would work as a junior engineer."

"That's impressive," Dad smiled. "Is it close to home, or...?"

"It's not close." Renee unzipped her gown, and a hand grabbed her shoulder. She did not look but allowed whomever to give her help. "It's not too far from home, but it's not around the corner."

"It's in Delaware."

"How did you know?"

"Oh, hi, young man," Renee's father addressed Vincent.

"Hi, Sir, I'm..."

"...leaving," Renee said. "I appreciate your help but let my family and I celebrate. I'll catch up with you later."

Vincent handed her the gown. "Yeah, sure, but I wanted to say congrats." With a frown, he said, "Have a great life." He walked to the street without looking back. *One day, one day, I will...*

"Why were you so hard on the guy with the bow tie?" Candi asked.

"He's annoying."

"You should be more aware of how you treat people." Mom frowned. "You may regret being harsh one day."

"But, Mom, some men don't get the message."

"I'm sure he got it," Dad added. "Heck, I'd never come around you again."

"Unless he's so far gone...you know," Candi giggled, "if he's remembering something."

"Don't you dare." Renee tapped Candi on the shoulder. "You better not..."

"Come on, you two, let's get going. We have dinner reservations." Dad pressured.

***

Tuesday night Renee laid in bed closing her eyes doing whatever it takes to fall asleep. Counting newborn turtles crawling to the oncoming beach waves didn't relax her. Especially since seeing birds sweep a few of them in their talons or beaks. She tried repeating a childhood story but that didn't work. She breathed slow and easy, focusing on the cycle of her intake and exhale. It started working and she finally dozed off. Something in her mind triggered her eyes to open and she looked at the bedside blare of green numbers; 3:20 a.m. Renee closed her eyes again, did what she could to resume the resemblance of sleep. After an hour and a half, she opened her eyes, turned around to look at the clock only to see the time display 5:00 a.m. Her eyes were heavy again, but her mind consistently tricked her body driving her to wake up and don't be late.

Tuesday night didn't exactly meet Wednesday morning even though a slither of sunshine peeked through the window curtains. She sat up in bed, wiped her eyes, and looked at the clock; 6:55 a.m. danced on the same screen she scanned throughout the night. With her right foot leading the way, she rose from the hotel bed, ran into the bathroom, and stood at the mirror. Renee reached her right hand out to the reflection. "Nice to meet you." She smiled and imagined the interviewer sitting in front of her. Her voice changed to a lower tone. "Nice to meet you." She giggled. *No, not like that.* She went to relieve body pressure by siting on the toilet. She returned to the mirror and grabbed her toothbrush and toothpaste, brushed her teeth and replaced the brush in the case. She stepped from the sink in search of the clock on the nightstand. 7:10 a.m., laughed at her though it was hours before the afternoon interview time. Renee returned to the sink, rinsed, and finished her oral care routine. She put the toothbrush in her travel kit before she looked in the mirror again. Her left hand brushed her hair back and she smiled, practicing being cheerful and enlightened, like she had rehearsed multiple times.

"Renee, you're going to knock'em dead," she said aloud. She turned on the television and listened to the local news, market data, and events around the city. Renee stripped off her pajamas and jumped into the shower. She washed with a song in her heart and a flashback to her graduation. "That man, oh that man...his eyes were cold, but his heart embraced me. I can only imagine how he would hold me—tough, but tender and secure. "Oh, that man, oh that man."

His image came to her—the MBA graduate. She remembered his shoulders and his dark hair; how his stride made her think of him coming towards her. She rinsed, allowing the water to flow over her body. *I don't know him, so why the hell am I so obsessed with that man? Stop thinking about him, even though I'm impressed. No time for that.* She wiped the water from her face. *Interview...think of the interview. I need this job.*

***

"Ms. Chadwick," the clerk called.

"Yes." Renee rose from the leather couch in the reception area.

"If you'll follow me?" The clerk led Renee through a door leading to the head office area. Renee did not recall this area when she interned with the company. Even though the office she had worked at was in Maryland, she traveled to the head office several times during the summer. "Please take a seat, and the human resources manager will see you shortly."

Renee followed instructions, sat in a comfortable seat and placed her leather satchel on the coffee table. She looked at magazines on the table, chose <u>The Young Executives</u>, and flipped through the first few pages. By the third page, she saw the man—the man who impressed her on campus. She raised her hand, covering her gaping mouth, and her eyes spread wide with lifted eyebrows. She held back a loud scream. Quickly, she looked at the magazine's cover and memorized the front image. Renee opened the leather satchel, grabbed a pen and folder, then printed the name and month of the issue on one of the folder's pages. She folded the page, returned the folder to the satchel, and secured it.

"Ms. Chadwick." The Human Resource Manager approached.

"Mr. Bentley," she responded.

He offered his hand.

Renee rose from the chair, buttoned the middle button of her suit jacket, and grabbed her satchel. "Nice meeting you, Mr. Bentley," she smiled and greeted him with a handshake and dropped her hand to her side.

"Good meeting you, too. Please follow me."

Renee walked into a conference room and waited for instructions. "Please sit there." Mr. Bentley pointed to the center of the conference table across from three occupied seats. "Good day, everyone." Renee unbuttoned her jacket and sat in the center chair facing the others. She laid the satchel across her lap.

"Good day, Ms. Chadwick."

"Mr. Ottman," Renee smiled, "nice seeing you again."

"I'm glad you're here." Mr. Ottman smiled and nodded his head. "As I was saying, this young lady was one of the best interns I've had in years. I'm sure, she'll perform well for us."

"Thank you, sir," Renee smiled. She placed her satchel on the table and opened it, then grabbed and centered a pen on a notepad and waited.

Mr. Bentley introduced the other two members of the interview board and suggested the questions begin with the far right. "Ms. Chadwick," the senior engineer addressed her.

"Yes," Renee responded.

"Are you ready for a serious challenge?"

"I am, without a doubt."

"Here's my question...when addressed with an issue, what process comes to mind that you'd follow for a quick solution?"

Renee wrote everything she had learned and named a couple of processes most engineers used. "If using a Six Sigma DMAIC assessment followed by the Ishikawa process for determining the issue, I'd find a senior engineer to discuss my findings and validate the fix." Renee looked him in the eyes and glanced at the others. "Did I answer your question?"

"You did, thank you." He took notes and tapped the next person on the shoulder. "I will have another question after you guys' finish."

Renee answered every question with skyrocketing confidence. She conveyed her experience working with Mr. Ottman during her internship and finished the interview with a few questions. She asked about the company, the executive mentorship, and the relative quirks she'd investigated that had happened in the market. Mr. Bentley rose from the table. "I think this concludes the interview. Please allow me to escort you too the main entrance."

"Yes sir." Renee stood, gathered her satchel and purse, and made eye contact with each member of the board. "Thank you once again for your time." She turned and walked through the door Mr. Bentley held open for her. He followed her, after securing the door. "Ms. Chadwick." He looked at Renee. "You did an excellent job in there. I am confident you'll hear from us."

"Thank you so much. I appreciate the feedback." She extended her hand. "Thank you again, Mr. Bentley. And, if you don't mind, would you share everyone's email address with me? I'd like to send them all 'thank you' emails."

"I can do that. Make sure you leave your email address with the receptionist."

"Thank you again." Renee walked the direction she entered returning to the receptionist's desk.

"Hi. I have been advised to leave an email address for Mr. Bentley."

"Sure." the receptionist handed Renee a pad and a pen. "I'll make sure he gets it."

"Thanks so much."

Renee got to her car and went over the notes. She straightened the folded page and read the magazine where she saw him (Young Executive - May 2009). She snapped on her seatbelt and took precautions leaving the parking lot pulling into traffic. Renee traveled on the route she used for home. She remembered passing a shopping mall off I-95. She exited and followed the signs to the bookstore. "Young Executive – May issue," she said aloud. "I hope they have a copy."

She parked in front of the store, grabbed her purse, and exited the car before locking it with her remote. With her purse on her shoulder, she entered the store and went directly to the magazine area. Her eyes searched for professional magazines. "Executive Management," she repeated, and then read "Management" on one cover. She thumbed through the stack, looking for the right magazine. She found it, pulled it from the back, and took a seat near the big window, on a wooden bench.

She crossed her legs and opened the magazine to his picture. She read the article title, "Young Executive Makes Industry Changes." Her eyes went to his picture, and she turned the page to another picture of him leading a conference. She read the caption, "Haines Building conference room, where staff executives plan the next big product."

Marvin Yarbrough, MBA graduate, makes a difference in the telecom business, devising a payment cycle charging pennies per any cycle - measuring the vice with a predetermined or negotiated fee structure to enhance monthly profit. His concept increases revenue using vice cost averaging.

"Smart man," she mumbled. The next page gave her more information.

He is the ideal young single executive, leading the industry for a better path to chief executive levels.

His quote in the article touched her. *"I'm ready for the world's challenges. I have no outside considerations to alter my goals, except my parents and one sibling. However, they support and encourage me to do everything I can,"* he laughed, *"and I'm sure it's for good reason."*

Renee grabbed a pen and paper from her purse and wrote; Marvin *Yarbrough, Junior Executive, Centicom, Haines Building, Delaware City, Delaware.* "Got it!" She returned the magazine to the shelf and put the note and pen in her purse. She went to her car, placed the purse in the front seat, and drove home with intermittent thoughts about Marvin.

Renee arrived home within four hours despite the heavy traffic. Just like her summers, she commuted to the job using direct routes and quick side roads. When she walked in the front door of her home, with her suitcase, purse, and satchel, her sister asked, "Did you get it?"

"I think so." Renee smiled.

"Dad wants you to," Candi shared. "I know. Believe me, I know."

"He's not expecting you to pay the tuition back."

"I know, but that doesn't mean I won't pay them back." She looked at Candi. "You have to make sure you graduate, too, alright?"

"Why do you do that?"

"Do what?"

"Make it about me and not you. Ugh!" Candi walked upstairs. Renee shook her head and mumbled, "She won't listen.

I know it."

Chapter 4

Her First Professional Job

Renee opened her eyes to darkness, looked at the blaring red 3:45 digits on the clock. Terrified of oversleeping on her first day of the job, she pushed her mind to consider resting, closing her eyes again, determined to have energy for the day ahead. She rolled over. *I've got to sleep. I can't have red eyes tomorrow.* Renee moved her foot in the bed, and the scratching noise woke her. She scanned the clock. 5:00 am. *This is not going to work. I'm not going back to sleep, and I can't be late. Might as well...*

Renee rose from bed and walked to the bathroom, trying not to wake her sister. After her shower, she went to the room, opened her closet door, pulled out khaki pants and a light blue blouse, put them together and shook her head. She grabbed a light-colored skirt, and a dark pullover, and shook her head. She selected her favorite loose-fitting maroon pants, white blouse, and a black blazer her father recently bought seemed right, according to the handbook. She dressed, ensured everything was picture perfect, and returned to the bathroom for the finishing touch.

She stood in front of the mirror, ran a comb through her hair before brushing it back to show her face. She patted blush, penned eyeliner, and powdered her nose. "That's good enough," Renee mumbled. "I don't want to look too sexy." She giggled, left the bathroom, and snapped the light off. Darkness didn't stop her progress through obstacles from her childhood home. She walked past the furniture to the blindfolded puzzle path game she played with Candi. Renee remembered left two steps, right one and turn sideways to get between the couch and the wall. She stutter stepped right into the kitchen, lifted her right hand and clicked on the light. "Oh!" Renee touched her chest. "You scared me. I didn't expect to see anybody."

"Good morning to you too," Mom said with an inflective chuckle. "I'm up at this time every morning."

"Since when?" Renee grabbed the cereal box from the cupboard.

"Before you left for school." Mom raised coffee to her mouth.

"Is everything okay?" Renee retrieved a bowl and walked to the table, placing it opposite of her mother.

"Everything is fine." Mrs. Chadwick looked at Renee. "You'll do the same before long—wake up and can't get back to sleep. You start doing things."

"Why sit in the dark?"

"Why not?"

Renee shook her head, poured cereal into the bowl, then secured the box. She turned to the refrigerator, opened it and looked inside. "We use milk substitute now?" she asked while scanning for real milk.

"It's better for your dad." Mom paused before commenting. "Why buy two types when one will do?"

"What about Candi?"

"She likes it." Mom sipped coffee. "You should try it."

"I guess so." Renee frowned. "I don't want to cook breakfast and smell like bacon on my first day."

"You look nice."

"Thanks, Mom." Renee smiled and poured the substitute milk into her cereal bowl. She picked a spoon from the utensil drawer, sat at the table, and began eating breakfast.

"Are you ready for your first day?" "I think so." *Crunch, crunch.*

"I'm so proud of you," Mom smiled. "I remember my first day on the job."

"What did you do?"

"Pay attention." She paused and sipped coffee. "I gave close attention to my surroundings, kept quiet and opened my ears."

"Good advice, Mom. I think I know what you mean." She ate another spoonful of cereal.

***

Renee rode to blaring music on the car radio. She peeked at the car's clock and took note to the flow of traffic on a Monday morning. She drove her preplanned route one street at a time and cruised at the same speed of other cars in front of her. Arriving at the office, she parked in a center spot a half-hour earlier than planned. From the car, she took note to who arrived at the same time she parked or who pulled in shortly after. She grabbed her satchel, pulled out the onboarding schedule she printed from her welcome aboard email and read what she needed for today.

Ten minutes later, she replaced the documents in the folder, zipped her satchel, and, with purse and satchel in hand, got out of the car. She walked into the office building 15 minutes earlier than directed, a habit her father had taught. *On-time means you are late,* she remembered him saying.

Her basic needs for starting the position were in her satchel. She scanned the office and realized her happy feeling from arriving as a full-time employee, which was considerably different than the internship she'd experienced. She smiled, walked to an assigned cubicle, and picked up the telephone before looking around to see if someone was watching. The dial tone hummed, and Renee touched the slot, seeing the extension with her name. *Wow - it's mine, all mine. I don't have to share, like during my internship.* She sat in the chair, hung up the phone, and opened desk drawers, organizing them in her mind.

"Excuse me." The receptionist stood next to her. "I am to show you to Human Resources (HR)."

"Okay." Renee stood from the seat and placed her bag on her shoulder. She picked up her briefcase and followed.

"It's easy getting to HR." She pointed towards the exit and walked ahead of Renee. Without turning to ensure Renee followed, she continued explaining. "Take the elevator to the 2nd floor, and we'll turn right towards the double doors." At the elevator, the receptionist pushed the call button. She glanced at her reflection in the shiny elevator doors and smiled at Renee. On the lift, the receptionist pushed 2 on the elevator's floor directory. "Usually, I like talking to one person who helps me the most. Or a person who will help me without breaking professional protocol. But I am sure you'll find someone who is responsive. I know it's based on personality, but I didn't say this." She smiled.

"Oh, ah, I'll make sure I remember your advice." Renee glanced towards the receptionist.

"It will help." The elevator doors opened, and the receptionist went first, turning towards the only double-door set.

"Hi." Renee smiled at the clerk sitting up front. "I'm Renee Chadwick." Renee turned to wave at the receptionist who escorted her. "I'll talk to you later. Thanks," she said, waving her hand.

The HR clerk went into her desk drawer and retrieved a blank card badge with a clip chain. "Please sit over there," she pointed.

Renee followed instructions and took the seat. "Is this okay?" She adjusted herself.

The clerk inspected the camera. "It's perfect." She nodded. "You can smile if you want."

"Oh, okay." Renee smiled and the camera flash caught her by surprise.

"It's done. You can relax." The clerk pressed a button and a machine hummed. "This is your key to everything in the building," the HR clerk clarified. "I mean, it's your access badge based on your job and security level." She grabbed the key card and chain combination and handed it to Renee. "You have a welcome session later today. Make sure you're here around 1 pm."

"Thank you, I will." Renee grabbed the badge, holding back her happy smile. *Look professional,* she reminded herself. Once at the cubicle on the 4th floor, her manager approached.

"Hi there," Mr. Ottman greeted her.

"Hi, sir," Renee smiled. "I had no idea I would be in your section."

"I played my cards right and won." Mr. Ottman smiled. "I look forward to getting a lot done."

"I do too, sir." Renee placed her bag and leather satchel on the desk. "I'm ready to go."

"We'll set you up with your equipment. It should be here this afternoon." Mr. Ottman turned. "Over there is the supply closet." Mr. Ottman nodded in the direction. "If I were you, I'd grab a pad of paper and a couple of pens and get to the 11 o'clock meeting in the conference room at the end of the hall."

"Yes sir, right away."

"Oh, and let Ted show you around." He pointed to the next cubicle.

Ted rose from his chair. "Yes, Mr. Ottman. I'll make sure she knows as much as I do."

"Good man, Ted." Mr. Ottman returned to his office.

"Ted Smithers." He offered his hand. "You are?"

"Renee Chadwick," Renee smiled. "I won't be a bother." She shook his hand.

"I didn't think you would be, but I have to show you around as Mr. Ottman directed." He turned towards the entry door. "Let's go to the cafeteria and work our way back upstairs."

"Okay." Renee followed Ted through the secured doors and to the elevators.

"The elevators get busy during lunch and around 5. If you need to leave by 5, I suggest you get out by 4:45 at the latest." He pressed the call button. "Or like many of us, use the stairs. They too can get a bit busy."

"God advice," she nodded. "I'll remember that."

"You were an intern here, right?"

"Not exactly this building; but the company, yes."

"Oh—then you know the standards, so I don't have to go over them."

"No, you don't unless something has changed within the last year."

"Change?" he snickered.

"That normal, huh?" Renee sucked her teeth and followed Ted onto the elevator.

"Press 1 for us, will you?"

Renee pressed 1 and stepped to the rear. She glanced at Ted and got a good look at his demeanor and appearance. Pretty solid gentleman, not too big of a man. "How long have you worked for the company?"

"It's my third year and I kind of like it, so far."

"It was my first choice of places to work." Renee gloated.

"You are fortunate to get here. I've known a lot of experienced people trying hard to get a position with us."

"I think my internship paid off."

"Mr. Ottman thinks so. He mentioned you were coming at the last section meeting."

"He did?"

"He did an excellent job of selling you to us."

"Selling me?" Renee smirked and frowned at Ted's comment. "What do you mean, selling me'?"

"Your skills and what you can do." Ted stepped through the opened doors. "You have talent at finding and solving issues."

"I guess."

"According to Mr. Ottman, you do." Ted walked to the double doors to the right of the elevators. "Here's the lunchroom." He pressed the doors open and she saw a serving bar, tables and chairs, a wall television, and a drink machine.

"You don't have to pay for drinks—the company takes care of it. And there's a drink machine upstairs, too."

"On our floor?"

"On every floor in each break room."

"Wow."

"Yeah, you get used to it. What a benefit, if you like commercial drinks."

They returned to the 4th floor and completed the tour of the building and required areas. When Renee sat at her desk, the technology person came with a laptop and key lock, connected her to the system, then gave her a key fob for security.

"Here, let me show you how it works," the techie said.

Sure." Renee gave her undivided attention to the refresher course on laptop operation and network security. "Is the network available from any Wi-Fi connection?"

"Yes, it is. Just remember to connect to our main network through the secure router."

"Okay, thanks." Renee shook his hand and grabbed her purse, after glancing at the time. "Ted, are you going to the conference?"

Ted looked at his laptop schedule. "I'm not in that one."

"Oh, okay." Renee gathered her pad and pen before heading to the conference room. Upon entry she took a seat at the table near the center. She discretely scanned members around the room doing her best to recall who she had met as an intern. When Mr. Ottman entered, most members stopped side conversations and sat at the table.

"It's a good day to be here, everyone," Mr. Ottman greeted.

"Let's go around the room and make introductions." He paused. "Name and section are good enough."

The team followed his instructions, and at Renee's turn, she stood. "I'm happy to be here," she added.

"Welcome," Ottman said. "Now, let's get this project introduced." He laid out the goal and explained the engineering plan, as well as the product development challenges noted by the executive board analysis. "It's going to be a profit hound when we finish, but we only get one shot at making it to the market."

"One shot?" asked the lead designer.

"That's it; because our competitors will overwhelm us if we make a mistake." Mr. Ottman stood and pushed his chair back. "I'm off to another meeting. I suggest you read the handouts I gave and come up with questions." He stepped towards the door. "Better yet, send your questions to Renee. She can compile them and make sure we aren't redundant." He left the conference room.

"I'm Renee Chadwick, and I should be on Outlook by the end of the day." She stood like everyone else who rose from the table and stepped back watching everyone leave. After the last person walked out of the conference room, Renee strode around the table, rubbing it with her hand towards the end. *I will have my own project soon.*

After lunch, she returned to HR for her in-brief. Her badge unlocked the conference door and after entering, she sat at the conference table facing a big bay window. She saw the reflection of her smile in the window.

***

Six months had passed since Renee started the job. Like she had imagined, her name became synonymous with quick answers, effective design processes, and issue elimination. Ted had moved up to team lead and chose to have her on his team. She was known for being a heavy hitter for process improvement and was keen on creating detailed analysis. They worked while Mr. Ottman kept his focus on the bigger picture.

Renee entered her cubicle and sat at her desk after lunch. She opened an engineering and industry trade magazine. The first article was improving manufacturing while tackling the dynamics of team building.

"Damn, someone beat me to an idea," she mumbled.

"No, they didn't. Someone beat you to writing the article," Ted said, standing behind her.

"Oh." Renee turned. "I didn't see you." She paused and looked at Ted, patiently waiting for him to share project work with her. "Is there anything you need?"

"Well..." Ted looked at the magazine. "You know who wrote that, right?"

"No, actually I don't."

"The guy is a serious jerk—kind of chauvinistic, with an ego the size of the Pacific."

"You know him?"

"Actually," he laughed, "I don't. But I know he's a jerk."

Renee snickered. "I thought you were serious."

He chuckled. "I have some information for you. Human Resources wants you to discuss their intake process with them. I know it is not what our project has us doing, but if you do this for them, they will be in our pocket when we need something. I told Mr. Ottman you had a little room to take it on."

"I don't see why I wouldn't help HR." Renee picked up her notebook and a pen. "Who is the contact?"

"I think you met one. He interviewed you for the job." "You mean, Mr. Bentley?"

"He's the one." Ted turned to his cubicle. "He's not the most fun person to work with, but I'm sure you'll do well."

"No sweat. I'll email him now."

"Good. Let me know if you need help." Ted returned to his chair. He rolled from his desk, peeking his head beyond the cubicle and faced Renee. "Oh, and how are you with re-engineering the quality process for the production line?"

"I've completed my part and I'll get it to you now, if you want it. But I wanted to give you the completed process. I am waiting on the others to send me their parts. I'm sure they'll have it to me before the end of the day."

"If we get it today, we're ahead of schedule."

"We'll get it. I've talked to them about it."

"Good deal." Ted held his thumb up, rolling to his desk.

Renee looked at her watch before scanning her Outlook calendar. She sent Mr. Bentley an email and a meeting invitation, as suggested, then looked for input emails from her team. Renee stopped and peeked at the top of the magazine for articles. She read the author's name, Marvin Yarbrough. She nodded and thought, *He's got a lot going on.*

***

Three weeks into the Human Resources Process Re-engineering effort, Renee sat with Mr. Bentley, reviewing the process changes she'd suggested. "Sir, it's more efficient if you have your team begin with this package in comparison to what you currently have."

"Oh, really?" Mr. Bentley responded.

"Yes, because it's more efficient on time and gives less redundancy in paperwork. I mean, I remember doing this."

"That wasn't too long ago," he smiled. "No, no, sir—it wasn't long ago."

"Okay, you think it saves us time and reduces paperwork." Mr. Bentley touched his chin and said, "I see. So, let me help you introduce your changes." Mr. Bentley called his lead clerk inside his office. "Please take Ms. Chadwick to our processing group. She has a new process to share."

"Yes, Mr. Bentley, will do," the clerk responded. "Please follow me, Ms. Chadwick."

Renee stood from her chair and shook Mr. Bentley's hand. "Thank you." She smiled and followed the clerk. "Call me Renee," she grinned.

Chapter 5

The Meeting

Marvin Yarbrough strode through the hallway, shoulders rolled back and walking smooth without wrinkling his sports coat. His slacks never showed his socks and didn't touch the ground when he stood still. His shirt was slight snug, enough to reveal the workout regime he lived by and swore to uphold for business appeal. Marvin sported the Spanish style zapateos, known to impress and admired for people who wants to look good and have comfort. His stride to the conference room, was no different than his regular glide to any location. Here, he had been to the company so many times, his lack of a badge didn't throw his ability to enter the room and prepare his presentation and connect to the room's technology.

Marvin arrived at the conference room with a laptop and a connection cord to the overhead projector. His early arrival found the empty room perfect for his rehearsal and afforded the opportunity to review in-house equipment. Marvin had done these types of meetings enough to know the importance of being early, to ensure everything ran smoothly. Though he had led his section with software sales, he had not yet achieved non-travel status. His sharp wit kept him one step ahead of his customers.

Marvin stood in the back of the conference room and pushed the cord into the overhead connection on the table. The control panel had been his favorite setup. He loved the simplicity of connecting. Push, push, press—and the hum of the overhead started. He pressed the 'on' button to his laptop and watched the forward screen display the booting cycle on the screen in front of the conference table. He tapped his laptop and a PowerPoint display appeared. He sat at the conference table with the laptop and viewed each slide, reviewing the content and rehearsing his pitch in his mind. Marvin efficiently went through the slides, returned the presentation to its first display, and rose to greet Mr. Ottman, who walked through the door.

"Hello, Mr. Ottman. How are you?"

"Doing well, Marvin. Nice to see you again."

"Good being here." Marvin adjusted the picture on the board with the remote to the overhead projector. "The view looks good." Marvin pointed at the display. "What do you think?"

Mr. Ottman looked at the screen. "Looks good to me." "Perfect." Marvin walked to the center of the table and opened his notebook. He grabbed 20 printed agendas and carefully walked around the table, placing one at each seat. "I think you'll like what I have planned today." "It's why you're here, and why no other company was invited," Mr. Ottman assured him.

"I appreciate your continued business."

Marvin smiled. "I wish I had other clients who were as loyal."

"Success is your second name." Mr. Ottman smiled. "The sad thing is: the greater your success, the less time for vacations."

"Vacation..." Marvin paused with his last agenda placement. "...what's that?"

"Ha, ha, ha," Mr. Ottman laughed. "It's almost a foreign word, but eventually you'll get a perfect job that supports vacations."

"Sir, I have the job, but not enough clients. I guess when I get the right number of clients, I'll take off. But right now, you're it."

"Seems like you are very busy." Mr. Ottman glanced at one of the handouts on the table. "How many trips are scheduled for this week?"

"I think one trip every day this week and multiple flights next week." Marvin looked at his silver blue-faced watch. "I can fill you in more after this meeting." Marvin watched six members enter. "Hello, folks."

"Hi." Marvin heard a voice but did not notice who spoke. He went to the chair he had selected, sat down, grabbed the remote, and typed on the laptop in front of him. He watched empty conference chairs fill with attendees until none were available. He rose from the table and stood at the side of the projector screen. "Hello, everyone," Marvin said, and he pointed at the projector with the control. "I can't imagine anyone in your department not being here for this new tool." He clicked the remote for the next slide.

"Has anyone ever glanced through their email in search of an acknowledgment notification, where the content was more important than who sent it?" Marvin waited for a response. "I do it, have done it, and if I didn't have this tool," he snapped the remote, "I'd have to do it again." He looked around the room and glanced into the eyes of every attendee.

"I'm Marvin Yarbrough, Senior Sales and Training, of Mims Specialty Technologies." He paused. "I'd like to have everyone introduce themselves. A simple name and position works for me." He pointed.

"You sir," he nodded. "Can we start with you?"

Mr. Ottman raised his hand. "You can call me Al," he said with a smile. A roar of laughter filled the conference room. Marvin smirked. "Okay, sir, thank you."

He pointed to the next person. "Fred, Andrew, Marcus, Anna, Belinda, Erin, Brook...Philip." A silent moment passed, with everyone looking at one member. "Renee," she said. The rest gave their name, one after the other. Marvin scanned the room, his eyes meeting the eyes of others. "Thank you," he continued. "Since we're formally introduced, I can get down to business." He pointed the remote for the next slide.

***

Renee positioned herself two seats from the far end and had a full view of Marvin, especially when he stood in front of the screen. *Damn, he hasn't changed since graduation,* she thought. His slacks were fitting below his sports coat, leaving room for the imagination of perfectly curved buttocks. Renee focused on his lips after a full-body scan. She raised an eyebrow, watching the way he used them in his facial expressions. She watched his eyes position themselves, and how they aided his words, delivering messages with clarity. Renee crossed her legs and looked at the table in front of her.

If I can get close enough to find out if he is really that attractive. Renee felt a tap on her right arm. "Say your name," Philip whispered.

"Oh, ah...Renee," she responded.

Renee watched his response and was eager to move into his work. She looked at the handout and scanned the content while listening to Marvin. She closed her eyes and heard his voice - the tone, the pitch, the speed - and imagined how she could listen to him over radio airways. With one eye, she glanced at the screen and captured his topic for discussion. Her mind jumped.

"I have a question!" she shouted in the middle of his presentation.

"Can you hold that until I finish this point, please?" Marvin responded.

"Yes, sure." Renee looked down again.

Marvin continued, "Therefore, you can use this tool with your everyday functions. Processing Human Resources support is what its best used for, from healthcare to finance — one tool for all of your business needs. Now, I have time for questions." He paused, looked, and smiled. "Um — Renee, I believe. Do you have a question?"

Renee smiled. *He remembered my name.* "Uh, yes — and it's about the process part of your tool. Why is it not linked to shipping?"

"Well, Renee, I don't think HR has a shipping component.

Well, I've never heard where Human Resources needs logistics."

"Actually," Renee said, "in our business, we rely on multiple sources for shipping goods. Those sources of inclusion will help us budget and streamline a shortfall."

Mr. Ottman interjected. "I think you have a point, Renee, but this a generic tool that can be modified for unique environments."

"Yes, exactly." Marvin nodded his head in agreement. "As a matter of fact, I'd love to discuss the module with you and see if I can help you understand the tool."

Renee looked at Mr. Ottman.

"Sure, I'll make it your project," Ottman responded.

"Thank you," Renee said.

***

Marvin continued entertaining questions and discussions on the tool. He showed process improvement areas where the software aided the company's perspective. "So, when you find fault in the software tool, it's easy to make a change through our submission for modifications. I know it works because we are flexible and focused to ensure that we support you."

"Are you with us every step of the process?" asked a member.

"Ah, yes—I start the process, but then I turn it over to more seasoned technology folks in our company. However, I'll be your major point of contact and will continue the involvement until it's completed."

Renee looked around the room and counted six modifications,

most identified. "Mr. Ottman, will all six mods be under one project?"

"Renee, I think it's a great idea." He nodded before adding to his response, "Everyone, write your modification requirement and give it to Renee. She will develop our modification goals and will make sure our process upgrade integrates with this tool. Please support her by giving her your full cooperation."

"Thank you," Renee smiled and nodded.

Mr. Ottman looked at his watch and rose from his seat. "Thank you, Marvin, for the tool introduction and pitch. We'll get back to you on modifications."

"You're welcome, sir," Marvin responded. "I look forward to them."

"I'm off to another meeting." Mr. Ottman grabbed his notepad, rose from his seat and vacated the room. All other attendees followed suit except for Renee.

"I guess you need my contact information," she suggested.

"Actually, I have it." Marvin paused and smiled at Renee. "I'm not a stalker."

"I hope you aren't." Renee grinned. "Then how did you get my information?"

"The company listed attendees. I get to know who plans to attend my presentations before I arrive."

"I almost didn't attend." Renee tapped her arm. "I wasn't sure if it would be worth my while."

"But Mr. Ottman directed you to come, right?"

"Yes, he did."

"He's my source on who was attending." Marvin smiled.

"Seems like you two know each other pretty well."

"We go back." Marvin walked to his laptop and closed it. "Not that I'm bragging but he's like a mentor."

"You guys worked together?" Renee raised her eyebrow.

"No, but he showed me the ropes in software sales and then got me my first big client." Marvin wiped the laptop with the palm of his hand. "And, of course, I won this contract, too."

"That says a lot about you two." Renee stepped towards the exit. "Well, Mr. Yarbrough…"

"Please call me Marvin." He walked to the door. "I hope we work closely together." He offered his hand.

"I suspect we will." Renee smiled, shaking his hand. "And send me an email when you get a chance, since you have my email address."

"I can do that." Marvin released her hand and stepped back. He watched every step she made, swaying her cheeks to a rhythm only he heard. His eyes peeled on her until she was out of sight. He turned his head in acknowledgment. "Damn, she's…" he nodded.

Renee walked, sleek with a little extra effort swaying her hips, hopeful he would watch. She slightly touched her hip before turning at the hallway. She stopped just past the turn and leaned to peek around the corner and saw Marvin turn from looking her direction.

***

Rene picked up her cell phone from her desk drawer and walked to the lady's room. She went into a stall, tapped her cell unlocking it, and placed it on the chrome industrial toilet paper holder. She removed clothing, sat on the toilet, grabbed her phone and opened a text screen. Renee tapped a number and began texting *I met him, that hottie from graduation. Tell you more tonight.* She pressed 'send'. Her reflective smile covered 85 percent of the black screen.

Renee swiped the screen and touched a camera application. Snap'—she took her shoulder-high picture, capturing the smile she had just seen. The toilet flush startled her, and Renee quickly got herself together, vacated the stall, and headed to the available sink. She placed the cell phone on the counter and washed her hands. She glanced in the large wall mirror and stopped in her tracks. Her mouth extended at the corners, showing her full glare of porcelain. Renee's heartbeat pepped face to brighten her stand in front of the mirror.

"Whoever got to you did a good job," a bathroom attendee noticed.

"Excuse me?" Renee responded.

"You're blushing."

***

Renee entered her childhood home. "Mom, I..." She walked into the kitchen, scanned it and briskly moved to the family room, dropped her cased laptop on the couch. Renee rolled her shoulders back, giggled, and looked towards the back sliding doors where she saw silhouettes of her parents sitting in their respective chairs. She slid the door open. "Mom!" She grinningly yelled, "I finally got to meet that fine man I saw at graduation."

"Who?" Mom quickly turned, leaned forward nearly rising from her chair. "Who?"

"Marvin Yarbrough, the guy who graduated with a Masters. You've got to remember."

"Renee, you know I only have eyes for your dad." She giggled, relaxing in the chair. "I don't look at men."

"Mom," Renee smiled. "Sure you do, Mom."

"Okay," Mom smiled. "You're talking about that chiseled guy with the dark hair?"

"Oh, and here I thought you only had eyes for Dad," Renee chuckled.

"Well, I wasn't the only one." Mom looked at Renee. "How did you meet him?"

"He came to our company presenting a software package." "A what?"

"A tool package for our computers."

"Oh." Mom looked at the back yard. "Was he impressive?" Mom crossed her legs.

"Quite impressive…he's smart, great looking, and a gentleman."

"You got close enough to notice all of that?"

"Mom," Renee smiled, "and then some."

"No, you didn't." Mom leaned her head back, gazed at her

daughter with serious eyes and encouraging words saying, 'tread lightly on your way.'

"Not yet," Renee giggled, "not yet." She used her open hand to fan her face on the way to her bedroom, changed her work clothes and returned to the kitchen. Her mind clamped onto his image, remembering his voice, a unique baritone sound, and recalling the last words he'd shared... *"I'll send you an email."* Renee retrieved the laptop in the family room and turned it on. She signed in, connecting to her office network. Her email application automatically charged the screen. Her finger traveled the mouse pad, and her eyes followed the pointer move to the email inbox. She clicked the mouse and her eyes sparkled like a kid seeing a corner of colorful paper boxed gifts, waiting for the full screen to appear.

"Marvin Yarbrough, Marvin Yarbrough, Marvin Yarbrough," she whispered. "Nothing—not one thing from him."

Mom entered the room. "What are you doing - more work?"

"Not really. I'm checking for an email."

"Oh." Mom walked to the kitchen. "I'm going to make dinner. Are you up for pasta?"

"Sure, I'll help you." Renee closed the laptop, placed it on the couch, and walked to the kitchen. "I'll prep the sausage for the sauce."

"Okay," Mom responded, and added, "we haven't done this together for some time now. What gives?"

"Just wanted to cook with you. Is that a terrible thing?"

"Not a sad thing." Mom increased the flame under the pot of water. "You have been so busy, lately—and of course, with your job."

"It's going great, Mom." Renee sprinkled seasoning over the sausage she had de-skinned. "But I need to be independent."

"Yes, you do."

"What?" Renee raised her eyebrows.

"It's time you find your own place." Mrs. Chadwick nodded her head.

"Wow, Mom. I…"

"You shouldn't be surprised. It's time you do, and we are here to help you. Dad and I don't understand why you haven't yet."

"It's on my to-do list." Renee turned towards the fryer. "I feel like it's time." "And we do, too." Mom smiled. "Renee, it's not that we don't want you around, but you've been to college, and you haven't thought about moving out. We thought it's kind of strange."

"All in good time, Mom—it's what you taught us girls."

Mom retrieved the pasta from the storage bin. "I did, and you're right. Now is an appropriate time because we figure you're more than responsible."

"I'll start looking this week. Excuse me." Renee walked past. "I need to put this on the stove."

Mom moved aside, holding dried pasta shells.

***

Renee walked into the conference room with her teammates. She sat at the center of the table directly across from Mr. Ottman, who arrived earlier than usual. He stood when the last person entered. "Okay, team," he said, "I have some particularly important news." He touched the remote and the board screen lights grew bright. "Look at this and tell me your first thought." He walked to the side of the screen and pointed with a red laser pen. "This area right here," he highlighted. "We can't afford to drop the ball because it's bad for our business and it will cost us more to maintain our people."

"Does that mean we can't use the new tool we're purchasing?" a team member asked.

"No, that's from another budget. However, we may think of a way to manipulate the cost," Mr. Ottman responded.

Renee frowned when she looked at the board and reviewed the highlighted area. She remembered a project she'd studied in college. "Mr. Ottman, I think we can readjust our healthcare cost by changing our policy. We learned this technique at the university and I'm sure we can make better options, but if I remember correctly, we have to sell the company on it."

"You are right," Mr. Ottman spoke. He touched his chin before raising the pointer. "This is the option you're pushing." He pointed with the red laser to another section. "See the policy note? We've done that, to this point. The question now becomes, what's next?"

"I guess we'll have to see what the execs decide. I don't know what to suggest," Philip said.

"We are feeding the execs information, so they make a decision." Mr. Ottman gazed at Philip. "I think we should create a think tank and come up with three solutions. Mr. Philip, you're leading one."

"Yes sir. I'm on it."

"That's good." He looks around the table. "You two," Mr. Ottman points at two members sitting together, "Go to Andrew and Brook. You three select your team and get a solution presentation in two weeks. We have to get this done."

"Can we use unconventional solutions?" asked Renee.

"We use the best solution regardless of convention." Mr. Ottman pointed to the next point. "See, it's about the bottom line. Let's see how we can get this cost responsive to our needs."

The team rose from the table and one by one exited the conference room.

"Renee," Mr. Ottman called, "how are you with the software modification objectives?"

"I'm ready with them, sir."

"Get them to Marvin and let's work to make sure we don't lose momentum on the software upgrade. We need this."

"Yes, sir." Renee walked past Mr. Ottman, exiting the conference room. She walked down the hall, looking at empty space in front of her, regardless of who passed her. She stopped at the elevators, looked at her reflection in the clean steel door, and her eyes met the ideas running on her mind. Leaving the elevator, she strode to her cubicle and Andrew approached. "You should be in my think tank group. We can use a fresh look of ideas."

"Okay, I'll be there."

"Good." Andrew walked to his cubicle.

Brook stopped by Renee's cubicle. "Got a minute?"

Renee turned around from her laptop. "I think so."

"Come to the huddle room with me," Brook suggested.

"If it's about the think tank, Andrew asked me to be in his group."

"No, that isn't it." Brook turned and walked to the huddle room (an oversized closet with two seats, and usually private), opened the door, and sat in one of the seats. She watched Renee sit in the chair across from her. "Look, I wanted to tell you something about your coming project with Marvin."

"Really?" Renee's eyes widened.

"I am giving you something to think about. I don't want to be involved or anything. I mean, I have seen you hustle. I know you'll do well, but with this guy, you may want to watch your step."

"Watch my step?"

"Yes, watch your step. The last person he worked with quit. She said it had a lot to do with Marvin and the way he treats people."

"That's it?"

"Look, I'm not telling you to be afraid, but I thought I'd share this before you get deeply involved."

Renee looked into Brook's eyes. "Did something bad happen to her?"

"I have no idea about the depth of her actions, but I get that she was quick to resign and move."

"Move?" Renee looked down, breaking eye contact. "I guess she may have gotten a better job."

"She was happy before leaving. But who knows? It happened after her project with Marvin." Brook paused. "Maybe, just maybe, it was the project...?"

"Some project." Renee shook her head. "I can only imagine how he must have had her work so hard, when he's an outsider."

"No, I don't think Ottman won't push you for him. He's serious about success at all costs."

"I can tell." Renee touched Brook's arm. "I appreciate your concern. I'll keep my eyes open for anything and everything."

"Don't be afraid to ask for help if something gets difficult. I'm here." Brook rose from her seat and stepped towards the door. "And let me know long before you resign, if you're going to."

"Resign?" Renee stood, leaning her head to one side. "I don't quite get it."

"If you think about leaving, let me know. I may have a few contacts for you." Brook stepped into the open floor on her way to her cubicle.

"That was an interesting comment," Renee whispered, walking to her cubicle.

***

Mr. Ottman sat behind his desk, tapped the Instant

Messenger (IM) on his laptop, and chimed Renee. *Can you visit at your earliest?* he typed.

Renee heard a chime and saw the yellow icon flash. She tapped the mouse and opened the IM. She typed, *On my way.* She rose from the cubicle, checked to see if Philip had left, turned and stepped with haste towards the office area. At Mr. Ottman's office, she tapped on the door. "You wanted to see me?" she asked while standing in the doorway.

"Yes, come on in." He watched Renee enter. "Take a seat, please." He pointed.

"Yes, Mr. Ottman, how can I help?" Renee said, sliding into the chair in front of Mr. Ottman's desk.

"I reviewed the software modification objectives. Excellent job. They look reasonable. But..." he paused, "I don't think Marvin can pull these off without your help. Are you ready to get serious with the project?"

"I'm ready for anything you assign Mr. Ottman. If working with Marvin is part of the assignment, I'll take it and do my best."

"Good, because you're the point of contact for the business and you will work with Marvin as the subject matter expert for us. Don't get caught up on every aspect of those objectives. You have other resources that I've directed to be at your call." Mr. Ottman stood and grabbed a user's handbook for the software. "Learn this as soon as you can. Play with the modules and become familiar with it." He walked around his desk and handed the book to Renee. "Don't be afraid to ask questions or dig for information."

"I won't, sir." Renee stood. "Thank you for the chance."

"Don't thank me. It was your internship that got you into this mess," Mr. Ottman chuckled. "You can handle it."

Renee rose and stepped towards the door. "Thanks again for the vote of confidence. I'll get it done."

"Oh, before you go," Mr. Ottman said, "you're not on Andrew's think tank group anymore. The software modification has priority."

"Yes sir," Renee answered, and walked through the office door into the passageway. She returned to her cubicle and logged into her email. Her fingers exercised over the laptop keyboard, zipping letter characters into a methodical message.

Marvin,

Let's get together and review the process ahead of modification requirements. Let me know your availability for this afternoon and tomorrow before lunch. I'll send three meeting invitations to make it simple.

Thanks,
Renee

Renee tapped 'send' with her mouse and the email disappeared from her screen. She set up three meeting invitations like she had written in the email and sent them off, creating one phone conference call per session. She then reviewed the modification requirements document and made notes of contacts working on it with each section. *I'm ready*, she smiled.

***

Marvin's cell phone pinged, acknowledging an email arrival. He picked up the cell phone from the coffee shop counter. He looked at the face of it and read: *Renee Chadwick - Software Modification Meeting*. He put the phone down and picked up his coffee cup, looking beyond the big glass window in front of him. He sipped coffee and allowed his eyes to scan past the cup's rim. He watched people and their style of clothes, addressing their appearance. A cloud covered the sun, and the reflection of his light color shirt contrasting with his dark blazer, caught his eye. He looked down to his stylish jeans and soft leather loafers. His casual-sexy look, always ready to meet a potential customer or date.

Marvin placed the coffee cup on the counter, focused on his cell phone, and tapped on the phone's screen. He read Renee's email, scrolled to his calendar, selected the afternoon, and sent a confirmation for the late afternoon. He put the phone down and picked up the coffee cup.

***

Renee returned to her cubicle after passing documents to Andrew's group. She sat at her desk, clicked the mouse and logged into the network. She saw Marvin's response for an afternoon call - in 15 minutes. Renee smiled, went to the restroom, walked into a stall where she sat on the toilet and giggled. She looked at her watch and quickly walked out of the stall, stopped in front of the mirror, washed her hands, and looked at her reflection in the mirror. She turned her head left, then right, in hope no one saw her teeth glare as bright as the sun.

"Umm, umm." She cleared her throat and went to

her cubicle, put on headphones, and dialed her conference bridge number. She waited for the sound of a high pitch bell, announcing a joiner to the call. Soft music filled the airspace while she retrieved supporting documents, opening them onto her screen. DING!

"Marvin Yarbrough, joining the call," the system announced.

"Marvin?" Renee called into the headphone. "Yes – Renee, right?" Marvin responded. "Glad you contacted me, because we don't have much time to get this done."

"Yes, Mr. Ottman suggested we get right on it, as it's a priority for the company."

"Good ole Mr. Ottman. He's a sharp guy."

"Yes, he is." Renee paused. "I'm glad you could get to me. I have these documents ready to go through and get the detail we need on what's expected."

"I don't have them, so I need to get a copy from you."

"Oh, I'm sorry, I forgot to send them." She looked at her laptop and created an email, attaching the documents.

"I'm sending them over now."

"Good. And I hope those requirements are straightforward. I can then explain them to my development team."

"That will be great, because I need to report back to Mr. Ottman when you can get these done."

"I think," Marvin paused, "I can't get them to download on my phone, so I'll get to a laptop or find a way to get a printed copy."

"I'm sorry. I thought you might have been able to get them now. Maybe we should reschedule our discussion?"

"Yea, give me a little bit to read these and get back with you." Marvin paused. "Maybe you can meet me tonight?"

"Tonight?" Renee nodded her head, looking at the screen. "I get off around 5 or so. I didn't think you'd work late."

"I'm sorry. I tend to take every client's goal as an urgent mission. I am open this evening and will have read these documents once I get to a laptop. Unless you want Mr. Ottman to think you guys aren't that important, then I don't mind waiting. But I'm sure I know his sense of urgency."

"Well, I think..."

"...Didn't he say this is a priority?"

"He did." Renee looked at her watch. "Where do you want to meet?"

"How about the coffee shop on Hall Stream? Do you know the place?"

"Actually, I don't, but if you send the address, I'll use Waze to get there."

"I can do that. Let's get there around 6, if it's okay with you," Marvin encouraged.

"Okay, the coffee shop on Hall Stream, got it. I'll be there at 6, and don't forget to send the address and print those documents." Renee reiterated.

"See you at six." Marvin disconnected the call, typed the address in an email, and pressed 'send'. He downloaded the documents to his phone. He walked to the nearest Office Supply store, scanned, and printed the documents before reading the first paragraph of each page; after his pass through, he defined the goals they needed to meet.

***

Renee packed her laptop in the carrier and placed a folder in one section before heading to her car. She put her phone on the dash and pressed the Waze icon, input *Hall Stream,* and followed directions. She took off driving as directed. "Turn left at Phipps Avenue," Waze directed. *I hope this is worth it. Hell, I am sure it is. This man, this guy...* she thought, remembering her first full look at him and the impression all the other women had of him at the meeting. She flashed to graduation and the impact he'd had on her.

"Turn right on Reid Street in 400 ft," Waze directed.

I can't believe it! I am meeting him... right now! Renee's right hand became moist, and she dropped it from the steering wheel, and wiped it on her pants and swapped with the other to do the same. She stopped at the light and turned as directed.

"Your destination is on your right, in 1000 feet," Waze informed her.

Renee slowed so as not to miss the coffee shop. She scanned each building marquis and the logos in the windows. She carefully drove each block paying attention to the road and the traffic, while searching address numbers on the buildings. She arrived at the front of a strip mall where the coffee shop is at the end. She pulled into the lot, parked in front of the coffee shop, and picked up her laptop case before exiting the car.

***

Marvin watched her exit the car, placing the laptop case over her shoulder. She walked in haste, displayed a frown, walking with a mission on her mind. He noticed her height, her slender build, and her caramel complexion. He smiled at the way her shoulder-length hair bounced with her movement. Marvin's eyebrow lifted, dropping his smile while she approached. His mind flashed to ideas of passion. He walked to the door and pushed it open for her entry. "Hi," he greeted her.

"Hi," Renee responded. "This is your office?" She looked around, noticing the setup and décor. "It looks interesting, but I couldn't work here all day," Renee giggled.

"Over here," Marvin directed. "I have a table by the window."

"Okay." Renee followed, glancing at the bay window. "You saw me come in."

"I did."

"Oh," she smiled. "It was nice of you to open the door for me."

"Makes it easy." Marvin pulled a chair out for Renee. "Please."

"Wait—this isn't a date, you know."

"Huh?" Marvin raised an eyebrow. "I'm sorry if I offended you. I do this out of respect."

"You do this for all women?"

"Sure, why not?"

Renee sat in the chair Marvin selected and retrieved her

laptop, laying it on the table and opening it. "I wanted to pull up the document."

"I have a printed copy. You don't need to."

"I want to make it easy for changes. I think working on the document during the review helps clarify our requirements."

"Oh, I'd better mind my manners. Do you want anything to drink? Maybe a coffee or latte?"

Renee looked at the counter. "Can I get a latte and maybe a snack? I'm missing my workout class."

"Oh, I'm sorry about the class." Marvin raised an eyebrow. "You look pretty good."

"Thank you. I try to keep my girlish figure." Renee smiled behind her laptop. "I should order."

"No, I'll get it." Marvin rose from the table and walked without looking back at Renee.

Renee watched Marvin walk to the counter, remembering what she saw at graduation and comparing it to this point. She smiled. "Ugh, ugh," she coughed. *I can do this man.* Her heartbeat slightly rose in rhythm. Renee connected her laptop to the Wi-Fi while listening to the soft music playing in the shop. She heard Marvin order her latte and a slice of cheesecake. "Good guess, Mr. Yarbrough," she mumbled.

Marvin returned to the table with a latte and cheesecake, utensils, and napkins. "I hope you don't mind if we share."

Renee glanced over the laptop. "Thank you." She picked up the latte and sipped. "Nice." She raised the cup towards him. "Thanks again."

"You're welcome." Marvin sat at the table and opened a preset folder for the meeting. "I read your modifications and have a few questions." He sipped his coffee and put the cup back on the table. "I'm not so sure we can modify the landing page. Or are you saying you want a different starting page?"

"I will note that. But from what I understood in the discussions, it is the landing page they must go through first, before getting to what we need to see. If the user could just get there upon login, it'd be faster and more efficient."

"Good, now I see." Marvin scribbled notes on his document.

"Okay, I'm looking at your fourth modification…Hmmm, I can't see how we can do this, but I'm not a techie. I understand enough to know we need a database, but making it bring up different data points will need a major change."

"I can't explain it, either. Well," Renee paused, "I think we have to get the techies in a meeting to explain this."

"Agreed."

Renee typed on her laptop, creating notes of their discussion. "I think we've covered the main points so far. The others are pretty much self-explainable."

"I don't think so. I wanted to ask about number 8 - it is a major change and will cause your company to have to buy the newer version. It's something you should report to Mr. Ottman."

"I can do that. I will bring it to his attention tomorrow, but I'll draft an email tonight when I get home."

"Why wait? We're here now."

"I don't want to take up much more of your time."

Marvin smiled. "I don't mind, unless you have someplace to go." His eyes met her gaze.

Renee broke her gaze, looked at her watch, and glanced at the window, seeing bumper to bumper traffic. "I can...yeah, why not now."

"Good idea," Marvin smiled.

She clicked on the email application and opened a blank draft. Renee typed Mr. Ottman's name on the subject line and looked at Marvin.

"How should we start?"

"Simple." Marvin touched his chin. "I usually make it direct and to the point, discuss what I want and need. Then I outline the problem, giving him heads up on what we're facing."

Renee nodded and started typing. "I'll just say, 'Problems ahead on the application modification. I'll send you a meeting request and share depths of the problem during our discussion.'" She signed it *Renee*.

"That was quick. Why did you keep it short?" Marvin shook his head.

"I need to research it before I send him a solution."

"It's a waste of time, but he's your boss."

Marvin looked at his watch. "Whatever you needed to do, I guess you still have time to do it."

Renee pressed the off icon watching the laptop screen go black and while waiting she glanced at Marvin over laptop's edge. "I can, and I need to." She giggled. "I don't keep this figure without effort, you know." She closed the laptop and placed it in the briefcase.

Marvin nodded in agreement. "You aren't so bad." His eyes rolled from her waist to her face. "I admire your discipline." He raised his coffee cup. "I think we should meet again," he said. "Um, maybe next time..."

Renee picked up her laptop briefcase and stood from the table. "Next time?"

"We'll see something different." He grinned and rose from his seat. "Please keep that in mind." Marvin walked to the coffee order counter. "I'll see you next time." Renee glanced at Marvin's butt while he moved along. Marvin turned, catching her stare, waved at Renee and returned his focused-on ordering.

She rushed to the exit.

Chapter 6

Developing the Chance

Renee drove to the office earlier than what became her habitual arrival. She pulled into the partially empty parking lot, selected a rarely available parking place stopping short of the white line. A thought crossed her mind: *Maybe I'll meet Marvin Yarbrough at the coffee shop.* She turned the car off. "That fine witty man has a sexy voice, and he smells great...I would have, if he'd asked...what am I to think of this guy?" she mumbled.

She reached for the rearview mirror, turned it towards herself, and eyed her reflection. Renee touched her eyebrow, pushed hair from her eye, and checked her makeup again. She readjusted the mirror, removed the key from the ignition, and gathered her things before leaving the car. On her way to the office door, she saw Mr. Ottman enter the building, followed by a gentleman she recognized.

The second elevator on the right arrived upon her call. She looked at the floor before the elevator doors opened, stepped forward, and in the corner of her eye stood a silhouette. Tingles ran down her spine and the sensation stopped her feet from responding to her mental command. She dared to lift her head in embarrassment.

"Good morning." A familiar voice entered her ears.

"Oh." Renee looked up. "I didn't see you. Good morning," she smiled.

He looked at his watch. "You're early."

"I can say the same for you." Renee stepped aside from the elevator doors. "I'm surprised to see you." The elevator doors closed before rising to the next floor.

"I typically get here early to see my customers." "Really?"

"Yes. I spoke with one of the executives in your company."

"Well," Renee smiled, "I guess catching executives early can make them listen." She paused and looked at Marvin. "Who knows, I'll have to arrive early more often to watch you in action."

His glare focused on Renee's eyes, noticing one eyebrow is above the other, and slightly bit the corner of her bottom lip, "Success waits for no one," he said, rising smile and calm eyes, stopping short of full show of pearly teeth. "I learned that from years of hustle."

"Really," Renee snickered. "You find time to see important people and sell. I get it." Renee looked at the elevator call selection and pressed the floor button for her destination. "I guess your other half doesn't mind your focus." She moved her back to the elevator's wall, facing her business companion.

"It doesn't matter because my time is my time. Regardless of a woman being involved, I get to do what's important." He raised his eyes towards the top of the elevator. "Sales."

"The first in, beats the competition." Renee shared a quote from a college business session.

"Sometimes it's that simple." He glanced at his watch. "I've got to get going." He stepped forward, timing the opening doors, and looked back. "Will I hear from you later?"

"Sure." Renee pressed the close button on the door of the elevator. *That's how he does it...non-stop working. No wonder the magazine highlighted his story.* The elevator door opened at her floor, and she stepped off, gazed around, and found the office scarce of people. Renee looked at her watch, noting the time of her early arrival. She realized after conversing with Marvin that her arrival was hours before the majority being in the office. She sat at her cubicle, popped her laptop into the docking station, and logged into the network.

She walked into the break room for coffee, grabbed a packet of grounds from a drawer, retrieved a paper filter, and prepped both in the coffee machine for the morning brew. She pressed the button and watched the machine activate.

"Good morning, Renee," Mr. Ottman greeted her.

"Good morning, Mr. Ottman," Renee responded. "You're early."

He looked at his watch. "It's my regular time." He smiled. "I have to find my quiet time before everyone arrives."

"Oh, I didn't know."

"You'll see the importance when you climb the ladder." Renee smiled. "Do you think I can get to your level?"

Mr. Ottman stepped in front of the refrigerator, retrieved a flavored creamer, and sat it on the counter by the coffeemaker. "Do you like this?" he pointed.

"I'm not a fan of cream." Renee smiled.

"That's my point. I was not either, until I stepped out of my box. And now I love it." He looked at Renee. "I read your email, and I think it's a clever idea to get both groups together. Make sure you have Steve, our lead techie, involved in each meeting."

"I can do that, sir."

"Good. And don't let Marvin push you too much. I know he is good at what he does, but do not allow him to run the group. Remember: we're his customer."

Renee flashed to an earlier conversation about the previous person assigned to work with Marvin. "Umm, Mr. Ottman, what happened on the last project with Marvin?"

Mr. Ottman picked up a coffee mug from the mug tree. "If you're asking why Ms. Angler quit, it was not because of Marvin."

"Okay," Renee frowned. She watched Mr. Ottman pour coffee and add creamer. He tilted the coffee pot, offering to fill her mug with the black gold. Renee nodded and Mr. Ottman filled her cup before replacing the pot.

"Thank you," Renee said.

Mr. Ottman smiled. "You're welcome," he said, a moment before he left the breakroom.

"That was odd," Renee mumbled.

***

Renee entered the conference room where she would

coordinate the meeting. She dialed the table phone and pressed the communication control box for the video conference link. The projector screen activated, and a picture of a conference room across the country appeared. Other attendees' images were aligned on the far side.

"Hi, everyone," Renee greeted them. She looked at her watch.

"We're a little early, so let's wait a few minutes for everyone to join."

Marvin walked onto the screen of the conference room across the country. "Hi, Renee, nice seeing you again."

"I didn't know you were there."

"I…" he chuckled, "I didn't know you had tabs on my travel."

"I don't," she frowned.

"I'm only kidding," Marvin smiled. "Don't take it seriously." "Yeah, he gets around," a team member laughed. "Always on the go. You never know where he'll join us."

"I'm wherever you think I'm not," Marvin responded with a smirk.

"I see." Renee opened her laptop and typed those in attendance and watched who else entered each room. She started the meeting and took roll, then started with the agenda she had sent days earlier. The major discussion led them into the software gap, and Marvin spoke. "I discussed the modification with these guys, and we have a solution I think you all will like."

"It's been a few days since our last meeting." She paused,

looked at her laptop, and retrieved the last notes from her meeting. "See?" She displayed the meeting minutes on the main screen. "You guys said it will take four weeks to modify."

"We found a faster solution," Marvin's lead team tech spoke. "Yeah, it's a simple modification and we'll have it to you this evening."

"I assessed it myself and it looks great," Marvin added.

"I think..." Renee looked at her technical advisor. "What do you think, Steve?"

"Let's see how it performs when it arrives." Steve looked at the screen. "When do we expect the push?"

"Again, we'll have it to you by our close of business." A technical lead spoke from Marvin's group.

"That's late night, for you folks. So, let's say when you arrive in the morning, it will be ready," Marvin presented.

"Okay; and that covers every modification?" Renee asked.

"Every one of them," Marvin responded.

***

Renee's desk phone rang. "This is Renee, how can I assist you?"

"I can think of a way you can."

"Marvin, I'm surprised you called."

"Why?" Marvin waited for her response. His mind spun defensive, flashing to a moment he heard his dad said to his mother.

"I usually get emails from you...it's been a month since we last talked."

"This isn't a business call, even though it's on your desk phone." Marvin paused, looked out of the window at the coffee shop. "I was thinking about you and wondered if you'd like to have dinner with me?"

"I..." Renee smiled, covered her mouth, and looked around her cubicle. "I'd like that. Why don't you text me when and where on my cell?"

"I would like that. Let me get a pen." Marvin reached into his blazer pocket. "Okay, I'm ready." He wrote on a napkin from the coffee shop, where he was sitting at the bay window.

Renee shared her cell number and waited for his acknowledgement.

"Got it. I'll text you." Marvin nodded and tapped his phone off. "It's going to be a momentous day."

Renee put the phone receiver on the base. She rose from her seat and walked to the lady's room. She went to the mirror and leaned over the sink. "Finally!" Renee smiled and her cheeks became rosy. "I'll get that text."

Brook stepped from a stall and walked to the sink. With one hand, in sequence, she pressed the water and liquid soap dispenser. "Hey, you're going to the luncheon tomorrow - right?"

"Yes." Renee looked at Brook in response. "I'm not missing it."

"You survived Marvin." Brook shook her hands at the sink, freeing them of water.

"Yes, I did." Renee turned, facing the open area with her back to the sink. "I didn't see a problem with him."

"That's a good thing. You know what you're doing." Brook grabbed paper towels from the wall dispenser. "Oh—fantastic job on it, too, by the way." Brook smiled on her way out.

"Thanks." Renee went into a stall. *What was that about?*

***

Marvin received a call from the Director of Sales. "You need to come to Corporate this week."

"Yes sir, I'll set up my flight for Thursday."

"Marvin, I need you tomorrow morning. Your flight is set. My assistant sent you the itinerary. If it is not there within the hour, call me."

"Is there an emergency?"

"You'll see when you get here."

"Yes, sir." Marvin disconnected the call before his phone chimed the email's arrival. *What the hell did I do?* He looked at his phone, reading the itinerary, thinking about what to pack in case he needed to entertain executives. Marvin went to his car and drove to his condominium. He went inside and selected his suitcase, placing it on the bed. *A week at corporate.* His chose two suits, multiple slacks, and one blazer, and a mixture of shirts. He packed his Stacy Adams, a pair of running shoes, and leather belt; then socks, underwear, and workout clothes. He ran to the bathroom and pulled out his travel toiletries kit, then checked his unique batch of colognes. His quick preparation gave him some free minutes. He walked to the kitchen and sat at the counter. He picked up his phone and called his friend Tracey. "Hey, I got called to Corporate. Can you check on the place for me?"

"Yeah, no problem," Tracy responded, and then asked, "How long, this time?"

"A week," Marvin paused. "Man, I have no idea what I did this time."

"Knowing you, it's another award or something."

"I don't know, but thanks for looking out for me. I will hook you up when I get back."

"Yeah—this time, include dinner."

"Damn, you just reminded me...dinner...got to go." Marvin tapped his phone off and pulled the napkin from his pocket. He selected the text message application on his phone and punched in numbers. He wrote, *"Sorry, but can I take a rain check on dinner? I've been directed to attend a conference at Corporate for a week. I leave in two hours."* He pressed 'send'. Marvin returned to his bags, grabbed his laptop bag, and drove to the airport.

Marvin arrived at the terminal gate with 20 minutes before boarding. He observed his surroundings and watched how effectively the airline managed the boarding process. He grabbed his phone and jotted lines on the note's app, marking his improvement ideas to pitch the company's software. He smiled at the counter assistant when he approached with his ticket in hand.

"Hi," Marvin spoke.

"Thank you, Mr. Yarborough," she responded, suddenly blushing.

Marvin took the boarding pass from her hand and touched her arm. "Have a wonderful day," he said, and stepped into the walkway. She sighed before turning to the next passenger.

"Oh, I'm sorry." He apologized to the woman he'd stepped in front of.

"No problem," she smiled. "I hope we're sitting in the same row."

"Good luck," the counter assistant said, grabbing another boarding pass.

Marvin approached the row and sat in the aisle part of his assigned seat. He placed his laptop under the seat in front of him and did not secure the seatbelt. He was fortunate to have a seat in business class. He took his phone from his pocket and tapped on the text application. He located Renee's number and typed, 'I wanted to see you tonight, but my misfortune takes me on business. I want you to know that my intent is pure.' He pressed 'send'.

***

Renee turned her phone on after it charged. She had forgotten to put the phone on the charger the night before and had left it charging when she attended the last meeting for the day. It chimed with multiple notifications. She looked at the front of her phone and swiped the screen. The first message from Marvin appeared. She puckered her lip in disappointment and responded, 'I understand. Things happen. I guess we'll see each other when you return.' She pressed 'send'. *I should have asked...no, if I had asked about where he's going, it's being nosey. I don't have to think I should ask...not yet.* Renee opened the second text from Marvin. She smiled. *He likes me.* Her fingers ran over the keyboard. 'I am happy you explained your intent. I can't wait until we *have a chance to talk.'* She pressed 'send' and sighed. *He is so sweet,* she thought.

Renee completed her workday, focused on her next assignment. After leaving the building, she got into her car, started the engine, clicked on the seatbelt, and turned on the radio. She looked before moving forward through the empty spot in front of her. Her cell phone chimed. She stopped the car in the easement and looked at the screen of her hand-held device. *'I'm free this evening. Can I call you?'* Marvin texted. She quickly responded, *'Yes, anytime.'*

Damn, I hope he doesn't call late. I have to work tomorrow. Renee drove home.

***

Marvin arrived at the hotel, his home for the coming week. He signed in at the counter and retrieved the access key to his room. He rode the elevator to the 38th floor to a suite with a view. When the elevator door opened, the hall was lit with golden wall lights, as if hand made from Spain. The carpeted marble floor reflected sparkles, and three side wall tables sat below landscape portraits. Marvin walked twenty feet from the elevator to his room, swiped the key, and pushed the door open. The sparkling chandelier took him by surprise. The white leather couch position in the center, flanked by matching chairs, unique to an English tavern. The gigantic wall screen television set in front of the couch and chairs. Over near the huge bay window is a table set for four. He looked at his feet, quickly slipped out of his loafers, and peeled his socks off. He sighed, looked at the ceiling, and whispered, "I've arrived." Marvin smiled and took his luggage to the bedroom where a king-size bed centered the room and glass walls gave a remarkable view of the city.

He shook his head in disbelief "How did I deserve this?" He frowned and sat at the foot of the bed. "What did I do?" He looked in the fridge and scanned the bar. Marvin selected Scotch and poured it into the available glass. He grabbed two ice cubes from the filled ice bucket, dropped them into the glass, and moved to a chair near the large window. He sat with the phone in one hand, Scotch in the other, and stared into space. He sipped, watching the glitter of streetlights mirror the bright stars in the night. His hand raised to his face, holding the lifeline to the outside world.

The buzz surprised him, startling him with the text alert. He put down the whiskey glass on the table next to the chair before smiling. He frowned at the screen and while he read, his face relaxed and the corners of his mouth pulled in separate directions. Marvin placed his fingers into action for his response. *'I appreciate your patience. I look forward to our dates.'* He read his response before sending it. *No, that isn't quite what I should say.* He paused for a moment before pressing the backspace key and erasing his first response. He typed, *'I can't wait to see you,'* and pressed 'send'. He put the phone on his knee, picked up the Scotch, and sipped. His eyes focused on the picturesque view a large metropolitan city offers at night.

***

Renee woke early, repeating Marvin's response, 'I can't wait to see you.' Her mind played a game of if...*what if it is good, or what if it is bad...*

She went to the bathroom, brushed her teeth, and washed her face before taking off her pajamas. She selected her outfit, dressed, and returned to the bathroom to style her hair. *I might like this*, she thought. *If he's anything with a relationship like he is with his work, I might enjoy his focus...No, no I won't. He's a workaholic.* She put the hot comb down on the sink's counter. *Maybe he is working so much because he doesn't have anyone in his life.* Renee looked into the mirror and brushed her blouse with her hands. *You know... I never asked if he's dating anyone. Maybe I should?* Renee finished styling her hair, unplugged the hot comb, and tapped the bathroom light switch off while passing through the doorway.

***

Marvin arrived at the corporate office and presented himself in front of the vice president's executive assistant's desk. "Good morning, I'm Marvin Yarbrough," he reported.

"Good morning. He's expecting you." She rose from behind her desk. "Follow me," she instructed, and walked to the office door. "Sir, Mr. Yarborough," she announced.

Marvin passed the assistant, "Thank you." He looked towards the Vice President of Sales and posed a slight grin.

"Marvin, good to see you." "Thank you, sir. Good to be here."

"Sit down, please." Mr. James raised his hand and pointed to a lazy boy-type chair. He moved from around his desk and sat next to Marvin. "Coffee or tea?"

"Nothing, Mr. James. I'm okay, thank you."

He reached to the phone next to him and buzzed the assistant. "Black coffee please," he requested, and released the button. "Let me say thanks for coming on short notice."

"I'm glad to be here."

"Good, because what I'm about to tell you is extremely important."

"Sir?" Marvin sat still reflecting on his curiosity. "I..."

"... I'll answer everything during the week you're here."

Marvin nodded and heard. "Excuse me, Mr. James," the assistant said, before she placed a cup of coffee in front of the vice president.

"Thank you." He nodded and instructed her, "Close the door behind you."

Marvin sat on the edge of the chair, leaning towards Mr. James, giving him his undivided attention.

"Sit back, we have a lot to discuss."

"Yes sir." Marvin pushed back into the chair, crossing one ankle over his thigh, slightly above his knee.

"Marvin, you've done an excellent job for us, and you've represented the company as best as I've seen. You bring our business a new eye to success."

"Thank you, Mr. James."

Mr. James picked up his cell phone and swiped the face of it. "Here are a few achievements you've made." Mr. James read the entire five years of Marvin's history to him, including setting new sales records and his magazine articles. "These are important to a company like us." He placed his cell on the coffee table near the desk phone. "I haven't seen this type of performance from someone with so little experience in a lifetime of working in sales."

"Thank you for saying so. I never thought of them as achievements. They were acts of making the sale."

"Well, tell me—how do you manage to not only sell, but have repeat contracts come to us?"

"I don't know exactly how to explain the results, but I do collaborate well with people."

"I suspect so. You have a certain characteristic we need in our company, and I explained our need to the CEO." He paused, reached for his coffee cup, and sipped the contents before looking at Marvin. "Did you ask why you're coming here for a week?"

"No, sir. I follow instructions well," Marvin admitted.

"I see—and without questioning."

"Sir, I was going to ask why; but you said you'd explain."

"Oh, that's right, I did," he smiled. "Okay, let me get to the meat of what's going on." He placed the coffee cup down and stood, walked to the large window, and looked at the scenery. "The company is growing, but not with the same young, vibrant leadership it needs to sustain the next decade. And what you've shown in your efforts makes us think you're a great candidate to join the ranks."

"Join the ranks?"

"We had a few of you come here for the week to see if you cut the mustard and can endure our level of business decisions. Based on what you do and how you respond, this will tell me if I am making the right choice. Every senior vice president in the company will mentor and evaluate a team member in their group and report their findings to the CEO." He turned to Marvin. "If you complete the week and impress us, there will be a substantial change in your future."

"So, I'm being evaluated for a promotion." Marvin sat forward. "I'm grateful you selected me, sir."

"You've earned it, but we'll see how it works for the week." "Yes, sir." Marvin stood and asked, "When do I start?" "Hold on, I have more to explain."

Marvin sat down and listened to Mr. James explain his expectations.

Chapter 7

His Move

Renee drove home in the middle of a rain shower after spending hours in the gym. She took the long route, imagining it would have less traffic and safer streets. She turned the radio to the local news, which shared the location of a huge auto accident three blocks from the gym. "I'd be in that mess, had I not come this way," she told the radio. Her phone rang. She pressed the answer icon on her car audio. "Hello?"

"Are you busy?" "Marvin?"

"Yes, it's me. Are you busy?" Marvin asked.

"You don't say hello or anything, from being out for a week."

"I need you." He spoke in a muffled voice. Marvin breathed into the mic before he said, "Can you come by the corner of Plural and Comanni?"

"Yeah, I was just near there. My gym is on Comanni. I know where it is." Renee reached to disconnect and thought, *The accident.*

Marvin tapped his phone and ended the call. He looked at the bouquet in his hand and the corner table where the receptionist had taken him. *Oh, gym...*he thought. *No worries, she will look great* His cell phone rang. "Hey."

"Were you in an accident?" Renee asked.

"No, not exactly." His voice sharpened.

"What? Not exactly? What do you mean?"

"Pull into Mexi's when you get to the corner, and you'll understand."

"I know the place. See you in about 10 minutes." Renee turned the corner and stopped at the traffic light. She went left instead of right, remembering the accident two blocks down, near Mexi's. Her drive took her three blocks in the opposite direction. *I should have said 15 minutes,* she thought.

***

Marvin looked at his watch and signaled for the waiter. "I'll have a house margarita and a Mexican coffee."

"Sure thing," the waiter said, and left the table.

Marvin looked at his phone and retrieved an email. While reading the content - especially the second paragraph - he smiled. *Once I show her this, she will be ecstatic.* His eyes glanced at the restaurant, past the empty tables and few patrons, focusing on the quaint decorations reflecting the picturesque life in Mexico. *I should take her there, to a villa along the beach. That will impress her.* His eyes focused on his phone again, reading the email's second paragraph. Rubbing his forehead with his right hand, wiping away the sense of perspiration, he thought, *I have not felt this since...I can't remember.*

"Marvin!" Renee called, upon her approach to the table. "Hey," she greeted him, and touched a chair.

Marvin looked up, put his cell phone down, and rose. "You look great."

"I'm not dressed. I'm coming from the gym."

She checked his dress from head to toe. "You don't look like there is a problem."

"There is," Marvin responded, and pointed to the chair in front of him. "Please sit down."

"Okay." Renee pulled the chair from the table and sat. "What's going on, and why did you call me like it's urgent?"

Marvin waved his hand above his head. "After you get a drink, I'll share what's going on."

"I...I don't know if I want a drink." Renee placed both hands on the table and crossed her fingers. "It's not what people normally do after working out."

Marvin reached for her hands, touching them with his palm. "Please have a drink with me."

Renee looked into his eyes, noticing a different image of a man she'd once seen as magnetic and powerful. "Okay, I'll have a glass of red wine."

"Good." Marvin smiled turned to the approaching waiter. "A glass of red wine for the lady." The waiter nodded and turned around.

"Now, I was sitting here thinking of what I should say, or if there's something I should do with you."

"Do with me?"

"That didn't come out right." He dropped his head. "I mean...I'm a little nervous, but I'm happy."

"Nervous and happy." Renee uncoupled her hands and sat back in the chair. "You? Nervous? If I didn't know you, I'd swear something happened during your travel."

"Something did, and I don't have anyone to share it with. Well, I mean, I have one person in mind." Marvin gazed in her eyes. "And I thought about you."

"You mean to tell me; you don't have much of a life outside of your work?"

"Not really, and not many women find me as attractive or interesting. I usually focus on work."

"I can tell you that isn't true."

"Me not working isn't true?"

"No, the attraction. Women find you incredibly attractive." Renee held her smile, pressing her lips inward.

"Do you find me attractive?"

"I... wait, I thought we were talking about you?"

"I am." Marvin caught her eyes with his and reached for her hand. "I'm asking for a reason."

Renee took in a breath, looked at his hand, and back into his eyes. "I think you're scaring me."

"Don't be afraid. I have good news, and I couldn't think of anyone better to share it with."

The waiter approached the table holding a tray with one glass of red wine, a margarita, and a Mexican coffee. "Excuse me." He put the wine in front of Renee and the others in front of Marvin. "Are you ready to order?"

"Can you give us a few minutes?" Marvin asked.

"Yes, just wave when you're ready."

"I will. Thank you." Marvin watched the waiter leave and then turned to Renee, grabbed his margarita, and raised it to toast. "Here's to my new job."

"New job?" Renee picked up the wine glass and met his margarita. She watched him sip while placing the wine back on the table. "I didn't know you were looking for a new job, but, then again, we were going to have dinner and you left." Renee tapped the table. "Did you go for a week-long interview or something?"

"You are a very smart woman." Marvin sipped the margarita.

"Yes, yes, and yes. I asked you out for dinner—and this is not what I had in mind, by the way. I did have a week-long interview. And I had to tell you because it's something I have to share with someone I am interested in."

"Interested!" She looked into Marvin's eyes. "Before I get to the interest you have for me, let me congratulate you." Renee raised the wine glass and waited for his response.

Marvin tapped her glass and sipped his margarita. "Thank you." His cell phone chimed.

"You need to get that?" Renee looked at his cell phone.

"It can wait." Marvin turned sideways and crossed his legs, then angled his arm over the back of the chair, locking his fingers.

Renee had seen him sit like this before when they worked together, and remembered it is his witty position.

"I don't want to know what you're thinking." She shook her head. "I need to go home. I have a long day ahead of me."

"You didn't ask what kind of job I got."

"I'm not so sure it will impact me — or will it?"

Marvin scanned the ceiling before he looked at her. He took in a breath and said, "I hope it does impact you."

"What?"

"Remember, I'm interested in you, and I hope you're interested in me, too. I've thought of you all week, every free moment. Once I got the news, you were the first I wanted to call. Then I realized we hadn't gotten to that point. Driving home, I said to myself, 'What the hell, why not call her?' So, I did. I asked you to meet me here."

"I see." Renee sat still, holding the wine glass with both hands.

"As I said, I don't have many friends or relatives." His eyes pierced her pupils. "You are the most important person I want to share my news with. So," Marvin paused waiting for a response. "I hope this information has an impact on us."

"What happened to your family?" Renee looked at the wine glass before raising her eyes towards Marvin.

"It's a long story, but maybe one day I'll share it with you." Marvin picked up the margarita and sipped. He put the drink on the table and swallowed. "Maybe I can share a little now, so you understand why I want you to know."

"I," Renee nodded, "I'd like to know."

"Okay." Marvin picked up the margarita and placed it on his lips. He raised the glass' bottom to her eye level and emptied the content. "I grew up in a weird environment. It wasn't the best, because I ended up doing things alone. Even as a kid, I was pretty much by myself. My mom remarried because my father left when I was a child. My stepdad, well, let's just say he wasn't really influential." Marvin pushed the empty margarita glass aside and grabbed the Mexican coffee. He pulled it close and looked at Renee. "It's why I want us to celebrate this news."

"There is no us," Renee responded. "I mean, we're friends, and that may develop into something."

"I'm taking a chance." Marvin sipped his drink. "We should become an item, and I hope it's as good as I imagine." He reached for the flowers in the other chair next to him and offered them to Renee. "Imagined?" Renee nodded her head before smiling. "Thank you." She lifted the bouquet to her nose. "They're lovely." Renee sniffed before lowering them from her face. "But I have to think about this. I know you are very energetic, and you put a bit of thought into what you do. I saw that while collaborating with you." Renee paused and looked at the bouquet. "But you've imagined us being a couple already. I don't know how to take that."

"As I said, I had a vision." Marvin raised one eyebrow and lifted the coffee cup.

"Ah..." Renee put the flowers on the table and picked up her wine glass, drank its content, and put the glass in front of her. "I suggest we have that dinner date." She rose from her chair, grabbed the bouquet, and stepped into the aisle. "Let me know when, and please give a girl time to get ready."

Marvin stood from the table. "You got it."

***

Friday's office luncheon with Mr. Ottman included the introduction of Marvin's replacement. He also shared the promotion of Marvin to Executive Vice President of Sales for the region. Renee's eyes widened, realizing Marvin had not explained his promotion or what it entailed. She picked up her phone and texted Marvin, '*I had no idea of you were being promoted. WOW, Marvin, Congrats!*' Renee placed the phone on the table in front of her and finished eating.

Marvin looked at his cell phone while sitting at his desk. He tapped the screen and read Renee's text. His thumbs danced over the keyboard. '*Saturday night. Pick you up at 7. Send me your address.*' He opened his calendar and blocked off the time. He calendared the entire night; in case they had fun. His mind wandered to fleeting work challenges, and automatically he scribbled on a notepad on top of his desk. He ended up writing a plan for the date.

Marvin called a friend's company to set up a personal touch for entertainment. He later called his favorite restaurant, making an appointment with a personal chef. He tapped the pen on paper as if a drumstick landing on the head of a snare drum. Tap tap, tap tap. Marvin stared into space, imagining what he did not want to have happen—failure to launch the opportunity with Renee – becomes a norm. He cringed at the thought of a nightmare dating experience with her. He did not want a flurry of weak impressions for a long-lasting memory.

***

Sunrise came with calm, sun rays saluted Renee through the

window blinds. Her eyes met light, through an odd occurrence since days before she woke to darkness and got out of the house before dawn. Her rise after daybreak took her mind to an exciting place. "The Caribbean." She smiled, put her feet on the floor, walked to the curtain, and glanced at the blinding sun. Renee closed her eyes and allowed her mind to imagine a sunny beach, a clear blue sky, and turquoise water, a view in travel magazines. She broke the sun's barrier and brightened the room with natural light.

"I have a date." She laughed and twirled towards her closet, looking inside the square space and selected a fitting dress. "You are the one," she told it, held it against her body, and looked at her reflection in the mirror. Renee looked at the clock on the dresser and realized the Saturday spin class is approaching. She dressed in her workout gear, washed her face and scrubbed her teeth, put her hair up in a ponytail and left the apartment in haste. Renee arrived five minutes earlier than class, which allowed her to set up her bike and briefly pedal before the instructor got the class going. She pedaled into the sunset display behind the instructor. Her sweat puddled on the floor, and at the end of class, she grabbed paper towels from the dispenser and cleaned what she could. Courtesy was a practice she didn't take for granted. She tossed the wet towels in the trash on her way out, skipping her routine weight training.

Renee went home, threw her wet exercise clothes in the hamper, showered, and changed into shorts, and tee-shirt set, wearing sandals. She jumped in her car, leaving the apartment, and drove to a nail saloon for a pre-date mani-pedi. She followed with a visit to the hairstylist, ate a light lunch, and finished with a bubble bath of soft oils and perfumes. She considered herself well prepared for a night she hopes to remember.

***

Marvin sat at his office desk; his eyes peeled on the laptop screen, scrutinizing a sales strategy for the region. He tapped his fingers on the desk while he read, leaned forward, and typed actions to implement. He turned from his desk, leaned back in the luxurious leather chair, and looked at the city through the glass wall of his office. He acknowledged the sparse pedestrian and street activity for a Saturday. He glanced at his watch, closed the laptop, and grabbed his sports jacket, before going to the elevators. Marvin pressed the down call button and waited. He examined his reflection in the sterling silver door - the shadow under his eyes, the wild hair and long drawn chin. He frowned before the elevator doors broke his reflection when sliding apart. Marvin stepped in, press the L button, and rode the elevator to the ground floor. He walked to the café before he remembered it's closed on weekends. He turned for the nearest exit and left the building for a local restaurant.

In his car, Marvin set his direction to a local pub that served his favorite sandwich and soup. He parked in the shopping strip mall and walked into the pub. He was not surprised at the busy foot traffic because, regardless of the day, it always had patrons. He sat at the long heavy dark wood structured bar and ordered the soup and sandwich before looking around the establishment. His eyes stopped at an elderly couple sitting at a table and saw how they shared a meal from one plate. Marvin smiled at the idea and his mind imagined Renee by his side doing the same.

"Here you go." The bartender placed his order in front of him.

"Thanks." Marvin picked up the sandwich, dipped it's edge into the soup and bit into it. In between bites, he looked at the mirror in front of him and watched people, especially noticing couples who shared moments—a little laughing, shared affection and even one in an intense moment. He turned towards the bar keep. "Hey, Scotch on the rocks?"

"Sure." The bartender made the drink and brought it over. "Can I fill your glass of water?" "Please." Marvin sipped his scotch and placed it on the bar. He remembered his youthful moments. *My Stepdad never took Mom out for dinner or drinks, but she had bruises from their interactions. I guess she loved it.* He pushed the half-eaten sandwich aside, finished his cocktail, and placed the glass on the counter. He lifted a credit card from his pocket and put it on the counter. "Whenever you're ready," Marvin said to the bartender. After signing the check, he rose from the barstool noted the dark wood tables, the big glass-stained window, the dropping table lights, and the booths along the side of the wall. His eyes glanced at various couples in the restaurant. He smiled, walked to the exit, replacing the credit card in his pocket.

The office became a ghost town, quiet and empty of the few people who were around before he left for lunch. He approached the security guard and a janitor who stood at the security desk. "Hey, guys," he spoke to them.

"Mr. Yarbrough," the security guard responded. "Always on the job."

"It's a good thing, right?" Marvin nodded and smiled.

"On the one hand, it must be, but your family must miss you."

"I don't have…" Marvin stopped midsentence. "I'm working on that." he smiled.

***

Saturday evening arrived at the end of a full day of pampering and preparation. Renee looked at her reflection in the full mirror. The semi form-fitting light blue chiffon dress, her dark hair, and glowing eyes (where the makeup artist had made her look exceptional) pleased her. Her smile added to the treasure of her appearance. Her hands slightly shook, and her heartbeat wouldn't slow, even though her pace to the dresser was not in haste. She grabbed a diamond center set antique bracelet – an heirloom passed to her from her grandmother and put it on. She chose a uniquely compiled necklace of sapphire and diamonds, a brilliant piece her mother gave her, giving a distinct contrast to her dress and put it around her neck. The only thing she imagined missing, making her dress complete, is a diamond ring on her left hand's fourth finger.

***

Marvin left the office prepared for his arrival on Monday. He arrived at his condominium right at dusk. Before leaving the car, he scanned his phone for messages from Renee. He walked inside, went to his bedroom, and tossed the phone to the center of his bed. He stripped, walked to the shower, turned it on, before stepping inside the transparent glass walls. The stream of hot water rolled down his body. He pulled out his scented soap and matching shampoo and began scrubbing his body. He rinsed, picked up the shaver, dunned lather, and shaved to his reflection in the glass. He rubbed his face, ensuring he'd gotten everywhere, and rinsed before turning the water off. Marvin put the shaver down on the counter and grabbed a towel, dried off, and wrapped it around his waist. His imperfect body showed the scars of his hustle, yet the definition of his muscles reflected the physical investment which kept his body and mind in unison.

He stood over the sink and rubbed his hair before he looked into the mirror. He grabbed his favorite fragrance, slapped some on his body and went into the bedroom to put on silk underwear and silk socks. He walked into the closet and stood in front of various clothing suitable for all occasions. He selected dark slacks, a light tan-colored shirt, and a sports coat to match. He grabbed his tannish brown shoes, a matching belt, and went to lay the clothing on the bed. He slid on his pants, put on the collared shirt, buttoning only to the second button from the top leaving his neckline exposed. He picked a necklace from his jewelry case, a classy watch from his collection, a ring from school, and one special piece awarded to him from an earlier job.

He looked himself over to make sure nothing was out of place. He searched for perfection, and what he saw missing was the one thing he would love to have - a gorgeous woman complimenting his good looks. Marvin walked down to his front room before putting on his jacket. In one swoop of his arms clearing the sleeves, he grabbed keys with one hand and the wallet with the other. He exited the front door, locked it, and waited for his chariot to arrive.

***

Renee heard the knock at her door. She walked from her bedroom to the front door and grabbed her purse from the couch on the way. "Hi, Marvin," she greeted with a smile.

"Wow!" Marvin grinned. "You look amazing."

"Thank you." Renee nodded. "That's exactly how I wanted you to respond."

"I feel like I'm underdressed," Marvin said. "I'm sorry I didn't know you'd go this far."

"This little dress?" Renee smiled. "It's not overdressed for you."

"Oh, you ...I mean...you are." Marvin raised his elbow. "The limo awaits."

"Limo?"

"It's perfect for a night with you." Marvin led the way to the limousine. The driver opened the door when they arrived. Renee entered, followed by Marvin.

"I didn't expect this," Renee admitted.

"I guess we're exceeding expectations." Marvin snickered. "There's more, of course."

"Like." Renee placed her purse in her lap before smiling. "What are we doing?"

The driver took off as planned. He drove to Marvin's choice reservation for dinner. "Well, I thought we'd enjoy fine dining, followed with a show and cocktails for the evening, to get better acquainted."

"That sounds nice," Renee said. "Really nice." She looked at Marvin and grabbed his hand. "I knew you'd be interesting, but for a first date, I had no idea you'd... "

"...like my plan. You know, drinks and dancing." He swallowed. "But I thought you deserved more than a simple outing for our first."

"This is perfect." Renee relaxed, sat back, and grabbed his hand, linking her fingers with his. Within 30 minutes, the car stopped, and the driver opened the door for Marvin. He exited and helped Renee out of the car. "We'll be done in an hour," Marvin instructed the driver.

"Yes sir," the driver responded. "I'll be waiting for you."

Marvin nodded. "Madam." He raised his elbow and walked with Renee into the restaurant. He walked upright with respectable charm and wore a stylish blazer, doing what he had developed to project a unique type of man. They arrived at the Maître De and shared, "Yarbrough, reservation for two."

"Yes sir." The maître de looked at the screen, pressed it with his finger, and pointed at a waiter. He whispered to the waiter, who eagerly listened.

"Please follow me," the waiter instructed.

Marvin and Renee sat at a table within the fine restaurant. Marvin ordered a bottle of wine and the waiter walked from their table.

"Is this your 'impress her' restaurant?" Renee asked.

"Actually, it's my second time. The first was for business."

Who? Renee's thought, and continued thinking, *I wonder why here?*

"This place has rave reviews, and I know it firsthand. I want you to have a piece of what I think you deserve."

"I see," Renee looked around. "I'm not stuffing crackers in my bag. My purse isn't large enough." She giggled.

"Renee." Marvin laughed. "Seriously, though, I think you deserve the best."

"You have a plan, don't you?"

"I have intent—not necessarily a plan." "What's your intent?"

"I'll get to that in time."

"Okay." Renee looked at the menu. "What's good?"

"From what I understand, everything." Marvin smiled. "I'm sure whatever you'll choose is an excellent choice."

"I think lamb suits me well, tonight. Medium well, please."

"Perfect," Marvin responded. "Maybe I'll have the T-bone...looks great."

"What's your family like?" Renee questioned.

"Huh, ah...I'll explain my folks. They're not here anymore. I'm the last of my father's and mother's existence. I am an only child."

"Oh, I didn't know."

"I never told you. It's our first real personal conversation."

"I agree, it's our first." Renee looked at Marvin's eyes beyond the flickering candle flame. "I got the impression you were never alone." She smiled.

Marvin watched the waiter pour water into glasses before informing him, "I think we're ready to order."

"Yes sir," responded the waiter who stood fast. "But first, please allow me to share the three house specials." The waiter proceeded to outline them. "And the last is the white fish, sautéed with a special sauce local to the area. It's served on a bed of white rice with a garden-fresh vegetable medley, and I suggest a white wine from a French Chateau."

"That sounds like what I'll have," Renee said.

"Okay, we'll have two." Marvin closed the menu and handed it to the waiter.

Renee followed his lead and gave the waiter her menu. "And I think a bottle will do," she suggested, and looked to Marvin. "I hope you don't mind."

The waiter paused for Marvin's answer.

"No." Marvin cleared his throat. "I don't mind." Marvin raised an eyebrow and interlocked his fingers in front of him.

The waiter responded, "I'll serve the wine first and, shortly, I will get your salads." He left the table.

"Good, thank you." Renee smiled. "I didn't mean to say it out loud, but I kind of figured you'd want a full bottle, since we're eating the same dish."

"I'll ask you, next time." Marvin looked at his interlocked hands.

"Oh." Renee reached over the table and touched his clasped hands. "I'm sorry if I overstepped a boundary."

"It's okay." Marvin smirked. "I didn't think you stepped too much. But I have a question."

"Sure, I don't mind. You can ask me anything."

"Good." Marvin waited a moment before getting to the point. "I want to know if you are an alpha woman?"

"You mean Alpha female?"

"Yes. It seems you're as dynamic as I am at taking charge. I saw this when we worked together."

"I..." Renee pulled her hand from covering his. "I don't think of myself like that. But I do kind of know where I want to go."

"Don't get me wrong, I like a confident woman." Marvin smiled. "I tend to find a challenge in the kind of woman you are. I can see my life never getting boring."

Renee gazed into Marvin's eyes and pressed her lips before she shared her thought. "Challenge for life. Did I hear that right?"

"Yes, for life." Marvin placed his open hand across the table. Renee looked at his open hand. *Do I like him that much?* Her eyes met his stare, and slowly Renee placed her hand in his.

"I'm not promising an organic garden in life, but I think we can start something that creates a world of beauty."

"I... well maybe we can." Renee smiled. "I think tonight is a start."

"Really?"

"Yes, I do." Renee pulled her hand to her side of the table while the waiter lifted one wine glass off the table.

"Excuse me, sir." The waiter poured a small amount of wine in a glass and passed it to Marvin. He waited for a response.

Marvin sipped and nodded his head, looking at Renee. "It's good." He looked at the waiter and smiled. "Good suggestion."

"Thank you, sir," the waiter responded, and poured two glasses. "Your dinner will be here shortly." The waiter placed two salads on the table. "Pepper?"

"No, thank you," Marvin responded.

"Sure." Renee waited for the waiter to sift pepper onto her salad. "Thank you." Renee picked up her fork and paused for Marvin.

"I think you're going to like the rest of our first date." "So far, I'm impressed."

"Good. I had hoped I wasn't moving too fast."

"Not at all."

***

The limousine met them at the front of the restaurant, and like a gentleman, Marvin entered after Renee, closing the door behind him and sitting back.

"We're right on time." He looked at his watch. "The next part of our date starts in 30 minutes."

"The next part?" Renee asked.

"Yes, I think you'll enjoy this."

"I don't know if I will — what is it?"

"I take you for a cultured person. The way I observed you during our interactions. I'm impressed with how you take on things. So, I took the liberty of setting this up."

"Umm, setting this up?"

"Sit back, relax, and be surprised."

Renee looked out of the window and waited for clues to where the limousine driver was taking them. She looked at the intersections and buildings. "I thought you were a more direct person."

"I guess I can be direct when needed. But this is not work, and it's my first date with someone I'd like a future with."

"Wow, you're dropping hints pretty heavily." "I'm confident in my choice. Besides, you have impressed me on multiple levels. I don't find women like you—I mean, you're one who takes my mind away from business or any other thing."

"I had no idea."

Marvin placed the palm of his hand in between them, an invitation to interlock their fingers. Renee placed her hand onto his with a smile of acceptance.

The limousine stopped, and shortly after the car settled, the driver opened the door. Marvin got out and held his hand for Renee. She maneuvered in the best way possible from wearing a form-fitting dress, doing everything to not reveal the very excitement she subconsciously desired. Her exit struck Marvin with warm charm, classy in her approach to his indelible courtesy. He placed her arm into his before they crossed the sidewalk to the entrance of the Delaware Theater Company. Their appearance together gave onlookers no misconception of them as a couple. Renee's eyes sparkled at the venue and became more accepting of Marvin's taste. She was impressed with him being right on about her likes and dislikes.

"I didn't know you knew." Renee nudged him with her elbow.

"I do my research," Marvin smiled. "I'm glad you like my selection."

"Perfect." Renee moved closer. She watched Marvin pull tickets from his breast pocket and hand them to the doorman.

"Right this way," he said.

Renee held Marvin close while they walked to their seats. She released his arm only to grab his hand while they walked stairs to their private booth. She took her seat, a direct sight to the center of the stage. "Great view," she said, touching his shoulder. "I have never been here before, and it's an amazing place." She glanced around at the décor.

Marvin smiled and opened the program pamphlet. He looked at the actors' profiles. "You're going to love this show."

"I watched the movie," Renee responded.

"You did?" Marvin laughed. "I did too, but it's nothing like a stage show."

"You like cartoons?"

"Don't all kids?" Marvin laughed. "I watched cartoons like every time I got a chance. My mom would get angry about how I was dazed while watching the shows. I remember her calling my name, and I pretended not to hear her so I wouldn't respond."

"I could never not respond to my parents."

"I did, until I felt a hard smack on my head," Marvin giggled.

"What?"

"Mom threw her shoe and popped me." He glanced at her and laughed. "I did the right thing from then on." Marvin looked at Renee. "I responded."

"I bet you did."

The theater lights flashed, a signal for the show to start. Calm and quiet, people sat down and watched *The Lion King* develop on stage. Marvin's eyes focused on the woman next to him and saw her attentive stare. In the dim light, he could see her smooth skin, view her perfect cheeks, and follow the curvature of her lips. He watched her laugh and respond to antics on stage. His eyes met hers when she looked at him and she smiled with her face nearly blushed.

At the end of the show, Marvin led Renee to the waiting limousine. He opened the door and aided her entrance. "One more thing, unless you're ready for bed."

"I'm ready for whatever else you have planned for our first date." Renee grinned.

"Good." Marvin tapped the driver. "You know the place."

"Yes sir," the driver responded.

"Where are we going?" asked Renee.

"I thought we'd enjoy a few cocktails to end our night. I'd like to get to know you on a different level."

"You mean, get me drunk and take advantage."

"Well..." Marvin paused before he touched her hand. "Yeah, of course. It's what men do." He chuckled.

Renee giggled. "Let's have a drink. I don't mind." She held his hand tight and sat quietly for the rest of the ride.

***

Renee held her martini, sitting forward at the edge of the leather love chair while Marvin sat back, holding a glass of Scotch whiskey. "What did you like doing as a kid?" Renee asked.

"I liked playing baseball and soccer and I ran track in high school." Marvin placed his arm on the edge of the backrest.

"Nice," Renee responded, "but those were older years than I'm asking about." She sipped her martini. "What about your childhood years...? You know—9, 10, 11...?"

Marvin leaned his head to one side, closed his eyes, and took in a breath when he opened them. "I don't like those years."

"Why not?"

"They were very difficult for me. I kind of found out what my dad was really like."

"Oh." Renee raised an eyebrow, gazing at Marvin. "I think you should tell me."

"I can't." Marvin sipped his drink. "Not yet, anyway."

"Not yet! Why not?"

"We have to be close before I let you in on my secrets."

"But this is getting closer."

"I agree." Marvin raised his drink towards Renee. "Cheers." Marvin finished his drink right when the waitress delivered two more to the table. Renee chugged the last of her martini before picking up the other. "I didn't know we attended the same college."

"What? I went to college with you?" Marvin sipped his drink before looking at her. "I was there first. So, technically, you followed me." Marvin touched Renee's far shoulder. "I graduated twice from that university."

"I know. Remember, I saw you on campus."

"How would I know that?"

"Didn't I tell you when we were working together?"

"You didn't." Marvin rubbed her back. "How does this feel?"

"Nice." Renee dropped her head, giving full access to the back of her neck. "How do you like this dress?" Renee did not wait for his answer and blurted, "It's nice, isn't it?"

"It is, and you look fantastic." Marvin encouraged her to sit back, pressing her to release tension so he could place his arm around her.

Renee leaned back on the love seat while she held the martini in her lap. She leaned closer to Marvin, snuggly fitting her shoulder into his armpit. She looked into his eyes and their noses nearly touched. Marvin moved his lips in front of hers and waited for a response. She pushed closer just enough to rub Marvin's lips with hers and he advanced, gently pressing his lips to hers. After she placed the martini on the coffee table in front of them, her free arm pulled Marvin closer. Renee kissed him harder, explored his lips longer, and didn't let go of her exchange. Marvin obliged her reciprocation and enjoyed making out with her. "Maybe we should take this to someplace more relaxing."

Renee pulled back and raised her martini. "Good idea." She tossed the content into her mouth and put the glass on the coffee table in front of them. She swallowed. "I'm ready," she slurred and scooted forward on the love seat.

Marvin finished his drink and waited for Renee to move ahead of him. He rose from the chair, placed his glass down on the coffee table, and offered his hand to Renee. "Let's go." He clasped her hand and led her out of the bar onto the street. Marvin pulled out the cell phone with his free hand, punched in a quick dial with his thumb, and put the phone to his ear.

"Hey, please bring the limo," he instructed, and put the phone into his pocket. Marvin embraced Renee, the woman he'd entertained and had hoped to explore. He kissed her on the cheek and kept one arm around her waist, then broke his embrace long enough to step to the edge of the sidewalk, looked both directions, before turning back to face Renee. "The limo should be here in a minute," Marvin said.

"No problem." Renee staggered and said, "But I hope he gets here fast. I need to sit down."

"Good, here he comes." Marvin took the initiative and grabbed her hand. He stepped to the edge of the sidewalk and aided his new girlfriend into the limousine. He sat next to her with his arm around her while his other hand fell to her hind cheek. She caressed his leg, periodically placing her soft lips upon his chiseled face. Marvin returned the affection, squeezed her firm buttocks, and pressed her closer to him. He enjoyed the mounds of her breasts against him. Within what seemed like an eternity, their arrival at Marvin's surprised them.

Renee had gotten comfortable in Marvin's arm, cuddled close enough to hear his heartbeat. She nearly fell asleep in the limousine, and when it stopped, this startled her. She looked at their destination and wasn't surprised.

"Is this your place?"

"Yes, it's my place," Marvin slurred. "It's perfect for our escape."

Renee exited the car and walked with Marvin to the front door. She watched him pull keys from his pocket and unlock the final restriction to finishing their quest. Renee melted when he embraced her with his muscular arms wrapped around her. His ability to kiss her with a gentle touch of his lips sent a message of affection and desire, the longing to get closer. He weakened her legs with the caress of his body against her sensual influencers for his continued advances. After the door closed, he pressed her against the wall in his foyer. The moonlight glistened through his undressed windows and touched them as if the soft ray was a spotlight from heaven.

Marvin released his clutch and led her to his sanctuary, a bed of restful down pillows and a comforter spread. She fell onto the bed, kicked her shoes off, and found a sweet spot of comfort in between throw pillows. With one pull, she had Marvin closer to her body. His tongue danced with hers setting a rhythm movement enticing her response. He maneuvered one hand under her while the other massaged her breast. He stopped kissing her and lifted her as he stood.

He unzipped her dress and pulled her arms from the arm opening. The dress fell to the floor, exposing her bra and matching panties. Marvin unzipped his pants and Renee unbuttoned his shirt before she removed both shirt and sports coat. He dropped his pants to the floor. Her lips met his and her hands rubbed his defined chest. She was surprised he had found time to dedicate working on his muscular body. Renee had assumed he would be in shape and touching him was all the verification she needed.

Marvin pulled her tight in his arms, spinning them around and laying on his back on the bed with her on top. He embraced her, moved his pelvis in a rhythm and grabbed her bottom pillows of excellence, directing her response. He stopped grinding and kissed her neck, moving his hand upward to center of her back to unsnap her bra, and lifted the colorful control. Her breasts were exposed right where his lips could kiss each nipple and his tongue dance with them. He got on top, rolling them both over, having her on her back before he put his lips between her breasts, slowly kissing along a journey south. His kisses stopped at her navel and showered her with easy lip caresses and a simple tongue dash before he moved trailed to a destination of ecstasy.

Renee lay in wait, enjoying the attention and the feeling she was experiencing. Her mind played with her movement, responding to everything Marvin did. She lifted her bottom to unveil the lily of enjoyment and the tomb of future life, feeling his breath upon her. Renee felt moisture in the tunnel of connection, coupled with a sensation of pulsating nerve endings anticipating the excitement, her flow filled her for a hopeful expulsion. Her inner thighs tingled from the sensations of Marvin's kiss and her toes danced with a layer of prickled skin.

Renee sighed, covering her mouth to muffle her noise. She moved her hips upward with a push of Marvin's hand, and the gentle invasion of a soft muscle danced with the inner wall of her channel of life. She wanted more, and moved her hips faster than he directed, but Marvin pulled back and focused on the swollen mound. He swiped one side, then the other, and twirled his tongue around as no other had ever done. Renee screamed through her hands.

Marvin lifted his head from kissing her, moved back from his knees, and pulled his underwear off, releasing the painful restriction of his loins. He laid down to kiss her middle section, leading to her lips. He stopped short, rolled to a nightstand, and retrieved a condom. Renee, relieved to see him be responsible, touched his back and ran her fingers down the sun kissed part of his neck. Marvin returned focused, ready for diving. Renee opened her arms giving him a full invitation.

Chapter 8

Committed

Marvin sat at his desk the day after returning from a leadership meeting for the region. He turned his back and looked at the festival of streetlights battling the arriving dusk. He cupped his chin with two closed fingers touching his face and looked hard at the multiple sparkling lights. His mind flashed to a conversation with Renee.

"Why not?" she'd asked.

"Why not? Let's just say, my life is not easy to share. You know, I'm driven to be the best," he'd responded, and remembered the message he had hoped she would receive.

"Why can't you understand how I'm capable of supporting you? I'm driven, too, but I..." Renee swallowed, "...I'm your greatest supporter."

"It's changing. I mean, you've come into my life, and I can't see tomorrow without you, but it's not easy for me to depend on others." Marvin repeated, "Depend on others."

What if I can't depend on her? What if she fails when I want more, and is she okay with the way things are? What if she wants to be competitive? What if she isn't compatible, after all? Business decisions are much easier, he thought.

Marvin stood at the bay window and watched the glow of the sun disappear. *Making business easier means no added concerns. I don't know.* He shook his head. *I want her, but...do I?*

Nine o'clock attacked with a lightning flash over the dark sky. Marvin looked at his watch, retrieved his sports coat, and gathered laptop case. He disconnected his laptop from the docking station and placed it in the carrying case. "I'm late." Marvin pressed the Velcro tight, pushed his arm through the carry strap, and hurried to the elevator. He pressed the call button and waited and looked at his watch.

"I don't like being late, damn it." Marvin rocked back and forth, staring at the elevator doors. When the door opened, he was surprised.

"What are you doing here?"

"I'm learning and you're running late, so I brought things to you."

"I..." Marvin smiled. "I guess you know me."

Renee lifted her bag of takeout. "Very well, I should say. I know you damn near like..." Renee paused, "... let's say, quite well." She smiled before adding, "Almost as well as you know me, these days."

"These days? Is there a message about timing?" Marvin moved closer to Renee, grabbed her with his free arm, and pulled her close. He pressed his lips against hers. "Thank you so much. I thought I was late meeting you for dinner."

"Baby, I know you're busy. I don't mind bringing our dinner

here."

"It's not necessary but I do appreciate it." Marvin moved aside from their embrace and pressed the elevator call button. "Why don't we go to my place?"

"I thought about that, but I have a better idea." Renee lifted the takeout.

"Okay." Marvin held the elevator door and waited for Renee to enter. "Are we taking one car, or am I following you?"

"One car, but it has to be mine."

"Are you kidnapping me?" Marvin looked at her with a raised eyebrow.

"You can say that I'm doing what you've done to me."

"What's that?"

"Impress me with your heart."

Marvin's eyebrows rose and his eyes widened. "I did – didn't I?"

"I'm here with dinner for two, aren't I?"

"That you are, my dear, that you are." He smirked. Marvin followed Renee into the elevator, exiting at lobby level. He shadowed her out of the building to her car, where he placed his laptop in the back seat and took refuge on the passenger side. "I don't have to know where we're going. Do I?"

"Sit back. Relax. I'm driving." Renee snapped the seatbelt and put the key into the ignition. "I don't want to hear you complain. Go with my flow." She drove onto the main street.

"I promise, no complaints." Marvin secured his seat belt and looked at the streetlights. "I have something we should discuss."

"Okay." Renee stopped at a traffic light.

"You and I have been dating for a while. I'm fairly sure it's been over three months."

"Three months and 20 days, to be exact," Renee giggled. "I'm not counting. I've enjoyed every moment."

"So, have I," Marvin responded. "I'm not counting." He snickered. "Anyway, we should think about being more serious."

"More serious?" Renee turned on the car radio, pressed the steering wheel controls and selected a classical radio station. "I have been serious. I made you exclusive. I don't date anyone else."

"You were dating when we started dating?" "I thought you knew."

"Are you serious?"

"Of course not. I was always available to you, long before our first date," Renee chuckled.

"I didn't know."

"You were too busy to notice." Renee turned the car towards a park.

"I didn't know this place would be open at this time of night."

"It's open for us," Renee responded. She drove further, near the cliff, and stopped the car near its edge.

"What a view," Marvin said. "Look, there's the office building and the bay. I didn't know this was here."

"A girl at the gym told me about it."

Marvin leaned over the middle console and waited. Renee moved closer and kissed him. "Thank you, baby, it's beautiful."

"Oh, we're not done." Renee put the car in park and turned the engine off. She reached into the back seat and grabbed the takeout bag.

"I hope not." Marvin unhooked his seatbelt. "Do you need help?"

"You can bring the blanket from the trunk." Renee pressed the trunk release button, unsnapped her seatbelt, and opened her door. She rose with the bag in her hand, walked to the front of the driver's side of the car, and waited.

"Spread the blanket here," she pointed.

"What about something wet?" asked Marvin. "In the trunk."

"I am so surprised."

"At?"

"How you continually surprise me."

"It's easy." Renee sat down on the blanket. "You tell me everything, and since you've been all about business, anything I do is new to you."

"Well, it's why I want to tell you." Renee patted the blanket. "Sit."

"Okay." Marvin sat in front of Renee. "I usually don't say this…" He swallowed. "I am seriously in love with you."

"I know," Renee said. "I've known for a while."

"How could you?"

"My Marvin, I'm a woman. A serious woman who was not in search of a relationship, but you...you waltzed into my life during college."

"I remember. You told me about us crossing paths on campus."

"You have been my man since then, even though I didn't know you. But I pledged to respond, if ever the opportunity knocked."

"Bam, bam, bam," Marvin laughed.

"Exactly."

"When was the confirmation you loved me?"

"On our trip to Antigua." Renee opened the box and grabbed two forks. "I didn't put plates in the bag."

"No problem." Marvin grabbed a fork from Renee. "You first."

"Okay." Renee dabbed into the box, looked at the view, and took her first bite. Marvin followed suit. "You know, Marvin," Renee swallowed. "I have never fallen for a man."

"You haven't?" Marvin said, holding his chew. "Honestly, this is amazing to me." He swallowed.

"I think we're..." Renee grabbed another fork full. "...chickens in the same coop."

"I'm the rooster," laughed Marvin.

"I would hope so," Renee giggled. "What do we do now that we're in love?"

"I say we build upon it, like the time we laughed until sunrise about nothing. Absolutely nothing."

"Proof we're meant to be together." Renee chewed.

"I know, right? Who does that?"

"We do." Renee giggled. "I enjoy you even when we're home, just because we're together. I love it so much; I can't wait until it's more often."

"That's why we're...well..." Marvin bit into another fork full, chewed, and swallowed. *I hope I am not rushing things, but it sounds like a great idea*, he thought. "I want you to move in with me."

"Marvin." Renee reached over to him, pulled him close and hugged him tightly. "Yes baby, I was thinking the same thing."

***

Marvin arrived home and dropped his suitcase and his laptop near the king-size bed. He unraveled his tie and pulled it through the shirt collar. "Hey, Renee, can you get me a glass of wine, please?"

"Sure thing, babe," Renee answered. She reached into the cupboard for a wine glass, went to the wine rack, and opened a bottle of merlot. She poured a medium amount into the glass and put the bottle onto the counter, plugged it with a cork, and walked to the master bedroom.

"Here, sweetie." She handed him the glass. "Thank you so much. I needed a drink." Marvin pulled up his lounging pajama pants. "It's been a tiring week."

"You told me." Renee moved closer and tiptoed for a kiss on his lips. "Welcome home, baby. I would have done more, but I had to focus on a project." Renee stepped to the doorway. "As a matter of fact, I need to get back to it before I lose momentum."

"What about dinner?"

"There are leftovers in the microwave. I didn't know what time you were getting here, so I had an early dinner and made sure you had a meal ready in case you were hungry." Renee left the bedroom.

Marvin picked up the wine glass, sipped wine, put it on the dresser. He grabbed a t-shirt, put it on and picked up the wine glass before taking in a deep breath. With pressed lips he nodded, while exclaiming, "Damn it!"

Renee sat on the couch in the sunken front room, placed the laptop on her lap, and continued typing her thoughts. She used a wireless mouse to manage her screen movement from one application to another. Another 15 minutes had passed when she completed one section and finally saved her work. Marvin sat next to her and tapped her shoulder with a finger.

"Oh!" she screamed, "you scared the crap out of me."

"I'm home, baby."

"I know, baby, I know. I must get this out. Bear with me."

"I've been here for 10 minutes," Marvin looked at his watch, "and you haven't noticed me."

"I am so sorry." Renee looked Marvin in his eyes. "I had to focus." She pushed the laptop aside. "I need to get this done before Monday morning, or we'll lose a client who agreed to support the company."

"I understand, but I'm your client," Marvin smirked.

"What?" Renee raised an eyebrow. "Wait, I...no, you aren't." She giggled. "I get it." Renee reached out to him. She pulled him towards her. "Baby, I know you're here and yes, you are my number one client." She pecked his lips as if a mother would greet her kid, 'smack.' "I know you are home. Can you give me a half hour?"

"Yes, but under one condition," Marvin responded.
"Sure, what is it?"

"You have to dress impressive and come with me."

"But you just got home."

"So what?" Marvin stood and broke their closeness. "I want you to be with me, dressed to look good, and ready for whatever."

Renee looked at his frown and a chill ran through her. "I can do that." She nodded, picked up the laptop, and refocused on work. *That was intense,* Renee thought. Her eyes glanced at the bottom corner of her laptop screen, noting the current hour.

Marvin went to the kitchen and refilled his wine glass before returning to the master bathroom. He turned on the water spicket filling the bath, threw in bubble relaxing mix, stripped his clothing, and eased into the hot, sudsy water. He remembered a night she welcomed him home, enjoying dinner overlooking the city during sunset and sharing the experience. He wanted to set things in motion. Marvin turned the water off and flashed to a smile Renee once shared with a unique glow of her eyes during sunset. He remembered how the light of the full moon left the adorable image of her smooth caramel complexion, complimenting the soft beam of excitement. Marvin smiled, lifted the wine glass, and sipped. He wet his lips with his tongue and imagined kissing Rene's glistening red lips. With his eyes closed, he lowered his body in the soothing water and imagined her smiling, the same way she penetrated his heart with her pearly whites. Marvin lowered his head in the water to just below his nostrils. *I need her in my life. I need her.*

Renee walked into the master bathroom and saw Marvin still in the tub. "Babe are you awake?"

Marvin did not respond. She leaned to him and stroked his hair. "Babe, you okay?"

Marvin moved. "Yeah, I'm okay…you woke me from my dream."

"What were you dreaming?" Renee sat on the edge of the tub.

"How beautiful you are and how I'm grateful having you in my life."

"Aw, you're trying to get me in there with you, aren't you?" Renee splashed water on Marvin.

"You better watch it. It's easy to pull you in." Marvin raised a hand. "On second thought…" Marvin pulled her in. "OOOOOH!" Renee yelled when she fell into the tub. "You little devil." Renee kicked off her house shoes and lay facing Marvin. He embraced her and his lips landed right where he wanted them… against hers.

"You know how much I love you don't you?"

"Yes." Renee laid her head upon his shoulder. "I love you, too."

***

Marvin dressed in slacks, a tailored shirt with cufflinks, a unique handmade belt, and Italian shoes. Marvin went downstairs and placed his sport coat over the couch in the living room, in anticipation for their departure. He paced the room. "Renee are you ready?" he shouted.

"Coming!" Renee looked at her reflection in the mirror. "I'm good," she whispered, giving herself approval. She walked with confident gait swaying her hips to an imaginary rhythm and her eyes looked straight ahead to the sunken living room. She saw Marvin and smiled, noticing how he stood in amazement. "You look...better than the definition of beautify." Marvin complimented.

"Thank you." Renee smiled, approached Marvin, and scanned him from head to toe. "You are stunning too."

"You know that men aren't usually called stunning – right?"

"In my eyes, it's what I see. Isn't it all that matters?" Marvin held a steady hand towards Renee and waited for her response. She accepted the offer and interlocked her fingers into his. "You are right," he said. "You are all that matters."

They paused at the front door long enough for Marvin to grab his keys. He opened the door for Renee who walked to a black Ferrari and stood in front of it. "Someone is parking in your space." Renee said.

"No, I didn't tell you." He pressed the key fob and the doors rose towards the roof. "Let me," he approached Renee, "Help you get in." He smiled.

"As you always have." Renee took his hand and found a way to enter with her bottom first before sliding her legs around. Marvin closed the door and walked around. He watched Renee connect her seatbelt while he took his sports coat off and placed it over the seat before he got into the car. He pressed the ignition button and buckled in. The car's engine hummed before Marvin pressed the gas, encouraging a sharp engine roar.

"That's how you got me." He chuckled. "I'm roaring to go."
"Corny joke." Renee shook her head. "Sometimes you're so awkward."

"You laughed." Marvin drove to the main intersection and turned right to the expressway. "I thought we'd do something fun tonight."

"I'm with you, and I'm happy to do anything you have in mind."

"Anything?" Marvin looked at Renee with a raised eyebrow.

"Let me...baby, I mean anything as long as it's with you."

Marvin turned the stereo on to soft music. "This sets the stage." He drove north to Philadelphia and exited near Center City, onto a major fairway. He stopped at a five-star venue. "This wasn't my first choice, but since you're the definition of good-looking, I needed to upgrade my plan a little."

"I've never been here."

"You'll love it." Marvin stepped out of the car, taking a ticket from the valet.

Renee exited the car and watched her man put on his sports coat. She flashed to a moment where she saw him on campus nearly two years ago. "You are one handsome man." She met him at the walkway and put her arm into his before they walked to the entrance.

***

Marvin got into the car after tipping the valet, looked at his beautiful woman and set the car into motion once she snapped the seatbelt. "I think you'll enjoy the second part."

"I'm enjoying every moment now." Renee beamed, tapped her foot and didn't sit all the way back in the seat. Her anxiety to get out subsided when memories of shared moments gave her the ability to trust him and blindly follow. "Is it someplace we've been?"

"No, but I hear it's exciting and can be fun."

"Really?"

"Of course." Marvin paused, glanced at the speedometer, and snapped a look at Renee. "You know, I do my homework. I want the best for you, the best for us, every time."

"I love how you take care of me."

"You are my dream, and I want you to feel appreciated forever."

Renee touched Marvin's arm. "Did I hear you right?"

"What?" Marvin glanced at Renee and returned his focus on the road. "Did I say something wrong?"

"No, you didn't." Renee interlocked her fingers into his when he dropped his hand from the steering wheel. She didn't let go when Marvin drove into the valet entrance to the art museum. She looked out of the car window and her eyes lit up with intrigue seeing well-dressed people enter the nearest door.

Marvin released Renee's hand, exited the car, and ran to Renee. He offered his hand to assist her out of the car. When she stood next to him, he pulled her close and whispered, "No one has ever been more beautiful than you are tonight."

Renee embraced him holding her purse, smiled, and let one tear fall. She heard the car door close, jetting her attention. They walked into the museum to the decor of South America and Latin Caribbean, in sync to the beat of a live band.

The main floor was scarce of tables, where couples danced to Latin music. "I don't know how to dance like that." Renee nodded in the direction of dancers.

"No worries, we'll learn together."

"You mean," Renee swallowed. "You don't either?" "I tried once but I never got it down." Marvin looked at Renee and touched the arm she'd interlocked with him with his left hand. "We can do this, and who cares if we don't. It's about us, right?"

"Yes, it is." Renee shadowed him to a table and sat in the chair he pulled out for her. "Babe, I think I need a good one before getting out there."

"Gotcha." Marvin dodged tables and dancers on his way to the bar. He ordered two drinks, turned to look at Renee, and saw her nod her head and rock in rhythm of the band. He looked closer to the floor where she sat and noticed her feet moving. He chuckled. *This is going to be fun,* he thought. He took the drinks to the table and set one in front of Renee. "Here, I think you'll like this."

"What is this purple-looking concoction?" Renee frowned. "Try it and we'll see if I need to drink it."

"Okay." Renee sipped and nodded. "It's not bad."

"Great, glad you like it." Marvin leaned closer to her. "Are you ready to try?"

"I don't want to embarrass you." "Now, how the hell will you do that?"

"You know me." Renee rose from the table. "But I don't mind making people laugh."

"Yeah, you're right. I forgot about that." Marvin grabbed her hand and led her to an open spot on the dance floor. "We're here now." He held her hand while holding a dance pose, right foot sturdy, left foot slightly forward and shoulder width apart. One arm forward and hand higher than the shoulder. The other hand touched Renee's waist. "I saw people do this on the big screen. I don't know what to do next, but I thought it looked good." He laughed, looked left and right, and with one hand on her waist, he stepped off with his left foot.

"I thought you didn't know how to do this." Renee followed his lead as best she could.

"I watched and remembered." He looked at other dancers. "I say we go with the music." Marvin pulled her tight. "Follow me." One arm around her, the other close to his chest and held her hand tight. He side stepped, 1-2 along with the beat of the music. He moved his hips and kept his shoulders stiff and upright, perfect for her breast to dance with his chest. "You're doing great." Marvin smiled.

"I...I like this," Renee grinned. "You do?"

"This is so...sensual." She grabbed him around his waist and did what she could to follow his footing. When the song ended, she held onto him and did not move from his embrace. A bachata song filled the air and Marvin moved slowly, regardless of the moderate rhythm. They danced to a mixture of fast and slow songs, performed sensual moves and teased their erotic zones.

He led Renee to their table where their watered-down drinks waited for them. "I'll get you another." Marvin chugged his drink and placed the empty glass on the table before leaving.

"I'll come with you." Renee grabbed his hand and walked with him to the bar. Marvin ordered another round and Renee added, "A glass of water too, please."

Renee put her arm around Marvin, waiting for their order. She leaned over to his ear. "You are an amazing man. I have never had anyone so exciting in my life."

"All of this, and I wonder why you chose to work instead of being with me when I got home from my business trip."

"Was this to show me something?"

"Yes, of course." Marvin paused, pulled her tight, and whispered, "I want you to know what you have."

Renee smiled. "I get it."

Marvin released her, took one drink from the bar, and gave it to her. He picked up the other and offered his free hand to Renee. They walked to the table and enjoyed each other's company. The band went on break. Marvin rose from the table. "Will you dance with me?"

"The band is…" Renee looked and realized the DJ was filling in with a love ballad. She stood, took his hand, and followed him to the floor. He grabbed her, giving her enough room to breathe where his rise of his excitement made an impact. She felt the power of a penetrable presence, unjustly matching its movement, and justifiably realize a heightened thrill.

"Oooh, I think we need to go," Renee whispered.

"I think you're right." He stepped away from Renee. "Let's

go."

***

Marvin's travel placed him on the last day of a business week when his cell phone alarm blared louder than an old man's snore. He looked at the hotel room's ceiling where a flickering light sparks reflective thoughts of weekends with Renee. He saw moments where Renee grabbed his hand while driving, or times she attached her hand to his while walking, and when he saw her radiant smile that brightened the room. The smile on Marvin's face stretched as wide as the Mississippi bridge. He raised his hand and wiped his face before he flashed to when they shared a blanket in the park. Sunlight beamed through a crack between two window curtains. Marvin sat up to the stream of light, without repeating the first thing he did from habit, picking up his cell phone to view business emails.

Friday, he smiled, *Friday. I get to see Renee.* His heart increased its rhythm and his palms moistened. *Her touch, her smile, her lips, her laughter – it's my life. I can't go anywhere without her, regardless if she doesn't quite get me…. she will learn.*

Workout, breakfast, and pack was Friday's routine when Marvin traveled. After packing, he pressed quick dial for Renee on his cell phone.

"Hello, baby," Renee answered. "Hi, babe. I can't wait to see you."

"We can video chat. You know, I'd like to see you."

"Okay." Marvin pressed his app and saw his reflection. Renee's image came online, and she appeared exactly as he enjoyed since moving in together. "My God, aren't you beautiful."

"Thank you." Renee blushed. "What time are you landing?"

"I get home around 6, if everything goes as planned. But I have to make a stop on the way home."

"Is it anything I can do?"

"No, baby. I have to do it."

"I am here if you change your mind. Remember, I have things for us, so don't make dinner reservations."

"You got it. Home it is."

"Good. I love you."

"I love you, too." Marvin snapped his video chat off, put the phone in his pocket, and put his laptop bag onto his rolling luggage before he exited the room. At the lobby desk, he checked out of the hotel and sat in the foyer before a cab arrived. He periodically looked at his watch and imagined Renee with him, as she had done in earlier times. He waited as if a test of patience and watched cab after cab announce specific customers. When he heard his name, he moved to the open door of the cab, entered the back seat, and waited for the driver to get in. "Airport."

"Yes sir," the driver responded. "Ah, which airline?"

"US Air," Marvin replied, and glanced at his watch, noting the time. He was hours ahead of schedule and had hopes of being lucky enough to catch an earlier flight. He retrieved his cell phone and visited multiple websites, shopping for a unique item. His fingers swiped and tapped, tapped and swiped, and later he placed the phone into his coat pocket, exited the cab, and stood at the curb for his luggage. He reached into the back seat to grab his laptop bag, set it on the carry-on luggage, paid the driver, and walked into the airport towards ticketing. Marvin approached the airline's counter and stood in the customer service line.

"Hi, I'm looking to get to Philadelphia this morning. When is the first available flight?"

"Sir, the next flight is an hour and a half from now. Would you like a ticket?"

"I have one." Marvin pulled out his cell and retrieved his boarding pass. "I hope I can pay the difference between the two. I would prefer not to, but this is an especially important occasion."

"May I see your reservation number?" the counter attendant reached for his cell phone.

"Sure." Marvin put his phone on the counter. The attendant recorded the reservation number and typed the data into the system.

"Looks like you won't have to pay anything if you downgrade to coach."

"How much is the difference for maintaining a first-class seat?"

"You can't, it's full," she informed him.

Marvin looked at the ceiling and thought, *Sit closer to other people.* "Okay, I'll take whatever you have."

"Good. And you'll arrive before noon."

"Perfect, right-on time." Marvin waited for his boarding pass.

"Here you go." The counter attendant smiled. "Have a great flight."

"Thank you so much, I sure will." Marvin grabbed his carry-on and laptop bag, put his phone into his pocket, and walked to the screening area. After passing through TSA Pre Check, he arrived at the terminal with enough time to settle in. While waiting for the flight, he opened his laptop, used his hotspot, and continued online shopping. By the time he'd completed shopping and constructed a plan, the flight called the third boarding group.

"Calling Zone B," the desk attendant announced.

Marvin closed his laptop, secured his bags, and retrieved his boarding pass on the way to the terminal gateway. He pressed his boarding pass on the scanner and walked down the jet way to the plane. Once inside, he texted his office assistant. *Taking a day Monday. Please cancel all meetings and appointments and reschedule them for Tuesday through Friday.* After putting his phone into airplane mode, he buckled in and relaxed for the flight.

***

Renee looked at her watch and nearly panicked. "Oh, crap! I have got to get to the airport." She ran from the conference room to her cubicle. "I can make it if there isn't much traffic, but…" She looked at her watch. "Damn it!" Her hands became sweaty and moved fast and breaking into a sweat from nervous energy. Her laptop flew into her bag and her notebook followed, right before she secured the zipper. She threw the carrying strap over her shoulder and rushed through the area's exit door to the elevator.

Downstairs, Renee dashed to the car skipping her routine greeting with the security guards. She pulled out the key fob from her laptop bag and pressed 'unlock'. The car responded, and within seconds she put the key in the ignition, started the engine, and snapped on her seatbelt. Her cell phone chimed sweet nothings.

"Hey, I thought you were on a flight?"

"You don't have to pick me up. Come home instead," Marvin encouraged.

"Okay. I have something planned, so don't cook anything," Renee reminded him.

"I promise. See you when you get here."

Renee turned at the intersection and headed for Marvin's condominium. She slowed her car and breathed easier than minutes before. Her mind flashed. *Special, be special for his homecoming. I hope he likes what I've planned. I should have left earlier. No, wait. Why did he get home early?* She moved onto the interstate, drove the speed limit, and exited within 15 minutes. The car followed her instruction, slowed after she passed the breaks before the traffic light, and turned right onto the roadway. She drove into the parking deck to an assigned space.

"I love this," Renee grinned upon her arrival.

***

Marvin landed at the airport, shuttled to his car, plugged an address in his navigation system, and drove to Wilmington, following the information. He exited into the city as directed, went to a florist, and bought a dozen roses. He looked at his phone, entered A. R. Morris Jewelers' address into the navigation system, and followed the voice's directions. He stopped in front of the store, parked, and went inside. He pulled up a picture on his phone while he stood in front of a glass display.

"Hi. How can I be of assistance?" asked the salesclerk.

"Hi, I need this." Marvin pointed at the picture.

"And can you size it today, while I wait?"

"I think we can find one that may not require sizing." The

clerk looked in the display. "Here it is." He pulled out the jewel. "It's a seven. Is this close?"

"I know she wears an eight."

"How about this one?" The clerk pointed to a similar cut which was a little more expensive. "If you like that one," the salesperson pointed, "about a hundred dollars more will get you this style, which is a unique cut only designed by us."

"Oh." Marvin put the other jewel on the counter and took the unique cut from the salesclerk. "I can see why you think it's unique. I haven't seen one like it, and I researched the style I know she likes."

"Let's see the size." The clerk took the ring and flipped the tag. "No need to size it, and if you want it, we're ready to go."

"Perfect, let's do it." Marvin retrieved his Black American Express card and handed it to the clerk. "Could you box it?" "A box comes with it, sir."

"I'm sorry, I've never purchased one before."

"I bet you won't ever again. She is going to love you for this."

"She already does."

"Lucky man." The clerk smiled and handed Marvin a pen and purchase slip.

***

Marvin arrived home, put the flowers in the closet, and placed the jewel box in his coat pocket. He hung the coat in the closet. He went into the master bedroom and undressed, entered the shower, turned on the water, and the massage of life ran down his body.

I only get one chance, maybe I'll set up another time? he thought as he washed. *Maybe a night on the town overlooking the bay, or maybe a drive to Philly, or a trip to the Caribbean?* He pondered the options. He grabbed a towel from the rack and wrapped it around his body while still in the shower stall. He warmed up since he toweled dry in the shower avoiding the cool breeze of his air conditioning. He wrapped the towel around his waist, opened the shower door, and walked to his side of the twin sinks. His reflection in the mirror froze in time exactly as the sweeping of his second hand stopped moving on his watch. His eyes locked in a stare, and he did not move a muscle. *It is now or never,* he thought. *Renee is doing exactly what I expected. She trains well.*

***

"Marvin!" Renee yelled, closing the door behind her. "Marvin, I'm sorry I didn't pick you up."

Marvin sat at the foot of the bed without giving a response. He waited for her to enter the master bedroom and smiled at the sight of her when she entered.

"Didn't you hear me?"

"Hi, baby, I heard you." Marvin looked into her eyes with raised eyebrows. "You get it."

"Get what?"

He opened the towel displaying himself. "Me."

Renee looked at him, walked closer, and captured his lips with hers, sampling his flavor before saying, "Yes, I caught a big one."

He reciprocated kissing and pulled her on to the bed. He held her tight while her knees were on the bed and her torso was bent over him.

"Stop, we have things to do, you'll ruin my surprise." Renee rose from his embrace.

"Surprise?"

"Your welcome home." Renee smiled and stood clear of his path.

"Oh, I see." Marvin rose from the bed and walked into the bathroom with his towel. "I'll go with it."

"Please do." Renee changed into yoga pants and a top. "I'm going to finish dinner and then we'll have your surprise."

"Okay," Marvin replied from the walk-in closet. He selected a polo shirt and relaxed jeans, dressed, and went to the front room. He watched Renee move from one side of the kitchen to the other, pull items from the cupboard and fridge, then chopped on the counter. He flashed to a childhood moment where he watched his mother move like Renee. His eyes grew large in anticipation and Marvin closed them tight with a frown. He grabbed the remote and tuned in to classical music on the radio, sat back on the couch, and closed his eyes, placing the remote beside him.

"Dinner will be ready in 20 minutes."

"Okay," Marvin replied. He heard Renee leave the kitchen, and when he didn't hear footsteps, he rose from the couch, walked to the kitchen, grabbed two wine glasses, set the roses in the middle of the table, opened a bottle of wine, and placed it next to the flowers. He went to the closet, grabbed the box from his jacket, and put it in his pocket. He returned to the couch, sat back, and closed his eyes.

Renee walked into the kitchen, saw the table setting, and walked to the roses. "Thank you." She lifted the dozen roses and smelled them. "Thank you so much, my sweet man."

"Baby." Marvin turned and saw Renee dressed in a maid's outfit. "What the...?"

"Welcome home, baby." Renee went to him with the dozen roses in hand. "I love you so much."

"I..." Marvin kissed her lips. "I need you to sit down." He escorted Renee to the table and pulled out a chair. "I need to talk to you."

"Is this a bad idea?"

"Oh, hell no. It's an impressive idea." Marvin's eye lit up. "I see you know me as no other woman has ever gotten to know me. He swallowed. "It's why I need to talk to you." His head shook before grasping the wine bottle. He poured, shaking enough to interrupt the calm of a waterfall, filling wine in her glass and then his.

"You..." He swallowed. "You know..." He paused. "Ah, we've been together for over a year now."

"Something wrong?" Renee asked.

"No, no, nothing at all" Marvin sipped wine from his glass "I was saying, we live like no other couple I know, and I've never loved a person as much as I love you."

"I love you, too." Renee raised her hand to touch Marvin's face. "There is…"

"…I need to say this."

"Say what?" Renee dropped her hand. Looked into Marvin's

eyes, doing what she can to stop her tear filling eyes. "Are you tired of me?" Renee covered her mouth and a tear fell from her right eye.

"No, no, give me a minute." Marvin touched her shoulder. "I love you. and can't ever get tired of you." Marvin picked up her wine glass and sipped a little before replacing it in front of her. "I can't see my life without you. I can't see not having you support me or ever lose my love for you." Marvin paused. "I absolutely love your family. I love everything about us, you, and our future." Marvin moved closer dropping to one knee, pulled the box from his pocket, and opened it, showing Renee. "Will you do me the honor…" He paused. "…and marry me?"

PART II

Current

Day

Chapter 9

The Coffee Shop

"Love is a fool's journey, and it hurts, but when it is good it's amazing." Renee Yarbrough fell on the bed remembering what her mom always told her. She pounded the mattress in anger with her fist. She repeated her mother's mantra before rising to her feet shaking her head. Renee crossed her arms walking to the dresser. Renee grabbed jeans and a tee shirt and changed from her pajamas. She made her way downstairs to the kitchen and stood in front of the sink. Her eyes locked on her image in the window while raindrops scattered the sky and hunger sounds of God amplified. "I get it mom," she whispered. A flash of light illuminated the sky wiping away her image in an instance. Marvin disappeared from her life. Marvin… Marvin, my *handsome man, why did you leave?* Her eyes swelled, her lips trembled, and she dropped her arms to her side. *"If I hadn't answered your knock, I wouldn't be here."* She raised her hand wiping the tear from her good eye. "Will I ever love again?"

Renee moved from the sink; her eyes peeled on the ideas of yesterday, her look of today, and a lost energy towards tomorrow. Her painful scars burn from the salted tear traveling through the crevasses of her incident … *Damn it, I did everything right. I graduated from college like my parents and grandparents. Even though it wasn't a Historical Black College or University, like they wanted, I still graduated.* She turned inward and faced the kitchen table. "I found a great job, let my heart go to the man I thought was my forever, and now... look at me!" Renee stared at the empty seat, filled with hope to steal a memory of the man who invaded her world. Raindrops danced on the roof loud enough to change the room's ambiance and the storm's rumble broke silence with an off rhythmic sound. "You didn't have to." Renee shook her head. "You didn't have to do either... leave nor hurt me." Renee touched her chest, applying a comforting pressure held by her imagination. She closed her eyes taking shallow breaths, and her head dropped to the hands. "I can't," she told herself. "I can't." she paused. "Turn around Renee." She instructed. With swollen eyes, tear-filled enemies of reflection took to the slopes of her cheeks, and raced on different terrains, one side smooth as beauty allows and the other side rugged like the moon's surface. She stared at the window watching raindrops disfigure the reflection of her smooth skin. She heard a loud rumble and saw lightning strike the ground. Renee closed her eyes, clenched her fist, swallowed, and cringed, and stiffened her body before one hand wiped the tears away.

She opened her eyes and hoped her defenseless garden survived the lightning strike. Renee looked for her nurtured lifesavers, more colorful than Christmas decorations, and brilliant as new blooms in Spring. Lightning flashed the sky with enough light for a glimpse at the friends who gave her multiple reasons for a beautiful existence.

For months, those plants got her out of bed at sunrise. She pampered the soil, fed seedlings, and nurtured each one. They created a unique partnership saving one another for the life ahead.

Renee waited at the window with hope the sky would give her

another glance at her prize. She stopped worrying about what she missed in her relationship and gave focus on her hobby and partners. When the storm stopped, the clouds moved to a full radiant moon which brightened the garden. The luminescence danced on the rain droplets upon each petal, a mirror to the stars in the sky. Renee smiled, walked to the corner of the kitchen, and grabbed her camera and tripod before heading where magic frolicked. She snapped, lifted the camera and tripod to another angle, focused her lens, and snapped again. A cloud covered the moon and Renee stopped with the pictures. She returned inside, put the camera in the corner, and secured the back door. Renee walked to the foyer and grabbed a windbreaker from the coat closet. She went to the family room, laid the breaker across the back of the couch and sat prim and proper. Her eyes darted to magazines on the coffee table, looked to the window and scanned past her reflection of the hall mirror. Renee opened her legs, sat forward, and closed them before her head went to her hands.

 She agreed to meet her mother and sister Candi at a coffeeshop within the hour. *I don't want to go.* She shook her head. *I hate going out looking like this*, she thought. Renee adjusted her position to avoid her reflection in the mirror. Her cell phone on the kitchen table rang her mom's unique ring tone. Renee rose from the couch and retrieved her cell phone, swiped the screen, and answered. "Hello."

 "Renee, I'm running a little behind," Mom said. "I'm driving as fast as I can."

 "It's okay Mom. I have nothing else to do." Renee walked to the window and opened the blinds. Sunlight beamed into the room.

 "I'll be there in 10 minutes." Mom stopped her car. "I'll call your sister and tell her to leave in 10 minutes."

 "Okay Mom." Renee paused, wondered if her presence in the

world will ever return to normal. Hesitant in her response, "See you soon." She disconnected the call and stood silent. She heard the rhythm of her breathing and slow thump of a heartbeat.

Mom grabbed Renee's free hand and led her to the car. "You don't have to be scared, Renee. Keep holding my hand."

"It's not about fear, Mom. It's about what's right." She paused, walking slower than normal. "Mom, it's about people seeing me…"

"You'll get used to it, Renee. I have faith, and before long you won't care anymore."

"I'll care, Mom." Renee rearranged her scarf with her free hand and covered most of her scarred face. "I can at least be mysterious."

"Listen to what you look like." Mrs. Chadwick shook her head. "You're beautiful." She paused, smiled at Renee, and touched the hand she held with her free hand. "You are always beautiful."

"Thanks, Mom. It's what mothers tell their kids." Renee sat in the car, readjusting her scarf before snapping on her seatbelt. She looked at the window and ensured she did not have a scary reflection. Renee moved the front blinder to the side window. She created a shadow towards whomever glanced at her.

"One day," Mom sighed. "You'll be confident and I pray it's soon."

"It will never happen, Mom." Renee shook her head in disagreement. "It'll never happen."

"I pray it does." Mrs. Chadwick nodded and put the car's transmission to reverse. "We're meeting your sister when we get to the coffee shop."

"Is she okay?"

"She's Candi; doesn't that explain how she's doing?"

"At least she's still beautiful, Mom."

"You both are."

Renee's eyes glanced at passing cars and sized up pedestrians at street corners. She reached for her scarf and wrapped the scarf around her face leaving enough gap to show her eyes. She had not raised her left hand since she had gotten into the car. The silk material irritated her facial nerves even though the mixture of scars had healed well. With her hand in place, Renee looked at her mother. "Mom, are you sure about this?"

"You have to get out, and the more you do, the easier it is."

"But..." Renee's focus went to her lap. "I don't think it's a great idea. I mean, people will conclude I'm some sort of freak."

"No, they won't. Trust me."

"I do, Mom, but..."

"... mothers know best." Mrs. Chadwick changed the car's gear, drove down the main street to a large six-lane intersection, and stopped at the red light. Renee glanced out of the window before releasing a sigh. She felt relief that no other cars or pedestrians were in sight. She smiled.

"Stop paying attention to who's beside you." Mrs. Chadwick encouraged. "Do me a favor and look straight ahead."

"What if I'm noticed?"

"So what if you're noticed? Let them look. They may think you're an Arabian queen riding in a poor man's Cadillac." She giggled.

"Are you serious?"

"I am." Mom smiled. "Imagine you're the princess of a harem."

"I know from where Candi gets her wacky ideas."

"You had them, too." Mom laughed. "Remember when you ran after the boy who used to run across the backyard? You jumped the fence and tackled him."

"You saw that?"

"How could I miss it? And when his mother called, I had to give her an explanation why you didn't stop slugging him with your fist."

"That's different. I had my reasons. I swear he was a peeping Tom."

"If he was, he isn't anymore," Mrs. Chadwick laughed.

"At least he wasn't like Candi's creepy high school boyfriend. You didn't find peeping Tom in the house when you and Dad came home early."

"Candi got hers, too."

"After I left for college, I'm sure," Renee smirked.

Mrs. Chadwick turned the car into Oak Street and pulled into the parking lot for the Tip of the Cup Coffee & Snacks, a quaint coffee café-style bakery with strategically spaced wooden tables and wooden multicolored chairs. The hardwood floor squawked at the weight of each person. Bells rang when a patron entered the pane glass front door. Members of a local Boys & Girls Club created the multicolored 'open' sign. Behind the counter was a chalkboard with a menu of coffee drinks and a glass presentation shelf to the left of the counter, filled with pastries. Mrs. Chadwick walked to the counter and read the menu board.

"Can I help you?" asked the barista.

"I would like a mocha with an extra shot." Mrs. Chadwick looked at Renee. "The Arabian Queen will have a black hazelnut."

Renee shook her head and walked to the far table in the corner. She sat next to the wall, avoiding the window, and her back was to the wall. She glanced left, ensuring no one had direct sight of her, then looked at her mom, who stood at the counter, waiting for their order. Mrs. Chadwick waved with one finger, beckoning her presence. Renee shook her head left to right. She mouthed, "No, Mom, I'm not."

"Mom!"

Mrs. Chadwick turned towards the direction of the noise. "Hi, Candi," she greeted her approaching daughter.

Candi hugged her mother. "Did you get the masked queen?"

"She's over there." Mrs. Chadwick pointed at the corner table.

Candi looked in their direction and waved. "Will she ever let that scarf drop to the floor?"

"No, she won't."

"I'll get her to." Candi touched Mrs. Chadwick's shoulder and walked to Renee at the back corner table. "I don't believe you." Candi covered her mouth.

"What don't you believe?" asked Renee.

"You look like a million dollars, covering everything but your eyes." She made a V-shaped slit with her fingers and slid them across her eyes. "The dance, my dear…. ha ha ha." Candi giggled.

"Stop that, just stop." Renee frowned. "You're making a scene."

"As if you already haven't?" Candi pulled the chair closest to the window a little distant from the table. "I'll block the lookers from the window."

"Thanks."

Mrs. Chadwick arrived at the table with two cups of coffee. "I didn't order for you."

"It's okay, Mom. I can get my own." Candi looked at the wall behind the bar. "Maybe I'll get what you're having, Renee."

"I'm having something simple - black coffee." Renee took the cup from Mrs. Chadwick.

"Keep that figure. It's been a year and you haven't gained an ounce."

"Why do you do that?" Mrs. Chadwick asked.

"Mom, it's true. She should be more confident. She's a survivor, and I admire her for being one."

"Now is not the time." Mrs. Chadwick frowned. "Get your coffee." She touched Renee's arm. "No worries, baby. You'll come out when you're ready."

"Thanks, Mom." She paused. "I will." Renee looked at Candi. "Get the hazelnut, it smells good."

"I'll do that." Candi stood, grabbed her purse, and walked to the bar.

"Mom," Renee addressed, "try not to defend me. I think I can manage Candi's comments."

"Look - it's my child being unthoughtful. I'll correct her," Mrs. Chadwick responded.

"But, Mom, she's no kid. She's my sister, and I can manage it." Renee lifted her coffee cup, lifted the scarf and sipped it. "This is good." She smiled.

Candi stood at the counter and chose a special coffee flavor for her order. She gandered around the shop before walking to the cake display and pointed at a slice. "I'd like this one," she said.

"Yes, and can I add a raspberry cream to it?" The melodic voice asked from behind the clerk.

Candi raised her eyes smiled. *Damn, he's handsome.* She glanced at his left hand. *Single, too.* She thought before saying. "I haven't tried cream with this cake. Is it good?"

"It's a mouth-dancing experience," he said.

"I shouldn't, Mister…?" Candi waited for a name.

He tapped his clerk and said, "Make sure you give her the sauce."

"Yes, I'll do that," smiled the barista.

Candi watched the toffee complexioned slender build, brown eyed man with black hair and perfect lips. Her eyes followed him towards the back. "Does he always ignore people?" she asked without looking at the barista.

"He doesn't answer personal questions." She shook her head. We don't know anything other than he owns a few of these shops around town."

"Really?"

The barista pulled the pastry from the case and grabbed the sauce from the cooler before placing it on the counter. She poured the special flavored coffee into a travel container and rang the final charge. "Card or cash?"

Candi looked at the Point-of-Sale display and pushed the credit card into the slot. "Here you go."

She paused and took the printed receipt for signature. "Can you tell me if he's married or not? I didn't see a ring." Candi signed the receipt and returned it to the barista.

"Ma'am, I can't. We don't get into people's business," she grinned.

"I…" Candi stopped short …*why would she tell me?* she thought. "Never mind."

"Thank you." The barista put the receipt in the cash register and turned to another customer. Candi picked up the tray with the coffee, pastry, and sauce before walking to the table. "Hey, did you see the guy behind the counter?"

"There you go again. Aren't you happy with the men you're dating?"

"I wasn't thinking about me." She looked at Renee. "It's time you get back in the saddle."

"I will when I think it's time." Renee lifted the scarf and sipped her coffee. She placed the cup on the counter. "You have no idea if anyone would like my new face."

"I know they will." Candi turned towards the mirror. "But who can see it if you keep hiding?"

"Mysterious is good." Mrs. Chadwick picked up the fork and sliced the pastry Candi placed on the table. "What is this?"

"I have no idea, but the guy said to add this sauce to it. He said it was amazing." Candi pushed the sauce closer to their mother.

"Mom, after this, I'm ready to go."

"Why?" Candi asked Renee. "You get out after being behind closed doors for over three years, and now before you can enjoy people, you're ready to leave."

"I'm not ready," Renee responded. "I don't think people are ready."

"You are my beautiful Renee. When anyone talks to you, they'll know the beauty inside and not from some scarf."

"Easy for you to say."

"I believe it," Mom chimed in. "I believe you'll find that one person who will embrace you for being you, and not something you had."

"I thought I had that, too." Renee dropped her head as if the wind from her lungs escaped through her chest. "I..." She paused. "...had no idea he was like that."

Mom gently touched her on her reconstructed shoulder. "You survived, and you're here with us. We're so grateful you fought back."

"Mom, Candi, thanks for being here for me. I couldn't do it without you two."

"I only wish we'd known sooner." Candi frowned. "We could have gotten you out before this happened."

"I know." Renee glanced at their mother and dropped her head. "I know." She gritted her teeth behind tight lips.

Mom took a second bite of the pastry with the sauce. "Oh, my goodness, this is so good."

"Mom, can't you see we're serious, here?"

"Don't beat a dead cow to life. Renee knows we wish a lot of things would have happened." She licked the fork. "This is so good."

"Let me try." Candi shook her head after watching her mother's response. "Let me get a new fork." Candi walked to the counter, retrieved a fork, and returned to the table. Her first bite danced on her tongue and tickled her taste buds. The explosion tickled the roof of her mouth, and when she breathed in, the air made it stronger. "Oh!" she exclaimed, "Mom, this is amazing."

"It's almost a drug of choice," Mom giggled. "Renee, you should try it."

"No thanks, I'm not...lifting my cover to eat something out here."

"You drink coffee with that thing," Candi reminded her.

"But it covers the cup." Renee sipped coffee, pointed towards Candi, showing her how it's done. "See?"

Candi walked to the counter. "Is the guy still here?" she asked the barista.

"No, he left a few minutes ago."

"That pastry with the sauce, was it his idea?"

"He makes it every day."

"Tell him…"

"…it was divine, right?"

"How did you know?"

"Most everyone says it. I mean, everyone who tastes it for the first time says something like that." The barista smiled. "It's our best seller."

"I can see why." Candi walked to the table. "Mom, the owner makes this himself."

"Really? We should get his recipe."

"I don't think that will happen." Renee said. "It's a unique product and I'm sure he's a shrewd businessman. No one will give their recipe, especially to a stranger."

"I'm not just anyone," Candi smiled, "and neither are you."

"I'm not asking." Renee looked out of the window and her brown eyes sparkled in the reflection. She dropped her chin to dodge the light in her eyes.

"Mom, we have to get to my next therapy session." Candi looked at her watch. "You should come with us, Renee."

"I don't think that's a good idea." Renee glanced at Candi. "I have my own in a few hours, and I prefer going alone."

Chapter 10

The Coffee Grounds

Mr. Vincent Mathis walked into the office and picked up a clipboard with the list of supplies and supplier contact information. He called from his cell phone. "Hey, Leon, I need to make an order in addition to what I bought last month."

Leon opened his laptop. "Okay, Mr. Mathis, give me a minute. My laptop is booting."

"Good. I'll get started when you're ready. Just say the word." Mr. Mathis pointed at the data on the clipboard. "Are you ready?"

"Give me a moment, this laptop is slow. It's almost booted."

"I get it." Vincent tapped on the clipboard. "Some laptops are slow and it's a shame we can't use pen and paper like we used to. We have a machine and software for nearly everything, these days."

"Yep, we do…almost there."

"If I could automate the coffee bar, I'd think about it." Mr.

Mathis shook his head. "Naaa—on second thought, we need people. Machines won't give the delicate touch most folks need."

"Okay, I'm ready," Leon said.

"I need an additional 8 boxes of Raspberry, 5 boxes of Hazelnut, and 12 boxes of Blue Mountain," Mr. Mathis breathed. "Did you get that?"

"I did."

"Oh, and you can't ship those here. I need you to deliver to this address."

"Are you opening another shop?"

"Yep, this time closer to the industrial area. You know where I'm talking about, right?"

"I know...who doesn't? It's the only multi-industrial complex in town."

"I figure it's a gold mine—easy for breaks and after work, out of the office opportunities. I know it's in competition with company café shops, but as I remember in college eight years ago, you couldn't wait to escape campus."

"Good point. Knowing you, Mr. Mathis, your touch is gold."

"Thanks for the compliment." Mr. Mathis took a breath. "You got the order, correct?"

"You know what? Since you're one of our best customers, I'm going to throw in a box of chocolate-flavored coffee."

"Oh, thanks. I'm sure it'll come to good use."

Mr. Mathis tapped the red phone icon, ending his call. He placed the clipboard on his desk and looked out the office window at the traffic. He noticed the woman who had asked his name and watched the scarfed woman walk to the passenger side of the elder woman's car. He tilted his head towards the right and frowned at the older woman. *I swear I have seen her before.* Vincent watched the women enter the car and drive off. *I have seen her before...where?* he thought, turning to the door for his next business measure.

The next store's inventory report got him riled. "Damn it, what happened?" He looked at his sales report and deposits, compared them to his inventory, and decided to review the store's film. "Customer traffic is fine." He watched. "I know the location is good." He rescanned the sales report and noted the norm. "What the hell happened to the coffee?" He retrieved his cell phone from his pocket and dialed the westside location. "Hey, is Harry there?"

"He stepped out. Can I help you, Mr. Mathis?"

"Maybe..." Mr. Mathis paused before asking. "Who usually closes the store?"

"That depends. Harry tries to share that responsibility with everyone. I think it rotates with the few employees scheduled on the last shift."

"That's what I need to know." Mr. Mathis coughed. "Please tell Harry to give me a call when he comes in."

"Sure thing, Mr. Mathis."

Mr. Mathis disconnected the call and watched the film in detail from the last month of operations on his laptop. He rewound and forwarded, then rewound to spots he felt suspicious over. He especially watched if there was waste and if bags of coffee grounds were disappearing. "Damn, no wonder we're upside down."

He was into the third hour of watching tapes before he finally picked up a pad and drew plans for a better process. He imagined doing it himself, going from one item to another and attending to each process. What he configured was the old college try. On his laptop, he created a process flow chart and accountability checkpoints that worked for his business. At each step of the process, he highlighted a data entry point. He created intense instructions and planned to distribute them as an employee handbook in a printed binder.

Sunrise forced darkness to repose giving way to an eye wakening glow through the office window, an alarm to the morning rush. Vincent heard the chime alarm from the back entrance where employees entered the store. *I haven't worked like this since college.* Mr. Mathis rose from the desk and stretched while yawning. *Renee worked our tails off for that paper.* He laughed. He stepped to the window, looked beyond the panes, and watched the increase of passing cars and multiple patrons enter the coffee shop, sounding the doorbell. He nodded his head. *Great location, just as I thought.*

Hours into the day, Mr. Mathis walked into the main serving area, grabbed a cup of coffee, and returned to his desk. He did not speak to the workers because of the effort he saw serving guests. At his desk, he surfed the network for food critics, especially of baked goods. Featured pictures of cinnamon buns, red velvet cakes, and multiple fruit pies flashed at the top of the page; and on the bottom of the screen, a perfect presentation of carrot cake jumped to his attention. He clicked on the picture and read the entire review and printed the name and address of the bakery. Vincent visited the bakery's webpage, reading the highlights and reviews and sipping coffee while researching and envisioning the products they sell in his stores. Mr. Mathis walked from his office to the display cases showing the multiple pastries he sold. He shook his head. *It's time to change,* he thought.

It was nearly the afternoon when Mr. Mathis got into his car, looked at the address of the new bakery, and tapped in the location on the navigation system. After buckling up, he started the engine and went on his way. Vincent followed the navigation voice that directed his every move. "Turn right in 200 feet," the voice instructed. "Travel this road for three miles. Your destination will be on your right." Mr. Mathis slowed his car and followed the last of the navigational instruction. Arriving a little before one, he parked the car, grabbed his laptop, and typed in a list of goods he thought he would like.

He walked into the building and stood at the front counter. He looked at the pastry display and smiled at the woman. "Hi. How are you?"

"Good morning, Mr. Coffee," Candi smiled. "Do I know you?"

"I don't think so, but I have seen you before." Candi raised her eyebrows.

"And where might that have been?" Mr. Mathis walked to the display case, eyeing the pastries he would like to try. Candi followed on the other side of the glass counter display.

"I saw you earlier, when I met my sister and mother."

"Oh?" Mr. Mathis said, without losing focus.

"You suggested the pastry, and I asked for your name." Candi sighed. "You didn't answer."

"I see." Mr. Mathis lifted his forefinger to his lips. "I don't typically share my secrets."

"Oh, I, uhm...understand."

"If I did, no one would come for my specialty."

"I thought your touch was coffee." She retrieved an order pad and picked up a pen. She gazed at Mr. Mathis.

"I realized coffee is only one draw to the shop, which is why I'm here." He focused on the pastries in the display.

"More baked goods. I am ready when you are."

"Go for it." She put the pen to the pad and waited.

"I have chocolate pastries, but I think we should do this one." He pointed. "Carrot cake, is it?"

"Yes, it's good, too. I would definitely purchase a slice in your shop." Candi smiled. "Would you purchase the entire cake, or slices?"

"Oh, I'm ordering for the entire eight stores. The whole cake, and four per store."

"You own eight coffee shops?"

"It's what I do."

"Oh, my." Candi raised an eyebrow. "I had no idea."

"Most people don't." Mr. Mathis bent to the bottom row and pointed. "What's this?"

Candi looked where he pointed. "It's a fruit tart, but with citrus as its main ingredient."

"That's different. We usually get berries. Add this to the list."

"Okay, I can do that." Candi wrote his selection. "What about the strawberry twist? I made it myself."

"Uhm, I don't think our customers will enjoy that."

"Really?" Candi stood frowning. "You know every person's taste and you won't offer a variety?"

"I had strawberry tarts, and they didn't move much."

"I see, but that wasn't my strawberry twist." Candi touched her cheek with the pen. "You know, like your berry syrup and cake mix, I put my best into that twist." She looked into Mr. Mathis' eyes. "It's as good as or better than your best."

"I still don't think I'll take the twist, but thanks for the try."

"You don't take challenges, Mr....?"

"Mathis. Call me Mr. Mathis."

"Mister Mathis, I get that you're a shrewd businessman."

"Not shrewd. I know my customers and what moves." Mr. Mathis looked at the next row of pastries on display. "Let's see the lemon tart." He pointed. "I think we'll order this, too."

"Okay," Candi responded. "Are you single?"

"What does being single have to do with a pastry order?"

"I'm asking for a friend," Candi smiled. "She's as stubborn as you."

"Oh, really?" Mr. Mathis shook his head. "I'll have to take your question as a compliment." He went to the cash register. "I'll have six dozen each, delivered at these locations on the day you bake them. I don't suspect that will be tomorrow?"

Candi wrote the order and rung the cost on the cash register.

"Give me a minute, please, while I ask the lead baker."

"Sure." Mr. Mathis walked to the baking supplies aisle, picked up a bag of flour and nut mix, then placed them on the counter. He looked at the cash register display and calculated the price point for each item, for a profit margin. He returned to the isle and chose more ingredients: salt, sugar, baking powder, and baking soda. He placed the items on the counter and checked them off on his iPad.

Candi arrived. "You want me to add these to this, or make it a separate purchase?"

"Please add these to my list. It's my experimental supplies."

"You create pastries and have bakeries reproduce them in bulk?"

"That's what normal business is like, right?" Mr. Mathis raised one eyebrow. "I, um…never mind."

"I know someone who'd love you." Candi scanned the items. "She's adorable."

"I beg your pardon?"

"You aren't married. I don't see a ring."

"Oh, we don't have to talk about my relationship status." Mr. Mathis looked at his watch. "When should I expect delivery of my order?"

"I think we'll have the order ready in two days."

"That's a long time, for my stores. How about tomorrow?"

"It's a tall order for a 24-hour turnaround. Give us 48 hours and we'll have your order delivered. All of our ovens are in use. But we can do it if you give us a little time, if that's okay."

"Is this your first big order? Don't you have another method of filling an urgent order, like borrowing ovens from another bakery?"

"You'd have to talk to the owner about the baking. I'm not the decision-maker, but I know we can deliver your order in 48 hours."

"You can, in 2 days."

"48 hours." Candi smiled. "I, uh, I'll give you a try."

"You mean me personally, or the baking?" Candi's eyes brightened. "I was talking about the person that's perfect for you."

Mr. Mathis shook his head. "How much?" "I'll have your total in a moment." Candi focused on adding numbers into the system. She mumbled, "32 cakes, 32 dozen, plus baking supplies." She pressed the machine for a total and a number appeared on the screen in front of Mr. Mathis. "There's your total cost, including delivery."

"Fine." Mr. Mathis retrieved his business bank card and slid it into the slot. "I'll get you the delivery addresses once I'm done here."

"Yes, I was about to ask for them."

He picked up the order sheet from the counter and filled in the information. He turned the paper over and added the other four addresses before signing it.

Candi handed him the credit charge receipt and pointed at the signature line. "And this one, too," she said.

"Thank you." Mr. Mathis signed the slip. "The bag?"

"Oh yeah, your supplies." Candi pushed two bags to the front of the counter. "I put the order receipt in the bag. I hope you have a great day."

"Thanks." He took the bags. "You do the same."

***

Candi completed her shift at the bakery, walked to her car and dialed Renee on her cell phone. "Hey, Renee."

"What is it? I'm busy." Renee responded.

"I met him."

"Who's 'him'?"

"The guy who created that pastry at the coffee shop," Candi smiled.

"Oh, good for you." Renee paused. "Did Mom tell you to call me?"

"What?" Candi's voice deflected curiosity.

"They're going out of town, you know."

"What…oh, I know, you are taking them to the airport."

"Yes, I will, but next time you should."

"That's not why I called you."

"Why did you call me?" Renee's voice spiked. "You're not shopping for me."

"No, I'm not." Candi sighed. "Will you listen?"

"Okay, fine." Renee smirked. "What's up?"

"I met the guy from the coffee shop, and his name is Mr. Mathis.

He's a handsome guy, really business-like, and I know he's your type."

"You mean, he didn't bite on your flirting."

"Why do you do this?" Candi frowned.

"It's who you are, and I know it. Why do you think he's my type when I told you I'm not looking, and I'm not some mental case that needs to find a man?"

"But you need this."

"According to who, Mom?" Renee took in a deep breath.

"No, according to me. I see you suffering, and this can help."

Renee slowly breathed before responding. "I didn't know you cared."

"You're my sister, and I care about your happiness."

"I..." Renee spoke in a soft tone. "I'm not ready yet—not yet. Maybe in a few years."

Candi heard her tone and covered her mouth. "Okay, we can try later." She dropped the phone from her ear and pressed the red icon, ending her call. One tear fell from her right eye.

***

Renee walked into her backyard, picked up the hand hoe, and kneeled near her first vegetable row. She hacked, pulled, and tossed weeds. *I never knew Candi cared.* Her good hand rose slightly shoulder high and, with effort, the hand-sized hoe pierced the soft ground. *All these years, I thought...she was self-centered. How did she change? Where was she when I needed real help? How can she pretend to care now that I am free of that man?* Renee worked in the garden during the heat of the day.

Chapter 11

One Step at a Time

Renee woke with flooding tears cascading down her face while she shouted "STOP!" at the top of her lungs. She sat in bed grabbing her bad arm as if holding an imaginary teddy bear. Her back felt the soaked pillow pressed against her, which encouraged her to get up. Before moving, she remembered her mother's voice.

"It's going to be okay, one step at a time." Renee repeated, "One step at a time." She wiped her tears, rolled, placing her feet onto the floor before standing. She walked pausing between steps. Renee wiped her forehead with her good hand, remembering Mom's advice, *One step at a time.*

In the master bathroom, she whispered, "I'm going to be fine." Her soft voice bellowed a magical command to her reflection in the mirror. "I'm going to be fine." Renee pointed her finger at the woman's gaze. "I am going to be fine!" Her voice lifted to the ceiling and the message echoed against the bathroom walls.

It was mid-morning when Renee put on long blue overalls, a white tee shirt and walked to the garden. She grabbed the hand size hoe, kneeled, and touched the dirt before gloving her hands. The gritty dark earth, danced between her fingers and in her palm. The fresh fertilized granules tickled her nose, and she breathed easy. She gripped the hoe, spinning it, reflecting the sun like a lighthouse on the beach giving warning of rocks. The hoe's sparkle ignited an eased heartbeat. Renee dropped the hoe and picked up gardening gloves she left at the edge of the row where she kneeled.

The miniature handheld hoe went higher than her shoulder and knifed into the soil in front of her. She chopped at the path she moved, digging around the roots of each seedling. She imagined Marvin at every place the hoe slashed into the ground, inflicting a small amount of revenge. She exerted herself, dug at the dirt, and felt her fight. The garden is her place of escaping hatred, and simultaneously feeling love from each plant.

The garden was the only place where her husband left her alone. He hated dirt or anything to do with gardening. Her haven to void his anger. She retrieved the water hose, grabbed a plant energy container, hooked it to the nozzle and sprayed liquid energy on her plants. The rush of water pressure through the hose, reminded her of the defense she imagined using if Marvin invaded her sanctuary. Peace and harmony. "One step...my garden."

Mrs. Chadwick drove into driveway of her daughter's home. She parked short of the front porch, exited the car and walked to the front door. She rang the doorbell and waited for Renee. Moments later, Mrs. Chadwick glanced at her watch and glanced through the side flanking French door window. She rang the bell two times more, peeked beyond the crack of the side curtain and knocked on the door. Mrs. Chadwick grabbed her keys, put the key in the lock and entered through the front door. "Renee!" she called walking through the living room. "Renee!" she repeated, exploring the kitchen, seeing the empty container on the table. She looked through the kitchen window and stood in observation.

My daughter, the prodigy, is now a gardener. She smirked and frowned. *I can't get her to leave this house or get her out of this fenced yard.* Mrs. Chadwick placed her purse on the kitchen table and walked to the backdoor. She called, "Renee!"

Renee looked towards the house. "Hi, Mom."

"Just as I thought," Mom responded. "If you're not in the house, you're in this garden."

"It's my baby." Renee smiled. "You know why."

"One step at a time," Mom said, reminding herself of the message she had told her daughter, only to repeat what the therapist had suggested. "You do this so much; it has to soothe you. It's like a religious ritual."

"Mom, it's my therapy. Before Marvin shared his secret, it was my escape. Out here, I feel safe."

"That was then." Mrs. Chadwick approached Renee. "That was then, Sugar." Mom hugged her. "I wish I had known."

"You're here now, Mom." Renee used her good wrist to wipe a tear away. She dropped the water hose and walked to the faucet. Her right hand shut off the water supply. She reeled the hose in the turnstile on the water hose holder.

"Did I interrupt you before you finished what you wanted to

do?" Mrs. Chadwick asked.

"No, Mom, you're right on time."

"I'm driving you to your doctor's appointment."

"I'm not going."

"Why?" Mrs. Chadwick raised her voice sharing her concern.

"I have my garden. He said it's my therapy. I like my therapy."

"But you should go…" Mrs. Chadwick sighed. "He's helping you see life since the accident."

"You mean, the attempted murder. I've talked about it enough, and it's not helping me when I relive that moment. Mom."

"Yeah, I'm sorry but… it's not enough… You have to get over it."

"I'm not going." Renee walked to the backyard sink and washed her hands before she sat at the patio table. "I don't think seeing the doctor will help my face. I don't think seeing him will heal my hand." Renee touched her scarred cheek. "I know he can't do anything."

"He's your therapist. He knows how to help us get you back to being normal."

"Sure, Mom, he knows. It's not working. And you know why it's not working." Renee dropped her head before saying, "My body can't take the memories. I can't take the pain mom, though it's psychological. I can't take the punch in my chest at the top of the stairs because I didn't get there fast enough. I can't take the stab in the hand for spilling coffee grounds on the counter."

Renee shook her head, raising her eyes to meet her mother's. "I can't and won't remember the isolation from everyone that he put me through."

"It's..." Mom shook her head in disgust and stared beyond Renee's eyes imagining her daughter is transparent. "...anyway, I didn't tell you. Your father and I are traveling to the Caribbean soon. I suggest you think about what you want for groceries."

"What I want for groceries?" asked Renee. "How long is your trip?"

"We're going for two weeks."

"Okay, I'll think about my list." Renee looked into the house through the sliding glass door. "Which island?"

"An island that your dad chose." Mrs. Chadwick reached over and touched Renee's arm. "Who's going to check on you?"

"I don't need anyone. I'll manage."

"I'll have your sister check on you."

"No, Mom, I can manage. She has a lot to do."

"Like what? She doesn't have anything to do but work at that bakery."

"At least she has that." Renee nodded and perked her lips. "But it's not better than my garden." Renee rose from the table and picked up a sprouted pot of liquid plant food from the shelf. She walked to the end of her garden and poured the plant food over selected plants. "I don't think she'll have time anyway; you know she's chasing some guy."

"She'll do the shopping. I'll call her." Mom went into the house for her cell phone. She dialed Candi, only to get her voice mail. "Call me when you get a chance. I need you to look after your sister." Mrs. Chadwick touched her cell phone, ending the call.

Renee moved down the line watering plant after plant in a pattern she had developed – step left, one back, step right, wide step, pour, and repeat. Mom walked from the kitchen to watch Renee's process. "So now you're dancing with your plants? I've never seen you do that."

"You weren't around when I fed them."

"What? Fed them?" Her mother shook her head. "I think you should come with us to the island."

"No way." Renee turned towards her mother. "I would never." She pointed to her scarred face.

"One day," Mrs. Chadwick muttered, "I'll get you out of this God-forsaken memory."

"What was that?"

"Nothing." Mrs. Chadwick opened the sliding door, entering the kitchen, picked up the blender, and sat it on the counter. She grabbed the fruit bowl, got a knife, and sliced apples and cut bananas, putting them into the blender pitcher. She then placed strawberries, blackberries, and seedless grapes inside of it. Ms. Chadwick poured almond milk into the pitcher and added ice cubes. She blended the mix and poured two glasses. Her voice pitched a perfect melody after she walked to the back door and, like hundreds of times, calling her daughter to come inside. She bellowed, "Renee, I have a smoothie for you."

"I'll be there in a few," Renee responded.

"Okay." Mom sat at the table with her fruit smoothie, sipped a little of it, and waited. She picked up her cell phone and tapped the screen. She pressed 'redial' and waited.

"Hey, Mom, I'm sorry I missed your call. What's up?" Candi asked.

"Your sister needs you to shop for her while your dad and I are traveling. Can you get a list from her and make it happen?"

"She can get her own groceries. Ma, you need to stop babying her, and push her. It's been a year since her last surgery and, regardless, she has to accept what she looks like in public."

"That's harsh, Candi, damn it."

"It's worse because she's hiding."

"You would, too." She frowned and raised her voice in response.

"You would be worse because you're the vainest child I've raised."

"Is that a compliment?"

"You little shit!" Mom yelled. "You're about to… "

"…piss you off?" Candi giggled. "You have no idea how to get her out, Mom. You baby her too much. She's a grown-ass woman and the sky is her limit."

"Like you didn't go through your problems and was babied. I'm so damned…" Mom paused.

"Get her damn shopping done." Mom tapped the read icon on the face of her cell phone. "That little shit." Mom sipped her smoothie and placed it on the table. "Now, where is my oldest?"

"I'm here, Mom," Renee responded, walking through the

doorway with garden gloves in her hand.

"You know, I can help you save a lot of worrying. Candi doesn't have to help." Ms. Chadwick shook her head in disagreement. "You won't go out."

"Mom, maybe I can if I need something. You won't be gone that long, so I don't need anything, and I can stretch whatever I have."

"Do you know what you have?"

"Mom, I can order it if I need it."

"You need to get out. Life isn't about staying wrapped like a gift; nor is it living behind closed doors. You should get out." Mom rose from the table and walked to the counter. She retrieved the fruit smoothie and handed it to Renee. "You have to try this."

"Thank you, Mom," Renee smiled. "You didn't have to make this for me."

"I know, but you need your strength for working in that garden of yours."

"I do, but it's not that difficult."

"I think it is. You haven't stepped out by yourself, and it's long after the surgery. You're much better than before." "Mom, that doesn't say very much." Renee sipped the smoothie and swallowed. "I am nothing near better than before."

"You don't give yourself credit. Think about your accident."

"Accident – Mom!" Renee shook her head and folded her arms without adding pressure to her injuries. "I never thought you'd look at what I've gone through as an accident."

"Well, that's my cue to leave." Mom chugged the smoothie and put the glass on the table. She grabbed her purse, stood up from the table, and walked stopping short of the front door. "We need a ride to the airport; can you do that?"

"I'll take you."

"At least you can do that without an argument."

Renee stared at her glass and waited for the sound of the front door. "Sometimes Mom can be so deceived." Boom! The door closed. Beads of sweat appeared on Renee's forehead, her injured hand twitched, and she closed her eyes.

"No, no, no... don't do it... STOP, STOP, STOP!!!" Marvin grabbed her t-shirt collar, ripped it to shreds, and pulled her up on her heels. "Bitch, you will never fucking question me," Marvin pressured her. "Never fucking question me." Marvin's open hand met Renee's face with a force greater than the slammed car door of a potential buyer. WHAP! "Smartass." Marvin released his grasp. Renee dropped to the floor and her body bounced before sticking to it for comfort.

Renee opened her eyes, looked around the kitchen, and wiped a tear from her smooth skin with her good hand. Her mind stopped imagining the horror of Marvin and she realized she was sitting at the table where Mom left the smoothie she had made. Renee stared at the smoothie, focused on its contents, and took her mind to the fruity mix. She handled the glass, sipped, and rose from the table. Renee looked out the window at the sun beaming on the plants and watched steam rise from the damp ground.

It's getting too hot to work in the garden, she thought, before she mumbled, "I'm going to shower."

***

Renee's cell phone rang when she stepped from the shower. She grabbed the towel, wrapped around her, and picked up the cell on the sink. "Hello?"

"What time are you going to be here?" Mom asked.

"You didn't tell me," Renee responded, shaking her damp hair and trying to keep dripping water from falling into her face.

"I was telling your dad you'll drive us. Then I forgot to give you our flight information. We leave next week Tuesday morning at 8. I think we have to arrive about 2 hours before our flight time." Mom paused. "Are you sure you can take us?"

"Mom, that's perfect." Renee rubbed her hair with the towel, holding the phone to her ear with her shoulder. "I can do that. I'll spend the night, and we can leave before sunrise."

"Good, and we return in the afternoon, in 10 days." "I don't think I'll pick you up. Candi can do it." "She's working and you aren't. You can't pick us up?" "Mom, it's mid-afternoon, and I…"

Her mother responded with a high pitch. "… you can be seen in public, damn it! Be there—and I expect you to be on time!" Mom screamed. She exaggerated her tap on the red icon on the phone's screen.

Renee looked at the face of the cell phone, shaking her head before she placed it on the counter. "She can be a bitch." Renee screamed. "DAMN IT!"

After she toweled herself dry, she went into the master bedroom and dressed for the day in jeans and a t-shirt, finding her way to the front room. She picked up a book she had been reading, <u>Rising After the Fall</u>, <u>A Self -Help Journey to Recovery,</u>

Reckoning With Reality.

***

Days later on the eve of her parent's travel, sunset over the garden shared nature's special colors. The orange glow of the sun hitting green leaves and colorful flowers danced in the eyes of onlookers. The evening was no different than any other summer day ending for Renee. She watched the glistening plant leaves, those she had watered minutes earlier, sparkled. She smiled before touching her face with her good hand, rubbing the smooth skin of her right side. "BUZZ – Demonic Sounds!" Renee jumped, her eyes widened, and her heart raced. She breathed in, tightened her body for defense of whatever it is in front of her with the sound. She relaxed, picked up her cell phone, and swiped the face killing the alarm. She forgot she had set the phone to announce the perfect hour to chance driving to her parent's home. It's the first time going on the road alone, for a 40-minute **drive that immediately** seems like an eternity. She nodded and tapped the address on the cell phone in search of a faster route than she remembers. She smiled at the part on the expressway but frowned at cruising down major fairways.

I can do this. **She** walked to the coat closet, got a scarf and a pair of white cotton gloves from the top shelf. Renee sighed in front of the mirror **adjusting** the scarf around her head. She widened the length to cover everything below her eyes to the bottom of her neck. The tucked scarf showed enough to intrigue the imagination to see her perfection.

She entered her car, placed her purse on the passenger's side, and put her overnight bag on the footboard in front of the passenger's seat. Her hands hit the steering **wheel and** she looked at the scar on **her** left hand. She picked up the left white glove and gently slid her **hand inside, extending** one finger at a time. She deliberately left the right hand free of wearing a glove and turned the ignition key bringing the car engine to life.

Streetlamps hit the car's windshield spotlighting her appearance while she drove, and oncoming car lights accentuated her image from all angles. She smiled, confident of her coverage. *Perfect timing,* she thought before she stopped at a major intersection, **pulling short** of the bright streetlight. The distance between the lead car and she was two extended car lengths. When the light changed, she crossed the fairway and entered the express lane, only to see the person peeking at her scarf from the right side. She pressed on the gas pedal, moving ahead of the onlooker.

Renee focused, taking the fastest routes dodging nearby cars and getting to her parent's **home** as quickly as possible. She pushed the accelerator moving the car faster, slightly turned right, changing l a n e s to the next exit, and moved ahead of the cars going her direction. She entered the far-left lane **and** turned left, leaving the expressway. **Renee** turned onto the street she had traveled for years. She flashed through the corner onto the six-lane road and finally arrived at the neighborhood.

She pulled in without hesitation and removed her scarf to freedom. She rolled the window down and slightly smirked at feeling the wind against her surviving nerve endings. She stopped the car in front of her long-time residence, parked, and grabbed her things before closing the door. She pressed the key fob and the car lights flashed, giving her **the** sign all was secure.

"Mom, I'm here," Renee said, entering the house.

"Good." Mrs. Chadwick dropped the last of her clothing inside the suitcase and closed it. "I'll be right down."

"No, Mom, I'm going to bed. I'll be ready before 5."

"Sleep well, and thanks for doing this." Mrs. Chadwick pressed her carry-on case closed and set the alarm clock. "Do you need an alarm clock?" she shouted.

"No, I'm fine," Renee answered.

***

Morning hours without the sun advanced like a reckoning sweep of time. Renee jumped from bed and ran to the bathroom, like she had done a thousand times. Her eyes didn't stare in the mirror because her mind was on the mission ahead. She dressed, wrapped her scarf to perfection, and went down to the kitchen. "Good morning, are you two ready?"

"Yes," Mr. Robert Chadwick smiled. "You look marvelous." He hugged Renee.

"Dad, you always know how to make me smile."

"Yeah, he's such a charmer." Mrs. Chadwick giggled. "Hey, the suitcases are at the door. Open your trunk, and Dad and I can put them in there."

"I can help, Mom."

"We can do it—but if you insist." Mrs. Chadwick placed her hands on her hips.

"Let the child help, it's okay. We all can carry a bag," Mr. Chadwick suggested.

"If her arm hurts…" Mom warned without blinking an eye.

"… She'll put it down and we'll get it. But if she doesn't use it, it will get worse."

"Mom, Dad, I'm right here. I know my limitations. If they are too heavy, I'll tell you." Renee shook her head.

"Grab that one in the middle," Mrs. Chadwick instructed. "We'll get the others."

Renee shook her head but followed her mother's instructions and grabbed the smaller suitcase. She walked through the front door going to went to her car. She opened the trunk and set the smaller suitcase aside. Her father followed with both larger suitcases, one in each hand. "I knew I'd do them all, anyway," he said.

"Yeah, Dad, I did, too," Renee snickered. "It's almost funny how that is…"

"I'm right here, you two."

"Seems to run in the family." They laughed. "Okay, let's get things going. To the airport!"

Renee got in the car and started the engine. She retrieved her white driving glove from the center console. "Is everything in the house secure for your trip?"

"I think so." Mrs. Chadwick looked at the front door, then her purse, and tapped her pants pocket.

"I can go check." Dad stepped out of the car and went into the house.

"You can come by here every couple of days," Mrs. Chadwick suggested. "I have your sister doing it, too. Just in case one of you can't, the other should."

"Mom, everything will be okay. You've done this before."

"I know, but we're being safe, like always. Just in case you and Candi want to coordinate visiting."

"I will, Mom. I will do it at night, but I will check. I think."

"You made it this far, and I'm proud of you." Mom touched Renee's good arm. Dad returned and sat in the back seat. "We're all set," he said.

"Great, let's get to the airport." Renee put on gloves and snapped on her seatbelt. She drove down the road. Traffic was scarce, and her intersection antics did not play into the early morning hours. Which meant that no people were watching. At the airport, traffic picked up and her eyes darted across lanes. She readjusted her scarf to make sure it's set with a purpose. Her breathing rhythm increased, and her face became stiff. Without turning towards her mom, she said, "Mom, Dad, I'm dropping you off here."

"But we're at the other end."

"I don't think…"

Mom interrupted. "You're here, and you need to drive down there. People do not care if you are wearing a scarf. **Just do it.**" Renee cringed, put on her shades, and followed her mother's instructions. She stopped the car at the far end.

"See, that wasn't so difficult, now - was it?"

Renee pressed the trunk release button. "I hope you two have a great trip. Please text or send me an email telling me you're okay. I will check the house while you're gone."

Mr. and Mrs. Chadwick exited the car and retrieved their bags. Mom **waved**. "Love you."

Renee moved the car into the flow of airport traffic. She looked at the rearview mirror and saw her parents watching her drive away. She returned focus on the road and glanced once more at the rearview. Marvin was standing on the sidewalk. Her hands started shaking and her grasp at the wheel tightened.

"No, it's not him!" she shouted. With a quick turn of the wheel, she drove onto the exit road with bright streetlights leading to the highway. She pressed the gas pedal and speed became her console. Within minutes she noticed her exit ahead and lifted off the gas pedal. She slowed the car to turn at the exit closest to her home. The morning light grew brighter with every passing moment. Even with shades, a scarf, and wearing white gloves, her nerves danced with the idea of being seen. Her heartbeat and a bead of sweat formed on her forehead. She pressed the gas, moving the car faster than the speed limit in her neighborhood, getting to her home before the streets became busy.

Renee had not replaced her shades since she left the airport, and the facial scarf was loose. Her mind feared the reaction of any onlooker. She turned down the main intersection and ran through the yellow light. She pressed forward, only to slow to 10 miles above the speed limit. She stopped at the corner and turned right onto her street. Her heart's rapid pace and quick breathing slowed with her approach to her driveway. She reached up to her scarf, pulled it free and smiled.

The sun reached morning peak and she pushed the car door open, grabbed her purse and bag, then pushed the door shut before zipping to the house's entrance. "I made it!" Renee sighed. "I made it," she repeated, touching her chest, breathing at a slower pace. "That was close."

Chapter 12

The Divider

Mr. Mathis followed his manager, Rick, during the walk through of his first store. He stopped for a moment, put his cell on the customer counter, and keyed data into his iPad before scanning the furniture arrangement. He stepped forward and accidently hit his leg on the side of a table. "Damn it!" Vincent moved the chair, pushed the table, and continued sizing up the area. He nodded, frowned, and crossed his arms, moving his head from the entrance to the customer counter. He shook his head before sitting at the table. His fingers tap danced across the screen of his iPad.

He stood, walked to the counter, and picked up his cell phone. He swiped the photo icon, and turned around to snap pictures before filming, imagining a patron enter the shop, move to the counter, and finally get a table. He returned to the table, sat, and added notes to his iPad. *Find a better flow to aid in-house service at the counter.*

His cell phone rang. He swiped the screen and placed it to his ear. Before he could speak, a woman's voice addressed him.

"Mr. Mathis?"

"Yes, how can I help you?" he answered.

"It's Candi." She paused and waited for a response. While Mr. Mathis kept quiet, she spoke again. "Remember me?"

Mr. Mathis closed his eyes and shook his head. "How can I forget you?" Vincent opened his eyes. "What can I do for you?"

"I think your order is ready."

"You *think*?" Mr. Mathis frowned.

"Well, I know your order is ready."

"I thought you guys would deliver." He exhaled. "It was the deal - you would make the delivery."

"I didn't say you had to pick anything up. I said your order is ready, but I wanted to make sure this is your cell number."

Mr. Mathis looked at the face of his cell phone with a scowl, then tapped it to end the call. "What a pain in the ass."

"You said something, Mr. Mathis?" Rick's right eyebrow rose on his arrival at the table.

"Not you. But, since you are here, I think…" Vincent paused and looked at Rick. "…we need to rearrange this configuration. It isn't good." He pointed to the tables along the wall. "I think we can adjust for better efficiency."

"No doubt, more efficient." Rick wrote in his notebook. "I can see the difficulty."

"It's something I expect you to change, and it's something we need to remember." Mr. Mathis keyed in his laptop and retrieved the monthly sales report to his screen. "You're doing a fantastic job here. It's why I like having you run the place."

"Thanks, Mr. Mathis. I love working here. It's the best job for my situation."

"How's that going?"

Rick closed his notebook and clicked his pen, hiding its fine point. "Its hard some days, but I get through it; especially after my infusion." He closed the pen inside the notebook. 'Snap,' the sound echoed.

"Know you're going to get better." Vincent looked at Rick. "You're important here, and I want you around as long as I'm in business."

"Yeah, and thanks for keeping me around." Rick touched Mr. Mathis on the shoulder. "It's not often that employers keep ailing folks around. I mean, I've heard of so many people being terminated."

"You're welcome. I am all in to help you fight. I can't speak for others, but small business owners who aren't supportive have the reason of affordability. Most can't seem to afford it."

"I appreciate you, Mr. Mathis."

"No sweat." Mr. Mathis rose from the table and walked behind the bar going to the supply closet with Rick shadowing. He looked inside. "There's a shipment coming today, so let's make room for it." He looked at Rick. "I have to get to another store. Let me know when the shipment arrives."

"Will do," Rick nodded. "I'll walk you out."

"No need, I know the way." Mr. Mathis grabbed his iPad, walked to the front door, and turned around before exiting. "Rick, we'll catch up again soon," he shouted.

Rick nodded. "Sure thing."

***

Vincent arrived at his second coffee shop, the original store that Paul Sattler had started. He parked in the back row of the parking lot, watched foot traffic, and took notes with a pad and paper. His eyes followed patrons headed to the shop and he remembered most of their facial expressions upon leaving the store. He recorded a tick mark for smiles and another for frowns, as well as those with neutral expressions. He created a success and failure definition based on his observations.

After two hours, Mr. Mathis walked into the coffee shop and looked around. He sat in the back, closed his eyes, and listened to the background music, the tone of conversations, and the hustle of his staff. He remembered Paul, the coffee shop owner who had given him a chance during college, saying, *'Use your senses and you'll know how to satisfy your customer.'*

Mr. Mathis opened his eyes and noted the people lounging, conversing, and enjoying coffee and pastries. He referenced the full spectrum of the shop's operation, in comparison to his recent report. He raised his cell phone for a picture, capturing his view, documenting his bases for future comparisons. He sat back, reflecting on the years he'd been one of the staff during college, and how he had camped in the closet during summer vacations. He rose and walked to the front counter.

"Hi, Mr. Mathis," the clerk greeted him.

"Hi, Samantha," Vincent responded. "Having an enjoyable

day?"

"Well..." Samantha paused. "So far." She looked at the back of the store. "I arrived just in time for the daily shipment." She pointed and showed Vincent the packing list. "They sent us the wrong order."

"Huh?" Mathis went to the shipping label on the first box, peeled it from the plastic, and unfolded it. He read it, before touching his chin. "It's the right shipment." He counted the boxes. "It's all here, but the problem is, it's all at one store. The delivery was slated for every store." He retrieved his cell phone from his pocket and dialed the bakery. "Hello." He paused for a response.

"Thank you for calling, how can I help you?" Candi asked.

"This is Mr. Mathis."

"I know who you are." Candi smiled before asking, "What's wrong? Didn't you get your shipment?"

"Is the owner available?"

"Yes, he is. Is there a problem?" Candi pitched her voice higher.

"I need to speak to the owner."

"I'll get him." Candi frowned, tapped the hold button on the counter phone and walked to the back of the bakery to the owner's office. She knocked on the door three times. "Are you in?"

"Yes, I am," the owner responded.

"You have a call from Mr. Mathis regarding the large order for his eight coffee shops."

"Thank you." He placed the desk phone receiver to his ear. "Hello, Mr. Mathis. What can I do for you? "

"I requested delivery to my seven stores, and it showed up at one location. How in the hell did this happen?"

"One shipment?"

"I paid for multiple shipments. When will you have your truck return and ship...never mind, where's my shipment refund?"

"Wait, let me rectify the situation before you ask for a refund. Can I call you back with a solution? I promise, five minutes."

"Five minutes?" Vincent paused. "Okay, five minutes." He pushed the red phone icon on the cell phone screen to end the call, then looked at his watch.

"Any progress, Mr. Mathis?" asked Samantha. "I'm giving them five minutes to respond. Meanwhile, we will have to take these to our stores, or end up having a huge sale."

"They will spoil before we sell this many. I don't think that works."

Samantha looked at the substantial number of boxes. "You ordered for the entire city."

"Yeah. It's going to waste if we don't do something quick."

"How about I put some in my car and I can drop them off to at least three stores."

"That can work, and I can take as many in my car. But I can do a double trip. Will you call someone to cover you while you're out?" Vincent walked to the back of the storage area and divided the boxes into delivery routes to capture the fastest path to each store. He calculated his loss, since he did not have a refrigerated truck, and traffic could make his morning delivery turn the pastries into day-old products.

"I think we can make the best of the situation with a few turnaround shipments." He paused and rethought the situation. "But I don't think we can do that."

"Why not?" Samantha responded, holding her head to one side.

"I can only take one at a time, and we have seven shops."

"Won't we refrigerate these, anyway?"

"Refrigerated pastries..." Vincent looked at Samantha. "I don't think it's a clever idea to refrigerate pastries. I wouldn't want one cold - would you?"

"I guess its day-old bread we're delivering, even though it's baked within the delivery time."

"A day-old sale is what we'll have to do." Vincent smiled before he lifted one box. "I'll load this in my car, and you grab what you can."

"Got it, Vincent," Samantha replied, grabbing a box of pastries.

***

Vincent walked into his second favorite coffee shop; the store he'd helped open with Stanley years ago. The original furnishing décor worked well with the wood beam ceiling and oil light fixtures that stood firm regardless of burn spots. Every table was positioned where Stanley had decided, which kept the feel of comfort and ergonomic perfection. Vincent held the box of pastries and listened to the murmur of patrons' voices. He smiled before he took another step towards the bar.

"Hi, Vincent," the barista greeted him.

"Hi." Vincent smiled. "Looks like things are going well here."

"Yes," she responded, while pressing grounds into the preparation cup. "I couldn't ask for a better day." She smiled. "What's in the box?"

"Pastries I ordered for the shop."

"Why are you delivering them?" The barista's eyes lifted.

"The truck…"

Vincent explained the mishap and walked to the preparation room. When the swinging door swung shut, he placed the box on the prep table. He opened it, looked inside, and took out the first set, inspecting them for damage. The hissing sound of the coffeemaker took his mind to his youthful days. *I can't believe it has been ten years since I started working here.* He looked at the door with expectations of the old man walking through it. His mind focused on the swinging door. His eyelids lifted and a smile grew as big as a rising sun over the horizon.

"Are you going to share what's in the box?" The barista nodded and pointed to the brown box Vincent held.

"Ah…" Vincent paused, looked at the box, and straightened his face. "Yea, I was just about to sample the contents."

"Can I share the sample with you?" The barista giggled. "I would love to give you my opinion."

"Ah, I sure think I made an excellent choice." Vincent

maneuvered the box, retrieved a pastry, and offered it to the barista.

"Thank you." She smiled before she grabbed the pastry with two fingers. She bit the corner, closed her eyes, and savored the taste. "Wow, people are going to love this."

Vincent grinned, sharing his approval. He removed the contents from the box and positioned a dozen on the tray. He gave the tray to the barista, walked to the refrigeration area, and placed the box on a shelf. He left for another store with his box-filled car.

***

Early afternoon before the lunch rush, Vincent arrived at the third coffee shop and found a parking space closest to the back door, where deliveries were common. This is the busiest coffee shop, with the best location, and produced twice the revenue at peak hours. The store continually made remarkable profits, and its first acknowledgment of success came from Jack, Vincent's mentor, who never fathomed a coffee shop could reach that level of profitability. Jack had quickly offered a partnership to his proven apprentice. Vincent's eyes watered while he remembered Jack and recalled events with his father. He gripped the steering wheel with his left hand and used the other hand to wipe a falling tear from his cheek. He turned off the car and grabbed his keys, pulling them from the ignition slot. His door swung open before he touched the handle. "Vincent, we're almost out of pastries and we're running short of coffee because we didn't get the coffee order today," a trusted barista said.

"Help me with these boxes," Vincent quickly responded. He got out of the car and said, "We're okay with pastries. How much coffee do we have left?"

"If business slows within the hour, we'll make it- that is, if the shipment arrives at lunch. But I can't be sure."

"In business, we never are," Vincent laughed.

"Jack's words, if I ever heard them."

"Huh?"

"Never mind." He paused. "Let's get this inside."

"Okay."

***

Vincent shook his arms to increase the blood flow. Regardless of his effort, his arms pained, and his breathing was slower than usual. His heart rate played like a ritardando of a symphony's dedication, matching the rise and fall of his chest. His relaxed body was ready to accept sleep if it knocked on his door. During his last delivery, he had zigzagged across town to all eight of his stores and completed the job he had ordered the bakery to do. Business, to him, was more than checks and balances. It was his stability and love, much greater than any relationship with a woman. The business was his bride, and he treated each store as an extension of his love.

Vincent arrived at his townhouse condominium and, like all other nights, sat on the sofa in darkness - no lights, no music, no pets around to greet him. He reached for the laptop on the coffee table and reversed his action. Vincent decided to review numbers and research ideas to attract more customers another night. He closed his eyes and relaxed.

He heard her voice call his name, never as clear as the moment she gave instructions, leading the group project they shared in college. After a short breath, Vincent opened his eyes and glanced at the digital clock. The green light of numbers interrupted perfect darkness. *Three twenty-seven*, he read. He rose from the couch, walked to his bedroom, and fell onto the bed. He waited for the alarm to sound before a morning shower.

Chapter 13

What's Missing

Vincent's squinted to day light after the radio alarm sounded. He placed his feet on the floor, rubbed his eyes, and then stretched. "I'm not ready for this," he murmured. He pondered about the day. "If Jack were here, I would call in for a morning off. Those were the good days." He chuckled, stripped off his shorts, walked to the shower, turned the water on, and waited for the perfect temperature. He reflected on his image in the shower glass door. "I can use a little exercise." Tapping his stomach. "Actually, a lot of exercise." Vincent stepped under the spraying water that danced on his skin with its massaging thrust. He held his arms against the back shower wall, exhaled and remembered moments of an earlier relationship.

She would jump in with him, sparking the joy of sharing with the assumption of preparing for a workday ahead. He smirked and washed his body.

Vincent met his love after college. Right after graduation he waltzed into a full-time position, becoming a partner with Jack. It took him two years to let things go after the heartfelt rejection with

Renee. He gave up winning over the woman he truly wished had his heart. It's when you took on a new love, any woman whoever seemed interesting in comparison.

Gloria Stonham, a pinup beauty, sparked in Vincent's eyes. She was slender with a tight athlete's dancer build. Slender sides, long defined legs, and tight arms. Her green eyes could guide your imagination, and mixed with her strawberry blonde hair, she gave off the promise of adulteress intimacy. What nailed Vincent was the smile of a million dollars on a wet Sunday. Gloria entrusted Vincent with her purest emotions. She had worked at store number three before the other five opened. Her discipline to keep a part-time job while in school said much about her drive for success, or so Vincent thought.

Gloria had a way with Vincent. She showered him with love, constantly being by his side, providing the graceful ear, and pushing him to focus on his passion. Though she was years younger and a better extravert, she knew how to speak her mind without fear. Her heart splattered the best of light showing him love on distinct levels. The greatest contribution to Vincent, he thought, was her engaging mind. She talked to him for hours about anything imagined. He loved dancing with her between the sheets. Gloria took his heart on a journey he thought would never happen.

For two years, Gloria kept her claws into Vincent. After her college graduation, she pursued his heart with her plan. The picket fence syndrome lived, and her view of happiness saw greater things than what Vincent offered.

When compatibility between the two showed its head, her ardent desire for wealth surfaced. Gloria's consistent disappointment in Vincent's lack of entrepreneurial drive led her to harass Jack in his toughest moments. Vincent had no tolerance for this, nor did he want a life in corporate America, which she pushed. Spectacular moments happened during the few years despite the conflict. His memories of their intimate excursions rose at Vincent's lowest moments.

Stepping out of the shower, Vincent toweled, wrapped the towel around his waist, went to his bed where he sat on the corner and listened to silence. He turned his head scanning the room, starting with the mirrored oak dresser, a memory of Gloria's content usually on top. He looked at the space above the hutch where pictures of their lives stared into space. He listened for her voice, the same as the day she'd said good-bye. He closed his eyes, only to view a setting sailboat under the open sky and calm water—a scene he'd relived a million times since she left; and one where he remembered the moment, he fell for her.

The picture-perfect environment in which his heart sailed into troubled waters picked up a strong wind, and the boat sped across the ocean. Gloria literally fell at the punch of speed as the vessel jolted. Vincent caught her head before she hit the helm. She looked at him with piercing green eyes and a smile of confirmation that he had saved her from a painful experience. He pulled her up by her hand and placed it on the helm before he moved behind her. "The safest place on the boat." He grabbed the helm and locked her in between himself and the ship's wheel.

His eyes slitted while he gazed into the mirror at his reflection. He Inhaled deeply and stood motionless to regain his unclouded vision. With one forward step, he retrieved a shirt from the dresser drawer and sighed. "It was good until." He shook his head, pulled the shirt over it, picked up a hairbrush before pressing its bristles over his scalp.

She left me, and that is the end of it. She just left. Vincent put the brush on the dresser, pulled up his trousers, and buckled his belt. "I won't do that again."

***

Twenty minutes into his drive, the cell phone chimed. He tapped the phone icon near his steering wheel. "Hello, this is Vincent Mathis."

"Vincent, it's Candi."

"Good morning, Miss. is there a problem?"

"Ah, no, there isn't," Candi answered quickly. She took a breath before making her pitch.

"Oh, good." Vincent changed traffic lanes. "What can I do for you?"

"We have a special at the bakery. I'd like to know if you're interested."

"I beg your pardon. You didn't tell me about a special."

"Here's the deal." Candi smiled. "If you give me your secret recipe, we'll make it for you in bulk and give you a fifty percent discount on any order."

"Are you kidding?"

"I talked to the owner, and he's up for it. I told him how my sister, mother, and I loved it. I know it will sell faster than any other pastry we make. And if you want more, then maybe I can have the boss share part of the profit with you, or we'll purchase the recipe."

"No, I don't think either option is good."

"My sister and mother loved it. Can you at least share the recipe with me?"

"I don't think that's possible." Vincent slowed the car, exiting the expressway. "You know, if you love it so much, tell me when you think you will visit the coffee shop, and I may have some on the day you arrive." *Why the hell did I say that?* He slightly shook his head in disagreement.

"That sounds great. I'll let you know." Candi smiled. "I will make sure you know soon."

"Give me at least a week in advance. I don't normally stop working to bake."

"I will. And if my sister doesn't show, can I take some to her?"

"I don't see why not. It's your purchase."

"It's not free?"

"Good-bye, Candi. Have a wonderful day." Vincent pressed the cell phone to end the call. *The nerve of that woman. I can't believe she would push for free stuff when I run a business.* Vincent parked his car at the least profitable store. He entered with the iPad and assessed the store. He noticed patrons scattered about before he stepped to the barista. "I'll have a mocha special, please."

"Large or medium?" she asked.

"Make it large," Vincent asked.

"Large it is." She smiled before ringing up a price. "Sir, that will be $3.70."

"Is that the usual price for a large mocha coffee?" Vincent reached for cash from his pocket and handed her a five-dollar bill.

"It is, and I think it's great, because the closest coffee shop sells it for $5."

"Oh, really?" Vincent laughed. "Good answer."

"Sir." She handed his change to him with a raised eyebrow. "I don't understand?"

"Mr. Mathis," Ted called out, "how are you?"

"I'm good, Ted." Vincent looked towards the young lady. "New barista?"

"Yes." Ted nodded, "Veronica." He moved to the counter and stood next to the new hire. "This is the owner I told you about." Ted introduced him. "Mr. Mathis, this is Veronica.

She's always on time and gives her best at learning everything about the shop." "I see." Vincent smiled. "Nice meeting you." He raised his hand for the traditional handshake. "Welcome aboard."

"Sir, I had no idea you…"

"…no problem. You were fine, and I like your style." Vincent smiled. "Very pleasant."

"Thank you." Veronica stood at the counter.

"My coffee…"

"Oh, yes, I'm sorry." Veronica processed the large mocha coffee.

Vincent looked at Ted and nodded. "You have time for a chat?"

"Sure, no problem." Ted walked to a corner table in the store.

He waited for Vincent to get his coffee and join him. Vincent grabbed the coffee from Veronica, sipped, and nodded his head. He smiled at Veronica. "Good job, it's perfect." He put cash in the tip jar.

"Sir, that isn't necessary," Veronica added.

"As a customer, for a perfect brew, it's necessary." Vincent raised his cup and walked to the table where Ted waited. "You hired a special one. I'm impressed."

"Thank you." Ted nodded. He looked Vincent in the eyes and asked, "So, what's on your mind, sir?"

"I wanted to review our numbers from last month and see what we can do to increase traffic and sales."

"I wanted to talk to you about this. I'm always brainstorming how to pull people in."

"Oh, really." Vincent sipped his coffee and opened his iPad to his revenue chart for the store. "I guess you would know better than most. What do you think would help this store?"

"Well, we have a competitor that recently had a sale that damn near made us a ghost town. I mean, they offered more things like events and celebrity visits and had radio and social media advertising. I thought we could do better in every category."

"I'm open to some advertising ideas. But what events are you talking about, outside of discounted sales?"

"I had the idea of sponsoring book clubs, giving them discounts on goods for meeting here."

Vincent listened to Ted before he responded. "I can see meetings. But who knows how to contact book clubs?"

"Using a marketing strategy." Ted paused before adding. "You know, they meet at someone's house or an apartment clubhouse, every so often. If we sponsored multiple book clubs, and market to them, we would pick up more traffic. And I believe we'll do well with regular traffic if we do it right."

"Okay, book club meetings. Or any type of group meetings that come here." Vincent closed his eyes and sipped the mocha coffee. "From your idea, we can make it a meeting special for groups in general." He looked at the iPad and retrieved the pricing model for every item. "If we give a discounted percentage and sell the appropriate amount, the store will get out of the red."

"Yes sir, but marketing to the organization is only one function. I want to bring in wine as part of our evening product line."

"A coffee and wine bar?"

"Think about it. If the book club doesn't want coffee, then serving wine is our next best product. The reason our numbers are bad is that coffee sales are high for morning and noon, but by evening, the store is practically a hangout, but not much coffee is sold."

"What sells in the evenings?" "Mostly pastries and water. But it's not enough to make us reach revenue goals." Ted's eyes focused on Vincent's facial expression.

"I see." Vincent sipped coffee. "I see where you are going with this, but I'm not so sure how we should approach it."

"It's being done in other cities, but not here in Baltimore."

"There is a licensing situation and legal age standards we must adhere to. And there are additional things we'd need to structure in doing so." He touched his iPad and typed in the idea.

"I've made a note to research the concept."

"Mr. Mathis, you know this opens another opportunity for growth, especially since we're close to residential areas."

"Yes, what is that?"

"Spoken word, poetry sets, and even live music on the weekends."

"Poetry? Read poetry?"

"Yes, exactly. It's not that hard to do and start. I can see it happening, and with the coffee/wine/bar set, it will go off amazingly well."

Vincent sat up in his chair. "Amazing, huh?"

"I'm not just talking marketing now, but I'm seeing real growth." Ted moved his head in agreement.

"That makes sense. I like the subject. Real growth, which the store desperately needs."

"I think the potential is staring us in the face. I can help you if you decide to go in any direction."

"Sounds good." Vincent smiled. "I don't think I'll be able to do it alone. So, your offer to help is perfect. How about we schedule things to work on, and track our effort?"

"Will it be okay if I include Veronica?" Ted asked.

"Does she know about the business?"

"Mr. Mathis, she knows more than the average barista working in the business. Let me say, I am impressed with her knowledge and skill."

"Ted, I will leave that up to you. I'll bring her in, and you two can work it together."

"Thank you. I'm sure we won't let you down." Ted smiled, pleased at Vincent's agreement.

"It seems you won't. I'll get back with you with a plan, later this week after I research the concept." Vincent finished the coffee, shut down his iPad, and placed it in the carrying case. He stood and reached across the table. "I enjoyed our conversation, and I'm sure you know the numbers that we didn't get a chance to discuss. I'm glad you are focused on raising the business."

"Sir, you are pretty fair. I only ask that you let me run it."

"As much as I can—heck, I'll even add incentives, to make it work."

"Incentives?"

"Let me work out the plan, and we'll see what I can come up with." Vincent shook Ted's hand as he rose from his seat. "I will get back with you and we can talk about how to move forward."

"Thank you." Ted smiled. "You won't be disappointed."

"I hope not." Vincent said, "Don't count on it as a sure thing just yet," Vincent smiled. "I'll get details on what it takes to make it happen." Vincent released Ted's hand, took the iPad and empty coffee cup, and walked towards the store's front exit. He dropped the empty cardboard cup into the trash, turned towards the barista, and said, "Nice meeting you, Veronica."

"Nice meeting you, too, Mr. Mathis." Veronica waved and

smiled.

***

Vincent left the coffee shop with excitement for reviving his business. Ted's suggestion lingered on his mind, remembering the coffee wine bar concept. *Wine and coffee... coffee all day, wine after noon... wine in the morning too... No. Who drinks wine in the morning?*

Vincent opened his car door and saw the potential of increased traffic for the store. *Ted's a smart guy.* He entered the car, started the engine, secured his seat belt and set his course to another store that wasn't doing well. In traffic, his heart thumped an extra beat, remembering how Ted's enthusiasm led to where he's headed today.

Mr. Jack Sattler did the exact thing with me. He let me drive the change for our business. Thank God it worked. Vincent zipped down the road. He saw different bars and clubs, coffee shops, and bakeries along the route. He noticed the lack of coffee and wine combination shops at every strip mall or stand-alone coffeeshop building. *Ted is onto something.* Vincent approached the city and noticed a few wine bars. He also noticed the lack of daytime traffic at each one. Empty parking lots in front of those bars helped his decision to not delay analyzing the wine bar concept. He passed the strip mall with a wine bar near the bay, slowed the car and turned into the parking lot. He drove to the wine bar and stopped in front of the entrance. Vincent exited the car and saw a shadow behind him. He ignored the dark silhouette and stepped to the dark glass wall before peeping inside. He looked with his hands cupping the sun and tunneling the view.

A homeless man stood next to him asked. "Spare change?"

"You should never sneak up on a guy," Vincent smirked taking his focus off of the dark wall. "Are you hungry?"

"Yes, I am. I'd like whatever you can spare so I can eat something."

"Uh, if you walk with me over there, I'd get you a meal

"That's it? Walk over there with you?"

"Sure. Is that asking too much?"

"No, not at all. Should I do something else before I walk with you?" He paused. "Most people tell me to wait here or wash their car windows."

"I want to ask questions." Vincent looked at the gentleman and waited for a response. Before he got an answer, he asked. "Do you come around here often?" Vincent leaned his head slightly to one side.

"I do, but mostly during the day. I sleep over there," he pointed, "next to that park, most nights."

"I see." Vincent walked towards the Morning Rise Restaurant he saw earlier on the corner of the strip mall. "I would say this is perfect for brunch. I'm starved."

"Excuse me. I'll wait for you here."

"Why?" Vincent's eyebrows lifted and ears perked. "I am inviting you inside for a meal."

"I am not so sure." The man pulled back his arms and stood with his feet short of a shoulder's width apart. His eyes gazed at Vincent and with his right hand, he cupped his chin.

Vincent recognized the guy's insecurity. "It's okay. I gotcha. I don't think they'll mind you coming in. Besides, we need to chat, anyway. Come on in."

They entered with a direct path to a booth towards the rear of the restaurant. A waiter approached with menus. "Welcome, can I get you water or coffee, or a glass of juice, to start?"

"We'll have all three," Vincent said. He looked at his companion. "Is that okay?"

The man nodded, picking up the menu.

"Any specials this morning?" Vincent looked at the waiter.

"No, just the usual on the menu. "

He left the table for the drink order. Vincent looked at the menu, decided on what to order, and placed it aside. "Well, partner, what shall I call you?"

"Dave; my name is Dave," he responded.

"Dave, I'm Vincent. Nice meeting you." Vincent offered his hand.

"Thank you for doing this." Dave released his hand. "You are a kind man."

"No problem, Dave. I usually eat alone, and I'm grateful you're here."

"Oh, you don't seem like the lonely type." Dave peeped over the menu. "I'd have guessed you are married, with kids."

"If I had the…" Vincent coughed. "Excuse me."

"I touched a sore spot." Dave placed the menu on the table. "I don't know what happened, but if you had a chance to relive it or go get her, you should do it."

"It's not that simple." Vincent looked out of the window. "I wish it were."

"Simple isn't always the best route to take. But if you had a chance to have a good woman, and someone to share life's treasures with, you should go for it."

"Sounds like you've loved and lost."

"I've loved, lost, and lost again," Dave admitted.

"Oh, that hard of a fall."

"Fall?" Dave covered his mouth. "I'm below the lowest point in my life."

"It can't be so bad, to live the way you do."

"Don't go to churchy on me. I have a reason I am here. And since I am here, I promised myself that if I could ever help someone avoid my path, I would."

"I bet you have a story." Vincent looked at Dave, imagining a cleaner version of the man. "Was it drugs and alcohol?"

"No, neither of those. But love and bad decisions were the root of my fall. Don't take love for granted; nor try to buy a good woman."

"Buy a good woman?" Vincent sat back into his seat and saw the waitress place drinks on the table. "Thank you."

"Sure, can I take your orders?" The waitress pulled out a pad and pen in preparation of taking their orders. "What are you having?"

Dave ordered bacon, eggs, and pancakes for breakfast. Vincent ordered French toast with a side of bacon. "Can you make the eggs over easy, please?" Dave asked.

"Sure, no problem." The waitress repeated the order and left for the kitchen.

"Depression and wrong decisions, one after another. Bad decisions with my wife, kids, and job. Then I served time without a path to redemption. I tried hard to return to the American dream. But I didn't love the right way. I didn't embrace the goodness God created for me. I stole and paid the price."

"I see." Vincent drank orange juice. "I don't think you'll be down forever."

"I don't know — really, it's safe over there."

"Begging for meals and handouts is safe, and a way to live?" Vincent frowned.

"Carefree, and no responsibilities for me to screw up again. Yeah, it's good; all good." Dave sipped his coffee. "It's the best cup of coffee in the world, right now. I haven't had one in ages." He sipped again. "Thank you for this."

"Dave, I heard your story, and I don't want to ask the details, but I get the idea that you're much better than you portray."

"I'm paying for my debt of the heart, and a crime. Love your dream girl if you can. I found mine but lost her to my stupidity."

"I understand; I do." Vincent drank from the glass of water and placed the glass back onto the table. "You are a man of substance. But that's another story?" He paused before his eyes stared out of the window. "Do you watch that wine bar from time to time?"

"Yeah, when I'm around." Dave looked at Vincent before he asked, "Is that what you want to know?"

"Yes, it's part of my research." Vincent continued his focus on the wine bar. "Does it get busy?"

"Weekends, mostly," he responded. "That's when I get the most change, on Saturday nights. Some on Fridays, but not as much."

"Oh, is it packed?"

"Cars come and go, and it's usually parking over here for that wine bar on Saturdays."

"Humm, that *is* pretty impressive."

"During the week, not so much. I haven't seen ten cars on any given night."

"Not much on weekdays. Got it."

"Are you going to visit? Is that why you're asking?" Dave inquired.

"Not in my immediate future, but I may." Vincent looked out of the bay window. "I hope you enjoy this brunch. I don't think this is a bad place."

"I'm grateful for the meal." He looked into Vincent's eyes. "You're a kind man."

"You are very welcome, and thanks for the information." Vincent smiled. "You reminded me of my mentor when you talked about relationships. He said the same thing after his wife died."

"But you?" Dave paused. "I get the feeling something happened to you, too."

"Well." Vincent gazed at Dave. His eyes were marble, frigid in his stare. He sat in silence, fighting a deep feeling of his lost love. He swallowed, sat back, and crossed his arms.

"Take your time." Dave nodded. "I know it can be tough. It took me years to face it, and even now I'm not doing so well."

"Did you get any help?"

The waitress arrived with their order and placed their orders in front of them before inquiring, "Is there anything else I can get for you?"

"No, not at the moment," Vincent said.

"I'll warm your coffee and bring more water." The waitress replied.

"Thank you." Dave spoke, surprising Vincent. He watched Dave nod his head before picking up his fork.

"Are you a religious man?"

"I believe in God, and I'm thankful for what I get these days." Dave paused looked down before raising his head and eyes locking with Vincent's. "I took so much for granted, and I am telling you, don't do it." Dave inhaled his first fork full.

"I appreciate the advice." Vincent looked at his brunch. "And information." Vincent dropped his head focusing on the food in front of him. His mind wandered to the beautiful soul he'd lost. The woman he thought would never leave. He took another bite, and his mind went to the morning he last saw her. The semi-shape fitting and beige dress she wore for work, beautiful and suitable for a summer's day. She styled her hair different, down like making a point to get noticed, and wore her special pearl necklace. *There had to have been a presentation or something, that day.... Yea, something.* When the coffee cup hit the table, the sound interrupted his thought.

"Is this good, sir?" asked the waiter.

Vincent looked up. "Yes, I think so. How about you, Dave?" He glanced over to Dave, who had finished his meal.

"I'm good," Dave responded.

"I'll leave the check." The waiter retrieved the ticket from his apron pocket. "Take your time. Let me know if you want more coffee or water." The waiter took Dave's empty plate and left the ticket on the table before walking away.

"Man, you were in deep thought," Dave commented. "You barely looked up even though you were moving."

"Just taking it all in." Vincent finished brunch with his last bite.

"Well, I'll let you get back to your thoughts." Dave rose from the table. "Thanks for the meal, and I hope to see you visit the wine bar."

Vincent went into his pocket and pulled out a business card. "If you ever want a chance to get back on your feet, give me a call." He handed the card to Dave.

"Thanks, I'll keep that in mind."

"I really mean it, Dave. I think we can help each other."

"I'll think about it. Thanks again, and I hope to see you around. The world needs more guys like you."

***

Vincent arrived at the most popular coffee shop in his chain, a location in the center of town. He entered through the back door into his makeshift office and opened the iPad. He researched Ted's idea of coffee and wine, serving in one of the locations. He investigated all legal aspects and noted them for his lawyer. He contemplated the information he had gotten from Dave, specifically on weekday patronage and weekend traffic. Every idea, he wrote on his iPad - marketing, events, and sale specials. He started crunching numbers such as modification costs, and how to create similar environments in all stores. He worked well into the evening before he rose for air. He stepped out into the coffee shop and was surprised to see the shop at sixty percent capacity.

The barista spoke. "Vincent, can I get you something?"

"No, not at the moment, thank you." He walked to the seating area and selected an empty table, sat in a chair, and looked around before his face lit up. He envisioned a wine list, and how patrons would enjoy a glass of wine during this time of day. He noted in this store, his main patrons are college students.

I don't think it will work here. The next step in my analysis is to visit other stores during evening hours. Vincent rose from the table and repositioned the chair. He returned to his makeshift office and tapped notes on his iPad. After working another hour, he shut the iPad, signed orders, and completed the pay invoices. His day ended with a drive home to an empty house.

Chapter 14

Sister's Surprise

Candi dialed her mom on her cell phone before rising from her desk. She walked out front for more privacy. "Mom, I did it," she excitedly shared.

"Did what?" Mom asked.

"I got the guy at the coffee shop to bake that pastry dish for us." Candi smiled. "Specifically, for us. I have to tell him when we're visiting his shop. He said to give him a week's advance notice. So, let's plan a time to go to the coffee shop and..."

"...wait a minute. You are way too excited. Are you trying something else?"

"Mom, you don't think I have other intentions," she paused. "Do you?"

"Candi, you are my daughter," Mom giggled. "But if you're not, then we should bring your sister."

"Good idea. She needs to get out of that damn house. I'll call her and tell her we're going next Thursday. It's enough time for him to make the pastry."

"Don't you think you should ask Renee first and see if she has anything planned?"

"Mom, Renee with plans? Come on." Candi shook her head. "She has not done anything without you in almost two years."

"Yes, but you still need to ask. Don't do anything to put her on the spot. You know she's still conscious about her scars."

"It's all she's conscious about. I can't wait to get her back."

Mom sighed. "Getting her back is going to be a journey, and it won't happen overnight. It won't happen until she's fully healed."

"If she fully heals." Candi exhaled. "Why the downer, Mom? Every time we chat, it becomes a downer about Renee."

"She's your sister, and I'm worried."

"Mom, she has to get out more often to help her adjust. Like the doctor told us. 'Make her life as normal as possible'."

"Easier said than done."

"I have a plan, Mom, don't worry. I'll think about something that may get her going."

"No men, Candi. Let her get comfortable with the idea." Mom waited for a response. "Do you hear me?"

"I heard you." Candi nodded. "Sure, Mom, I heard you."

"Let me know if it's Thursday and I'll pick her up and make sure she comes."

"Okay, Mom, I will. I'll call her in a few minutes. Bye – love you." Candi disconnected the call before her mom responded with additional comments. She returned inside the building and pulled the latest orders for Vincent Mathis' locations. Her eyes focused on the shipment schedule. She went to her boss's office, knocked on the door and entered.

"Hey, you know what? If we make an early shipment to these places, we can get Mr. Mathis to sell us his recipe."

"There you go again. I haven't tasted the pastry, and you swear by it. When I get to taste whatever you say he bakes, then we can talk about it."

"I'm telling you, it's great. Have I ever led you wrong?"
"You've never suggested a pastry."

"Ah." Candi paused. "Good point." She turned and exited the office. *Dang, what can I do without hurting business?* Her eyes went to the scheduled address of all the coffee shops Mathis owns. One shop looked more attractive than the usual location her mother and sister patronized. She went to her desk and planned when, where, how, and if, deciding on the best opportunity to enjoy her sister, mother, and the baked special Vincent had promised.

***

Renee stooped after setting the bucket of water next to the five-pound bag of fertilizer. She took out the miniature gardening tool and dug around the base of her plant. She grabbed a hand full of fertilizer and mixed it into the dirt. She picked up a cup of water and poured it into the soil she'd mixed. She repeated the process, going down the line of plants in her garden - one plant after the other - finishing one row and turning to the next. Her phone chimed, and she rose from the squat to answer.

"Hello," Renee greeted.

"Sis, I have an idea," Candi said excitedly.

"You have what?"

"Remember the guy at the coffee shop we went to the other day? The one we normally go to when we're with Mom?"

"Yes. Why?"

"I think we could visit another location soon."

"Why?"

"Why what?" Candi fell silent, waiting for a response.

Renee looked at the screen of her cell phone, shook her head, and tapped it off. "She's always up to something."

She returned to gardening and completing her task for the day. Renee put the tools away and walked into the house. She went to her bathroom to shower and clean up before cooking lunch for her mother's visit. She put on a flowered summer dress and sandals, rushed to the kitchen, and began to prepare potatoes, slicing the fresh tomato before she chopped celery. She pulled out the lettuce from the fridge's hamper, grabbed cucumbers she had picked earlier, and sliced them. Every vegetable was from her garden. She created a salad, adding store-bought carrots, onions, beets, and turkey to the dish. She toasted fresh slices of delivered bread adding croutons to the salad. And the last touch was putting homemade vinaigrette dressing in the fridge. Lunch was ready and waiting.

Mrs. Chadwick rang the bell before using her key to Renee's home. "Hello?" she yelled.

"Mom, I'm here. Why did you ring the doorbell?"

"It's a habit. You remember. I didn't want to interrupt anything you may be doing that I shouldn't see."

"Mom, who would that be with? You know how hideous I look."

"Hideous?" Mrs. Chadwick approached. "You are beautiful, and I'm sure there's a man out there who will accept you."

"Not likely." Renee walked to the kitchen and pulled the fresh salad from the refrigerator. "Look at this." She showed Mrs. Chadwick the fresh salad bowl she recently created. "It's ready, if you're hungry."

"Let's eat. I'm starved. I haven't eaten anything since six thirty this morning." Mrs. Chadwick walked to the table.

"Why were you and Dad up so early?"

"You know your father. Early morning is his normal time to wake up, so I get up too. It's making sure he doesn't burn the house down."

"Mom, it's so cute."

"Cute?" She chuckled. "I would guess so. He is my dream man, and I'll do anything for him."

"I know the feeling, Mom." Renee froze, closed her eyes and sighed. She slowly walked to the cupboard and retrieved two bowls. "Here, Mom." She handed one bowl to Mrs. Chadwick.

"I'm sorry Renee," Mrs. Chadwick said. "Baby you have to learn how to move on." She grabbed two forks from the utensil drawer and fluffed the salad before placing a chunk into her bowl. "Is this enough for you?"

"I will get mine, Mom, you go ahead." Renee turned to the fridge. "Iced tea, lemonade, or Coke?"

"When did you start buying Coke?"

"It was delivered."

"Who ordered it?"

"Mom, I thought you did."

"No, I didn't, but I told your sister to fill in your grocery list."

"Candi does it again. I swear, one day I'll get to her."

"You already do, Renee—you get to her. It's why she wants to go to that coffee shop and get another taste of that pastry."

"Mom, you know I am not going. I barely avoided people staring when we were there." Renee moved to the kitchen table with a glass of lemonade for Mrs. Chadwick. "Here, Mom. I know you don't want anything else."

"What are you drinking?"

"The same as you. Lemonade." Renee poured a glass and went to the table, where Mrs. Chadwick started her salad. "Mom, do you think Candi is up to something?"

"It feels that way since she insists on the three of us meeting at some coffee shop."

"What or who?"

"Maybe the barista or a manager, or someone she met. Might be the recipe she's after."

"I can only imagine which." Renee focused on her salad and

filled her fork with the luscious ingredients. "Mom, half of this salad came from my garden."

"Is that why it's so good?" Mrs. Chadwick took another bite. She dabbled a little of the fresh vinaigrette onto her bowl content. "I love the dressing, too. I suspect it's homemade."

"I do as much as I can, these days."

"You're doing great. Your progress is amazing. Two years ago, you wouldn't walk into your backyard in the middle of the day."

"It has been something, Mom. Two years ago, I felt my face burning and I keep remembering what he looked like before it happened." Renee looked at Mrs. Chadwick with a fork in her hand. She held the pointed prongs in her mother's direction. "Thank you." Renee smiled. "I couldn't have done it without you."

"I'm your mother, and I will always be your mom. I would never leave you alone to fight any battle."

"I know, Mom, I know."

Renee picked up the bowls and utensils and took them to the kitchen sink. She washed and rinsed them, placed them in the dish rack and returned to the table with a pitcher of lemonade. "Let me fill your glass, Mom."

Mrs. Chadwick finished the last of the lemonade and placed the empty glass on the table. "Sure, go ahead." Renee filled her glass.

"Mom, I don't think I'm ready, even after two years since…" Renee sat in her chair and placed the pitcher on the table.

"… let's not go to your wall by remembering Marvin." Mrs.

Chadwick gripped her glass. "There are better men in this world. Look at your father."

"I... I looked at him, Mom. Don't you think you two fighting and almost divorcing when I was in middle school had something to do with my choice of men?"

"What in the world?" Mom increased her grip on the glass. "I know you aren't comparing Marvin to your dad."

"I'm trying to understand why him, Mom. Why did I love him?"

"He swept your heart. It's the only reason." Mrs. Chadwick paused, raised her eyes, locking them on Renee. "Like the doctor said in counseling, 'You aren't a weak woman—his methods were just stronger.' So, don't try to blame yourself. You fell in love with his good side."

"In the beginning, it was beautiful." Renee's mouth tightened to nearly a smile. "Mom, he was handsome, charming, and a gentleman."

"And he hid every indication of being abusive." Mrs. Chadwick touched Renee's arm. "You survived, and here you are sitting next to me. I wouldn't know what to do if you hadn't made it."

"My life is..." Renee swallowed. "It's like I'm a monster. I'm hideous."

"No baby, life is beautiful because you'll make it out of this. Trust me. You will."

"Mom, how will I?" Renee leaned on her elbow before she touched the smooth part of her face with her hand. Her fingers avoided the wounds of love. "I don't think I'll ever have a man love me again." Her eyes swelled. "I don't see how anyone would look at me."

"Baby." Mom rose from her chair and walked behind her, placing her arms around her. "You are an amazing woman, and God allows love to happen. It will happen when you least expect it. But you have to get out of your house so it can. You can't stay behind these walls and think someone will knock on your door."

Renee touched her mother's arm. "I know, Mom. I realize no man will knock on my door."

"If you want it, it's like everything you've done in your life — you have to go after it."

Renee held onto her mother's arm while being hugged. She sat in the comfort of her touch and felt the security of her mother's love. Silence pierced the room, which allowed her soft sniffle to amplify. Mrs. Chadwick felt moisture on her arm, and she held Renee tighter. Feeling her daughter's need, she did not think about the length of time she sat next to her. Ten minutes later, she whispered, "It was something you both couldn't avoid."

***

Renee woke scratching her scarred hand. She had done this despite the doctor's advice and remembered to use the prescription ointment. In the bathroom, Renee rubbed the solvent into her skin to calm the itch. A glimpse in the mirror displayed her wild look, with wicked hair, dried saliva, and a trace where one tear trailed on the smooth side of her face. "What in the world?" She giggled. "Any man would run from this face." Renee stopped smiling while evaluating her reflection. "Would a man love this face?"

She turned on the faucet and cupped water with her hands, rinsing her face and quickly grabbing a towel to dry. She looked again at her reflection. "I won't know unless..." She paused before grabbing a toothbrush.

After brushing her teeth and styling her hair, she walked to her dresser, retrieving a tee shirt and brassiere, and matching them to a skirt she imagined wearing.

Chapter 15

Visioning

Vincent paced the best coffees shop location floor while the sun hid, and the moon shared its face. He gathered answered questionnaires from adult patrons, all of whom were of legal drinking age. He held those papers and looked over one after the other, pacing from wall to wall.

"It's going to work," he murmured. "It will work." His voice rose. He stepped twice more. "It will work!" he shouted before reaching the other wall and turning around. He stopped mid distance and looked for modifications he would have to make. He turned the papers over to their blank side and sketched changes he envisioned. He created a shelf, added a mirror, installed a camera, moved the bar out- just a little, creating space for stools. He added a stage on the left wall and removed tables for a couch and coffee table combination. The coffee shop space became smaller, but more ergonomically functional between coffee and wine.

He pulled a chair from a table and sat, focused on the bar. "It can work." Vincent turned the table, redirecting the view of his assessment. "I can't see another way of changing it, but I need to think about the number of people the store can support." He turned to another blank page and counted tables and chairs, adding standing room possibilities. "Nearly one hundred and five people at any given time. Wow, that becomes a revenue booster." Vincent put the papers on the table and laid the pen down before taking a seat. He paused, imagining how the flow of people would enjoy his coffee/wine shop. He imagined increasing sales moving product going from morning to late night.

Vincent rose from his chair, pushed it back in alignment with the table, and walked to the exit. With papers in hand, he stepped through the door and, locked it before walking to his car. Once inside, he looked at his watch and shook his head at the wisdom he had gotten.

He remembered Sam, the man who'd started his journey in the business, determined to make every customer enjoy the coffee shop experience by passing everything he knew to Vincent. His mind flashed to his ex, who said he would never account for anything if he did not work in corporate America.

Vincent smiled, started the car, and placed his seat belt across his body. "Sam would be proud. Especially when the changes go into effect...and that bitch can kiss my ass."

***

Morning sun attacked the shades of his bedroom window, blaring between the cracks, hitting his eyes. He squinted, even though he had not fully opened them. Vincent placed his feet on the floor raising his hand to cover the glare and allowed his eyes to adjust. He stretched with a loud roaring yawn. He didn't fall asleep early the night before because his mind wouldn't allow him to stop sketching the details of the change. He added five items in his drawings until 3 am, before making the decision to contact an architect to finish his idea.

Vincent dressed after his morning bathroom routine. He went to the kitchen, grabbed a breakfast bar, poured coffee, from his pre-timed coffeemaker, into his travel cup, gathered his sketches, and put them into a pocket of his laptop/iPad carrying bag. After securing the condominium, he entered his car and drove to the closest coffee shop.

Inside the shop, he sat at the manager's desk, logged onto the iPad, and searched for architect firms. He contacted three firms one after the other and discussed price and service, only to debate internally about which offer was better.

Suddenly, he remembered how he and Jack developed other locations throughout the city. He drafted a request for a proposal, placed details in the document, and reviewed the contents. Once satisfied, he gathered a list of architect firms and contacts within the city, developed a distribution list, and put a date for submissions in the body of the email.

After Vincent pressed 'send', pushed back from the desk, grabbed his cold coffee, and nodded his head in agreement. *Clever idea*, he thought. He rose from the chair, coffee cup in hand, and stretched before he walked out to an open table space in the coffee shop.

He observed the number of patrons who entered the store, noting what they bought and how long they stayed. His calculation placed the store in a profitable position, based on foot traffic. Again, he nodded in agreement and imagined how foot traffic would change when the coffee shop served wine in the evenings.

Vincent noted the time, rose from the table, then retrieved his business equipment. With his notebook backpack in hand, he waved at the staff and exited the store. Once in his car, he pulled out of the parking spot and glanced at the front of the shop, only to imagine how the new color scheme could be more inviting.

At the next coffee shop, upon entry, "One, two, three, four..." he counted until reaching the order counter. "Good day, guys," he smiled, with a wave of his hand.

"Do you need anything?" the barista asked.

"No, I'm good. Thanks." Vincent turned to an open spot along the far wall and faced the store's entrance. He sat in wonder. *Why did I open another store in this location*? He sighed, turned his head from side to side, and evaluated his own safe house of disappointment. *Stan would have loved it here*, he thought. *I wonder why, since I ask every time, I visit.*

Vincent watched people enter and watched the number rise as the hour grew closer to lunch. *This is why. I remember, now.* He rose from his table, giving the crew a hand, picking up empty coffee cups and small dessert dishes. The guys behind the counter were busy fulfilling orders and responding to drive-thru customers. At one table after the other, he helped the crew, even though they would have done it themselves. After ninety minutes, the crowd subsided, and the crew picked up where he had left off.

"This happens every day, right?" Vincent asked one of the crew members.

"Yes sir, every day like clockwork. It will pick up again by four and will be consistent until we close." The barista looked around the room. "I mean, the crowd at four is nothing like the office rush. Patronage in evening will keep us moving." He smiled before he left Vincent, shuttling dishware, cups, and papers to the back for cleaning and disposal.

Vincent nodded a second time, sat at the table where he had left his iPad, and retrieved his notebook. He made notes of his observation and imagined that he added the modifications of wine and coffee operations to this location. He never thought to change this location. By four in the afternoon, Vincent packed his iPad, picked up his notebook, and neatly put them away for travel. He waved at the barista behind the counter and left the store.

It was three days later during his routine when he waltzed into the main store, his home office, and acknowledged the woman he had met at the bakery. "Not you." He smirked. "Is there a problem, or are you stealing a recipe?"

"Nice seeing you, too," Candi smiled.

"What brings you here?" Vincent inquired, scanning her from top to bottom. "Are you meeting a guy?"

"Wouldn't you like to know?" Candi responded without hesitation. Her eyes caught his glance. "Actually, I'm meeting my mom and sister."

"Oh, the people you were with the time you wanted the recipe."

"Yes, those people," she sassed.

Vincent shook his head. "Okay, I guess I pinched a nerve." He scanned the shop and added, "I need to get to things, here."

"Oh, I wanted to tell you. I think you have a problem."

Before Vincent walked from Candi, he responded to her comment. "What?" Vincent leaned his head to one side, raised an eyebrow, and stared at her. "A problem with...wait, I don't want to know."

"That's your biggest problem." Candi pointed at him. "You aren't up to listening to anyone about anything."

"You know..." Vincent frowned at her words hitting home — he had heard this from his ex, who had been persistent about him needing to work in corporate America. "It's a familiar comment made by a lot of people. Especially from women I don't get along with."

"You don't get along with me?" Candi's eyes lit at Vincent's response. "Not particularly. I would think it's better being your customer than becoming your friend. But I do appreciate you patronizing the coffee shop." Vincent turned his back to Candi before hearing her response.

Candi frowned. "You have a lot of nerve. My family and I have been coming here since it opened. I don't think you can afford to piss off your best customers."

Vincent spoke over his shoulder. "No, you're right. I don't like the idea of pissing off customers. But when someone is annoying..." Vincent, cleared his throat and turned around. "...really a pain in the ass..." He pointed at the door. "When you're done, I hope the door slaps your ass on the way out."

"You still don't like listening to people. You have met your match, buddy. I'm not leaving until I am ready, and once my folks arrive, we'll stay as long as we like."

"I would hope so." Vincent returned to his trajectory, stepped from Candi, and didn't glance back at her. He walked to his office, sat at the desk, and opened his laptop.

Damn, she reminds me of Gloria. With one hand, he wiped his forehead to clear the sweat from his brow. "I promised never to get mixed up with a girl like that again."

***

Candi walked to the corner table, picked up her cell and dialed her mother. "Mom, you there?" she waited for a response. "Mom?" she called.

"Yes, yes, I'm here." Mrs. Chadwick answered. "Is there a problem?"

"Yes, Mom. Instead of meeting at the coffee shop, let's go somewhere else."

"Why - did something happen?"

"The asshole owner just pissed me off being arrogant." Candi sighed. "And he doesn't deserve our patronage."

"We've gone there for years and now you want to change?"

"It's the owner, Mom." Candi frowned. "He's an ass, and I don't like him."

"Are we talking about the same guy that you wanted the recipe from, for his fruit crumpler?"

"That's the one." Candi looked at the counter and did not see Vincent. "I would send you a picture, but he's not around."

"If he is not there, why can't we go and mind our business, and leave when we're done?"

"You never take-up for me, Mom." Candi raised her tone. "I

say one thing and you push another." Candi paused, lowered her voice. "And it's sad, Mom. Really sad." Candi pushed the red phone icon on her cellular. "Never fails!"

Mrs. Chadwick looked at Renee. "Your sister can be a pain."

"Mom, she's just Candi. She finds a way of fixing herself. I know she's one step ahead of us."

"Doing what?"

"I wish I knew, but she's like a cat. She never falls." Renee adjusted her scarf recovering her facial scars. She glanced out of the car window and saw a thousand images she had seen a hundred times. Her mind flashed. "Mom, do you remember when this was a two-way street and the only thing out here were trees?"

"Yes, that was a long time ago. Six lanes later, there more businesses and apartments than you can count in a day." Mrs. Chadwick pressed the brake pedal reducing car speed to a complete stop. "I remember when this light wasn't here."

"That wasn't long ago?"

"It changed." She giggled. "Now, are you going to tell me what's on your mind?"

"It's time I got back on the saddle, Mom."

"Saddle?"

"In my last therapy session, I told the doctor moments of abuse I endured; being stabbed and the knife going through of my hand, the rush to the emergency room with broken ribs and broken busted lip. I told her about the nights I didn't close my eyes and prayed he had travel. I finally got enough out that she thought I made great progress. It was the first time I didn't shake when talking to her about Marvin. The doctor said it's time I start being a part of the public. She is encouraging me to stop being afraid of what people may see and show them who I am."

Mrs. Chadwick turned the car into the coffee shop's parking lot. "I can't imagine how you'll do what the doctor suggested." Mrs. Chadwick smiled. "Unless there is one guy who would rescue a woman in distress."

"You've been listening to too many songs on the radio. No one is coming to my rescue."

"Besides, you're going out with us, and I believe you'll meet someone soon. It's your time." Mrs. Chadwick touched her daughter's arm before she retrieved her purse.

"But, Mom, who will want to date a defaced woman with horrendous scars?"

"You are the Renee we all love. He will find you. Love always does."

***

It was minutes shy of half-past three when he walked into the sitting area of the coffee shop. He finished the shop's schematic and made modifications as a backup if bids were extremely high. Vincent stepped to the center of the bar, held his pen up, and looked beyond the ink tip. He noted the height he would like the big movie screen he decided to add. After turning left, he maneuvered between tables and glanced at the location he'd pinpointed, to ensure a full view from the farthest corner. Turning around, Vincent quickly walked to the opposite end of the seating table. He stopped only when Candi spoke to him.

"What on earth are you doing?" Candi asked. "Look, my mom

and sister wanted to come here, so don't make their visit miserable."

"Ma'am, I am sorry you feel that way." Vincent smirked. "Ma'am...sarcastic, much?" Candi sucked her teeth.

"Oh no, ma'am. I treat every customer with the utmost respect. Good customers get better service, and you're not a good customer. You can let the door slap your ass on the way out, any time you feel like it." Smiling from ear to ear, Vincent turned towards the coffee bar.

"What an asshole!" She frowned. "You are so like my ex-wife." Vincent looked at the center of the bar and angled for a view from where he stood.

"You know, you'd be more accurate if you sit your ass down and looked," suggested Candi.

"What?"

"Sit down and analyze the view." Candi pointed to a chair.

"Gosh, you're dumb, too." Shaking her head before her eyes fixated on the entrance.

Renee walked inside the coffee shop, searched for Candi and walked to the table where she sat. "What is this guy to you?" she asked.

"I've heard that voice before." Vincent held his hand up in search of the source. "Excuse me—are you, by chance…"

"…No, I'm not," Renee interrupted. "But she is my sister." She pointed. "Maybe she would like a manager to greet her better." Renee held her scarf to hide the scars.

"Are you…" Vincent started to ask.

"No, I'm not," Renee quickly responded.

"Are you sure?" Vincent looked at her and waited for a response. He placed one hand over his mouth and the other hand on his opposite waist with his arm covering his midsection. "I know that voice."

"She's sure," Candi said. "Go do owner things." Candi pointed.

"I'm not a dog."

"Could have fooled me." Candi pulled the chair next to her from the table for Renee. Renee looked at Mrs. Chadwick and covered her face. "Mom, are you going to sit down?"

"You two aren't very nice to that guy," Mrs. Chadwick chided her girls.

"Just because he owns the place, doesn't make him a gentleman. It takes more than kind words to make us believe he's a good man."

"But how do you know he is?" Renee asked.

"He was standing in front of us, listening to you two ridicule him," Mrs. Chadwick responded as she placed her purse on the table.

"Mom, I know he's here, but does he have to treat Candi like a second-class guest?"

"No, and I doubt he started it," Mrs. Chadwick pointed out.

"Mom, how dare you say I started it?" Candi frowned before looking at Renee. "See, it's always me, Renee. Regardless of what's going on, mom blames me for everything."

"She doesn't." Renee looked at the table before glancing into

Candi's eyes. "Not even close."

Vincent pulled out a chair for Mrs. Chadwick. "Please, ma'am," he directed. "Your daughter said you come here often."

"Yes, we do. Thank you." Mrs. Chadwick sat down. "Do you know what you'd like? I'll get it for you."

"Yes. Mocha latte for me and Renee, and Candi gets a chai tea with soy."

"Sure thing." Vincent smiled, turned to the bar, and headed off to fill their order. When he arrived behind the bar, he went into action. He created one coffee after the other and, like six years before, he completed them with a decorative topping design. "Perfect," he said aloud.

"Looks good." His employee smiled at the topping. "I'm out of practice but it works." Vincent lifted the tray and walked to the table. He repeated the order and watched Mrs. Chadwick pointed to whom each cup went. After Vincent placed each cup on the table, he spoke. "These are on the house, ma'am. Thank you for your years of patronage."

"Thank you...uhm?"

"Mr. Asshole..." Candi responded.

"Candi, please," Mrs. Chadwick scolded.

"No, ma'am, I deserve that. You have a unique daughter with a fire-breathing spirit. Kind of like my ex-wife." Vincent scowled at Candi. "Really like my ex-wife."

"Lucky for you, Mr...?"

"Vincent—just call me Vincent, please."

"Vincent. We thank you again." Mrs. Chadwick smiled.

"Would you like anything else?" Vincent inquired. He glanced at the woman with the scarf.

"No, not now. I'm sure this will be enough."

"What about that blueberry surprise crump cake thing you make?" asked Candi.

"I'm sorry, that comes out once a week ... no wait, did I promise to bake some for you? Vincent dropped the empty tray to his side. I know I promised but, no way will I bake it for you." He scowled at Candi. "But for your mom and sister, I can." He looked at his watch. "Maybe on your next visit I'll have a batch made for you... if you haven't stolen my recipe yet." Vincent frowned when he looked directly at Candi.

"No worries, I wouldn't want your crappy mix anyway." Candi admitted.

"Good to know." Vincent frowned. "If that's all, ma'am, I'll get back to business." His warm smile glistened towards Mrs. Chadwick.

"Thank you." Mrs. Chadwick touched Vincent's arm. "Thank you so much."

"You're welcome, ma'am." Vincent grinned after she removed her hand. He returned the tray behind the bar and went to his office, sat at the desk before and leaned back in the chair.

"Renee." He whispered her name as if going into a trance, remembering his college years where his eyes experienced seeing the most attractive woman of his existence. The image of the woman with the scarf was vivid in his mind, bright and clear as a movie projection upon the silver screen. *Renee*, he thought. *She would have to be around 30-something now. No, it can't be the same* woman. Even though she sounded like the woman in college. I remember her voice like yesterday because she would practically scold us like she was our big sister.

He flashed a second memory of Renee and compared it to the woman with the scarf. "She didn't have a reason for a scarf." He recalled. "She was gorgeous and simple, nice hair, golden brown eyes, and caramel sun kissed skin." He looked at his laptop and his cell phone, breaking the imagery of his college classmate. "It isn't her," he whispered.

***

"You two are embarrassing." Mrs. Chadwick shook her head. "A man is being a gentleman and all you do is chastise him over his lack of interest in you."

"Mom, he's an ass," Candi responded.

"Why? Explain to me why...why do you think so?" Mrs. Chadwick asked.

"Maybe he didn't treat her with respect," Renee answered. "Don't you know your sister? She can be a smart ass, too." "Mom, I didn't even say anything for him to be mad over."

"But you must have done something." Mrs. Chadwick frowned. "He is a nice man, and even gentleman like. It's rare to see that these days."

"But Mom." Candi shook her head "He's really an ass. I took his order at the bakery, and he is harsh."

"Maybe he's a shrewd man who wants the best for his business. Maybe he works hard to make things better for his customers. Maybe..."

"...maybe you like him, Mom." Renee sipped her coffee,

placing the cup just past her scarf. "Maybe he impressed you."

"Well, he is kind." Mrs. Chadwick looked at her daughters, one after the other. "If either of you found him nice, I'd approve."

"Not me," Candi quickly responded. "I thought Renee would be a great candidate, but not today." She frowned before adding, "He's an ass."

"There you go again." Mrs. Chadwick shook her head.

"Not for me, Mom," Renee said. "I don't need a man in my life—not now, and probably never again."

"Don't say that Renee," Mrs. Chadwick said. "You never know when the right man will come." She sipped coffee and placed the cup on the table. "You don't know what God has in store for you."

"Right, Mom." Renee frowned. "You never know, and it's horrible I had to experience it firsthand."

Chapter 16

The Break

Vincent received six blueprints barely six weeks into the bidding process for changing the business into coffee shop/wine bar venues. He sat with each one, unrolling the first in the pile onto the desk, placing a stapler on one corner, a paper weight on the other, and a cup of coffee on the lower end. He held the last corner and scanned what he could from top to bottom.

He stared at the designs and imagined which would be most effective in matching his vision. He placed the first one on the side of acceptable and the second on the side of rejection. Vincent split the six into half and walked away from his desk.

"Good morning," he greeted a barista in his largest and oldest business.

"Good morning, Vincent," the barista responded while he replaced ceramic cups on a shelf. "It's a good day, and I'm ready for school."

"You are?" Vincent looked around. "Is there an exam today, or is there a woman you'd like to see in class?" He chuckled.

"How did you know?" the barista responded, smiling from ear to ear.

"I've been there," he smirked, "during my sophomore year."

"Was she gorgeous?"

"...and out of my league." Vincent stirred the coffee pouring skim milk into it. "Which didn't go well for me."

"Why not?"

"Too long of a story." He glanced at the barista. "But let me give you a little advice. Talk to her and see if she's even interested before you start fantasizing about the future."

"I can do that." The barista smiled. "I appreciate the advice."

"Good." Vincent returned to the office and reviewed the blueprints in the 'keep' pile. Unexpectedly, he thought of the barista. *I wish him the best.* Vincent flashed at moments standing in front of the Mexican Cantina at the college cafeteria, seeing Renee for the first time. He flashed to sitting in front of her in class. He remembered the group dinner sitting across from her and watching her walk on campus. Those flash memories of Renee had driven him wild over the years. *Man, I really wish him luck.*

***

Renee went into the backyard with a pail of water and watered her creative garden. The blooms were colorful - red, blue, and yellow. Her flowers stretched towards the sky and her vegetable plants bloomed and formed in unique beauty. On the third garden row, she stopped and smiled at her accomplishments. *Perfect,* she thought. *Why couldn't my marriage have been as perfect?* Renee shook her head in disappointment. She turned from her created beauty and walked towards the house like she had done a multitude of times, even as tears fell from her eyes.

She went inside to retrieve the NIKON D850 camera. Renee put the camera strap around her neck and checked the battery charge. She returned to the back yard and grabbed the camera stand leaning on the corner wall of the back porch. She set up the camera and her eyes focused on every detail of the garden, capturing multiple shots to remember. She repositioned the camera stand moving angle to angle, going row to row. She separated the camera from the stand and shot close-ups throughout the garden. She sent pictures to her mother and sister.

Candi loved the pictures Renee sent her, she printed and framed her favorite. She encouraged her boss to place eight pictures in the bakery. After multiple customers inquired about the various pictures around the bakery, it gave her the idea to price tag each one and offer prints for sale. Candi picked up her cell from behind the counter and dialed Renee.

"Hey, sis, what's up?" Renee answered.

"I have a surprise for you." Candi held her smile, doing her best to be serious. "I'm coming over after work."

"Did you meet someone?" Renee asked. "Don't bring him here."

"No, nothing like that." Candi frowned. "And why can't I bring him over, if I did?"

"You know why!" Renee responded. "I am in no condition to meet your friend."

"Sis, it's time you moved on. It's been almost three years plus."

"It's not important when...whose side are you on, anyway?" Renee responded before Candi answered. "Mom told you to say that?"

"No, Mom didn't!" Candi fell quiet. In a calm tone she said, "I will be over later. No man is coming with me. I will call before I get there. Okay?"

"Okay." Renee disconnected her line before Candi could punch the red phone icon on her cell.

"She is such a pain in the ass, sometimes." Candi shook her head and returned her cell phone to its storage place.

***

Vincent selected two blueprints and walked into the coffee shop. He sat in the back of the seating area, opened the blueprint on the table, and imagined the measurements and design. He looked at the business flow. "Not bad, for number one. Not bad." He rolled the blueprint, placed it in the carrier, and put in on the chair. He unrolled the second blueprint design and spread it on the table. His eyes widened, in comparison.

"This will not be as smooth," he murmured. "Looks great, but I'd have to move another wall and rent the next storefront space… Maybe not a bad idea, after all."

Vincent returned to the office and contacted the leasing officer of the strip mall. "What do you think?" he asked. "Can we do this and allow modifications in the space?"

"It's your cost, and I don't mind because it's coming available next month."

"What's happening to the tailor shop?"

"The old man had a heart attack."

"I'm so sorry to hear that."

"I know the widow isn't going to keep the business. I spoke to her yesterday."

"I'll give her my condolences."

"Next month, once it's clear, we'll sign the lease agreement."

"You've got it. Give me a call." Vincent disconnected the call, placed his cell in his pocket, and walked out front. He hadn't noticed the signs in front of the tailor shop. He walked to the florist on the edge of the strip, bought a bouquet, and headed back to the coffee shop.

It was the second time he had bought flowers there, for condolences. Rick, his long-time employee, had lost his battle with cancer two weeks earlier. Vincent stopped on the way to his office, looked at the parking lot, and held the bouquet in his hand. "They fall one after the other."

Vincent Mathis walked to the front of the tailor's shop, pushed open the door and walked inside. "Hello?" he shouted. "Anyone here?"

"Yes." The elderly lady walked to the front. "How can I help you?"

"Ma'am, my condolences to your family. I had no idea. I heard about it today."

"Thank you." She looked at the bouquet and smiled. "They're lovely flowers."

"I'm glad you like them." Vincent sighed. "I am so sorry, because your husband was a great neighbor."

"You're next door?"

"Yes, I am. Yes, ma'am, I am."

"He loved your coffee. It made his day."

"I am so glad he did," Vincent responded. "I loved his patronage."

"Thank you," the widow said. "I appreciate your kindness."

"If there is anything I can help you with, please don't hesitate."

"Thank you." She smiled and turned her back to Vincent. "Oh, by the way." She looked at Vincent from behind the counter. "If you're still single, you should find her before it's too late."

She turned listening to Vincent's response.

"Don't do anything without considering a woman. Yes, I get it, I think." Vincent frowned. *How could she know?*

***

Candi arrived at Renee's front door after an hour in traffic. She rang the doorbell, waited, and called Renee's cell phone. Instead of going inside with her key, she waited two minutes before her fingers redialed. The door opened and Renee shook her head. "Why didn't you use your key?"

"I am your guest," Candi replied. "Besides, I may be here on business, as a partner."

"A partner? Not you — don't even try it."

Candi followed Renee to the kitchen. "It just so happens…" Candi reached into her purse and retrieved an envelope, "… that you have a talent many people would like to explore…or, let's say, own."

"What in the world are you talking about?"

"I did something I thought was interesting, and it turned out, it's about you. You're interesting to me and to a lot of people."

"Yeah, sure I am. How would they know me from this face?"

"You have no idea how good you are."

"Good at what?" Renee reached into the cupboard for two glasses. "Tea or orange juice?" she asked.

"Tea," Candi replied. "Look at this." She held up a long envelope with Renee's name printed on the front. "Here, take it."

Renee sat the pitcher of tea on the table after pouring three-quarter cups in each glass. She took the envelope. "Who gave you this? Is it a note from a guy you are trying to match make me with?"

"No!" Candi replied. "Why would you think such a thing?"

Renee pursed her lips. "You are my sister. You think I don't know you?"

"Not now." Candi pointed. "Look at the envelope. Open it."
"Why?"

"Just open the envelope, and I'll chat with you about the content."

"Yeah, sure you will." Renee slid her finger under the glued flap. Rip! "Why is it so tight?"

"Why would you ask?" Candi frowned. "I mean ...sometimes I wonder about you."

Renee looked at the envelope's contents and pulled out a check. "I didn't order or sell anything."

"You sold a few things," Candi admitted.

"Like what?" Renee asked. "What did I do since being in this house? Get my ass kicked?"

"You planted a great garden." Candi walked to the sliding door. "And then had the idea of taking pictures of it."

"So?" Renee sighed. "A lot of people do that."

Renee watched Candi at the doorway. "What makes my hobby so special that I get a check?"

"Look at the amount." Candi had hoped Rene would be happy having people respond to her pictures. "They love your eye and your flowers."

"Who? And why $200's worth?"

"That's one framed print," Candi answered. "Oh, it was three hundred, but I took a hundred for framing and a sales commission."

"Sales commission." Renee shrugged her shoulders. "I guess you should take it all."

"What?"

"I didn't do this to sell pictures. I do it because I love it."

"But, sis, it's easy money," Candi argued.

"Easy money." Renee placed the check on the table and filled the glasses. "I can't believe you … How did you sell a picture? What was it?"

"Your first pictures of your blooms. The vivid colors made the print alive. I framed six of your pictures, and my boss let me place them around the bakery. Before long, people asked if the pictures were for sale."

"And you didn't ask me before selling," Renee scowled. "Typical."

"Why are you not seeing the appreciation of what you do?"

"Because I don't want the notoriety that comes with it."

"That's what you're worried about?"

"Isn't it the most important thing? I'm not looking for fame, I'm hideous with this." Renee looked at Candi and pointed at her face. "It's not for me anyway, it's *your* fame."

"But, Renee, it's income for your hobby."

"Income…does it look like I need income?"

"But you can use it regardless of whether you need it. Besides, it's everyone's dream of being paid for a hobby, right?"

Renee sipped her iced tea and stared at Candi before looking at the garden through the kitchen window. "It is beautiful."

"Yes, it is, and all you have to do is keep growing and take more pictures. I'll do the rest."

"You'll do the rest. What does that mean?"

"It's easy to get your prints out into the public. I can manage it. It was easy selling the first one, so I bet we can do more."

"You say it's easy. I…" Renee stopped mid-sentence and

remembered her enthusiasm for a challenge and working on a team, which was a long-gone opportunity. "Maybe I can help."

"Now you're talking." Candi raised her glass, indicating a toast.

Renee picked up the check. "Same incentive, to get these out. I'm giving you 30% of whatever we move."

"Hmm, that doesn't sound bad. I get to frame them the way I want, and you cannot argue with my decisions. All you do is take pictures and keep sending them. Deal?"

"Deal." Renee nodded and shrugged her shoulders. "Let's not tell Mom about our arrangement. Okay?"

"Why not? She would love hearing about us working together."

"Yes, but the next thing she'll say is I should get out in public. You can't keep this quiet."

"I guess you're right. If you aren't ready for that." Candi sipped tea. "Besides, we've only sold one picture. Aren't we getting ahead of ourselves with public appearances?"

"You haven't learned yet? Everything I touch..." Renee stopped. "... except marriage, turns to gold."

"Your day of finding another love is coming. Right after mine," Candi smiled.

***

Vincent visited the architect firm he selected as the winner. He spoke to the architect who originated the blueprint. "What gave you the idea?" Vincent asked.

"Well, sir, I visited your locations and thought about the theme. Wine and comfort, like a coffee shop setting on any given day. Also, I thought about the opportunity to stage a quintet-sized group without having it impact the flow of customers."

"Your vision is impressive. I couldn't add anything, and that was surprising for me. When I contract the construction company, will you be available throughout the modifications?" Vincent asked.

"It's our firm's policy to follow through on each project. I will definitely be there."

Vincent offered his hand. "I appreciate it, and I look forward to the transition."

The architect took Vincent's hand. "You are welcome. When do we start?"

"As soon as I sign the dotted line with the contractor."

"Let me know, and I'm there."

***

Renee took her camera to the garden at early dawn capturing the rise in daylight. "Perfect lighting." She smiled. One pot after the other, she moved the arrangement after a swap of color combinations and placed it where she could return each pot. She snapped a shot and reviewed it. "I should move them right here — blue, purple, and orange." Renee nodded while she looked through the lens setting for a timed shot. "Where did I put the spray bottle?" She looked around, let the camera timer set, and walked to the kitchen to find the water spray bottle. She got back to the flower setting and sprayed water on each petal. The camera clicked three times in session, click, click, click. "Oh, damn," she laughed. "I shouldn't be in the picture."

The camera sent the snapshots to Candi. Renee continued her snapshots, moving around the garden, creating floral arrangements and highlighting the unique blend of colors. *This is actually fun.* She smiled, feeling the excitement in her work, and the blood flowed through her as once before. Her mind was clear about what she wanted, and not a worry in the world clouded her view of her happy place.

Mrs. Chadwick walked in after 10 am. "Renee!" she called, walking towards the kitchen. "Where are you?"

"Mom, I'm in the garden," Renee replied. "In the garden!" she shouted.

"What are you doing out there so late in the morning?"

"I'm taking pictures."

Mrs. Chadwick placed her purse on the kitchen table and walked through the sliding screen door into the back yard. "You've come a long way with the garden. I can't believe it's so beautiful."

"Thanks, Mom...I think."

"Did you contact a florist?"

"What?"

"You should do this as a business, now." Mrs. Chadwick walked to the azaleas. "These are better than any florist in town."

"You know, Mom, they contract from large farms." "I know, but maybe..."

"I don't want to do this on a larger scale. I know my plants." Renee arranged the plants.

"Okay. I see. Are you ready for your appointment with the psychiatrist?"

"I forgot. Mom, give me a minute to change."

"Yeah, sure. I'll look around." Mrs. Chadwick walked to the morning glories. "Beautiful flowers."

Renee stopped moving plants, grabbed her camera equipment and walked into the house. She stored the camera gear and headed for the bedroom.

***

Vincent left the architect firm with a contract and payment receipt. He sat in his car, opened the iPad, and placed the papers inside. He buckled the seat belt while he sat behind the wheel of his car and set it in motion. He drove to the other side of the city, where he had an appointment with the contractor. When he opened the office door, the receptionist greeted him. "Hi, how can I help you?"

"I'm here for an 11:00," Vincent responded. "Mr. Mathis?"

"Yes, that's correct," Vincent smiled. "I hope I'm not too early."

"No, not at all." The receptionist stood. "Please follow me." She walked to the conference room and opened the door. "Please have a seat. Would you like bottled water or coffee?"

"Yes, water is fine, please," Vincent responded.

"Mr. Themes will be in shortly. They're expecting you." She closed the door just as Vincent responded, "Okay, thank you."

"Mr. Mathis." A gentleman walked into the conference room with a bottle of water in his hand. "I'm Jake, your project manager. I think this is for you." Jake handed Vincent the bottled water.

"Thanks." Vincent took the bottle, stood, and offered his hand for a professional greeting.

"Nice to meet you. Shall I call you Mr. Mathis?" asked Jake.

"Vincent is better."

"Okay, Vincent. Clark will be in quite shortly. He was finishing a call."

"Good. Right on time, I guess."

"It's how we do things here." Jake paused, opened the bottled water, and sipped. He replaced the cap. "Do you have the blueprint I can look over?"

"I do." Vincent reached into the iPad case and retrieved the document. "It's here, and I think the architect did an excellent job."

"I'll bet." Jake put the water bottle on the table and looked at the blueprint's rolled top. "It's a guy I've worked with before."

"This makes things a lot easier."

"It's as if we're brothers in the game. I know his work, and it's always on point." Jake opened the blueprint on the table and scanned the work. "Every location the same, right?"

"It's doable, and I like that idea. One mirrors the other."
"I know, it works. Good for business."

"Perfect, in my eyes." Vincent nodded and noticed Jake's focus on the blueprints. "How much do you think each location will cost me?"

"I can't give you an overview now, but I can say it's not beyond affordable." His eyes met Vincent's before he said, "It should be a 4-week process at each place— maybe sooner, if things are perfect. Which they never are." He chuckled.

"Will I have to close each store for modifications?"

Jake leaned his head left and placed his hand over his mouth before he said, "I would say, if you want less of a liability, yes – you should close the store. That is, if you do not want us to work around customers and slow the process. If you don't, it will cost more."

"No, closed is fine."

"Hello, Mr. Mathis, how are you?" Charles Themes said, entering the conference room.

"Mr. Themes, I am doing okay. You have a nice setup, here."

"Just call me Chuck." Chuck shook Vincent's hand.

"I see you've met Jake."

"Yes, we're going over the blueprint now."

"Good stuff, right Jake?" Chuck commented. "So far it's great, boss," Jake admitted.

"Sounds like a win already." Vincent added, "When can we start, if we sign contracts today?"

"As soon as we resource the materials needed and get them in our hands. Better yet, when can you close the business— and which store would you'd like for us to start?"

"I'll get back to you," Vincent responded. "But I will say that my objective is next month, on the 1st."

"A week from now," Jake said aloud.

"A week is perfect," Vincent responded. "I need the time to advertise the changes."

***

Mrs. Chadwick sat in the psychiatrist's waiting room and listened for her name in case the doctor wanted to converse with her. Like earlier times, the psychiatrist pulled her into the session for transition support. It was twenty minutes before the office door opened. Mrs. Chadwick rose to her feet. Out walked her oldest daughter, with her scarf a little more revealing. Mrs. Chadwick smiled. "It must have been a good session."

"Mrs. Chadwick," the doctor smiled, "I think Renee is on her path to a great life."

"Really?"

"Mom, don't make a scene." Renee touched her on the shoulder.

"I won't, but…"

"No buts." The doctor nodded her head. "Keep doing whatever it is you're doing, and I won't need you to come back every month. Maybe every quarter."

"That's marvelous!" Mrs. Chadwick clapped her hands. "Oh,

I never thought I'd hear you say this. Thank you, Doctor."

"Don't thank me, it's Renee."

"Mom, let's go." Renee turned her mother towards the door and looked behind her. "Thanks, Doctor. I'll see you next month...maybe." Renee smiled. "Mom, uhm, a latte to celebrate?"

"Sounds good." Mrs. Chadwick put her arm around Renee. "It really sounds good."

***

At the coffee shop, Renee adjusted her scarf covering her face as usual, but not so tight it wouldn't stretch from her face from time to time. Before, she would hold it tight to cover the scars.

"You're a new woman," Mrs. Chadwick remarked.

"No, Mom. I realize I have to accept the things I can't change. If someone is going to stare, it's going to happen."

"Confident, too." Mrs. Chadwick smiled. "I don't know what's happened to you. It's like something changed overnight."

"Nothing happened, really. I let the hate towards Marvin go, too. I had to."

"I'm so glad you are finally getting over the emotional hold he had on you."

"One step at a time, Mom." Renee looked at her mother. "Are we going to order, or just sit here?"

"I'll order," she replied.

"No, Mom, let me." Renee rose and walked to the counter. "I'll have a mocha latte and a regular latte, please."

The barista rang up the order. "Six forty-six, total." She turned from the counter and walked to the cupboard, retrieving two ceramic cups. Renee paid for the order on the kiosk. "Oh, by the way, you didn't ask for a name."

"I don't need to, ma'am. I know your scarf."

"Oh, I, umm." She coughed. "Thank you."

"I like your scarf. I love the colors," the barista complimented. "I will bring it to you."

"Thank you so much."

"Sure thing," The barista smiled.

Renee returned to the table, seeing her mother wipe tears from her eyes. "I knew that one day you would return."

"Mom, I never left…not really. Thanks to you."

***

Vincent reviewed the contract before leaving the conference room. He liked what he saw on the construction plan and enjoyed their honest approach. He called his lawyer's office and set an appointment for contract review. Vincent rarely focused on ideas to master the world, yet he enjoyed fair, quality idea exchanges. His mind never rested on mediocrity. He knew the roadmap to better business. Vincent walked to his car, got in, smiled, and drove to his number one store.

Arriving at the coffee shop, Vincent entered through the front, and a voice he recognized startled him. It was the voice recorded like his favorite song, carried for years, promising to sing in unison once heard. Vincent smiled acknowledging the unique sound that got him moving during a college class. It was noticeably clear, extremely crisp, and concise. As the volume lowered, her unique sound increased. "Wow." He moved to the counter right after a scarf-wearing customer left. "What's her name?" he asked the barista.

"I don't know, but she's always wearing a pretty scarf."

"What?"

"Yes, she comes in with other ladies, and she always wears a scarf. I think they are family, or related. I saw you talk to them one day."

"Oh, you mean Candi's mother?"

"Is that her name?" the barista asked. "I never get to use their names, but I know they are regulars. I see them at least once a week."

"Once a week." Vincent looked at the table where the woman with the scarf sat, and remembered the lady he'd given free coffee to, after he'd dismissed Candi. "I didn't remember her voice." Vincent had taken a step towards the table when his phone rang. He looked at the table and decided the phone was more important than getting into a discussion with a woman who may or may not prove to be the one of his dreams.

Chapter 17

Is it Really You?

Renee nodded towards a guy standing at the counter of the coffee shop. "Mom," she said. "Is that the shop manager?"

Mrs. Chadwick looked. "I think he's the owner." Vivian grinned at her daughter's inquiry. "Why do you ask?"

"He looks familiar." Renee leaned over for a better look. "He looks like a guy that had a crush on me."

"Renee, I can't believe you." "Why not Mom?"

"It's been over three years since you've spoken about a man."

"I'm not talking about any man. It's an old college classmate."

"That's even more interesting."

"Why so, Mom?" Renee asked, hoping not to hear about her hardship.

"Just days ago, you wouldn't care to be seen in public."

"I… you are right mom; I didn't want to." "What changed?"

Renee sipped coffee and while holding the cup in both hands away from her lips, she looked into her mother's eyes. "I guess I did. I changed because I don't care about what people think of me."

"Oh." Mrs. Chadwick touched her daughter's hand. "I... I am so surprised..." She paused, and her hand shook from the news. "It's taken you a long time to get to that point," Vivian mumbled losing a battle to restrain tears that trailed down her cheeks.

"Mom, it's not that important. Why are you crying?" Renee put the cup down and wiped the tears from her mother's cheeks. "It's okay, it's okay." Renee gripped her mother's hand, showing her scars without worry. "It dawned on me that people will ask, and if they do, I'm not afraid of the truth anymore. So many women go through it. Maybe..."

"... maybe you're just ready, and the doctor made an enormous impact this time."

"Actually, Mom, the counseling session was normal. It finally hit me that I have to live and learn how to get through it."

"It's just that simple? You finally want to live again?"

"I won't say it's simple, but I will admit that I'm surprised myself." Renee released her mother's hand and picked up the coffee cup. She glanced around without adjusting her scarf. "You see, Mom, I had a great life, before. I was confident, ambitious, and a person you were proud of."

"I'm proud of you." Mom touched Renee's arm. "I've never stopped being proud of you."

"You know what I mean." Renee placed her cup on the table and covered her mother's hand with her scarred one. "I realize I want it back, and I don't want you to worry about me anymore."

"How…I'm confused at the speed of your…"

"… Mom, I'm trying harder to be myself again. It's all I'm doing."

"Can I…"

"… Not yet Mom. No men. I just escaped my shell." Renee smirked.

Mrs. Vivian Chadwick smiled. "I was going to tell Candi."

She giggled. "I hadn't thought about men, at the moment." Vivian picked up her coffee cup before sipping its content. "You…" Vivian smiled. "You have to do that at your pace. I can only imagine how that's going to change your life." She shook her head. "I can only imagine."

"I will get there, Mom. I'm sure I will."

***

Vincent went into the office, reminding himself of the work he needed to complete. He didn't forget about running a business with multiple stores and decided to push the modifications aside. *I have to make a solid plan before closing each store and losing revenue it took years to achieve.* Right when he looked at his schedule, he heard a knock on the door. "Hey, anyone here?"

"Just a minute." Vincent rose from his desk and walked to the door, pushing it open. "You're on time today."

"Oh, hi, Mr. Vincent." A delivery person responded. "Yes, I'm on schedule, and I'd love to keep it." She smiled.

"How many boxes of coffee today?"

"Seven of your regular and five of your specialty brands." "Perfect." He pointed to a place inside the storage area.

"Place them there and I'll sign for them."

"Okay." She rolled over the dolly of boxes and set them aside as directed. "I'll get the pad for your signature."

"I'll follow you out, no worries." Vincent signed the order and waved the delivery person off. He returned inside to get a barista. "Hey, the delivery came. Can you replenish what we need from the back?"

"Sure," the barista nodded. "I have one cup to deliver to that table and then I'm on it."

"I'll deliver it, no problem."

"Thanks, Mr. Mathis." The barista gave him the coffee and pointed at the table.

Vincent looked at the two women with full recognition. He walked to the table. "Excuse me, here's your coffee." He placed the cup in front of the woman with the scarf and picked up the empty cup. "I can take this, right?"

"Yes, you can," Rene responded. "Thank you."

"I've heard your voice before." Vincent looked at her. "I think I know you."

"You may," Mrs. Chadwick said. "We come here all of the time."

"No, I mean I've known her from before." Vincent looked at her features and saw a glimpse of scars behind the scarf. "I'm sorry, but your voice is so familiar. It's like we've shared something together."

"I spoke to you earlier when you talked to my mother."

"I can tell you where I know you, for sure. Let me hear you again."

"Thanks for the coffee," Renee responded. "How much do we owe you?"

"That's it!" Vincent recalled. "We went to college together."

"We went to college together?" Renee responded. "What year did you graduate?"

"I remember, now. You were ahead of me and we had a class together."

"I took a lot of classes with a bunch of people." Renee grabbed her scarf and pulled it further toward her nose. "I don't think we crossed paths."

"Maybe you two can find another time to reminisce, but right now, I need to talk to my daughter. Do you mind?" Mrs. Chadwick looked at Vincent and nodded.

"No, ma'am, I don't mind at all. Enjoy your coffee." Vincent left and headed to the bar. He peeked at the table, getting a full glimpse of the woman whose voice, he recognized. *I'll never forget her voice,* he thought. *I will never forget her voice.*

***

Mrs. Chadwick watched Renee grab the end of the scarf and pull it over her scars. Frowning, Renee's mother said, "I didn't think you were fully ready."

"What?" Renee responded.

"The young man who spoke to you." She looked at the counter. "He didn't care about your scars. Why did you pull on the scarf?"

"Mom, I didn't."

"Oh, okay, I see." Mrs. Chadwick touched her daughter's hand. "I see." She smiled. "We'll keep working on that."

***

Candi reached for her phone on her work desk. She dialed Vincent's number. "Sir, your order is ready, and I'm informing you of the delivery schedule."

"Thank you," Vincent responded. "What can I expect?"

"The regular pastry list, plus a special blend you'll love. We're sure of it."

"Don't tell me…you guys figured out my recipe."

"No, not at all. It's the boss' recipe, which he is throwing in at no charge. It's only a baker's dozen."

"New product?" He paused. "I don't want to…No, wait. Okay, I'll see if it works."

Candi chuckled. "I am sure it will because it's so popular at other places that he's willing to give it to you." She paused for a response.

Vincent shook his head. *He's admitting he figured out my recipe.* "Okay, let's see if it's successful. I can't promise an order, but I will consider it with the other baked goods I get from you."

"Being a kind man, you sure are challenging." "Like calling me an asshole?"

"Oh, sorry about that." Candi covered her mouth and whispered, "You didn't deserve being called that." She swallowed before saying. "I apologize." Candi paused. "I hope you don't stop using the bakery because of me."

"There is a difference between professional and personal. Something my ex couldn't decipher."

"Your ex?" Candi removed her hand. "I don't' mean to pry, but you have an ex?"

"Why does that surprise you? Don't you have an ex somewhere?"

"I didn't think you were the dating type."

"Excuse me?" Vincent frowned. "I think you…never mind." "I'm sorry, I touched a soft spot." Candi smiled.

"When will you send the order?"

"It should be there tomorrow, as scheduled. I only called because I didn't want you surprised when you checked the inventory."

"Oh, thank you. Have a wonderful day." Vincent pressed the red icon on his cell, ending the call. "Nosey and disrespectful girl. I don't know how her mom could have had her. I don't understand."

***

Renee stood from her chair. "Mom, are you ready? It's time we get moving."

"I'm not so sure I want to go. Let's finish our conversation." "I'm doing fine, Mom. I really am. It's just that I'm not ready to get personal."

"What do you mean, 'personal'?"

"You know what I mean. I don't have to spill it for you."

"I thought the psychiatrist said you were ready. Or, at least, it's what you said to her when you showed a positive change." Mrs. Chadwick grabbed Renee's arm. "Sit down and let's finish this, so we know what's next."

"Mom, I'm not ready for this conversation." Renee sighed. "Didn't I show you improvement?"

"I agree, you did, but…"

"…but it's time to go. I don't want to stay here any longer." Renee stepped behind her mother. "I can help you get going." She grabbed the back of her chair, and as Mom moved, she edged it out. "See, Mom, that wasn't so bad."

"I'm going—don't rush me."

"Thank you," Renee smiled. "I'm glad to see you comply." She smirked.

"Our conversation isn't over, Renee. You cannot run away from changing and letting go. You have to."

"But can't I do it at my pace?"

"I thought you were." Mrs. Chadwick shouldered her purse and stepped in front of Renee heading for the exit. "You *are ready*, so stop fighting."

"Yes, Mom…stop fighting."

***

"That son of a bitch!" Vincent shouted in the storage room. He took out the latest item and saw its similarity to his creation. "I can't believe her." He bit into it and slowly savored the pastry, comparing it to the taste he knew so well. "Nope, not quite—good try." He chuckled after he swallowed. He called for one of his employees. "Let's put these out and sell them two for one and make it a deep discount—like, 50 cents."

"That is cheap." The barista took the box.

"It's a new product, and I'm not so sure I'll order it. But it's no cost to us." Vincent returned to his desk, grabbed his favorite cup, and walked into the coffee shop. He scanned the room, and, to his surprise, he saw Mrs. Chadwick and Renee exiting. He stepped quickly from behind the counter and went to the front exit. "Ma'am, thank you for coming." Vincent waved.

"See you next time," Mrs. Chadwick responded. "See, Renee, he's a nice man. You don't recall being in school with him?"

"Mom, let it go." Renee entered the car and snapped on her seat belt. "Besides, why would I remember an undergrad when I was a senior?"

"It's not like you to forget a person…see?" Mrs. Chadwick snapped her seatbelt and started the car. "I know you remember him."

"Okay, Mom." Renee sighed. "When are we having dinner with Dad?"

"What?"

"Dinner with Dad?" Renee glanced at her mother. "I don't see him much, these days."

"You can come home any time you like."

"Mom, I know that, but I thought we'd have a family dinner soon."

"You know, dinner together sounds like a great plan."

"Is there something going on with you and Dad?" Renee stared at Mrs. Chadwick. "It's like you haven't said anything about him, lately."

"Everything is fine," she responded. "I love your father, and we're just fine."

"Mom?" Renee touched her mother's arm. "Are you worried about something and not telling me?"

"I'm worried about you, dear."

"Outside of me, Mom, is there more?"

"Your sister."

"Mom, don't change the subject."

"No, really, everything between us is fine. I don't have anything to tell."

"Okay, Mom." Renee removed her hand from her mom's arm and looked forward. "I'll find out, if there is."

"Yes, I'm sure you will, if there is."

Twenty minutes of silence was not unusual for Mrs. Chadwick and Renee, especially after the incident. Renee did her usual, stare out of the window, close her eyes when she see's people near, and turn so the back of her head is shown when there is a car abreast to them. She rarely kept a conversation because over the years they would talk about the scars and how Renee got them.

Renee broke silence shortly before arriving home. "Mom, it's time you came clean."

Mrs. Chadwick pulled into Renee's driveway, parked the car, and looked at Renee with a raised eyebrow. "Come clean about what?"

"I was thinking…it's funny you haven't talked about Dad in a few days. I mean, nothing. He's the perfect guy, and haven't done anything annoying to you…Mom, I've been with you for ages, and there has to be something going on."

"No, nothing is going on." Mrs. Chadwick looked at the gauge cluster on the dashboard. "Nothing at all."

"See? You aren't making eye contact with me."

"I really mean it. Nothing is going on." Mrs. Chadwick stared at Renee. "Really."

"I don't believe you, but, okay, Mom. I'll call Dad and ask him."

"He'll love hearing from you." Mrs. Chadwick watched Renee leave the car and open the house's front door and enter. *He's going to love talking to her.*

***

`Mr. Chadwick rose from the family room couch, grabbed the remote, and pushed the 'off' button before he put it on the coffee table. He went into the kitchen and retrieved a glass from the dish strainer. "She has to feel my energy," he whispered. "God has to feel my energy."

"Are you okay?" Mrs. Chadwick asked after she walked through the front door. "Are you doing, okay?"

"I'm fine," Mr. Chadwick responded. "I'm fine," he said, "I don't think I could feel any better."

"How can you say such a thing?" Vivian asked. "Like I always do…I open my mouth." He laughed.

"Yes, you open your mouth a lot. And so do I." Vivian placed her keys on the wall hook and put her purse on the kitchen table. "Can I get you anything?"

"No, baby, not at all. I'm still doing great."

"Not with what I know about you. I have been with you for decades. Don't you think I know what you're thinking?"

"Forget about that." Robert smiled. "You know, everything going on…" he pointed at his head, "…is all about us."

"Now, that's our problem." Vivian frowned. "Your daughters are worried, just like I worry about you. Why aren't you serious about this?"

Robert moved closer to Vivian, put his arms around her, pulled her close before kissing her neck.

"Robert! I'm serious." Vivian held onto him. "Babe," He whispered, "It's like you've become my guardian, my sergeant, and my angel. But, you are my wife, who I love more than anything in this world. I know you shouldn't worry about me, but I can't stop you." He gazed into Vivian's eyes. "I think the best I can do is take your mind away from fear." He pushed her back without fully releasing her. "Life can be short and is even shorter when we worry. We've got this, we…"

"I can't Robert. I can't pretend nothing is going on."

"I never asked you to forget or pretend. I asked that you enjoy what we have, and let's be positive as much as possible. I've read, more than once, that being positive is the drug of choice."

"I…"

"I know." He pulled her tight before whispering, "I'll tell the girls when the time is right. But, right now, I need you to believe that there isn't a problem."

"I don't think I can." A tear streamed down her face. "I can't." She sniffled.

"If you do, then the girls will follow your lead." Robert ran his hand through her hair, starting from the top of her head and moving down to her shoulders, like he'd done a thousand times before when she was uncomfortable. "You can do this for us...baby you can do this with your eyes closed."

"I..." Vivian pushed from his embrace. "I can't believe you're telling me not to give a damn."

"I never said that." Robert shook his head. "I can't believe you would even think I could say such a thing."

"Oh, Robert, we need to tell the girls before things change. I mean, before my looks change."

"Beauty is within our hearts, regardless of time."

"There you go again. Why bother you, when I can do it myself?"

"I will tell them, in time. I will tell them. I just don't know how to do it without breaking my heart."

"It's your decision, but I think the news coming from me is better than watching you break down in front of them." Robert walked to the table, picked up his glass, and walked to the refrigerator. He retrieved a small amount of apple juice. "Would you like some?"

Part III

A Year Later

Chapter 18

Realization

Renee leaned on the shower wall. Her tears mixed in cascading water. With deep breaths, she inhaled and spat every drop during her wail of pain. She cried under liquid streams, over important memories of her life—the struggle to battle abuse, and the change from being a rescued woman to one who could live without fear. She remembered her mother's cry to get better, felt her mother's arms around her, and recited Vivian's words of wisdom that she will never hear again.

Renee struggled to stand, grabbing her waist with one hand, and turned the water off with the other. She pushed the shower door open pulling the towel from the rack. Her cries stopped while her mind continued recalling those challenging times between Marvin and her mom. She touched her chest after wrapping the towel around her body. Her frown remembering what Marvin caused, is nothing compared to the torment of losing her mother. She leaned on the vanity, hair releasing water droplets onto her shoulders, and looked at her red eyes. That bastard was nothing even though he hurt me and my mom.

Breakfast was no different than any other morning before tending the garden. She drank coffee and ate fruit with a bagel. Renee glanced at her staged camera equipment in the corner by the door.

She looked at the rising sun through the French doors, a gateway to the back yard. Renee gazed at the first row of sparkling roses, where sunlight danced on their moist petals. She retrieved the camera set and went to the garden. Her routine camera shoot today started without a stand to get natural sunlight. She later moved the stand, positioned the camera on it, and snapped more photos, capturing nature's beauty with a time-lapse approach.

Two hours into the morning, she took the camera and camera stand inside. She placed the camera on her desk and returned to the garden. With gloves covering her hands, she grabbed a five-pound bag of fresh soil, a gallon of weed killer, and moved to the garden. She returned to the porch for the five-gallon bucket of fertilizer and the scoop on top. She'd learned to use both hands, regardless of her injuries. She sprayed weed killer, and where she thought needed fresh soil, she managed to fill the plant's base.

Renee smiled after spending two hours in her garden. Candi arrived around one o'clock with lunch - two sandwiches and a slice of cheesecake their mother would serve on a special occasion. She rang the doorbell before using the key.

"Hey," she announced while walking inside.

"I'm in the kitchen!" Renee shouted, standing at the sink running water over her hands. "You're late."

"Ah, I am?" Candi placed the bag on the kitchen table and dropped her purse on one of the chairs around the table. "I'm right on time, thank you."

"Yes, like always."

"How'd your shoot go this morning; any masterpieces?" The business manager Candi asked.

"I had perfect sunlight this morning. It seemed like the sun finally visited us in the right way."

"Good." Candi pleasantly nodded. "Then you'll develop more prints I can sell." Candi pulled sandwiches from the bag.

"I think so." Renee smiled and turned off the water. She grabbed a kitchen towel and dried her hands, then folded the towel for the holder. "I'm happy you got here. We need to talk about the rest of this year."

"Are you wearing your business hat, or big sister cap?" "Why? Aren't they both the same?"

"Ah, nope—not even close."

"I think they are." Renee sat at the table. "Maybe we can start planning our next move."

"That works, as long as you listen to me." Candi paused and pushed a sandwich towards Renee. "I'm the one selling everything. You have to listen to me, or it's a moot point."

"Yeah, you wouldn't follow my instructions anyway."

Renee grabbed her wrapped lunch and peeled the paper away from the contents.

"It's not that. It's just a different side of doing business, outside of your education."

"It's why they call it education," Renee reminded her sister.

"Smartass." Candi unwrapped her sandwich and walked to the cabinet for a drinking glass. "I bet Mom would say you need to listen to me – if we asked her."

"Probably." Renee sat at the table. "Hey, grab me a glass - will you?"

"Yeah, sure," Candi went into the cabinet a second time.

"What would you like in it?"

"Water — tap water, if you don't mind."

"Not bottled? Did you run out again and forgot to go get some?"

"No, I didn't forget. I just haven't gotten any more."
"Scared, much?"

"Now, you know better than to ask me that." Renee shook her head. "Why do you insist that I jump in front of people?"

"Like Mom said, 'Isn't it time you move on?'" Candi placed a glass of water in front of Renee and sat directly across from her before placing her drink on the table. "I can't understand you. It has been a long time since Marvin left, and you are much better today. I see you barely wear a scarf these days. Why not get back into dating?"

"Who's going to accept me?"

"You know who." Candi bit into her sandwich and placed it back on the paper. After swallowing she said, "Why do you do that?"

"I am not pretending. I don't know if he's really into me or if he's sympathetic."

"I wonder." Candi shook her head. "Do we come from the same parents?"

Renee picked up her sandwich from the paper and said, "I wonder that too," before biting into her lunch. She glanced at her sister and imagined her mother had joined them, like she had done multiple times before. She swallowed a little and left room for a comment.

"You know, we need to get Dad out of the house."

"I called him earlier," Candi admitted.

"You did?"

"He's doing great. For an old man. He's riding a cross-country bicycle."

"What?" Renee stopped chewing. "That will kill him."
"Yeah, I wonder what Mom said about that."

"Knowing Mom, she would have talked about being safe. If nothing else."

"Dad knows when and where to ride his bike. He's not some kid."

"I'm glad he's busy." Renee bit into her sandwich.

"How do you do it?" Candi had watched her sister eat the same type of sandwich for the fourth day that week. "I don't call to ask what you want, anymore. It's like I know what you expect."

"Habits are good, you know."

"Like staying home every weekend since going to the coffee shop with Mom?"

"I have my work here," Renee quickly responded.

Candi shook her head. "I'm not surprised with that answer. I mean, your work has been pretty good, and I've sold more of your pictures these past months." She bit into her sandwich and put what was left of it on the paper. "Especially the flowers by moonlight shots." Her eyes scanned the room and stopped at a picture Renee had recently hung. She swallowed. "Oh, nice!" Candi pointed at the wall, picked up her glass, and sipped, replacing it on the table. "It's the number one print in demand."

"It is a good shot. I mean, I had no idea it would turn out so well."

"I see this picture almost everywhere. Even on plate settings." Candi smiled. "The chain store manager was happy to submit your picture as a design. I would have never thought you'd become famous."

"I'm not famous. The picture is famous. I didn't sell it, you did." Renee had eaten her sandwich down to a little corner. "I have to clean up and get out for my daily exercise."

"I'm impressed." Candi raised an eyebrow. "You can go to a gym and not get scared?"

"You know the answer; why would you ask?" Renee finished her sandwich and shook her head. "What makes you think I don't wear a scarf?"

"Oh, I know you wear a scarf, but you're still going. Don't you think it's time you got back on the saddle?"

"No, not on the saddle." Renee drank water. Holding the glass, she rose from the table, grabbed the sandwich paper, and went to the trash receptacle before arriving at the sink. "I swear, you never give up."

"Look, I don't want you to be alone when you're older."

"I *am* older." Renee placed the glass in the sink and turned towards Candi, staring at her.

"Yeah, all of thirty-two, now?"

"It's been a few years, but I'm not ready to ride the saddle. No, I'm not ready." Renee shook her head.

"Well, I'm not saying ride just any saddle." Candi nodded her head to one side. "You know who I'm talking about."

"Candi, please." Renee turned to the hallway. "You need to stop." She walked away.

Candi shouted, "You know exactly who I'm talking about!" She rose from the table and moved to the hall. "And Mom would approve!"

"My damn sister never gives up." Renee changed into gym clothes. She walked to the bathroom and picked up the hairbrush. "She can be a pain in the ass." She pulled the brush through her hair and pushed it aside. Twisted and turned, with a band, for the ponytail on the opposite side of her scarred face. She had done this hairstyle six times before, and found the scarf fit better with that hair design.

"Candi, you are not welcome in my house anymore." "Yeah, sure. I'm your favorite sister," Candi responded, heading to the bathroom.

"Damn you."

"You're thinking about it. I knew it." Candi stood in the bathroom doorway, watching Renee, and moved aside, and prepared to follow her sister.

"I can't." Renee tied the scarf before she walked downstairs. "I don't think he'll even look at me."

"Mom enjoyed talking to him, remember?" Candi followed and kept pace with Renee's shadow.

"I do, but I wasn't ready, then."

Candi walked to the table, picked up her sandwich paper, and threw it in the trash before she walked to the sink placing the glass in the middle of it. "I have something to tell you." She moved to the hallway towards the stairs. "Mom said to get you two together without being annoying."

"Mom said what?" Renee frowned at Candi. "Mom said to get us together."

"When Mom was fighting liver failure, she and I went to the coffee shop…"

"…and?"

"Mom and Vincent had a serious conversation about you. They figured out where you two knew each other."

"They did?" Renee stood in the foyer before picking up her car keys.

"What did she find out—do you remember?"

"Yep, I do, and I vowed to get you to at least talk to him."

"How long ago was that?" Renee looked at her watch.

"Never mind, I have to run if I'm going to the Zumba class."

"Now Zumba? What happened to Jazzercise?"

"You have to change to keep going!" Candi followed Renee outside. "I'll be back in a couple of hours. Don't touch anything on my desk." Renee waved before she got into her car. Candi closed the front door and watched through the side decorative window as the car left the driveway.

***

Vincent groveled with the entertainment manager. "Why can't we simply put a speaker in front of him instead of across the lounge area?"

"We need both for sound balance." The manager pointed at the far corner. "Especially over there. The playback will be great."

"No one will sit there because there's no view of the stage."

"But the sound will carry. Trust me, you can't afford to not have a speaker set up over there." He pointed. "And over the entrance."

Vincent shook his head before he responded. "I'll look at the cost of adding those speakers. Knowing you, it has to be top-notch—meaning, more than I'll collect for the night."

"No, I disagree. Once the word gets out that you have a great venue for live music, the house will always be full."

"Yeah, that's what the last guy said at the other location." Vincent raised his eyebrows and shook his head in disagreement.

"It's marketing for their boss."

"I pay you for solid advice." Vincent frowned. "It better pay out, Mike. It better pay out." Vincent moved from the entertainment manager, and waved at Candi, who'd entered the coffee shop.

"Changes, changes, Vincent," she noticed.

"Hey, what brings you here?" He hugged Candi. "Nice

seeing you. It's been a long time since you and your mom were here."

"I need to talk to you." Candi looked at Vincent with her eyebrows pointed inward.

"Yeah, sure." Vincent raised his arm leading Candi to a quiet and secluded area. "Have a seat." He pulled out the chair. Candi sat in the chair and pulled her purse from her shoulder placing it on the table. She looked at Vincent. "It's nice to sit without fighting." Candi smiled.

"Unless you have something to argue about." Vincent chuckled. "I can find you a better adversary than me."

"That isn't necessary." Candi glanced around the bar. "You've made progress."

"Yes, we have. It's not like I thought it would be, but I'm not always right about things, you know."

"I know, right!" Candi smiled, "Mom was right, you're the right man."

"I haven't seen your mother for some time now. How's she doing?"

"That's why I'm here." Candi touched Vincent's arm. "She's no longer with us."

"Oh." Vincent grabbed Candi's arm and placed it over his. He looked into Candi's eyes, and his eyes filled with tears. "I'm so sorry." Vincent paused and wiped the tear buildup. "She was a beautiful woman." He looked from Candi. "How did it happen? When did she…?"

"'Fourteen months or so, not long after we were here. Her

liver finally stopped working and there was nothing we could do to help."

"You mean, we laughed and joked together while she was sick?" Vincent shook his head in disbelief.

"She didn't look sick at all. Rarely acted sick, but during her final stages, her health failed, and my poor father watched her deterioration firsthand. It was the worst."

"I can't imagine." Vincent removed his hand from Candi's. "Is there something you want me to do?"

"Yes, there is." Candi placed her hand on the table, looked around the bar and focused on Vincent. "My mom liked you." She paused. "She really liked you."

"I liked her, too." Vincent smiled. "She was a kind and classy lady."

"She told me to encourage you." "Encourage me?"

Candi grabbed her bag and retrieved her cell phone. She held it in her palm and tapped the screen before opening the photo gallery app.

"Look at this." She turned the phone towards him. "This is Renee's graduation picture."

"I remember," Vincent shook his head. "That was a rough day for me."

"I know. Remember, Mom placed you there. She remembered that you bought flowers for Renee."

"Your mother and I had that laugh, and I told her... "

"...you would not chase any woman that hard." Candi switched photos. "Yes, I know, but look at this picture."

"This is the same sister?"

"The one and only." Candi scrolled to another photo of Renee, with her scarf. "She needs your help."

"Help?"

"I think so, and so did Mom. Believe me, I thought about this, and it's perfect."

"I am supposed to date your sister because you asked me?"

"No. I'm saying she needs your help, and you want to give it to her."

Vincent sat back in the chair, gazing beyond Candi. "You know, I had a serious crush on her. But she pushed me past my limits of accepting bitchy behavior."

"Love has a way of healing." "Who said I was in love?"

"You did." Candi giggled. "It's why Mom wanted you to step up and find that love again."

Vincent glanced at his watch and looked at Candi. "Coffee break? I can get you a cup on the house."

"No, thank you. I need to get back to Renee's house before she returns from the gym." Candi rose from the table, dropped the cell phone into her bag, and placed the bag straps over her shoulder. "Raincheck, maybe?"

"Oh, ah, yes. A raincheck is perfect." Vincent stood and moved from the table. He followed Candi to the front door. "How am I supposed to get in touch with you?"

"Here." Candi pulled a business card from her purse. "Call me if you have questions or when you're ready to meet Renee."

Vincent took the card and placed it in his pocket. "I'll call you when I am ready."

"Don't wait to make contact. Do it before it's too late," Candi smirked. "Remember, Mom liked you, and I…"

"… you like me, too." Vincent chuckled. "Have an enjoyable day." He watched her disappear through the glass door exit. Vincent went to the counter and asked a barista for a cup of his favorite coffee. "I'll drink a cup with Mrs. Chadwick."

***

Renee arrived home in time to see Candi exit her car. "I thought you were working on something."

"I had to run an errand." Candi closed her car door. "It' not important or about the business."

"We're doing pretty good, right?" Renee followed her sister to the front door.

"Yes, why do you ask?"

"I was thinking while on the treadmill, after the Zumba class, that it's time we go somewhere."

Candi opened the front door and went to the office, where she put her purse on the extra chair near the window. "Will you take your camera and shoot while we're gone?"

"There you go." Renee sighed. "I was thinking vacation and you're thinking work."

"Why can't we do both? I mean, wherever we go, there must be something worth sharing. And you have an eye for pictures."

"I was thinking, just to enjoy something different." Renee moved from the office door. "I'm going to take a shower. Don't touch my camera."

"Okay, I won't touch your camera." Candi watched Renee leave, stood from her chair, and walked to the desk. She picked up Renee's camera.

***

Robert Chadwick stood at Renee's front house wearing biker shorts and a tank top. He parked his bicycle near the bottom of the stairs. He walked to the door and rang the bell.

"Dad!" Candi yelled, after peeping through the peephole. She opened the door. "What brings you here?"

"I can't visit my daughters?"

"Yes, you can." Candi smiled and embraced him. "And you rode your bike here, too. That had to be dangerous, on the road."

"Have you forgotten how much fun it is to ride a bike?" Mr. Chadwick hugged Candi before asking, "Where's Renee?"

"She's in the shower. What's on your mind?"

"I want to chat with you two." Robert walked into the office and went to the chair by the window. He pushed Candi's purse aside before sitting. "I remember your mom doing the same thing, putting her purse on the best chair in the room."

"It's a woman's thing, Dad."

"Not so sure every woman does the same thing." He relaxed before adding, "But I don't want to find out."

"What's on your mind, Dad?"

"Well." Robert scanned the walls, admiring the pictures Renee had taken. "You two are doing fabulous together. Mom would be proud."

Renee entered the office. "Dad, nice seeing you. You look great, biker shorts and all." She giggled and hugged Robert while seated. He stood after Renee released him and positioned himself between both daughters. "I was thinking about how large our house is...I mean, your childhood home, the place of so many memories, including some I'd like to forget."

"I think I know where you're going," Renee quickly added. "I still live there, Dad," said Candi.

"But you're very busy, and I love seeing you home, but it's not like you are always here."

"He's right, Candi. You are here a lot, these past months."

"It's business." Candi added, "It's not like I've moved my stuff from home."

"Maybe it's time you did."

"I left once, you know," Candi reminded him. "I had Mom help me move me home when I lost my apartment."

"Tough times fall on everyone. You were fortunate we were there for you." Robert moved from the center of the desk to the window behind the chair. "Your mom did it all." He swallowed before his voice softened. "And I loved her so much."

"We know, Dad." Renee rose from behind the desk, moved beside her father, and placed her arm around him. "We know." She placed her head on his shoulder. Candi rose from the chair and positioned herself on the opposite side of their father. She added her arms to the mix. "I support your decision."

"You do?" Robert sighed. "I didn't think you two would."

"Look," Renee spoke. "It's difficult because we lost Mom, but it's harder on you. We want you to be happy, and whatever it takes, we'll be here."

"You two are amazing. It's the second-best thing I've ever done."

"I was the first," Renee chuckled.

"There you go, Miss Competition," Candi responded. "Why don't you show Dad your new pictures."

"What new pictures?" asked Robert.

"Those on the camera from this morning," Candi suggested. "Dad, you're going to be impressed."

"With you two..." Robert kissed Candi's forehead and then Renee's. "I have always been impressed."

***

Three days into the week, Candi's phone rang. She walked from her bed to the lamp next to the reclining chair where she left her cell charging, picked it up, and swiped it before she said "Hello." She turned on the light and sat in the recliner with the phone held to her ear.

"Hey, I decided to call you." Vincent fell silent.

"I guess you did." Candi wiped her eyes before asking, "Why so late?"

"Is it?" he hesitated, "I didn't look at the time." He gasped for air. "I'm sorry, you're right. We can do this tomorrow."

"No, it's fine, go ahead and tell me what's on your mind." "I wanted to find out about Renee."

"What about her?"

"Anything you can share, because I haven't talked to her in years."

"You've talked to her, but not on good terms," Candi responded. "Well, not on the best of terms—but she knows you."

"Does she remember me?" Vincent sighed.

"She remembers…Mom and Renee had the best conversation before she died."

"I can't believe your mom is gone." Vincent dropped his head.

"It was a tough battle, but she's in a better place." "May she rest in peace." Vincent fell silent.

"She will when you get with Renee. It was her wish for me to help you two make it."

"Why me?" Vincent waited for Candi's response.

Candi didn't immediately respond; instead, she considered the twelve conversations about Vincent that she'd had with her mom. "She said for me to remind you of Renee's graduation. Get that sparkle in your eye, again."

"Your mom remembered that?"

"She remembered a lot."

Vincent swallowed and contemplated his next comment. "What is she like?"

"Really—from the things she's gone through, she's amazing, resilient, and dynamic." Candi repositioned herself on the seat. "She's funny, disciplined, and smart."

"Smart." Vincent laughed. "She was the smartest person in our group."

"You remember?"

"Yes, more than you know."

"Then why are you asking me about her, when you know?"
"People change, you know." Vincent paused.

"And often, some changes are not the best."

"That's what I have to warn you about. She's changed in appearance."

"I bet she has."

"No, you don't understand, but I want her to tell you - if she tells you; because Mom and Renee are the only two who knows exactly what happened." Candi paused, waiting for Vincent's response. After a minute of frigid air blowing through the vent, Candi spoke. "Renee is scarred for life. It's why she wears the scarf every time she's out."

"So that's why she's always covering her face." Vincent closed his eyes and recalled the college beauty. "She was amazing, in school."

"She still is, but it's a touchy situation now, since the accident."

"I see." Vincent looked at the cell phone. "How bad? Don't get me wrong, but I want to know before I put my foot in my mouth."

"You're asking makes a world of a difference." Candi responded, "I want her to tell you...better yet, show you."

"Show me?" Vincent asked. "Show me what she looks like at night, or in mid-day?"

"Why would that matter?"

"I guess it doesn't." Vincent paused. "I ask because my mother had scars. She was not exactly a beauty pageant runner-up, but she was the most beautiful woman I have ever known with the temperament of a Japanese angel. I mean," Vincent paused. "Like your mom, sweet and kind. I guess our mothers had something in common." Vincent closed his eyes before taking in a deep breath and exhaling. "I might be the lucky one, but I'm not so sure I should be the one pursuing Renee."

"Look, I am following Mom's instructions, and it has to work. She chose you to be in Renee's life. Mom wasn't always a great judge of character, but she believed in you. I promised her that you were going to try."

"I see." Vincent nodded, accepting Candi's explanation. "Good night. And talk to her soon, or I'll bring her to one of your coffee/wine bars." Candi pressed the red phone icon on her cellular. She turned off the lamp, rose from the chair, and set her phone on the nightstand before going to bed.

Chapter 19

His Move

Vincent moved from the kitchen island after pouring a glass of wine. He walked through the condo to his favorite recliner, grabbed the universal remote, and played easy listening music. With his eyes closed, feet solid on the floor and sipped wine. *I told them an old joke and they didn't laugh. Wasn't it funny?* He giggled at how dry it was hosting a conference of high rollers at his number one coffee/wine bar. *People with money don't have much of humor.* Vincent raised his wine glass to his lips, sipped, and put it down. *Why do I insist on being present at everything happening at the stores?* Rocking in the recliner, he's planning what's next to stay on the venue list of the city's best. He looked at his wall of old photos and stared at the latest purchase, a decorative framed photo of roses in the moonlight. The soft glow of the lamp made the picture stand out. He did not know why, but the lighting had the same effect on the painting as moonlight had on the rose.

He sipped from the wine glass, paused, and sipped again, nearly finishing the content of the glass. He remembered the last relationship he had and the pain he endured ending it. Vincent shook his head. "Damn, do I want to go through that again?" he mumbled. *I would rather not. She was a pain damn near the entire marriage. Always nagging about my lack of motivation to work when I was working my ass off with the coffee shop.* Vincent rocked with the rhythm of the soft music. *That girl was seriously a platinum digger. She nagged and nagged about making more, more, and more money. And then she hated me for not making her life extravagant. What the hell did she see in the beginning?* Vincent rose from the chair and walked to the kitchen. He placed the wine glass on the island. He stepped slower, turned the lights off, and made it to the recliner. *Let's say I get Renee going, will it end like it happened with my ex- wife?* He rocked in an up tempo despite the music rhythm being slower. *I hated walking on eggshells in anticipation of an explosion. Will Renee push me to that point?* Vincent opened his eyes to the green glow of the stereo. *Naw, she wouldn't do that. Not the Renee I know.*

Another thought countered and supported his delusion about any interaction with women. Dealing with Candi when she worked at the bakery was not his best effort, but recently, a chat with her had made sense. He recalled the attitude she had with him and how she supported his challenge of having conversational charm. *How am I going to talk to Renee?*

Vincent closed his eyes, reaching for his college days revisiting how he approached the hottest woman on campus. Those days he watched Renee from a distance. He questioned his character. What happens if Renee rejects me again? He remembered her graduation day and the disappointment having nothing more with her than a greeting that turned sour.

Vincent's rocking slowed; the music became silent even

though it played the same as earlier. He remembered a day in the college cafeteria where Renee sat alone near the corner. He'd made no effort to meet her. He was hesitant to approach Renee, regardless of his crush. Five minutes of thought led to a half an hour, and after three-quarters of the hour had passed, he recognized that his fear was about to change. The window of opportunity crashed, and she left.

He recalled the last time he made his move, and her rejection pierced his heart. He remembered Candi's comment. "Mom remembered you at the graduation." He had flowers, and Renee didn't want to accept them. *Why would she now?* He pondered. *Why now, and not then?*

Vincent turned off the music, stood from his chair, and walked to the light switch on the wall. He glanced at the photo with his night vision and walked to his bedroom. He pulled up his cellular phone from his pocket and redialed Candi. "Hey, I was just thinking?"

Candi answered with a question. "Why aren't you calling Renee?"

"I was getting to that. Instead of calling, maybe we can meet for lunch."

"No, call her, first," Candi suggested. "Trust me, just call her."

"What if she doesn't answer?"

"What are you – 15 years old?" Candi frowned. "What do you do when someone doesn't answer your business call? You call them again."

"I get it. I do, but you have to understand that it's been years since I've talked to a woman outside of work."

"Then, pretend it's about work." Candi shook her head. "I don't know why Mom chose you."

"Wait, what?"

"Yeah, I thought you were a confident man, a straight shooter, and no-nonsense. That's what Renee needs, now. You can't go flip-flopping before you get to her. Be the man my mom saw."

"I see. I ah, but..." Vincent murmured.

"No buts...do it." Candi disconnected the call.

Vincent's eyes opened wide, eyebrows lifted, and his mouth opened at Candi's abrupt disconnection. He knows she's right. It was time he stopped hemming and hawing about Renee and got to it. He looked at his wristwatch. *Tomorrow, mid-morning, is a better time to call.*

***

Vincent rose with the sun like he had done so many mornings. He jumped out of bed and dressed for a jog. He clicked on the coffee timer and put his jogging shoes on before going outside. He stretched without thought. On his Fitbit phone connection, he tapped to track his distance and heart rate. He jogged on one of his favorite paths through the nearby park. Ten minutes in, his wrist buzzed. He glanced at it and read a text. *Call her today.* He nearly lost his balance while stepping on a slight incline.

Vincent jogged through the forest and on intermittent paths of the paved and dirt walkways. His mind recycled his approach and what he should say on his call with Renee. "Hi, Renee, it's been years since we've talked." *No that's not it — we have spoken, but not only the two of us.*

"What will I do? What if she says yes to a date? What if she is shy about her scars? What if I am not feeling good about her scars? No, I'm not that shallow." Vincent sighed. He watched his footing on the trail. Five minutes later. "I know. I'll ask her to walk by the river with me, in the evening. That way, she will not be nervous about whatever she fears. At least, I hope not." Vincent smiled, cleared his mind of mystery, and completed a working plan.

At his condominium, he stripped from his wet clothes and jumped into the shower. He washed, imagining Renee as he remembered her. His jitters were abnormal behavior for the confident businessman.

Vincent splashed cologne on himself, the brand he rarely used for a workday. He put on favorite shirts that appealed to most onlookers and, of course, to himself. He chose his best watch, classy enough to impress but simple enough to not catch a robber's eye. His loafers were of soft Italian leather, usually worn when going on a date or to an office meeting with potential business ventures. He looked himself over in the full mirror, pulled his collar straight and gave himself a grand smile as big as the moon. Vincent brushed his hair forward with his hand, looking the low trim style, and waves like the ocean before crashing ashore. He smiled, turning himself to profile a three-quarter pose. "You're ready. No way she'll turn you down." He pointed with right forefinger.

In his car, looked in the mirror while putting on eye shades, and snapped on his seatbelt. Vincent, carefully eased into traffic, pulling off for the office. *I'll call her from the office. It will be perfect timing.*

***

Renee finished her morning routine before seeing her roommate having coffee in the kitchen. "I didn't think you'd be up."

"I'm always up at this time. I had to be here before eight-thirty."

"But you live here, now."

"Where can I put my furniture?"

"I think in storage. You can find a nice unit." Renee poured coffee into a cup. "I don't have room, here."

"Right, you don't. The garage is full of our prints."

"Unless you find a way to get them out, because I don't see the importance of moving them, outside of selling them, like we've planned."

"Even for me?"

"Even for you." Renee held the cup and walked to the window; she viewed the garden. "It's another wonderful day for shooting."

"Why don't we go someplace else to shoot, today?"

Renee's eyes caught Candi's while she held the coffee with both hands. Her head cocked to the side, and she responded. "You know," she said without a blink, "I was thinking the same thing. It's a nice idea." Renee smiled before glancing at the garden. "I'm ready to see whatever I can snap a few photos of."

"Yea, umm." Candi raised her cup to her mouth before she mumbled. "You can shoot a place, this time." She sipped coffee and kept her eyes on the cup instead of Renee. "You said 'a place¹?"

"Remember going to some old restaurant and seeing photographs on the wall? I mean, those old pictures of famous people, or the way the store looked long ago, or pictures of patrons?"

"Of course, those pictures are interesting."

"My exact point. Why can't those pictures come from your eye? I mean, you can do something similar, and I can sell them much easier."

"Don't you have to get permission for taking pictures inside the venue?"

"Leave that to me." Candi walked to the kitchen sink and placed the coffee cup in the middle of it. "I have a plan for the first location."

"I'm sure you do." Renee shook her head.

"I did," she murmured. "It's a promising idea." She walked to her purse in the office, listening for Renee's response.

Renee had never used her photography eye for a location or anything outside of plants and nature. "I don't think I have an eye for places, and I don't look at people." Renee walked to the kitchen table and placed the cup on the opposite side of her. "What makes you think taking a picture of a place will be the same as plants?" Renee's eyebrows lifted and her eyes widened. "Because you have an eye that captures the essence of everything you see." Candi smirked at Renee's facial response.

"Umph, you have to trust me on this." Candi smiled. "That's my point. I do trust you...but..." Renee took in a breath. "I'm still...well, you know. Something Mom and I shared when you got anxious about an idea."

"Didn't they work?" Candi retrieved her cell from her purse and tapped 'redial' before returning to the kitchen and holding the phone to her ear.

"That depends on how you define work." Renee giggled, leaving the kitchen for her office.

***

Vincent arrived at his second busiest coffee/wine bar in the city. He parked his car in the back corner of the plaza's parking lot, always allowing customers front-row parking. After retrieving his iPad case and his record-keeping booklet, he exited the car. His cell phone rang, startling him. "Hello?"

"Where the hell are you?" Candi asked.

"What do you mean?" Vincent replied. "Wait, you greet people that foul in the morning?"

"Formalities, schu-malities, why does it matter?" Candi looked to see if Renee is headed to the kitchen. "I'm bringing Renee to the shop."

"Why?"

"You're taking too damn long to get things going."

"I work at my pace."

"Look, Mom's gone, and I promised her to do this."

"Yeah, but can't we at least set up a time that's right?" Vincent walked through the store's entrance. "I mean, which location are you planning on?"

"What kind of questions are those?" Candi sighed. "For a guy who does business well, you sure are a schmuck at dating."

"I've been told that before." Vincent waved at his staff and walked to the back office. "I can't believe you have the nerve to say that to me."

"Look, she's going there this afternoon. I will have her bring the camera and start shooting at your place. I'll tell her you contracted her to do the shoot. That way, she'll go freely without feeling like I'm setting her up."

"I don't like that idea."

"Why not?" Candi shook her head. "Tell me why not!"

"I may have to pay you for something I hadn't budgeted for." Vincent placed the iPad and record book on the desk. "Besides, it's doing so well. Why would I pay for a marketing cost I don't need?"

"Because you need this for growth," Candi responded, "You're growing, regardless, and having those photos will do you some good."

"Let me think about it." Vincent sat in the desk chair. "Damn, there you go again. Focus! We have a mission."

Candi paused. "We'll be there after lunch. Few people are hanging around there, then anyway."

"I'll show up at 1:30. Start without me if you arrive first."

"Good man." Candi looked at the cell phone's screen and tapped the icon ending the call. "He had better show up." She watched Renee through the kitchen window, hoping that she had not given her plan away.

***

Renee picked up her camera and placed it in the camera case with the shoulder strap. She loved using this case because it allowed her to use the camera without taking it out of its protective leather. She lifted the camera to her eye, pushed a couple of buttons, and, snap crackle, the camera clicked. She removed the camera from her eye and whispered, "See, I can do this." She walked to Candi, sitting in the office recliner, and showed her the review screen on the back of the camera. "It looks pretty good, huh?"

"Yeah, not bad," Candi agreed. "See, I told you. You're just as good with things as you are with plants."

"I am starting to believe you." Renee uncovered her right eye. "My problem is going without my scarf. And sometimes it gets in the way."

"Your right eye is just as important as your left. You can use either for this job. It's perfect timing that no one is around."

"Are you sure?" Renee asked.

"I am sure. It's late after the lunch rush, and only four people, at best, will be there. Besides, he only sells coffee during daylight hours." Candi giggled. "You can't drink wine while taking these pictures."

"I didn't think I would." Renee shook her head in disbelief. "I'm never drunk on the job."

"This isn't a job." Candi's eyes grew. "I mean, it's a job, and we'll make good money if the shots are as good as the plant photos."

"You are up to something." Renee let the camera drop from the holding strap, which landed around her waist. She picked up her purse and maneuvered her scarf. "Let's get this over with."

"It's a little early." Candi looked at her watch. "I thought we'd wait a few minutes to let the crowd disappear."

"How much longer?" Renee walked to the door. "I want to do this before I change my mind."

Candi grabbed her purse and followed Renee to the front door. "We can go now; it's either now or never."

"My point exactly."

***

Vincent was on his third cup of coffee before he scanned his watch. He was surprised at the time, five minutes past one o'clock. He closed his record book, packed it with the iPad, picked up the cup, and walked to the coffee bar. He discarded the cold coffee into the sink and placed the cup in the washer.

"Hey, Steve, I'm heading to the main store," Vincent shouted. He waved at the other baristas on his way to the front exit. He unlocked the car door and swung it open, threw the book and iPad in the front passenger's seat, and got in. After his foot pressed the brake and his finger pressed the start button, he snapped on the seatbelt and pressed 'dial' on his screen display.

Vincent drove to the parking lot exit, looked both ways before he safely entered the flow of traffic. When he pressed the gas pedal to speed up, his auto brake assist stopped him cold.

What he saw next startled him, because no one had ever walked into the path of his car right when he did not see anyone around. He pulled the car over closest to the curb, put it in park, turned on the emergency flashers and exited the car. "Hey, buddy, are you okay?" he asked.

"Why did you stop?" The young man sat on the curb. "Why did you stop?"

"I don't hit people." Vincent explained, before asking, "Why on earth would you walk in front of an oncoming car?"

"I don't know," the young man said. "Actually, I...really, it's none of your business." He stood from the curb and with a balled fist, he swung at Vincent.

Fortunately, Vincent stepped out of the way and kept his arm from retreating and yelled, "What the hell are you doing?!"

Vincent frowned. "Why would you want to hit me?!"

"I don't know...actually, I do know." The young man raised his foot and kicked Vincent on his left thigh. "I need you to hit me."

Vincent pushed the young man back, stepped to his car, and felt pain in his left thigh. "Damn drugs." He got into the car, closed the door and quickly dialed 911. He gave information to the dispatcher at the end of the line. Vincent shared the address and the description of the man who'd tried to inflict pain on himself. He moved his car through traffic and returned to the plaza's parking lot. "Drugs can make a person do shit they don't understand," he said aloud, looking to the passenger side as if someone listened to his rant. "Damn it!" Vincent looked at his watch.

The police arrived in time to watch the young man walk to the middle of the intersection and stand in front of oncoming traffic. Despite the blaring horns, he didn't budge from danger. Vincent watched the officer run into traffic and speak to the pedestrian. "Hey, why are you here?" he shouted. Without a second thought, Vincent got out of the car, and watched the officer bring the young man back to the curb and put cuffs on him, then pushing the young man into the back seat.

"You did that pretty well," Vincent said to the officer.

"It's Jimmy," the officer said. "He's high again and does stupid things to hurt himself."

"Then it's a good thing not many people are violent." Vincent looked at his thigh. "This is his footprint, where he kicked me."

"You can press charges for assault, and that will lock him up."

"No, it didn't hurt. I'm just shocked that a young man like him would do that."

"I hope he stays in rehabilitation, this time."
"This time?" Vincent asked.

"Yes, it's his third that I know of," the officer responded. "Why is he doing this?"

"His parents left him as a teen and haven't opened the door to him, since. He has a foster family, but he's too old to be a part of that. So, he's a street kid."

"Street kid?"

"Lives on the street. I only know about him because I get to take him to detention every time, he does something stupid." The officer shook his head, looked at the back seat of the police cruiser, and moved to the driver's side of the car. "I gather you're the one who called."

"I am."

"Are you pressing charges from his kicking you?"

"I don't think I need to. I hope you can get him some help."

"Yeah, me too." The police officer clicked on his seatbelt and closed the car door. He waved at Vincent and drove off. Vincent followed the process and drove towards the oldest coffee/wine bar he owned. "Dial the last number called," he instructed his app.

Candi walked to the corner of the coffee/wine bar and distanced herself from Renee. She answered the call. "Where the hell are you?"

"I got delayed."

"Don't mess this up."

"How can I mess something up when nothing's started?"

"That's my point." Candi scanned the area for Renee. "You have to break the ice, today!"

"What's so important that it has to be done today?" Vincent stopped at an intersection. "You are pressing me as if it's just before the end of the world."

"Look, college boy, I promised my mom I will do this and you're screwing things up," Candi angrily whispered. "Don't get on my bad side."

"You don't have to go there." Vincent turned left onto the main thoroughfare. "I don't want to fight with you. I don't think you'll win."

"Like you don't want this?" Candi frowned before she looked at Renee.

"It isn't that I don't want it, but I've done without it for years."

"But Mom said…" Candi looked up. "Yeah, get here, and we'll see how things go." She ended the call.

Renee shook her head. "Mom said what?"

"You're going to be great, and I wanted him to know the talent before he sees your work," Candi replied. "Are you finished with shooting everything you want?"

"I think so. Not much more than chairs and a few baristas." Renee held the camera towards the bar. "I need to get their permission."

"I have the documents. Besides, it's their place of employment. If Vincent says its part of the job, we don't need a release."

"How did you get to be so smart with this?"

"I studied, and I've learned a lot about photos and marketing."

"Good, really good." Renee walked to the bar and asked, "Do you mind if I take pictures of you in action?"

"No, not at all," the baristas responded in unison.

Vincent arrived at the location and walked into the establishment. He looked for a woman with a camera. He did not see anyone who was walking around and took pictures. "I missed them," he said.

"Actually, no, you didn't." His employee pointed to the corner where two women were looking at a camera.

"Oh, thanks." Vincent nodded, heading to the table. "Hey, ladies," he said upon approach, with a smile bigger than Texas. "I am glad you're still here. Can we talk about what my ideas are?"

"Why would you talk about that?" Candi asked.

"Because it's my coffee/wine shop. Why else?"

"It's looking pretty good." Renee smiled. "Don't stress about what we'll do with the pictures before we show them to you."

"Why not?" asked Vincent. "I get scared of my pictures every month. You know — some review about the wine bar with a magazine, and they include pictures."

"You aren't held liable for a relationship break, are you?" "Why on earth would you ask that?" Vincent peeped at Candi and returned his focus to Renee. "Never mind, I don't think you're serious about that question."

"I most certainly am." Renee returned the focus to her camera. "This one should be good."

"Are you going to let me see it?"

"Not yet." Renee guarded the camera. "I'll make a portfolio for you and we'll sit down together and see what you think. It's better than seeing my work as if it's nude."

"Okay, I guess you know what you're doing," Vincent smiled. He walked from the table, abruptly stopped by Candi.

"Get to it, buddy. You broke the ice, now take advantage of it," she instructed him.

Vincent turned to the table and glanced at Renee, who fought not to stare at her scarf. "I understand that you now remember me."

"Of course, I do, because it was difficult trying to see myself, then. I was hoping that you wouldn't remember me differently from what you see today."

"But I remember you because I always thought you were impressive." Vincent smiled. "I remember our first encounter."

"You do?" Renee adjusted the scarf. "I bet you thought I was a bitch."

"No, why would I think that?"

"I had no time for junior classmen." She looked at Vincent.

"But it seems like I may have been mistaken."

Vincent pulled a chair from the table. "Do you mind?"

"No, go right ahead." Renee held her scarf with one hand, grabbed the camera with the other, and stared at the snapshots she took. "I think these pictures are pretty good."

"I bet they are." Vincent's eyes projected his thoughts, his heartbeat quickened, and his mind ran with ideas about Renee. He looked at the smooth side of her face. His smile grew and he covered his mouth, masking the flashback of what he remembered in college. His hand muffled his words. "I have a great eye for photoshoots." He dropped his hand. "I said, you have a great eye for pictures."

"I try, but my sister believes that I do."

"She's right this time." Vincent laughed. "I mean, she's a character."

"I know, and so was my mom."

"Your mom was a sweet woman." Vincent nodded his head. "You would know better than me, since she was your mother."

"I am glad you noticed." Renee sat the camera up on its side with the lens facing her and the back facing Vincent. "Push the arrow to the right and watch the slide show."

"Okay." Vincent followed instructions. "Oh, wow, great shot. Where is this?"

"Here!" she explained. "Turn around."

Vincent paused the camera snapshot review and turned to look at the coffee/wine shop. "You made it look different. How did you do this?"

"It's what I see."

"It's incredible. I can't believe a camera can make things look so different."

"I've learned a lot, since working on a few things." Renee's scarf relaxed while she picked up the camera with both hands. Turning the camera around and putting it to her good eye, the one she used to look through the peep lens, she pressed her trigger finger. Snap, the camera responded. Quick shots followed—snap, snap, snap. Renee pulled the camera from her face and leaned the lens towards the table. "Here, look at these," she directed Vincent.

Vincent could not believe his face was pixelated on the screen of the camera. He looked at the few shots and shook his head with surprise. "It seems like you have a great eye for people, too."

"You are the first person I've photographed."

"I feel special."

"I get a funny feeling that you are," Renee smiled.

Candi returned with the coffee and placed one ceramic cup in front of Renee and the other near an empty chair. "That's your time, buddy. I need to chat with my sister."

"What?" Vincent asked.

"I'm sorry, business calls," Candi responded. She glanced at

Vincent, winked an eye, and nodded her head towards Renee.

"Oh, oh yeah. I've got things to do, too." Vincent rose. "It's been nice chatting with you. I hope we do it again soon."

"It was nice. Thanks, and I hope you enjoy the photos. I'll send you those pictures of you when I get home."

"I'd like that. Nice seeing you too, Candi. We should talk about business when you get a chance."

"Yep, sure thing, Vincent." Candi smiled watching Vincent leave. From the corner of her eye, she saw Renee watching Vincent the same way. "Not bad, huh?" Candi asked.

"What?" Renee shook her head and quickly grabbed her scarf. "What did you say?"

"Not bad, and you know it. Stop acting like you didn't stare."

"I watched. I remember him - but not like I see him now."

"He didn't think about your scarf, did he?" Candi grabbed the bottom of the scarf. "I don't think you'll need this."

"I was surprised he didn't say anything about my scars...but time will tell."

"Interesting conversation?"

"Basic." Renee looked at Candi. "I knew you were up to this."

"Just looking out for my big sister."

Renee raised an eyebrow. "I don't need you to do that."

"Are you complaining, or thanking me?"

Chapter 20

Let's Talk

One week had passed since Vincent and Renee conversed at the coffee shop. Candi made sure Vincent did his homework to impress Renee. She drilled him on her likes and dislikes, her fears, and strengths, and how she loved her garden. Candi also prepared him about the way she appeared, with those dreaded lifetime scars. "Remember, Vincent," Candi said, "there is a beautiful woman behind the scarf."

"I know. Why don't you believe me when I tell you I remember her before the accident?"

"Because I know how fickle men are when it comes to looks."

"There you go again, putting all men in one basket." Vincent sighed. "We're not all alike." He frowned. "Nothing like gold-digging ass women." He looked at Candi with a raised eyebrow and waited for her response.

"Are you talking about me?"

"Am I?" He paused. "I think you get my point." Vincent walked to the coffee counter and pointed for the barista to pass his cup. "Why did you come here this morning?"

"To talk to you." Candi shadowed him. "How about being a gentleman and get me a mocha cappuccino."

"See? Gold-digging ass woman." Vincent laughed. "Gotcha!"

"No, asshole, you didn't get me." Candi shook her head. "What a bad way to start someone's morning."

"Really, you aren't so bad after all." Vincent smiled at Candi before ordering coffee from the barista. "And can you fill this with that flavor of the day, please?" He passed his cup forward. "Thank you." He retrieved a ten-dollar bill from his front pocket and placed it on the counter. "Take it from this and tip yourself."

The barista nodded. "Thanks, boss."

"See? You aren't so bad, either." Candi nodded before smiling. "Mom had you pegged right."

"Sweet woman, your mother."

"I wondered what she saw in you. I had no idea she'd like another asshole." Candi made a scowling face.

Vincent shook his head. "Another asshole?" He glanced at the barista before he turned his attention to Candi. "You mean. her husband?"

"I want her to tell you what happened, but I will just say this. She's widowed."

"Oh, snap. Why do I feel I'm being set up?"

"No worries. If he were alive, I don't think she would have visited the coffee shop as much."

Vincent grabbed the coffee from the barista and handed Candi the mocha cappuccino she'd ordered. "Here." Vincent walked towards an empty table in the back. He turned to see if Candi followed. "I want to know more about that relationship."

Candi sipped coffee before she arrived at the table. "I don't think it's my place to share."

"You've shared a lot to this point. Why not tell me?" Vincent held a chair for Candi and directed her to take a seat.

She sat in the opposite chair. "Save the courtesy for Renee." She placed the coffee cup on the table before she looked at Vincent, who sat in front of her. "I can't tell you what happened because only she and mom know the whole story. But I will say that if mom liked you, she had a way of making things right with Renee."

"What the hell does that mean?"

"Don't ask, act!" Candi sipped coffee and retrieved the cell phone from her purse. "I need to make talk about business."

"Make your call. I have things to do."

"No, my business is with you." She tapped her phone to open an app.

***

Renee arrived two hours late for the appointment. Vincent stood at the office door and watched her approach. He smirked at her appearance, brown boots, high legging socks- pushed-down to her ankles, cargo shorts, a tee-shirt, a cargo vest, a bush hat blended with a thin mosquito net, and her silk scarf, to cover her scars.

"Safari shoot?" Vincent laughed and shook his head.

Renee grabbed the camera strapped to her shoulder. "I'm sorry I'm late. I had a previous engagement that I had to make."

"Were you the model?" Vincent pointed at her feet and moved his finger upward. "I mean, you're a great model right now."

"Don't be silly." Renee looked around the coffee/wine shop. "I shot this location already."

"Oh, that isn't why you are here."

"It's not?" Renee released the camera allowing it to hang from its shoulder strap. "I thought for sure Candi said to be here for a shoot." She reached for her cell phone in the side cargo pants pocket. With quick fingers, she swiped the cell phone's face, and it lit brighter than a stage's spotlight. "I can't believe her." Renee's fingers tapped the phone screen.

"It's right here." She pointed and read aloud, "Coffee/Wine Shop Shoot - 9 am."

"Well, it's past eleven, and she's right, but it's not this location."

"Why did she say to come here?"

"We thought you'd like a sit-down conversation about what I'd like to see from your shots."

"That's not possible." Renee tapped her phone and it darkened. She put it back in her cargo pants pocket. "I shoot what I see, regardless of what you may want."

"No customer relations skills."

"I do this, and Candi manages the business." Renee turned. "Maybe you should call her and discuss what I do."

"We have, and I'm sure of what I want."

Vincent moved closer to Renee. He lightly touched her shoulder. "If you'd sit with me, I can explain."

Renee had not felt a man's simple, calm hand in years. She rarely hugged her dad since her mother had passed. She stared at Vincent's hand. "I think I can manage a few minutes. But make it quick." She glanced at her wristwatch. "I have another appointment in an hour."

"Let's sit over here." Vincent pointed to a back table. He led her with his arm. "Over here." He stepped aside and rushed to a chair. He pulled it out and stood behind it. "I thought we'd have tea or wine. Which do you prefer?"

"I don't think I'll have anything." Renee put the camera on the table and sat in the chair. "I don't have time to chat. I thought I'd get to shooting and be on my way."

"I wouldn't mind you doing that, but at store number 5."

"Why didn't you tell Candi that?" Renee watched Vincent sit across from her. "I would have gone there."

"Because..." Vincent paused, looked at the table, and scanned her scarred hand. His eyes rose slowly to hers. "I like you. I have always liked you. I would love to take you out. I don't care about your past." Vincent's eyes connected to hers, sparkling from the warmth within his soul. "I like you, and I hope you don't mind going out with me."

Renee sat back in the chair, her eyes caught his gaze, piercing the ideas she had about him. She flashed to college days when their interaction was distant. She lowered her chin to her chest. "I'm not so sure…"

"Sure, you are." Vincent quickly added, "I've watched you since your mom died. I have watched your confidence grow these days, staying busy and going everywhere. I've paid attention to you. I really have."

"But I'm not like other women." Renee swallowed. "I'm not a perfect-looking woman."

"And I'm a perfect-looking man?" Vincent touched her good hand. "Look at me. I'm nothing like I once was, especially since being a college sophomore."

"Thank God you aren't." She laughed.

"I'm not, but I *am* a man—a man who admires you. And I have admired you from the very first time I saw you on campus."

Renee met his eyes, moved her hand from under his, and spoke with a soft voice. "I've been broken, and I am not sure how anyone can fix me. I have gone through rough times, and I don't think I should be sitting here. If it weren't for my mother, I probably wouldn't be here now."

Renee breathed deeply before adding, "I'm not a perfect woman. I can't promise to be fair because I don't know what I'm capable of doing." She lowered her head and focused on the camera. "I haven't been with anyone since losing my husband, and the accident has stopped me from thinking that was possible." She waited for his response, and after moments of silence, she said, "I've accepted it."

She looked at Vincent, grabbed her camera, and rose from the chair. "I'm good, right now. Thanks for trying. I do appreciate it." Renee left the table and walked faster than usual to her car. Tears fell from her good eye and her hand shook in her pocket as she tried to retrieve the car fob. She whispered, "Why now?" as if asking her mother whose image stood firm in her mind.

Renee arrived home instead of going to her next photo shoot. Her phone chimed and she reached for it. "Hello," she answered.

"Mrs. Yarbrough," the client addressed her. "I'm sorry we're missing you."

"I had an emergency. I am sorry I didn't call you first."
"Everything okay?"

"It's going to be." Renee looked at the front door of her house. "It's going to be, as soon as I get inside."

"I hope so," the client wished. "We love your work, so as soon as you find the time, can you fit us into your schedule?"

"I'll get Candi to call you to make sure it happens." Renee grabbed her camera, purse, and key fob with one hand while she held the cell phone to her ear with the other. "I am sure we'll get to you within a day."

"That will be great." The client paused. "We'll wait for Candi's call."

"Sure thing." Renee breathed, put the phone in her purse pocket, kicked the car door closed, and walked to the front door. She put the keys in the door and unlocked it, then pushed the door open.

Candi stood at the foyer and asked, "Why?"

"I didn't feel like it," Renee responded.

"He is one of my…" Candi shook her head. "…I mean um, our…" She paused. "…better clients."

"Like Vincent?" Renee walked past Candi and headed to the

office. She placed her bag, camera, and cell phone on the desk. "If you want me to do a shoot, how about finishing everything before I get there?" Renee walked behind the desk, shook her head for confirmation, and like raindrops falling on hot coals, she seethed with steam. "I could have finished both jobs, had you been honest."

"I *was* honest. And I sent you with good intentions." Candi shook her head. "I bet you weren't listening to him."

"Don't you dare." Renee looked through the crack between window curtains. "I can't believe you'd try to set up a date."

"Did he say it was going to be a date?"

"Damn it." Renee turned to face Candi. "You did this without considering my wishes. You know damn well that I'm not ready."

"Says who?"

"Me. I said I'm not ready."

"Mom knew you'd avoid becoming fully normal."

"I am trying. Why do you think I'm out snapping photos?"

"You love it, don't you?" Candi shook her head. "He is perfect, and I'm not going to tell you how much of a perfect man he is for you. Don't blow it."

"Blow it?" Renee pointed at her outfit. "He noticed my clothes, and we talked about my outfit." She paused before saying, "And he laughed at me."

"Then why are you here?"

"You could have at least told me what the hell you were doing. I am a professional woman. I take shooting seriously."

"I know you do. It's why I schedule those shoots." Candi planted her fist on the desk. "Besides, you need to talk more with Vincent."

"I what?" Renee shook her head. "I don't want to get involved yet. Don't you know I'm not ready?"

"Did you hear yourself when you came into the door?" "I heard everything."

"Did you?" Candi approached Renee and touched her shoulder. "Did you hear the excitement in your voice? Do you realize that you came home despite having a scheduled shoot that you take seriously?"

"I..." Renee gripped her camera. "I know I'm not ready because I'm too focused on my work."

"Excuses, now." Candi grabbed both of Renee's shoulders and faced her. "You have to live. Mom and I agreed, it's time you do it now."

"Mom?"

"Yes, Mom." Candi's eyes focused on Renee's. "I made a promise to Mom that I'd do whatever it takes to get you involved."

"Mom?" Renee put her head on Candi's shoulder. "I miss Mom, more than you will ever know."

Candi caressed Renee's head like their mother did when she consoled them, while they were kids. "She wants you to give Vincent a chance. He is a nice man. He's crazy about you."

"Really?"

"Mom saw it. She believed it. And she told me to make it happen."

"Okay." Renee lifted her head and stared at Candi. "You're still a little shit." Renee stepped away from Candi, sat the camera on the desk, and went upstairs.

Twenty minutes passed, and Renee had not returned downstairs. Candi made four calls to reschedule the recent shoot Renee had missed. Other calls held personal goals, which included a chat with Vincent.

"What did you tell Renee today?" Candi asked.

"Nothing. I mean, nothing that would push her into leaving." Vincent admitted, "Maybe I like her."

"Call her when you get a chance. Make sure it's in the evening, so she doesn't have an excuse not to talk to you."

"I don't think I'll do that."

"Why?!" Candi creamed.

"What the hell?" Renee looked at Candi on the phone from the door. "Who pissed you off?"

"Nobody," Candi responded.

"I'll call you back," she whispered into the phone. "I was talking to a friend."

"Some friend who accepts you screaming like that. If I were that friend, I'd have hung up."

"You aren't." Candi frowned. "And that's a remarkable thing."

"Smartass." Renee picked up the camera from the desk. "I'm heading to the garden. I may see something I like."

"Yeah, do that. It has always helped you figure things out. I am sure you'll get a message before you come back inside. "

***

Vincent put the cell phone on the desk and walked to the main area. He shook his head while standing in the back of the wine coffee bar. He looked at the floor and up again, frowning at Candi abrupt with their call in the middle of a serious discussion. He didn't get the chance to explain why he hadn't talked to Renee. Vincent crossed his arms, frowning in disgust, and wondered if he'd made a grave mistake.

"Damn it. What is it? Why can't I call her?"

He looked ahead and walked toward the bar, grabbed a clipboard from the wall and stepped into the storage room. He counted the boxes, looking at each to distinguish wine from coffee. With every checkmark on the clipboard, he imagined talking to Renee. "You are amazing, from what I remember and observing you're fight today…." He tapped a box, reading the label. "No that doesn't work."

Vincent walked to another section in the storage room. "One, two, three, four…" He placed a note next to a column on the paper. He stopped counting.

"I admired you in school and I admire you now, even though we've changed." He smiled. "A better line." Vincent resumed counting at the third box. "One… I bet you're wondering what happened to me over the years. Let me tell you," He swallowed before he added, "that I've never stopped thinking of you." He heard a voice and snapped out of his thought process.

"Vincent," a barista called. "Can I have a box of coffee, please?"

"Oh." His curt voice rose. "Sure." Vincent grabbed a blend

he loved selling. "Here you go."

"Thanks." The barista grabbed the box and exited the storage room. Vincent noted the change on the clipboard and continued counting. "Ninety," he mumbled, before noting another notch on the report. I need to ask her out," he said aloud. "Yeah, just call her. Her answer will either be yes or no!" Vincent walked through the door, headed for the wall to replace the clipboard. "I'm going to call her." He went to his desk, grabbed the cell phone on the desktop, looked up a text from Candi, and dialed the number she sent.

"Hello," Renee answered.

"Hi, it's me, Vincent. I wanted to …" Vincent paused. "I don't know why I'm having such a tough time asking you out."

"You are?" Renee smiled. "Actually, I wanted to talk to you about that."

"You do?" Vincent's voice rose with excitement.

"I'm not ready, regardless of what Candi tells you."

"Ah," he paused. "I see." Vincent fell silent, the air from his lungs escaped, and he closed his eyes before responding. "I kind of expected that answer." Vincent took a deep breath. "Wait. Don't hang up, let me tell you what I have held in my heart for years." Vincent waited for a response, and after a moment, not hearing her voice, he continued.

"I've admired you from the moment I noticed you. And since then, I've wondered if I were the man in your life, would you have loved in return. I dreamed of treating you better than God's first kiss upon this earth. I dreamed I somehow influenced your mind to believe in us. I dreamed I grasped the passion in your heart. And I dreamed I danced with your soul to a song we understood. I had hoped my dream would become our reality. We would fall in love and share everything."

He paused long enough to add, "I've lived with the idea of you as my standard for women, and if any woman didn't measure up, she wasn't worthy of my attention." Vincent listened to death reckoning whispers no one could hear, hoping Renee would say something. "Are you still there?"

"I'm here," Renee softly replied.

"Good, because I have more to share." Vincent took a breath. "I haven't stopped thinking about you. I relive the moment you stood at the Mexican Cantina over and over again." He smiled. "You were my angel."

"My God, you remembered that?"

"Yes. You impressed me, and I haven't been impressed like that since."

Renee's response was curt. "I'm nothing like that now, Vincent."

"But you're better. Regardless of whatever accident." Vincent's confidence rose. "Your past is something we can work through. I want to be in your future."

Renee paused, touched her scarred face with her patterned hand, and whispered, "You've said a mouthful."

"Did I change your mind?" Vincent smiled, crossed his fingers, and hoped for the best.

Chapter 21

The Date

Renee answered the bedroom door in a dress hugging the curvatures of her exquisite body, something she had not worn since the first year she and Marvin dated. She wasn't motivated for an extenuating exclamation, inviting a man's territorial response, but she smiled in the mirror before closing her mind to enticing a male onlooker. Candi stood at the door, watching Renee walk in front of the mirror. She couldn't believe her eyes, seeing her sister dress in something so seductive without being forthright sexually appealing. The dress was nothing she had in mind for Renee's date. But seeing Renee smile prancing in the mirror, seeing how the dress looked on her, gave warmth in Candi's heart. Renee twisted and turned, in front of the mirror without care to distorted wrinkles of her skin. Instead, the dress applauded the way her fantastic gift held the dress's fit. Renee turned from one side to the other, rubbed her stomach to a smaller size, and turned the other way. Her smile, her glow, and her imagination reflected instantaneous beauty.

Renee nodded. "It's time I tried this."

Candi smiled in agreement. "You look amazing."

"I never thought I'd wear something like this again."

"I am so happy you are. It's like you haven't gained an ounce since college."

"Actually, I haven't." Renee giggled. "And you know what else?" Renee paused.

"No, I don't." Candi leaned her head to one side. "I really don't."

"I look like I deserve a night on the town."

"I wouldn't push that on you, since it's your first time in years." Candi reminded.

"I hope he has good plans that don't put me in a spotlight."

"I would change my dress if you don't want to be in everyone's eye."

"I want to be in his eyes, right now."

"What?" Candi's voice rose with excitement. "You what? Did I hear that right?"

"I need to get a life. You said it a hundred times." Renee smiled. "And you're right."

"Mark this day on the calendar." Candi giggled before leaving the room and headed downstairs to the office. She retrieved the cell from her purse and pressed autodial 8, calling Vincent.

"You better do something great tonight," Candi said with conviction.

"Why are you worried?" Vincent spoke with ease taking Candi by surprise.

"She's giving you a chance, and I don't want her disappointed."

"I don't want to blow it, either. Give me a break and trust me. I got this." Vincent tapped the red receiver icon on his cell phone. "Damn, who am I dating?" Vincent walked to the mirror that flanked his front door. He posed, smiled, and said, "I can't go wrong with this look."

He picked up his keys from the kitchen counter and walked to his car after securing the front door. He entered the car, readjusted the mirror, and pressed the start button. The car engine growled igniting his excitement. "It's happening!" He turned the entertainment system on, and music filled the car's cabin. His foot touched the brake, he clicked on his seatbelt, pressed the car into drive, and drove into traffic. He felt ants marching through his extremities and butterflies danced around his chest, making his heartbeat faster.

"Wow, she's finally going out with me." Vincent tapped the car phone and dialed Renee. "Hello Renee, I'm enroute," Vincent said when she answered.

"I need fifteen minutes before I'm ready. Can you give me that?"

"Sure. It takes me at least 30 minutes to get to you. I'm letting you know I'm on my way."

"I'll be ready when you get here." Renee disconnected the call.

Vincent sighed. "She doesn't sound enthused." He lifted his foot off the accelerator pedal and the car responded, slowing his journey. The song on the radio reflected the deacceleration of his act. *Damn, even the radio knows what's up*, he thought. At the next intersection, Vincent stopped at a florist, walked in and looked at the selection in the refrigerated section. "What are these blue called?" he asked the florist.

"Morning glory." She responded.

"What about the white one, it's kind of long leaf." Vincent pointed.

The florist picked it up, "You mean this one, right?"

"Yes. I think it would look good mixed with a couple of roses."

"Nice combination." The florist said, "I'll add baby's breaths to it for color."

"Huh?"

"The green with the little white tips." The florist smiled. "You don't do this often."

"A special night."

"I hope she loves it."

"I hope so too." Vincent watched the florist wrap the flowers together. When she completed wrapping, he retrieved his credit card. With flowers in hand, he returned to his car, and continued his journey to Renee's house.

Back in the car, he continued his journey, passing one of his coffee/wine shop locations. He smiled seeing multiple cars out front, something he had not expected, especially without scheduled entertainment. The smile grew greater than a full moon in spring. His spirits lifted before he pressed the phone icon on his steering wheel. "Renee, I'm about ten minutes from you." He disconnected after leaving a message.

Whatever happens tonight, happens. I at least got the chance. I'm happy that my business keeps growing, and if I can get Renee to share my success, it would be awesome. He pressed the gas pedal and accelerated through the streets while he reviewed his plan for the evening. Vincent tapped his phone list with his finger and dialed Le Chateau, a French cuisine restaurant. He confirmed his reservation, then dialed the Opious Theater that was playing Le Madeline, a musical, and confirmed his box office tickets.

So far, so good, he thought. *One more intersection and I am there.* He listened to his navigation. "Turn right." Vincent followed the instruction and looked for the house number. He followed the soft-lit street in search of even numbers. He slowly drove with a focus on every house until he arrived at Renee's driveway. He pulled into the driveway and took in the beauty of the wrap-around porch. With flowers in hand, he walked to the door and rang the doorbell.

And what he did not expect was Candi, who stood in the open doorway. His head nodded. "Hey, I don't have to tell you why I'm here."

"You're a smartass."

"Is she ready?" Vincent asked. "We have a short time to get to our reservations."

"She's ready, but you have to make sure she has fun. Or you'll never get a second chance."

"Pressure a guy - will you?" Vincent lifted the flowers in response to Renee's arrival. "Ah, wow!" His eyes watered. "You're…you are…I mean…"

"Yes, I thought so, too," Candi admitted.

"Beautiful!" Vincent handed Renee the flowers.

"Thank you, I love them." Renee took the flowers into the kitchen and looked for a vase. "It's important to do this now."

Vincent held his watch up and tapped on it. "Well, we don't have too much time to spare. With traffic, we'll arrive right at our dinner reservation."

"This only takes a minute." Renee stood at the kitchen sink and filled the vase she retrieved with cool water. "They love cool water."

Vincent waited in the foyer near the front door, glanced at Candi, and smirked. "No worries, I got this," he reminded her.

"You better." Candi pointed directly at his chest. "Don't disappoint her."

"I got this," Vincent smirked, which turned into a smile upon Renee's approach. "Wow. I mean, this is going to be my reaction all night – WOW!"

"I'm ready." Renee grabbed her small purse and a shawl. "Just in case it gets cool wherever we go."

"Oh, you don't need it," Vincent replied. "I'll keep you warm." He smiled and opened the door.

"What a line," Candi said. "Can you two get going? I have plans."

"Who's stopping you?" Renee looked at her. "Make sure you lock up."

"Yes, mother dear."

Renee turned to Vincent. "I'm following you."

He pointed his arm towards the car. "Your carriage awaits."

Renee giggled and stepped out of the doorway onto the few steps of her porch. Vincent scurried to aid her descent onto the driveway. He opened the passenger's car door, admiring the way Renee's tight dress accented her curves and long legs. He lightly touched her back and her arm, then aided her to the passenger's seat. He felt the soft silky material of her dress, and the touch sent a forgotten energy up his arm. When she sat down, he recognized a different scarf he had never seen, covering her scars.

Vincent snapped into the driver's seat, started the engine, and reversed into the street. He tapped a button on the steering wheel and classical music invaded silence. "I remember how beautiful you were in college, but wow—after so many years, you're still the most gorgeous woman who's ever blessed me with her presence."

"Vincent, you don't have to flatter me." Renee blushed. "I'm already in the car."

"But I want you to know what I am thinking." Vincent stopped at the intersection, delaying the car's movement, before turning. "You don't mind classical music, for now, do you?"

"It's your car. Driver's choice." She touched her scarf. "Besides, I had heard you never touch a man's car radio."

"I never heard of that." Vincent laughed and glanced at Renee. "I'm open to anything you would like to listen to."

"This is fine." Renee responded before asking, "What's the plan?"

"Well." Vincent kept his eyes on the road before glancing at Renee. "Dinner at a French restaurant."

"I like French."

Vincent smiled. "Okay, next is a show at the Opious – a French play called…"

"…Le Madeline." Renee smiled, after answering. "You're going all out, aren't you?"

"No, not all out. I mean, we didn't fly in a private jet to some beachfront or high-rise building with a view of the city."

"I could swear this is the same thing."

***

At dinner, Renee moved the candle past her glass of water. The soft light fell on her good side. She picked up the menu and read the entrees. "Do you have any suggestions?"

"Allow me." Vincent raised his hand, and the waiter came to the table.

"May I take your order?" the waiter asked.

"For starters, we'll have the Bistro Salad. For our main entrée, she will have the Coq Au Vin. For me, I think I'll have the Cognac Shrimp with Beurre Blanc." He handed the menu to the waiter, who took his and Renee's. The waiter repeated the order, and before he could ask about wine, Vincent interjected,

"Oh, we'll think about dessert when we're done." "Good idea," Renee said.

The waiter responded, "Thank you. I will get that order in. May I suggest a delicious wine for the table?"

"Renee, are you up for wine?"

"Sure, I don't mind." She smiled, noticing Vincent's

gentlemanly manner. She flashed to their last group pizza outing in college. He'd tried so hard then; and tonight, she thought, he had upped his game.

"Let's do a white Burgundy. I suspect you have 2017 Vins Auvigue Pouilly-Fuissé Solutré?" Vincent inquired.

"Yes, sir, we do." The waiter wrote in his notebook, waiting for the final decision.

"Perfect, for us." Vincent nodded and watched the waiter leave the table. "You'll like this wine, Renee."

"I probably will, since it's been some time since I've had any."

"Really?"

"Well, not outside of your coffee/wine shop, but really." "I'm privileged." Vincent smiled. "You're making me realize I've missed out on my dream years from long ago." He looked at the water glass on the table. "I thought about this—us on a date—a thousand times. I mean, probably more than a thousand. And here we are, living my dream."

"Yea, I never thought I'd be here, either," Renee admitted.

She looked at Vincent while readjusting her scarf. "I vaguely remember how you thought of me in college."

"Well." Vincent looked at her and the glow in her eyes from the candlelight. He swallowed, his foot started tapping, and his hands began to moisten. "I don't know where to start."

"I think you said that we met at the cafeteria?"

"Oh, no. I saw you for the first time at the cafeteria. But we met in class when we joined the group."

"That's right." She giggled. "You underclassmen were so green."

"Thanks to you, one group project got us past that stage. And, I mean, right away." Vincent smiled. "You should have been a professor."

"No, it wouldn't have worked," Renee said while grabbing the glass of water. "I liked what I got into after graduating."

"Did you?"

"Yes. It was exciting work."

"What was it - what type of work?"

"A process engineer at a large manufacturer. And I was fortunate because I got to use my business major. The company was amazing, and the people were dear to me. Especially Mr. Ottman."

"You remember your first employer? I guess that's a good thing, since you were treated well."

"Vincent, most people remember their first real job," Renee grinned.

"Funny you say that, because I'm still there."

"You are?"

"I started as a part-time barista with Stanley, who took me under his wing. After he decided to retire, he let me take over the business."

"Then, you aren't the owner?"

"Well, that's a long story. I'm not so sure we need to get into the details about how I became the owner." Vincent picked up his glass of water and sipped. He spoke while putting the glass on the table. "I am more interested in you. I mean, it's give and take, but I am like an open book that you already know. But I don't know much about you."

"Uhm, I see." Renee watched the waiter approach the table.

"Excuse me." The waiter placed two wine glasses on the table and opened the bottle. He poured a small sample into Vincent's glass and handed it to him. "Sir," he said.

Vincent accepted and sipped the wine. He swished it around his mouth for a moment before swallowing. "Yes, just as I expected."

The waiter poured more into Vincent's glass and followed the process for Renee. He placed the bottle on the table and left without a word. "Sometimes I think they are more mechanical than human," Vincent noted.

"So it seems," Renee responded. "But I notice that here, the wait staff seem very efficient."

"As I was saying." Vincent sipped from the wine glass. "I'm more interested in you. Let me find out how you continued to be an amazing woman."

"I wouldn't say amazing." Renee smiled. "I'm a simple gardener, now."

"And don't forget, a talented photographer."

Vincent nodded his head. "I have seen your work, so you can't deny your skill."

"It's still a hobby. But I am more attached to my garden than anything else. It's my best friend."

"Oh, really." Vincent's face gave away his surprise. "I mean, I would have thought that either your mom or your sister was your bestie."

"No one is like Mom."

"I really liked her." Vincent raised his glass towards Renee. "Here's to Mom."

Renee picked up her wine glass and leaned it towards Vincent. "The best mom ever." She placed the wine glass on the table, after sipping a little. She moved her scarf back in place.

"Let's get back to you. What happened after finding your job?"

"I got married."

"Oh yeah, I didn't expect that right away. Was that right after graduation?"

"No, it was a little after. We dated a long time before I accepted his proposal."

"Okay, I'm jealous." Vincent picked up the wine glass and drank wine again. He placed the glass down before asking, "Did you ever think about me?"

"Ah." Renee looked at Vincent before responding. She touched her scarf, looked at the wine glass, and softly said, "It wasn't an option to think about anyone."

"Not an option? Did I hear that correctly?"

"Not an option." Renee caught herself before responding, trying to keep the conversation light. "It's a long story, like the one where you got the business."

"I see." Vincent readjusted in the chair. "Huh, good answer."

He smiled at Renee and agreed to keep things on a lighter side. The waiter arrived with their salads, placed one in front of each of them, and asked if they would like pepper. Neither accepted, and both selected a salad fork.

"I'm so glad I paid attention to dining etiquette." Vincent snickered. "Comes in handy, to impress a beautiful woman."

"You know better than me," Renee said. "But I'm not too refined."

"If I'm lucky—if I'm fortunate—you'll give me a chance to show you what I know."

"Sounds nearly interesting—almost arrogant."

"It's a plan I have. That is, if you come along. I mean, without fearing my arrogance."

Renee dabbled with her fork in the salad. "I can see that happening." Renee smiled before nibbling.

After ten minutes of silence between Renee and Vincent, he managed to avoid an awkward moment. He filled her wine glass and waved to the waiter for a second bottle.

"You're okay driving, right?" Renee asked, after she pushed her finished salad plate from in front of her. "I can't drive, you know."

"I'm good. Besides, we don't have to travel far after dinner." Vincent looked at his watch. "We're good on time."

"I'm excited to see the play." Renee smiled. "I wanted to see it years ago but didn't get the chance. I'm really happy you chose this for me."

"Did you just deal me an ace card?"

"I may have." Renee smiled and looked left, past her scarf. "It's here, and I'm nearly starved."

"Yeah, the salad wasn't enough." Vincent moved his salad plate aside and made room for the entrée. The waiter placed Vincent's entrée in front of him and did the same for Renee. "Can I get you anything else?" he asked.

"No." Vincent looked at his plate and glanced at Renee. "No, I'm good," she responded.

The waiter took the empty salad plates and used utensils from the table before returning with a second bottle of wine. He poured a little in each glass from the new bottle after popping the cork. "If there's anything else, please let me know." He placed the bottle on the table.

"I think we're good." Vincent watched the waiter leave before he turned his attention to Renee. "Where were we?"

"I don't know," Renee responded. "But I like the way you make conversations easy. I think that even when it's quiet, I don't feel pressured to explain things."

"That's nice of you to say." Vincent chewed, and the flavor hit his tongue. "I love the French." He swallowed.

"This is delicious." Renee smiled in between chewing. "I can only imagine how yours tastes."

Vincent took the cue, lifted a fork of food, and offered it to Renee. "Here, try it."

Renee looked at his fork and became hesitant to accept his offer. She glanced at Vincent and thought, *Why not?* She took the bite, savored the taste, and said, "Wow, that is good."

"Glad to share - if you want more," Vincent suggested.

"My dinner is fine, thanks. I do like yours. I guess when we come back another time, I'll remember that dish."

"I would gladly have a second date with you."

"You would." Renee smiled at the suggestion. "Why didn't I pay attention..."

"...when we were in college?" Vincent picked up the table knife and used it. "I'd guess, because of class differences...maybe?"

***

After dinner, Renee sat in the car and watched Vincent walk around front. Right before he got to the driver's door, she reached over and pushed it open.

"Thank you," Vincent said. "You are a real keeper."

"So they say," Renee laughed. "Thanks for dinner. It was a really good."

"I wasn't sure you'd like French cuisine." Vincent snapped on his seat belt. "Besides, I only asked a little about you."

"You mean, my sister didn't spill her guts?"

"I'm not so sure she likes me," Vincent laughed. "Besides, I'd like to find out more as we go."

"You are much more interesting than I am." Renee relaxed in the car seat.

"Are you serious?" After starting the car, he changed the gear and drove to the next location, the theatre.

***

In their assigned seats, with an excellent view of the stage, Vincent and Renee watched the theater fall dim and light up, repeatedly for three times. The environment fell silent to the theater hearing a pin drop's echo, and the show began. After Act One, while the stage scene changed, Renee leaned closer to Vincent. "It's interesting so far, huh?"

"Yes, it is," Vincent replied. "I read the book, and it has a lot more to it. She was a dynamic madam, playing her part well."

"But it's not like she's on the street or handling women badly."

"I would guess it's not exactly a comfort house she's running." Vincent glanced at her through the corner of his eye.

"Yes, but the portrayal is about class back then."

Vincent nodded his head. "We'll discuss this at the next break in the show."

"You mean intermission?"

"Whichever comes first," he whispered.

The show continued with multiple acts leading to the intermission. When the theater brightened, Renee noticed how people whispered after staring at her and her scarf. Vincent looked at her, watching her expression and body language change in front of him. "You need a break?"

"I think I might use the lady's room," Renee said, standing. "Excuse me." She stepped from his side and walked towards the cleared aisle long end of the row. She arrived at the bathroom's entrance and waited in line for a stall. She again noticed the stares at her scarf, which covered a good portion of her face.

"I love your scarf," one lady remarked.

"Thank you," Renee responded without smiling. "It's a unique touch."

"Yes, I would have to agree." The woman in line could not hold her inquisitive nature and asked, "What happened?"

"Huh?" Renee responded.

"The reason you're wearing a scarf over your face at night. It's blocking something, right?"

"It is." Renee stepped forward and said, "I'm next. It's been a long time since I've used the bathroom."

"Go right ahead," the woman said, and followed, going into the next stall.

Inquisitive people were not unusual to Renee, since she'd escaped her earlier shell. She entertained questions, and some were more egregious than others. Regardless, the agony of coming forth with an explanation made her bitter. The inquiries often made her remember how those scars got there. Marvin's distrust, delivering agony from physical abuse with agonizing pain she can never forget. Regardless of her counseling, or practicing methods to overcome the horror, those who ask pressed play to a recording on a old tape.

She was out of the house and engaged with a man who could offer her a future, and still those questions rose from curiosity. On her way back to her seat things became very unnerving. Another woman saw the scarf hiding her facial scars. "What happened to you?"

"I'm not comfortable talking about it," Renee responded, "but thanks for asking." She grabbed the scarf and tightened it, she continued to her seat. "I am not leaving your side anymore, tonight."

"Everything okay?"

"There are too many questions to answer." Renee sighed.

"Huh?" Vincent whispered. "Oh, the scarf. I see. Sorry about that."

"It's not your fault. People aren't used to things outside of their norm."

"I think we'll get a lot of stares, especially how we look together. I get that stare from folks trying to figure out what I am. And I am sure you get stares because you look marvelous. I maybe exotic to some but I'm not nearly as attractive as you are." Vincent smiled, "I'm your lurker." he laughed. "Besides, if they haven't seen beauty before, they see it now."

"Thank you for trying to make me feel better."

"What's there to make better? You have a unique style going on." He scanned the theater. "I bet next week we'll see a lot of women wearing scarves like yours."

"Oh, stop," Renee giggled.

"No, seriously. Look how so many people have noticed you. I guarantee a lot of them will stop at one of the coffee/wine shops wearing a scarf covering one side of their face."

The theater ceiling lights flashed and dimmed right before the stage curtains opened. Both Renee and Vincent watched the second part of the show. During the act, Vincent laid his open hand next to the dividing chair's elbow and waited. He was surprised when Renee locked fingers with his and held his hand like they had dated for months. Vincent smiled while he clasped her soft hand in his. He dared to look at her, and instead slightly tightened his grip signaling his excitement.

***

Renee placed her palm into his inviting hand and locked fingers. It was a touch she had longed to enjoy. The last time she held hands was before her agony began. She smiled, realizing it was too dark for anyone to see her face. She eased tension on the scarf, and with the stage light reflections, she watched the man next to her become giddy.

He's cute, she thought. *Really cute.* She watched the show, periodically glancing at Vincent, and held his hand tight, responding to his tightened grip, loving every minute.

***

They watched the show without speaking a word. During one scene, Renee squeezed Vincent's hand with extreme pressure. She could not believe what she was watching on stage. When the actor slapped the leading woman, Renee lifted their hands to her face in defense.

"Oh!" she mumbled.

"Are you okay?" asked Vincent, during the scene change. "What's wrong?" he whispered.

"It's my reflexes. I'm sorry." Renee put their hands down and resumed the position they had held before her response.

Vincent leaned towards her. "Whatever shocked you, you're with me, and I won't let anything happen to you."

Renee heard him, and automatically remembered how she had hoped, during those agonizing years, that someone like Vincent would come to her rescue. But she didn't release the grip on his hand tightened with every repeated thought reminding her of a path she once walked. Her mind saw Marvin, the knife in his hand. She saw spokes to the banister rise and fall with her body rolling down each stair. She remembered the pain of her rib from the punch he landed. She squeezed Vincent's hand.

At the end of the show, when the lights grew bright and acknowledgments were finished, Vincent stood, assisted Renee and guided her towards the exit. Renee tightened her scarf and followed Vincent who securely held her hand. She glanced at his emphasis of not letting go, the one thing she wanted in life. A man to make her feel secure, like a child deterred from losing her parents in a crowd. The crowd was thick leaving the theater, down the stairs, and on the red carpet leading to the exit. Outside of the theatre, Renee kept her grip of his hand until she sat in the car. She opened his door and, like before, Vincent smiled.

"Thank you."

"What's next?" Renee asked. "I've enjoyed everything, so far. What should we do next?"

Vincent looked at his watch. "You know, I heard about a very cute and seductive coffee/wine bar that's still open at this hour."

"Really?" Renee laughed. "I bet you know the owner well, too?"

"As a matter of fact, I do." He snapped on his seat belt, pressed the start button and put the car in gear. They took off for the nearest coffee/wine shop. On the way, Vincent asked, "What were those intense moments about?"

"Another time, I hope to share it with you. Another time." Renee looked out of the car window and allowed a tear to trail down her face.

Chapter 22

When Hearts Pay Attention

Three weeks since their first date. Renee completed multiple marketing shoots. Vincent made a second effort dating Renee, surprising her with a picnic lunch during one of her shoots. He packed a picnic, a blanket, and chose a perfect setting in a nearby park. He called Candi to set things in motion, and with her help, Renee left the shoot in time for Vincent's arrival.

"Hi," Vincent smiled when she opened the car door.

"Candi said you were here for lunch." Renee sat in the car and buckled the seatbelt. "Where are we going?"

"Somewhere easy and peaceful." He drove down the road. "You're going to like it. Trust me."

"Are you sure?" Renee looked at the changing surroundings. "I know this park."

"Yep, it's our lunch destination."

"Grass and bugs?" Renee giggled "What am I? A horse?"

"Ha ha, just like you. Smartass." Vincent drove into a parking space to park the car. He tapped a button on his way out of the car and walked to the opened trunk. He pulled out a basket filled with trinkets of Renee's favorites. He closed the trunk, walked to the passenger's side of the car, and opened the door. "Here, let me help you." Vincent offered her his hand.

"Oh," Renee smiled. She looked at the basket and asked, "What do you have in there?"

"You'll see." Vincent led Renee to a picnic table near a large oak tree. At the wooden structure, he opened the basket and pulled out a cloth and two flowers in a vase and set them up on the table. He retrieved a pre-chilled metal 'winesulator' flask set and a bottle of Rosé, then positioned them, one in front of each person. "You should sit here," Vincent instructed her. Vincent pulled out Renee's favorite sandwich, wrapped in paper, and a fruit container. He lit a citronella candle, and then smiled before he said, "Just for you."

On another date, Vincent picked up Renee before sunrise. He drove to an open field, and in the dim light, Renee saw the magical round structure come to life— huge, colorful balloons, with large fires pushing them into monstrous round shapes. They climbed aboard, and in a whisk of wind, they rose to the sky. Renee covered her mouth with one hand and held onto her scarf with the other. Vincent watched her excitement, and when he touched her shoulder, he noticed a tear on her face when she turned towards him. "It's alright, Renee," Vincent consoled her.

"It's not bad," Renee murmured. Her arms swung around Vincent, and he responded with his lips touching her cheek. He whispered, "The height of my life has been spending moments like this with you."

Vincent continued his dating ideas. He bought tickets for

matinees that highlighted her work in local theaters. He played a tambourine with one of the entertainment bands at his coffee/wine bar while she watched. He sung out of tune for her in another set. He made sure every effort was made to share his excitement being with her and win her at his cost.

Renee's transformation with Vincent became profound with their knot-tying interactions. They enjoyed two Sunday brunch moments, with one being at Vincent's condominium. He created the ideal meal: buttermilk oatmeal pancakes, vegetable omelet, and turkey sausage, cooked to perfection. The fresh fruit presentation added to the mimosa and the unique blend of Jamaican coffee.

The second brunch was at the café near the third coffee/wine bar Vincent owned. The buffet was a town highlight, and most who experienced the unique meal waited hours to enjoy it.

Vincent pitched attending a minor league baseball game, which at first Renee rejected, but somehow, he got her to attend during a weeknight. He rung her doorbell and waited for Renee to answer.

"Who is it?" Renee shouted through the door. "You know it's me. Who else were you expecting?"

"You never know these days," Renee said while opening the door.

Vincent glanced at Renee…" Ha ha ha ha ha," he bent to his knee laughing so hard.

"Why are you laughing at me?"

"Did you look in he mirror?" "No, I didn't."

"Maybe you should." Vincent stood tall wiping tears from his eyes. "You can't go like that, you have to either lose the scarf or lose the baseball cap, and please don't wear it backwards."

"I thought it was cute."

"Maybe without the scarf but... I thought with your jersey on backwards, and the hat plus scarf, you were dressed for Halloween."

"You are so evil." Renee frowned and went inside to change her look. She turned everything around and wore the scarf under the hat, but loose fitting.

In the car, they drove to the park, chatted about their day and laughed about first impressions. Vincent had now seen the facial scars and without looking at her he said, "Maybe you can lose the scarf tonight. Be yourself, be comfortable in your own skin. I'm not leaving you."

"I don't know but we'll see when we go inside." Renee touched the scarf but didn't wear it as tight. And though she had gotten better with Vincent seeing the scars on her face and hand, she was still not as easy with the public noticing her damaged beauty. During the game, Renee loosened her scarf more, allowing the cool evening breeze to touch her face. The only reason she felt good about it, is their seating high in the stands away from everyone, an island of themselves. Renee appreciated Vincent's ability to cater to her with her seating choice. He pulled out binoculars to get a better view of the ball. He shared it with her, "Look, over right field." He pointed.

"I know baseball."

"You do?" Vincent surprised at her statement. "And the reason you wore the jersey backwards?"

"Now you get it."

"You got jokes." Vincent shook his head. "You are one of a kind."

***

With Renee and Vincent's increased interactions, they leveled through conversations about interests, life goals, and family. Though her trust increased with Vincent, Renee never once talked about the best conversation piece that hovered over them, nor did she comment on a woman's needs, since she'd invested so much of herself on one man. On Tuesday evening, she walked into Vincent's condominium with her camera and two bottles of red wine in her bag. "Hey, did you work out today?" Renee asked.

"I did this morning, around six. It was good, too—something I've learned to do since being with you."

"That's it—you haven't been with me." Renee frowned. "You haven't deeply kissed me once.

Not even grabbed my ass - even on the sly." She shook her head. "You don't want me as your woman; not as a girlfriend." She placed the bag on the counter and set her camera next to the bag. "You aren't trying to be my lover. Damn you!"

"I…" Vincent paused. "I mean, why in the hell are you so angry?"

"I mean it. It's time I became a woman." She pointed her finger.

"You're not helping me, and I understand why, now." Renee stood with her hands folded across her chest. "You have done a lot with me and made me feel special— but not special to where

I know I am yours."

"Oh, honestly, I never think of you as anything else other than mine. I mean," Vincent swallowed, "I mean, my girlfriend."

"Are you playing a game with me?" Renee frowned. "You know, it's been months, and you have not made one pass at me."

"I didn't think I should." *Boy, that sounds stupid.* "I mean, I didn't think it was important between us." Vincent paused. *That was just as stupid.* "I mean, I enjoy you so much that it's like I'm being pleased. I don't think of you as a woman I'd rush into something with." *Damn, I shouldn't have said that…another stupid comment.*

"You don't want to rush, with me?" Renee sat at the counter and spun around in the high counter chair, facing Vincent. "I'm not good enough for you to want me as your woman?"

"Wait, I didn't say that." Vincent lifted his forefinger, waving it from side to side. "I wouldn't say anything like that."

"Then you have a problem with my scars." She shook her head.

"I thought we'd gotten beyond my ugly face."

"I *have* gotten beyond your scars. I love your face. I mean, your looks. But that is not what I meant. I mean…I mean, it's going to happen; and when I start, I want to finish it right."

Vincent shook his head. *What the hell is wrong with me…am I that stupid?* "That didn't come out right. Give me a moment. Let me explain it better if I can." Vincent paused and kept his eyes on the woman he had enjoyed being with for nearly six months. He did not want to admit his sensual attraction because he thought that being physically aggressive was a turn off, to Renee. He didn't want to admit that he had dreamed of being intimate with her and falling in love, like he had done a million times.

Vincent walked towards his kitchen radio, flipped the 'on' switch, and music filled the silent room. "I like this song," he admitted. "Now, where were we?" He moved closer to Renee, pulled her to stand from the chair, and grabbed her into his arms. He swayed to the music and Renee followed before he gently kissed her neck. "Baby, I'm not sleeping with just any woman," he whispered. "You aren't any woman." He swayed. "You are Renee Chadwick, the woman I've dreamed of loving since my sophomore year in college." Vincent held her tight and swung her around before he looked into her eyes. "Do you realize that being intimate with you is the greatest event of my life? And I would rather wait for the perfect moment than make it an awful experience." He pulled her tighter to where her body touched his erogenous zone, and like the musical chord that feels soft, his strong erection pressed against her.

"Oh," Renee whispered. "I think I know what you mean." She relaxed, laid her head on his shoulder, and followed his lead. She responded to every sway and every grind. Her body temperature rose, and the moisture from his embrace wet her blouse. He kissed her forehead. "I hope you understand how badly I want you," he whispered. "I don't want to cheapen the experience." His lips touched below her ear.

"Oh, ah...I understand, but what about now?" Renee slightly palmed his ass. "I'm beginning to feel like a desired woman," Renee softly said.

"That's my point. I've desired you from the time I met you. You were desired when I took you out for the first time. You are desired right now, in my arms." Vincent stopped dancing and, with one hand, lifted her head positioning her lips for his. He moved with the slow imaginary breeze of the ocean, touching her lips like the mist blowing against dry skin. His lips met hers, gentle as a feather and smooth as the lily's petal. He kissed her soft and slow, moving his lips across her mouth, deliberate and passionately, while embracing her as if she is tomorrow's gift. He looked into her eyes, breaking his kiss.

"This is our beginning, the way I've wanted it since…" Vincent paused. "…as long as I can remember." He held her as tight as he could, nearly pressing the air from her body. "I want you in my life. I don't want a fantasy woman. I want you, the woman I truly admire."

"Don't play with me, Vincent. I'm really serious. I want to feel like a complete woman," Renee whispered.

"I want you, my complete woman. It's my heart's desire to love you…enjoy you, my one and only."

Renee heard his pitch and felt the spark of his heart reaching for hers. Her body relaxed in his arms and warmed to the first time he became affectionate and open. She remembered how long it had taken them to get to this point, closer to engagement and with something he offered, showed a deep feeling of commitment. It's what she'd needed more than what she thought she had, from her past relationship experience…love.

Vincent broke their embrace and stepped away from her. He walked behind the counter and took a bottle of wine from the bag. "I think this is reason enough to open this bottle now." He raised the wine to her sight.

"I would like that." Renee sat at the counter and watched Vincent's back while he retrieved the corkscrew and opened the wine bottle. Her eyes were on his butt, the solid basketball shape that she remembered being hard as stone. She looked at his slim shoulders and closed her eyes to a flashable moment where she'd felt the warmth of his embrace, something she desired. The excitement moved to the feel of heat below right were the moist experience mirrored an early menstrual cycle. She bounced her legs inward and outward, a movement that gently massaged her inner excitement. Renee opened her eyes and saw a glass of wine in front of her.

"Where did you go?" Vincent asked, with a wine glass in his hand and focused eyes on Renee. "You went somewhere."

"I never left you." Renee took her glass and, after one sip, kept her eyes on Vincent.

"I bet you…" Vincent put the wine glass to his lips, drank a small amount, and lowered the glass, shaking his head. "I had to stop because I'm ready to show you something more than a miracle."

"More than a miracle?" Renee nodded to her good side. "I don't need anything outside of being with you."

"It's okay, Renee." Vincent placed the glass on the counter. "I want this for us. I have so many things I want to show you, a million things I'd love to share with you. And most important is giving you love I've never had for anyone else."

"I didn't expect things to turn out like this."

Renee rose from the chair and approached Vincent with open arms. "I can feel your desire, now."

"Can you?" Vincent put his lips on her facial scars. "I'm going to love every inch of you. Because, to me…" He paused, kissing her again. "You are the most beautiful woman in the world."

"I believe you." Renee felt his magic. Her body trembled slightly, nearly noticeable to Vincent. She inhaled deep and fast before Vincent put his lips on hers. She let out a sigh as tears trailed down her cheeks. "I believe you, Vincent."

***

Morning streaked in, faster than a rooster's crow. Renee rose from bed with the biggest smile. Her energy rose her body heat to a drenching hot summer's morning, though the air conditioning had the house cool. Sweat beaded her forehead, the natural cooling process and by the time she walked to the shower and turned the water on, she was drenched.

Renee stepped under the cool waterfall of the big shower head. She closed her eyes remembering the moment they danced and enjoyed the cool water running over her head, cascading to her feet. Renee's senses rose and the excitement her body shared was how Vincent made her feel from his embrace. "Hmmm," she moaned, the pitch-perfect sound harmonizing with running water.

Her idea enticing Vincent did not turn out as she had liked, but it started something – something she needed to enjoy. Like past nights after the incident, when she wanted to feel a man's touch, she imagined Marvin, during their early years. As soon as she touched herself, the imagery stopped, and shame ran over her. But last night was different—entirely different. She saw Vincent, his eyes glued to hers, imagining his strong embrace, and feeling hopeful of power from his excitement when it touched her leg while they danced. She remembered having an increased heartbeat and was surprised at feeling the heat of pleasure. Renee smiled and replayed every moment before they took pictures.

***

Vincent went to his office after morning exercise without changing his wet, smelly, clothes. He walked into the coffee/wine shop receiving greetings. He smiled in response, approaching the counter and asked each team member about something personal. He spoke with a grin and talked, without asking for coffee. His team members were laughing at a couple of his comments before he left them for the back office.

His desk was organized like a Japanese rock garden, balanced with items east to west, sized for feng shui, and clean enough to enjoy a meal on it's surface. He liked all things to be perfectly arranged but his organized desk was nothing he had done. He gazed in awe at the natural perfection and magical emphasis on structure. He returned to the bar and asked, "Who reorganized my desk?"

"I didn't do it," the first barista responded. "But I know there was a lady with a scarf that went back there. I thought she was one of our new employees."

"Oh, really?" Vincent responded.

"Yes, it happened last night when I was working." "Wait— you worked last night and working this morning?" "I changed schedules with someone else." He paused. "You said as long as someone was here and the manager knew, it was okay."

"Yea, sure, I don't mind because you're here." Vincent turned towards the back room. Before he touched the door, he looked over his shoulder at the barista and asked, "Are you sure you saw a woman wearing a scarf go into the storage area?"

"Yes. A pretty, decorated scarf, too."

"Oh, okay, thanks." Vincent sat at his desk and opened the middle drawer, where he noticed a note. He unfolded it and the words danced in his head as he read:

Vincent,

You bring joy whenever we're together. I tried sharing what I think would put you at ease, but my words didn't quite come out as I would like. You see, when I was married, I had to be very careful of my words. You help me remember what it's like to be free.

Thank you,

Renee

"What it's like to be free." Vincent frowned, shook his head, and tried to understand what happened. He knew of an accident but didn't know the details. Curiosity milked his mind. *What happened?* He closed the desk drawer, picked up his coffee cup, and went for his favorite blend. On returning to the desk, he read the note again, re-read each word, and paced himself, as if he were reading it for a secret meaning. On the third pass, he read one part aloud. "You help me remember what it's like to be free." He placed the note on the desk, went to his car for privacy, and dialed Candi.

"Hey," he greeted her.

"What did you do to my sister?" inquired Candi.

"Huh?" Vincent responded. "Ah, nothing. Why do you ask?"

"She's singing in the shower," Candi smiled. "And that is not what she's done since…"

"…the incident?"

"Oh, she told you about the incident?"

"No, she hasn't, but she leaned towards it once or twice. It's why I am calling you." Vincent fell silent, growing strength to ask, "What *was* the incident?"

Candi didn't answer and waited for Vincent to repeat the question before she responded in a way that might settle his curiosity without revealing what happened. Vincent heard Candi breathing over the phone. "Are you okay?" he asked.

"I'm okay." Candi took in a deep breath. "Okay, here's something you have to know. Her marriage was painful, and it ended badly. That is the best I can tell you."

"The incident was the marriage?"

"I'm not giving you more than that. Let that be a discussion between you two. I'd get her relaxed, so she can tell you the details." Candi sighed. "I can't tell you anymore."

"Okay, got it." Vincent looked out the car door window at a barista, who waved him in. "Thanks for the info, and I will talk to her." He disconnected the call, rolled the window down, and asked the barista, "What's up?"

"I wanted to know if we're closing store number two?"

"Closing store two? Why would you ask that?"

"I heard about the strip mall being sold to a new owner, and he wants to tear it down. I hear it's going to be a work/play/live type of community."

"I hadn't heard about the strip mall." Vincent looked at his cell phone for a message from his property manager. "Thanks for the info. I'll let you know." The barista left the car. Vincent opened the notepad on his phone, typed a reminder to follow up on the latest information, and closed the app. He returned home.

***

Renee snapped a photo of a new mural near one of Vincent's stores. She was impressed with the artist's eye in his use of brilliant colors. Her camera snapped to the rhythm of her finger movement. Angling another shot, she snapped using natural sunlight, and the images jumped as if pushed from behind.

"Great shot!" she shouted after a good review of the panel screen of the camera. When she looked away from the panel, she saw Vincent's car zoom by. "I wonder where he's going so fast?" Within fifteen minutes of her eyes on Vincent's car, Renee dialed him.

"Hey, you." She smiled. "I saw you whizzing by - what's up?"

"Sorry." Vincent pressed his foot on the brake and streaming telephone poles became visible. "I didn't see you."

"I know. You were driving like things are on your mind." "Well, besides you, there is something important." Vincent stopped at the streetlight. "Yeah, I found out the strip mall is under contract. And it's being planned to change to a live/eat/play location."

"I've seen those around. Not a bad idea, if you ask me." Renee walked to her car with the camera in its carrier strapped to her shoulder.

"I don't think it's bad. It's just that I have a five-year lease on it."

"That long?"

"Yes. It's one of my most productive locations. Just last week, it paid enough for the month to cover all four locations." He stepped on the accelerator and the car moved through the intersection. "What are you doing later?"

"How much later?" Renee asked. "Whatever you need, I can change my schedule."

"Good." Vincent paused. "Can you squeeze me in for dinner - my place?"

"Since you have cooked for me, I should cook for you. My place, instead of yours? If you can get there around seven, that would be perfect."

"Of course, I can be there at seven. I'll see you then." Vincent pressed the car's phone icon ending the call. *I want to know what the incident means.* He arrived at his condominium after multiple attempts to see someone at the site. Inside his place, he showered and dressed well enough to engage Renee's attention: classic tailored medium collar shirt, creased slacks, and Italian loafers. Before he headed to the car, he put a call through to the property management contact he had written down from a sign on the property. Receiving no answer, he went to his laptop, booted it up, and drafted an email requesting a meeting. The email bounced back. "Those mother…" He breathed. Vincent called the number two coffee/wine location and asked if there were any word or packages left for him from the property manager. What he heard infuriated him. He dropped everything, walked outside, locked the condominium's door, and got into his car. He hit the steering wheel three times.

"Shit, shit, shit!" he screamed. He pressed the start button, connected his seat belt and put the car into motion.

***

Renee made it to her next appointment and finished the photoshoot regardless of her plans. She ignored her excitement about dinner with Vincent and put her enthusiasm into her work, as she had always done. At the location, her camera went into autopilot, as if her finger did not touch the shutter button snapping shots. At the last model of her appointment, she gathered her thoughts for dinner before the end of shooting for the day. Snap - snap! Renee looked at her results and returned to shooting, eyeing objects for a good shot. She contemplated a dinner menu. "Pork chops, sweet peas, and cabbage or corn." She shook her head and moved the scarf from her peripheral vision. "Scallops, white potatoes, cabbage."

An itch bothered her on the way to the supermarket. She pulled into the parking lot to focus on adding cream to her irritated spot. After parking the car, she heard gunfire – bang, bang. Her eyes widened and she ducked towards the passenger car seat. "Oh, crap." Her nerves stopped their irritation. Renee laid there for twenty minutes and rose when the sirens finally silenced in front of her. She looked up, backed out of the parking space, and drove to the grocery store nearest to her home. She bought dinner items: wild rice, baby peas, and New York styled beef strip steak; prepared with kindness and wrapped with affection.

Renee made it home in time to tidy things up and get Candi out, in case Vincent wanted to spend the night. She slammed the car door, which made her jittery. She breathed with ease — one, two, three. Renee counted on her way to the front door and got out her key to unlock the house.

A gust of wind pushed the door closed as if she had made a deal with the devil. Bam! She jumped, nearly dropping her bags, and screamed. "OH!!!" She turned and saw nothing, but heard Marvin's voice saying, *"I will teach you."* Renee's hand shook on the bag and rattled plastic loud enough that the sound took Candi by surprise. Before her sister arrived at the foyer, Renee thought, *I shouldn't have invited Vincent...not today.*

Candi ran into the kitchen from the office. "Why did you slam the door?" She waited for a response, only to hear Renee's bag make scratchy noises. She looked at Renee's hands before she moved close enough to grab the bags from her. Holding two grocery bags, Candi walked to the kitchen. "You went shopping?" Candi asked. "You should have called.

"It was on short notice," Renee said. "I am cooking dinner tonight." She placed the other two bags on the kitchen island.

"Oh, I bet it's a special guest coming." Candi put the bags on the island and stared at Renee.

"As a matter of fact, do you have plans tonight?"

"No, I don't, but I can find something to do."

Candi looked at Renee. "I can visit Dad; he'd love some company."

"I bet he would." Renee pulled items from the bag and set them on the island. "Is he back?"

"He got back last night. I thought he called you."

"No, he didn't. Unless I didn't hear the phone." Renee took the phone from her bag and put her camera on the island. She looked at the missed call list, revisited the message list, and read the text list. "Nothing from Dad."

"He's back, so I'll chat with him tonight while you do your thing with Vincent," Candi spoke as she turned to leave the kitchen. "I did tell him you were seeing Vincent, and maybe he wanted you to have some space."

"You think that's why he didn't call me?" Renee frowned. "You know we live together, and he did ask about you,"

Candi said, from a distance. After she retrieved her cell, she called their father and announced her plan for the night. She suggested a movie he and Mom had loved a meal he didn't have to create, and lots of conversation, like they used to do while she lived with him. Candi grabbed her purse before going upstairs to retrieve her overnight bag, filling it with clothes and pajamas before returning downstairs. She peeped into the kitchen where Renee was slicing and dicing on the kitchen island. *I haven't seen this much energy in Renee since Mom,* she thought.

"Hey, I'm going to Dad's. I'll be back by the afternoon in case Vincent doesn't want to leave." She giggled. "Have fun!"

"Okay, see you tomorrow!" Renee shouted. She grabbed the olive oil and added it to the boiling water preparing it for noodles. She chopped onions, garlic, and peppers, then cut shrimp into small bites. Renee created a tomato-based sauce from a recipe she had learned from her mother. She lowered the flame and scanned her counter space. She grabbed the spices and replaced them in the cupboard and put the leftover vegetables in the refrigerator. She wiped the counterspace before running upstairs to shower and change. By the time she returned to the kitchen, the aroma had blessed the entire house. She turned on the oven, set it for the right temperature, and waited. She stirred the noodles and tested them for consistency. With her sauce, she added the chopped shrimp and stirred the sauce to mix it well. After the oven alarm sounded, she prepped the bread and placed it in the oven before setting the timer.

Renee hurried to the dining room and looked at what she would like to do. She flashed to moments where she and Marvin sat down for dinner, six nights before the incident. She retrieved glasses from the cupboard, picked out a bottle of wine she had bought, grabbed the corkscrew from the drawer, and placed them all on the table. She grabbed napkins and utensils from the drawer, then positioned them at the opposite end of the table. "New territory," she whispered. The doorbell surprised her. "Already!" She rushed to the door smiling, giddy, without weary to a surprise.

"Vincent!" She gleamed. "You're early."

"I couldn't wait any longer." Vincent handed her a dozen red roses from one hand and held a bottle of wine and a bag in the other. He gently kissed her lips. "Smells great, where can I put these?" he asked holding up the bottle of wine and the plastic bag.

Renee's eyes sparked in the porch light, she looked at the roses. "They are lovely." She evaluated them for perfection. "I couldn't have grown them better myself."

"I hoped they would meet your expectations."

"Put the bottle on the island," Renee instructed him. "What's in the bag?"

"Dessert. I thought you wouldn't mind if I bought wine and dessert."

"Not at all. I didn't think of dessert." Renee stopped smiling and retrieved a vase, filled it with water, and placed the roses in it before she spaced them equally apart. "Dinner is almost ready." DING - the oven timer chimed. "Perfect timing."

"Can I help?" Vincent walked around the island. "I can do something."

"You can take the bread out of the oven and put it on the

stove. I'll do the rest. Thanks, Hun." She placed the roses on the center of the dining room table.

"Wow, that's a first." Vincent grabbed an oven mitten from atop of the island. "It's the first time you've called me by a pet name."

"Oh, really?" Renee walked into the kitchen.

"Yes." Vincent opened the oven, grabbed the pan, and placed the hot bread on the stovetop. "How do you turn the oven off?"

"Here, let me." She stood next to Vincent, brushing against him. He looked at her and realized that for the first time she didn't wear a scarf in his presence. Her hair was wavy like he remembered, full flowing and natural. He finally got a great look at her scars - their splashed pattern, big enough to follow but small enough to hide. He caught himself staring. "Oh my God, you are more beautiful without the scarf."

"Oh, oh, oh!" Renee said. "I was so busy, I forgot to put it on."

He pulled her close and pressed his lips onto her disfigured face. "You just did." He kissed her gently, then moved his lips on her neck.

"Hey, there's none of that until after dinner." Renee broke his embrace. She moved around him and retrieved plates out of the cupboard. "Ah, can you open the wine and put it on the table, please?"

"Ah yea, I can do that." Vincent grabbed the wine and left the kitchen to the dining room to fulfill her request. He peeled back the cork cover and used the corkscrew. He turned towards the kitchen and watched her move. She floated gracefully, spreading her butterfly wings, flying from one flower to the other. He had not noticed how sensual she moved, even though he had been with her on different occasions. The releasing cork pop snapped him from staring. He poured wine in each glass and set them down. "Where do you want me?" Vincent asked.

"Either place, it doesn't matter," Renee responded, holding plates in each hand, headed for the table.

"A man can get used to this," Vincent smiled. "If other things are as good, I can only imagine never leaving your side." Vincent grinned, gazing at Renee.

"Trying to sweet talk me?"

"I'm just saying. I know myself." Vincent stood as she arrived at the table. He grabbed one plate and moved to pull her chair out. "I appreciate a loving woman."

"I thought you didn't know love."

"I never said anything like that. If I did, it's because I wanted you to know I waited for you." He set the plate on the table and pushed in the chair as she sat. "I'm impressed." He looked at dinner. "Did you learn to do this in school?"

"Stop, you're killing me. It's just spaghetti."

She laughed. "Who doesn't know how to cook spaghetti?" Vincent sat across from her. "You have no idea, do you?"

He raised his wine glass. "To our first dinner here—and I am sure it's not the last."

"I hope it isn't." Renee tapped his glass with hers. She sipped wine fighting the urge to smile. She put the glass on the table. "It's been a long time since I've eaten in here."

"Oh, really?"

"At least a year plus, since Mom passed." Renee looked around. "How do you like it?"

"I love the place." "No, the dinner."

"Oh, oh yeah, it's good." Vincent turned his fork for another bite. "You're not going to eat?"

"Yes, I will." Renee twirled her fork in the spaghetti and lifted its capture to her mouth. She didn't close her eyes, fighting a memory of her past to appear, instead she blinked and held her eyes on Vincent. Her mind flashed to the last time she'd cooked this dinner combination, the night before the incident. The memory danced in her consciousness, and with every bite, it became vivid. Her hand trembled and she released the fork, which crashed onto the plate. She sat back in the chair and stared beyond Vincent. He looked up when he heard the noise and saw her gaze.

"Renee! What's wrong?"

Renee didn't respond. She sat motionless, lips tight, and calculative. Her eyes kept the thousand-yard stare without blinking.

"Renee." Vincent stood from the table, went to her and touched her shoulder. "Are you okay?"

"AAAAAAAAH!!" she screamed, pushing his arm away from her before jumping out of the chair. She ran full speed upstairs.

Vincent watched her run from him. His feet moved to catch her, but something sparked inside telling him to stop short of the stairs. "I'm here when you're ready to talk about it." He shouted. At the table, he filled his glass with wine before walking over to the stairs where he sat at the bottom. Vincent sipped before shouting, "I'm not going to bother you. Tell me what you want me to do."

Renee sat at the foot of her bed and breathed as if she had just run a hundred-yard dash in college. "Why can't he leave me to be happy?" she cried. "Asshole." She settled down before looking in the mirror above the dresser. She stared at her image and slowly reached up before she touched her scarred cheek with the same hand that stopped acid from burning her entire face. She placed her hand in the position completing the splash pattern. She sniffled, held her breath, breathed slower, and held back the tears. It didn't work and she yelled breaking silence, fighting pain inside, crying with the wail of a lost child, and wiping the trail of tears from her cheek.

The sweeping second hand on Vincent's watch rotated five times past twelve. He stared at his watch and patience got the best of him. He listened to Renee's crying and felt confused. *What the hell did I do to make her run from me?* Vincent did not hear anything. He rose from the stairs and set out on a trail into the unknown. He climbed each stair with a mission, careful not to create a misunderstanding, and eager to get to Renee. He arrived on the second floor.

"Renee, where are you?" He investigated the first room he came to, then the second. "Renee." He opened the third door and repeated his call. He walked faster to the last bedroom and looked inside. His eyes peeled on Renee sitting on the floor at the foot of a king-size bed. "Renee are you okay, baby?" he asked with concern. He squatted in front of her.

"I'm sorry." She looked at Vincent's facial expression, squinted eyes, tilted lip, and solid approach. "I am so sorry. I didn't know I'd remember."

Vincent rose and put the wine glass on the dresser before sitting next to her. "I am here for you." Vincent moved his hand slower than touching an unknown dog for the first time. He hoped his hand on her shoulder would not spark another outburst.

"I'm not going to be nosey." He rose to his feet. "I'll be downstairs when you're ready."

"No." Renee reached for him. "Stay here." She pulled him next to her. "I want to forget, and you can help me."

"Forget what?" Vincent's eyes focused on her. "Forget what?" he whispered.

Renee pulled him closer. Leading with her lips, she explored his irresistible features. Her kiss ignited the spark of desire and she pressed hard against his mouth. He put his arms around her and hugged her tight without losing their connection. Vincent fell back, took her with him onto the bed, and his hand roamed her body, feeling the surprise of life hidden under her dress. He reached for her neck, caressed her, and moved his hand to pull the dress from her shoulder. He kissed the newly exposed shoulder and traveled with his lips to the bottom of her neck, moving upward and stopping behind her ear lobe. He gently kissed her, and his tongue danced with hers. She pulled him closer, grabbing his butt and guiding his adjustment. She pulled him atop of her and spread her legs, gyrating her pelvis an effort to feel what she had missed for years.

He obliged Renee by following her lead with excitement and celebrated his erection. He darted with his movements - danced with her, responded to her rhythm, and allowed her control. He deeply kissed her and managed to move one hand under her, keeping the other above, only to wrap her neck with his elbow.

He stopped, broke his embrace, and stood before he pulled her to sit up where he could grab her dress, and remove it over her head. She allowed his disrobe and in turn, unbuckled his belt and unsnapped his pants before pushing the zipper downward. She yanked his pants, throwing them to the floor. He stepped out of them. She pulled at him, grabbed his shirt, and unbuttoned each button.

Renee looked at his exposed chest and the bulge in his underwear. She smiled before she stood, pushing Vincent to lay on the bed. She unsnapped her bra and slid out of her matching panties before she removed his underwear that blocked the rigid penis that she wanted to feel.

"Wait," Vincent said. "Let me get my pants." "Why?"

"I need to protect us." He moved aside, leaned down to the floor, and retrieved a condom from his wallet. He quickly zipped the cover and pulled it out. "It's better to be respectful." He positioned it and suddenly felt a hand over his. "Let me," Renee said, pushing him back on the bed, and she rolled the plastic down to cover the length his shaft. She lifted herself and took control, grabbing his fun stick and guiding it into her. She eased herself down. "It's been a long time." Her body stiffened in anticipation.

He moved his hips in a circular motion upward, and she bounced in rhythm. She went down and slightly up again, repeated and moved faster. She rubbed his chest and danced with an imaginary rhythm—fast, harder, short, slow—moving consistently until she lost the beat under a strained response within her erogenous zone. She moved harder and harder with her midsection and pressed so much that no sunlight could flash between them. Her nails grabbed his shoulder and Renee pulled him upward as she threw her weight onto his erection. Her teeth managed to pull out his bottom lip while her body shook. She slowed to a stop with a moan.

"Mmmm," she purred.

Vincent held her close, sat up without escaping from her embrace, kept his erection, and maneuvered them into a missionary position. He started with a rhythmic motion, created the imaginary mating dance, and explored her with deep strokes. He moved faster, darting his tongue into her mouth in sync with his thrust, in search of pleasure. He pressed the best part of him on a spot in her body that created a sensational buildup. She threw her pelvis upward, met his movement, then pulled his head to her ear and whispered, "Let go; don't hold back."

They cuddled in the center of the bed, motionless, and held each other. Each felt the depth of the emotions they both shared. He looked at her and watched a tear fall from her eye.

"I'm sorry, baby," Vincent said.

"You did nothing wrong," Renee responded. "I'm happy."

"A tear of joy?"

"A feeling of love. I've missed this so much, and I'm happy it's with you."

"With me?" Vincent smiled. "You mean, this was planned?"

"No, silly." She giggled. "I enjoyed you." She touched his chest and moved her hand to his head. "I didn't think it would be any different." Renee ran her fingers through his hair. "I haven't experienced this feeling." She grinned. "I read about it; I think."

"Love?" Vincent responded. "Is it love?"

"If that's what it is, I don't want anything else." She fell silent before saying, "I feel it's time we get serious." She dropped her hand from his hair.

Vincent sat up after he released his hold on her. "I'm thirsty." He rose from the bed and retrieved the wine he'd brought to the room. "Want a sip?" He tipped the glass towards Renee.

"Yes, do you mind?" Renee sat up, took the wine glass and drank part of the contents. "Umm, perfect."

"Yes, we are."

Chapter 23

The Incident

Light rays touched Renee's face from the blazing sunshine between the curtains' slit. She rose, gazed at Vincent, and enjoyed how the streak of sunshine lined across his caramel skin. Renee went to the bathroom, closed the door behind her, and ran water to wash her face like she had done thousands of times in life. Even after the incident, she'd learned to keep her skin clean and used certain agents to clean her pores. Having skipped her skincare last night, it was the second thing on her mind to do, after smiling because of Vincent. When she lifted from splashing water on her face, the bathroom door opened and there stood Mister Excellent.

Vincent saw her nudity in sunlight for the first time. His mind jumped to the throbbing desire he had in mind and body. He couldn't help having the idea of a second experience with Renee, enjoying the depths of her and repeating the affection the way he imagined for years. He went back to his pants and searched for the cover of safety to protect them both. He snapped his finger and shrugged his shoulders. *Damn!* He went back to the bathroom, touched her back and kissed her cheek. "Good morning."

"I didn't think you'd get up so soon." Renee kissed back. "I hope I didn't wake you."

"You didn't, but I missed you." Vincent rubbed her bottom. "Do you mind if I jump in the shower?" Vincent walked to the shower, turned on the water, and the rainforest showerhead came to life. He waved his arm inside it and waited for the perfect temperature.

"Nice," Vincent said. He entered the shower, closing the glass door behind him. He closed his eyes, feeling the water thrusting over his shoulders and rolling down his body. He opened his eyes and there stood Renee, in front of him. She embraced him, and together they let water dance over them while they entangled their bodies. He took the soap and washed her back, and she grabbed his penis and massaged it to an erection. She turned around and pressed her ass towards his pinnacle of life, inviting him inside. Vincent paused, jumped from under the water and moved his shaft against his better desire.

"Why? Don't you want me again?" Renee asked, standing with her back to his chest.

"I respect our commitment, but we have to be careful until you are my..."

Renee turned around, looked into his eyes and nodded her head. The water ran on her face, and her hair got into the stream. She stood under the thrust and closed her eyes. She shook her head breaking from the spreading shower. "You don't know what you're saying."

"I know what my heart is saying." Vincent smiled, grabbing the liquid soap and purple bath sponge. He washed her shoulder and moved the bath sponge over her body, covering each inch with care. He paid more attention to her nipples and followed under her breast. Renee sighed and raised her arms, leaned her head back, and turned to kiss him. Vincent appreciated the moment. "My dear, life has a lot of this for us ahead."

"Where were you?" Renee asked. "Why didn't you force me to pay attention?"

"Leave that thought alone." Vincent turned her around and scrubbed her back. "Let this be our moment to a new history."

Renee rinsed and grabbed the sponge from him. She filled it with liquid soap and washed the man who opened the door of change. She turned him around under the shower and watched soap disappear from his skin. Renee got out of the shower and retrieved two bath towels. She passed one to Vincent while he turned the water off. Renee dried his hair with her towel.

"I like the way we're connecting." Vincent toweled and watched her take care of her hair.

"Is that what you call it?" Renee wrapped the towel around her, covered her breasts, and showed her curves under terrycloth. "Connecting?"

"You know, I can't say it's not connecting. I mean..." Vincent pulled the towel tight around his waist. "It's like we're here." He pointed two fingers towards his eyes then to hers.

"Better, a lot better," Renee said, heading for the bedroom. "Get dressed and I'll meet you for breakfast."

"Meet me for breakfast?"

"In the kitchen, silly." Renee grabbed sweatpants and a tee-shirt from her dresser drawer, put them on, and went downstairs. She grabbed the coffee pot, placed the thin paper filter into the strainer, added grounds and pressed on, for the coffee maker to brew. Renee went into the refrigerator and got out turkey bacon and a loaf of bread, eggs, and milk. She started cooking the bacon and created French toast with the bread. Vincent arrived by the time she had completed the second set of toast.

"I could get spoiled living with you. Tell me this ain't normal."

"It's normal," Renee smiled glancing at Vincent. "I believe in taking care of the man who has my heart." She went to the cup tree on the counter, pulled off two coffee cups, and poured the freshly brewed black gold into each. She placed the coffee pot on the island.

Vincent went to the dining room table and retrieved the dishes they had left from last night. Renee nodded her head after noticing his aid without her asking.

"Thank you." Renee smiled. "You are a helpful man." "What do you mean?" Vincent asked while holding dirty dishes in hand, he placed one on the island and scraped one plate of leftover spaghetti into the trash. "Oh." He looked at her after setting the scraped dishes into the sink. "I get it." He did the other.

"Here, sit and drink your coffee. Breakfast is ready." Renee placed the bacon and French Toast she'd plated in front of Vincent. She poured a little honey on the toast. "Bon appetite."

"Thank you." Vincent bit into the bacon then sliced the toast with a fork. He swallowed the bacon, then bit into the toast. "Wow, nutmeg and cinnamon."

"Mom would add vanilla into the mix." Renee sat next to Vincent and carved a piece of French Toast with her fork. "Besides, it's better if you add nuts."

"Never added nuts," Vincent responded, between chews. "Nut lover, here." Renee took the bite with a shared grin. "I'm not so sure I know how to take that." Vincent laughed.

He noticed the window behind the sink and how the sun sparkled through the windowpane. "Isn't your garden in the back?"

"My original garden, yes; it is."

"Original garden?" Vincent asked before he put the coffee cup on the island counter. "I have never seen it."

"Let's take a look." She rose from the table and left her unfinished breakfast. "I'll finish later, don't worry."

"Not eating is your secret to staying in shape."

Renee walked towards the back door. "Come on." She shared the way her plants made her smile. She looked behind her making sure Vincent followed. "These plants saved my life."

"Saved your life?" Vincent questioned.

"It's a long story, but yes, these plants saved my life." She picked up the garden hose and turned on the water, filling the water bucket sprinkler. "It was more than therapeutic. It was like these plants pumped blood in my veins and entertained my mind."

"No wonder you love gardening."

"I had no idea until…" Renee paused and walked down the first row of plants.

"Until?" Vincent asked.

Renee's voice lowered. "I'll tell you later."

Vincent heard the melodic gargle of her voice. He remembered her scream and flashed to the moment she sprinted upstairs and left him alone. "Talk to me before you scream," Vincent suggested. "Tell me something, so I'm prepared. Please don't scare the crap out of me again."

"I…" Renee lifted the water pail and looked at Vincent. "I'm sorry, really; I'm sorry about last night."

"Hey, as long as I get a warning, I can manage it." Vincent smiled. "Especially after making love last night and sharing a shower this morning." Vincent covered his mouth blocking his grin. "Hell, you can whisper a warning before you scream, anytime."

"Really?" Renee chuckled. "I guess the outcome makes it better."

"Yes," Vincent nodded. "I know it's childish, but it's like a kid wanting ice cream. You know, we'd run a mile behind an ice cream truck, in summer."

"I've never done that in my life. But I get it."

"Okay, something else I've learned about you."

Renee continued watering her plants. "It's morning and not too hot, so water the base of the plant instead of the leaves, so the sun doesn't burn them."

"A life lesson," Vincent said. "It's like being too hot to make coffee—the same principle. Mornings are better."

"Aren't they?"

"There you go again." Vincent shook his head. "Naughty girl, you." He looked before stepping over to another aisle of plants. He touched one, and it moved. "Woah!"

"Plants are living things, you know."

"I've never..." Vincent put his hands in his pockets. "I'm not touching another plant in your garden."

"That one is important to me. She likes being talked to, and she'll respond."

"No way, come on...no way."

"It warned me many times," Renee whispered. "I wish I had listened."

"I heard that." Vincent's eyebrow lifted with his response. "Listened to what?"

"It's a long story." Renee sighed. "And I'm not quite ready to scare you from me."

"I don't scare that easily." Vincent walked behind Renee.

"You know, whatever you want to share with me, I'm all ears."

"Oh, speaking of sharing...what happened yesterday, that was so important?"

"Yeah, that." Vincent paused. "You know, I hate it when people screw you over. I mean, that property management firm could have done things better. They are closing my coffee/wine shop—the one that makes the most revenue."

Renee looked at him. "The number two store that I took the marketing photos for?"

"That's the one." Vincent shook his head. "All they had to do was include me instead of selling the strip mall out from under me. I thought it was a delightful place, and now I'm out."

"How's that going to impact business?"

"That shop could run the entire business for four months with one month of its revenue. That's how well that location did."

"Oh, I see." Renee placed the bucket down after finishing the last aisle. "I can see why it pissed you off." She walked towards the back door of the house and Vincent followed. "What are you proposing?"

"I don't know. I just found out yesterday, and the management company went out of business. They didn't tell me about that, either; especially since I had recently signed a five-year lease."

"Vincent, you can't let that get you down. We can come up with something huge before closing the shop. Besides, you can talk to the new owners about a new lease."

"I can't talk to them until they get things going. Plus, unfamiliar places and new rates...I'm not so sure I'll pay some ungodly amount for the lease. Especially when we aren't sure if the community will support a place for good music."

"Then keep the new place in mind, and maybe your skills can guide your business to something better."

"Let's hope so." Vincent grabbed his coffee cup and refilled it. "I like your blend."

"You should," Renee said. "It's from your coffee/wine store."

***

Vincent worked three days straight restructuring the financial plan to rebuild his business production. He searched for similar locations to the one closing - high in traffic, the right mixture of consumers, and the economic evaluation which supported the unique blend of entertainment, wines, and coffees. His conversation with the construction company did not lead him to the new property owners. Vincent became frustrated after his search through permits, deeds, and business licenses. He found one cover after the other and tried to understand what he could do if his plan did not work, or if finding who could lease the new buildings to him proved to be a tedious task.

Vincent arrived at Renee's house wanting her to be the sounding board for his new plan for the shop. He remembered her analytical mind from college and earlier discussions. With his laptop and notebook in hand, he knocked, then rang the doorbell. After a minute of waiting, he turned around to confirm that both cars were in the driveway and repeated the process.

He retrieved his phone and dialed Renee. *I should have called first,* he thought. The call went to voicemail. He dialed Candi in hopes she could tell him if they were available, or since both cars were home, if they were okay. Candi's voicemail answered. Vincent paced the porch and peered through a window. The blinds were cracked but he couldn't see anything out of the ordinary, in comparison to the few times he had visited.

His curiosity peaked and he walked around to the back, looking at the garden. He walked to the side gate, strolled to the back, and scanned for a living soul around the garden. When he did not see anyone, he walked to the back door, cupping his hands on the French Door, he looked inside. Nothing seemed different, yet there was still no trace of Renee or Candi. Vincent returned to his car and sent a text to Renee before he drove to his number one store.

***

"Dad, did you like the movie?" Candi asked.

"Yes, I didn't expect to laugh too much." He looked at his daughters sitting across from him. "I'm so glad you two got me out." He touched each simultaneously. "And you made me drive." He laughed. "You know, that took me back to when your mom was here."

"Aww." Renee touched her good eye, keeping her tears from falling. "I hope to have that love in my life."

"What?" Candi quickly responded. "Are you blind?"

"What are you talking about?" Robert was surprised. "I don't understand."

"Dad, she has a man who is crazy about her. The coffee/wine shop owner. The guy..." Candi informed.

"...your mother liked."

"Yes, she told you about him?" Renee smiled.

"Your mother wanted the best for you. I want the best for you both." Robert removed his hands. "But God knows, I'm hoping for men who are strong enough for you two. This Vincent guy I have met once, maybe twice; but your mom thought the world of him. She said he was the one."

"Mom didn't pick a guy for me," Candi frowned.

"You never bought one around, outside of Prom. While you worked at the bakery, you didn't think to get serious."

"I do appreciate you two for not being matchmakers." Candi giggled. "It could have been a mess."

Robert laughed. "Could have been, especially with your quirky personality." He looked at Renee. "Vincent showed you kindness from his first impression of you." Robert nodded in agreement. "Wasn't he the kid with the bouquet at your college graduation?"

"Dad, you remember that?" Renee asked. "Of course, because I felt bad for him. You didn't have a kind word for that young man, back then. I knew his pain." He looked around. "We've been here for a few minutes. Doesn't a waiter or waitress serve this table?"

Candi rose from the table and went to the receptionist's stand. "Hey, we haven't seen a waiter at our table."

"Oh, let me get you one." The receptionist walked in an opposite direction than Candi. A moment later, she heard her dad say, "I made a move on your mother when I first met her. I mean, it was a simple kind of gesture."

"And Mom rejected you," Renee responded. "She gave me a kind smile in return."

"You didn't go out with her then?" Renee asked.

"No, that came after she broke up with a guy who didn't treat her well."

"No kidding." Candi's eyebrows raised. "We hadn't heard about this," Candi said. "And Mom told me a lot of things. She never said anything about an unhealthy relationship."

"She didn't want you to think less of her. It's why she said you had to be strong at everything. And you two are really strong women."

The waiter arrived at the table and wrote down their orders. He waved his hand, and another person from the waitstaff brought glasses and a pitcher of water.

"I'll be back with your napkins and utensils." The waiter instructed.

***

Candi and Renee arrived home, walked into the house and dropped things in the office before settling for a night cap from the kitchen. Renee went to her recorder and reviewed whatever recorded from her home cameras. She watched Vincent on the porch and show up in the back yard near the garden. "What the hell?" she thought. She picked up her phone and the text message alert chimed. She quickly read: *I dropped by without calling. I panicked when you didn't answer the door. Please let me know you are safe.* Renee deleted the message. She looked at the missed calls list. Vincent's number was on top multiple times. She walked to her desk, sat on the desk chair, and contemplated what to do. *Should I call? Is he controlling? Or is he sweet? Does he expect me to cater to him? Is he going to be like Marvin?* She shook her head from side to side.

Candi entered the office. "Vincent called me. I'm sure he was looking for you."

"Yeah, he called me, too." Renee shook her head. "Here, look at him walking around the house."

Candi walked to the player and watched. "He's really into you. Look at his face. He was worried that something might have happened."

"I don't think it's that."

"Why wouldn't you?" Candi covered her mouth. "No, Vincent is nothing like him. This man is crazy about you, and he's different."

"Why did you say he's different?" Renee frowned while she looked at Candi.

"Because he's concerned for us. He saw our cars outside, with no message on us being out, no response from his calls, and he looked around to make sure we were okay." Candi moved from the front of the video. "Besides, you know the difference. Every man will not be like your ex." She left Renee in the office. *She better not blow this,* thought Candi on the way to the kitchen.

Renee reset the surveillance tape and walked to the kitchen. "Hey, I'm going out."

"At this hour?"

"Yeah, I need to see Vincent." Renee grabbed her keys and purse. "I'll see you later!" she shouted before she pulled the front door closed behind her. Renee got into her car and drove to Vincent's condominium. Upon arrival, she noticed there were not any lights on in his place. She retrieved her cell phone from her purse and dialed his number. When he did not answer, she knew where to go. She drove to the number three store. After parking, she went inside and walked straight to his office, behind the bar.

"Hey." Vincent rose from his desk and opened his arms as he approached her. "Why didn't you call me? I was so worried."

"Were you?" she asked from the comfort of his embrace. "I'm sorry. I didn't think you were that worried. I mean..." She paused, her head still on his chest with her eyes closed. "I didn't think you'd look for me."

"I love you more than I care to admit." Vincent held her tight. "I shouldn't say this but, I am in love with you, just like I knew I would be."

"Are you serious?"

"Would I panic about you if I didn't?" Vincent shook his head. "Not hearing from you had my heart sweating. I only came here to avoid thinking about terrible things." He held her tight. "What if I didn't get a chance to see you again? What if you decided to leave me and not tell me?"

"You don't have to worry about me leaving you. I like you, and I am sorry I didn't tell you about going out with my sister and dad. We went to a show, and I turned my phone off."

"Oh." He didn't release his embrace.

"I shouldn't have jumped to conclusions," Vincent whispered. "I'm sorry."

"No, I'm sorry for not sharing my plans with you." Renee pushed back from his embrace and looked at him, then touched his lips with hers. She kissed him before words left her lips. "I think we need to talk, because I'm ready for us."

"I can leave, now." Vincent released her and returned to the desk. He closed his laptop, put it in its case, and grabbed his book.

"I'll meet you at your place."

"No, let's go to yours, tonight."

"Say no more."

***

Vincent pressed the remote button opening the garage door to his condominium. He pulled in, parked the car, and waited for Renee before he opened the garage door entry into his home. He watched her pull up next to his car. "I could get used to this," Vincent said. Renee got out of the car and walked towards him. Vincent opened the door, allowing her to enter first. He shadowed her, flipped a switch, and darkness inside the condominium disappeared.

"Here's something for you." He pulled off a garage door opener from the key chain hook. "Keep this in your car."

"What does that do, without a key?" Renee asked. "Because that's next." Vincent walked to the kitchen drawer and retrieved the other key chain with the key, which he uses for guests. "Use it whenever you like."

"Vincent, are you serious?"

"After my heart went into a panic over not being able to contact you, I'm surer than ever. Especially since I want to share everything, I own with you."

Renee took the key and placed it with the garage remote on the kitchen island next to her purse. She walked to Vincent, kissing him on the lips. She hugged him as tightly as she could. "I think you're ready."

"Ready for?"

Renee let go before she moved to a cupboard. "Are they here?" She opened the cupboard doors. "Your wine glasses?"

"No, not there." Vincent walked to the opposite side and opened a cupboard door. "Here—all the glasses are here." He showed her, grabbed two glasses, and placed them on the table before he pushed the door closed.

"Here, sit down," he instructed. "I'll get the wine." "Just one glass, okay?"

"We'll have one glass." Vincent pulled the cork and poured equal amounts into two glasses. "What's on your mind?" He replaced the cork and set the wine bottle on the counter. "Something important, I guess."

"It is. I want to tell you, before we move on."

"No children you're hiding - right?" Vincent asked. "Hell, at this point, that wouldn't matter. I want kids, anyway."

"No, no kids, and we can talk about that later."

"What is it?" Vincent caught her eyes.

Renee saw his stare, looked at the wine glass before lifting it to her lips and sipped. She lowered the glass and said, "I need to explain my past." She sipped again and lowered the glass. "It's only fair that you know before we get serious."

"I *am* serious," Vincent said. "I know whatever you're about to say has to be important." He focused his stare between her lips and her eyes.

"I feel it is." Renee emptied the wine glass.

Vincent refilled her wine glass before his response. "This has to be serious."

"It is, and I need you to know."

"Know what?" Vincent put the wine bottle on the island counter and corked it. "Know what, Renee?"

"I had a wonderful marriage to a man who I totally admired.

He was charming, smart, energetic, and sweet." Renee paused and watched Vincent shake his head. "Wait, before you judge. I'm not finished." Renee took a full gulp of wine. She placed the wine glass back on the island. "It started when one day I didn't give him the focus he wanted. I had a lot of work to do, and he expected me to stop whatever and tend to his needs."

"Tend to his needs?" Vincent's eyes grew wide and one raised eyebrow. "Sounds like..."

"...wait, just listen." Renee interrupted. "I felt the air of his hand before I felt the sting. He hit me so hard, it knocked me out of the chair, and it startled me so badly that I didn't know how to respond." Renee looked at Vincent and her breathing took on a different pace. "He...he...apologized for that, and of course I stopped working on whatever I was doing. I couldn't yell at him because I saw the anger in his eyes. He was like I'd never seen before."

"I'm so sorry, Renee." Vincent frowned.

"He promised not to do it again." Renee paused, looked at the empty glass before continuing. "I should have left then, but love got the best of my logic. I thought it was because of something from the job." Her eyes met Vincent's. "He had a new position that brought on more stress. For the moment, it was my excuse. But I found out later that it wasn't. He punished me for anything he saw fit that I didn't do correct. If I didn't put a new bag in the trash can right away, he'd slam my hand. If I didn't clean the shower with lemon disinfectant, he'd punch my stomach. If I didn't have dinner ready when he got home, I would get kicked."

"That mother..." Vincent balled his fist. "Did you?"

"Tell anyone?" Renee lowered her head. "At first, I cried to my mother. But all I got was, 'it's marriage jitters'."

"No, not your mom." Vincent shook his head.

"That's not all. Because it got worse. I walked on eggshells in my house, afraid of what I did or didn't do. I thought of leaving, but I was sure Marvin would find me. He had resources. I went to the police after he pushed me downstairs. I didn't have the courage to press charges." She leaned forward on to the island and held her cheeks. "Plus, I loved him so much, and he kept telling me it would get better." Renee rocked back into the high island chair and reached for the empty wine glass.

Vincent noticed that her hands shook when she picked up the wine glass. He moved closer and put his arms around her. "It's okay, baby, no one will ever abuse you again." He reared back from the embrace grabbing her hand and asked, "Is this from…"

"Marvin?" Renee nodded her head. "It was a bad week for me. I had done nothing right. My leg was badly bruised from his kicks. My eye was blackened from a surprise punch, and I had a fractured arm, which I had no idea I had." Renee lifted her head, and Vincent saw where a tear had fallen from her good eye. "It was that night—the one night I didn't think I could take anymore abuse. I screamed at him that I was not taking any more bullshit. I had called my mother, and she finally supported me. I had her agree to let me move back home with her and Dad. I had set things into motion, and she would come for me. She told me to keep distance from him and avoid confrontation at all costs. Her exact words were, 'Do whatever he asks. I'll be there soon.' I remember them so well."

Vincent stroked Renee's head with his right hand and held her tight with his left arm. "I'm so, so sorry you went through this. I can't believe..."

"...I chose an abuser. Hell, who knew he was such a bastard?" Renee responded. "That night..." she sniffled. "That night, he didn't push me or ask for anything. I didn't think much about it, but my gut instinct said that something was going to happen." She turned her head, looking at Vincent. "I called my mom and tried to get her to drive faster." Renee leaned her head next to Vincent's.

"So, mom got there in time to get you out." Vincent kept their touch. "Right? Mom came to get you from this nightmare."

"Not soon enough." Renee closed her eyes tightly and the vivid picture of what had happened next became her movie screen. "Baby, it was horrible!" Renee cried, pushing back from Vincent and moving to the other side of the island. She pointed next to the sink.

"It happened right there. If we were at my house, you could see the burn stains."

"You mean..." Vincent pointed.

"Yes." Renee placed her scarred hand on her facial pattern of bumps and crevasses. "This happened." She pointed at her face with her good hand. Renee screamed, "AAAAAH!"

Vincent's eyes widened and he rushed to her side. "Baby, I'm here."

"Don't!" Renee yelled and screamed. "Don't touch me!"

Vincent stepped back and watched Renee drop to her knees with one hand connected to her face and her good handheld her body in a forward, prone position. Her back arched and her scream pierced the condominium's silence. "AAAAAH!" Her tears were like a stream of melted snow on the Rockies.

"It burned so bad; it burned so bad. My God, I thought my life was over." She said in between sniffles.

"Oh, shit," Vincent whispered. "That must have been hell." He moved over to Renee. "Baby," he said, "sit with me."

"No." Renee's quick response startled him. "No." She looked up at Vincent and saw the nervous tension he portrayed. "It was when Mom walked in."

"Where?"

"I'm not sure, but I heard 'Bam!' And I knew Mom had done something."

"I can't imagine what."

Renee sat on the floor and her hands covered her face. Her good side was still wet from tears, and her scarred side was noticeably moist. "I only remember that Mom stopped him from splashing me a second time."

"She stopped him from splashing you with…?"

"Some kind of acid concoction."

Vincent sat on the floor in front of her. "Baby, I'm so sorry." He put his arms around her and fell silent. Vincent was surprised and realized her reluctance to share her past during their early dates. "I'm here for you," Vincent whispered.

"When I opened my eyes, I heard the doctor say I was lucky it didn't get close enough to lose my eye. It was close."

"I noticed." Vincent didn't release his embrace.

"That's when Mom explained what had happened, and how

Marvin isn't here any longer."

"You aren't divorced?"

"Widowed." Renee said. "Marvin died from his wounds." "He was hurt. By whom?" Vincent said, "Oh, oh, oh—your mom."

"Yes, but I didn't see what happened. I only got wind of the police report." Renee paused. "Don't let go," she said.

Vincent held her while both sat on their knees, on the floor. Renee continued. "I read the police report."

"Yeah, what did it say?"

"Mom saw him with the container and watched him splash me. I don't remember hearing the door when she came in because Marvin was yelling. According to the police report, Mom had a bat from the car, and she swung it with all her might and connected with his head. The container fell to the floor, and he fell next to me. The report further explained it was in the defense of family, and she wasn't charged. From what I read; he died on the way to the hospital. Mom really hit him."

"I see." Vincent released his stare. "She protected her daughter. I know mothers will protect their kids regardless of conditions."

"If only she had come sooner," Renee said softly.

"I imagine you've thought about this a million times. If she had, you wouldn't have had these scars. Well." Vincent released his embrace and pushed her back far enough to see her eyes. He looked right into them. "I would hope to have been here with you either way, good or bad. And, right now, I'm here, and will be here for the rest of your life. It's my promise."

Author's Biography

Lonz is originally from Augusta, Georgia, is a graduate of Westside High School and retired Marine and a veteran of Operations Desert Shield / Desert Storm.

Lonz has a BS Degree and a MS Degree in Administration. He is a Technology Specialist and was an Adjunct Professor of Project Management. He is published in Project Management Institute Magazine. He resides in Atlanta, GA.

Lonz authored Good Guys Finish Last Series:

Good Guys Finish Last, When Love Evolves, Crossed Expectations, and When Love is Final.

He also authored A Choice to Yield (a full-length feature film), A Cyber Affair, and A Loss Too Great.

Let others read what you think. Leave a review on Amazon, Barnes & Noble, Goodreads or any website where books are sold.

Future release. Gus Blake – Pigeon Forge – A Marine Veteran Amputee Private Eye reluctantly takes a case fighting a small-town drug ring. He's skilled in surveillance and investigations, but not as cunning as the youngsters who hires him.

www.lonzcook.com